Divas DON'T YIELD

ONE WORLD | BALLANTINE BOOKS
NEW YORK

Divas Don't Yield

A NOVEL

Sofía Quintero

A One World Trade Paperback Original

Published in the United States by One World Books, an imprint of The Random House Publishing Group, a division of Random House, Inc., New York.

ONE WORLD is a registered trademark and the One World colophon is a trademark of Random House, Inc.

LIBRARY OF CONGRESS CATALOGING-IN-PUBLICATION DATA
Quintero, Sofía.
Divas don't yield: four chicas, one car, tons of baggage—: a novel / by Sofía Quintero.
p. cm.
ISBN 0-345-48238-7
1. Hispanic American women—Fiction. 2. Automobile travel—Fiction. 3. Women travelers—Fiction. I. Title.
PS3602.L24D58 2006
813'.6—dc22 2005054667

Printed in the United States of America

www.oneworldbooks.net

9 8 7 6 5 4 3 2 1

Para todas mis hermanas

who are

raising hell, redefining real,

and representing lovely

Change is a-comin' because you're bringing it

ACKNOWLEDGMENTS

It has taken a long time and much support for the story of Jackie, Hazel, Lourdes, and Irena to reach any audience. Even though I'm bound to miss thanking someone who over the years made this possible, I had to try. Much gratitude to:

My family, especially my parents *el Negro y Pura,* who never blinked when I decided to become a novelist.

Elisha Miranda, who supported my creative recovery—and this story in all its forms—from the very start.

Other sistergirls who had my back in one way or another: Janis Astor del Valle, Nicole Burrowes, Myla Churchill, Kim Davis, Kelli Martin, Mylaine Riobé-Heron, Rosemary Rivera, Ginger Romero-Pardlo, Andrea Schorr, Marta Urquilla and Aleeka Wade. All the friends and even acquaintances who went—sometimes more than once—to all the readings and performances.

The fierce sister organizations on the front lines, especially Sisters on the Rise, Sista II Sista, Casa Atabex Aché, the Young Women's Development Center, Hermana á Hermana, and of course, my heart Chica Luna.

All the wonderful people who made me feel at home during my time in Omaha, including Ricardo Ariza, Kimberly Gallion, and especially Maria Luisa Gaston of the Latina Resource Center and all the wonderful members of her book club.

The 5th Night Reading Series at the Nuyorican Poets Café for that first opportunity to bring this story to the public, as well as all the amazing actors and actresses who participated in readings of *Divas Don't Yield* when it was a screenplay called *Interstates.* Also, Montage Entertainment, the National Association of Latino Independent Producers and the San Francisco Black Film Festival for supporting the vision in its early stages.

Julie Barer, Johanna Castillo, and Jennifer Cayea, the literary *luminarías* who saw possibilities and weaved magic.

Last but hardly least, all the folks at Random House, especially Danielle Durkin for all her confidence, support, and most important, patience!

The journey that is this novel began in 1998, so for all who I might have failed to acknowledge, please know that the oversight is a consequence of time and not a reflection of ingratitude.

MEET THE CHICAS

Get in the car with these four chicas as they drive from New York to San Francisco and learn more than they ever bargained for about love, courage, honesty, and what it takes to accept yourself and keep your friends no matter what the road ahead may bring.

Jacqueline Alvarado (21):
With an interminable feistiness that radiates through her five-foot-nine-inch athletic build to the tips of her untamed hair, proud Afro-Latina Jackie is the undisputed leader of the pack. She's the first to yell "Black is beautiful," but these days not so triumphantly, when her boyfriend, Wil, keeps taking calls from his Vanessa Williams–esque ex, who still hounds him for playdates with her adorable son, Eric. Jackie's positive the ex is just using the kid to steal Wil back, but whatever . . . It's not like Jackie's, like, in love or anything.

Carmen "Hazel" Flores (21):
Bombshell Hazel can have any man she wants . . . if and when she wants one, that is. This lipstick lesbian (with only one foot out of the closet) has eyes for only one woman—Jackie. Never mind that they've been best friends since they were thirteen. Despite Jackie's

tomboyish ways, she is relentlessly straight and irreversibly in love with Wil. With that relationship at a crossroads, Hazel is convinced the time finally has come to get her woman. It's now or never.

Irena Rodriguez (19):
Yoga, numerology, Reiki, tarot . . . asthmatic Irena never met a holistic treatment, New Age philosophy, or occult science she wouldn't try. A borderline psychic (but don't call her that), her intuition has served her better than any old religion. The petite blue-eyed blonde hates speaking Spanish like a gringa and being likened to Cameron Diaz. Still suffering from a traumatic experience during her first year in college, Irena idolizes Jackie and envies her kick-ass attitude. Where the hell was her inner *chola* when she needed her most?

Lourdes Becerra (20):
Rich girl–turned–rabble rouser Lourdes will march as long and far for the perfect pair of Gucci sunglasses as she will for a woman's right to choose. She may be a devoted Catholic, but her God believes in live and help live. If her conservative mother in Denver only knew how often Lourdes threw her money at her working-class friends' problems! But Mamá doesn't even know that her pre-med daughter is snapping photographs of the immigrant neighborhoods in New York City when she should be poring over a petri dish.

Divas DON'T YIELD

TO: Hazel1985@hotmail.com, LuLuLinda@aol.com, DreaminginCuban@juno.com
FROM: imokurnot@yahoo.com
DATE: May 30, 2006 11:27 PM
SUBJECT: Cali Here We Come!

OK, gals, while procrastinating on my thesis, I banged out a potential itinerary. If we each drive at least two hours every day, we should get to Frisco in time for the opening ceremony on Wednesday the 21st. Here's how I think we should ride:

9AM—12PM:	Me
12PM—1PM:	Lunch
1PM—4PM:	Hazel
4PM—6PM:	Lourdes
6PM—8PM:	Irena
8PM—???:	Dinner and all the fun we can stand and still hit the road by 9 AM SHARP the next morning.

If we keep to this driving schedule, we'll spend the night in the following cities:

16th—Cleveland (I know this means missing the Emergency Brides' March, Irena, but we really need the extra day.)
17th—Chicago
18th—Des Moines or Omaha—I don't care either way. Omaha's another two hours west though and might be a better option, especially since the drive between Chicago and Des Moines is seven hours. Let's do as much as we can each day. Mush!
19th—Cheyenne? Denver? Someplace else?—Still trying to figure this out. On the one hand, I thought Lourdes would want to drop in on her family. But the truth is it's going to be really tough to make it there because there's almost 700 miles between Denver and Des Moines (or Omaha).
20th—Salt Lake City—I'm maaad curious, aren't you?
21st—San Francisco!

I suggest we stay in the same cities on the way back. Not just because this damned thesis is kicking my ass, and I don't have a lot of time to figure a completely different itinerary for the way home either. I'm just thinking that while going west, there's bound to be things that we're going to want to check out but won't have time to. So I say we hit the same cities again on the way home so we can do the things we couldn't on the way to Frisco.

Everybody, give an update on your tasks so we can see where we are before we meet on Friday. Haze and I aren't going to have a lot of time, since we have to leave no later than a quarter to one for our graduation rehearsal. So let's use lunch to iron out any last-minute details.

Peace,
Jackie

P.S. Anyone want a hundred bucks to finish this stupid paper for me?

TO: imokurnot@yahoo.com, LuLuLinda@aol.com, Hazel1985@hotmail.com
FROM: DreaminginCuban@juno.com

DATE: May 31, 2006 7:38 AM
SUBJECT: Re: Cali Here We Come!

Goddesses,

I'm so excited!

Jackie, I'm cool with the itinerary. Just one thing though . . . can someone switch with me? Since I don't drive a lot, I'd be a lot more comfortable if I didn't drive at night. But if no one else wants to do it, that's TOTALLY OK! It's summertime so maybe it won't be that dark when I start driving, right?

As your self-designated community builder, conflict mediator, and spiritual healer, I came up with a few ideas. First, I bought a notebook so we can collectively document our journey. Like a scrapbook or journal. I have supplies, but feel free to bring whatever you need to express yourself. No rules other than please make a good faith effort to contribute to it.

Remember to bring an item to offer as a gift to your sisters for our embarking ritual. Don't buy anything (I mean it, Lourdes!). It should be something that represents you and is small enough to fit into the box.

Oh, and please bring with you two or three questions that you want the others to answer. Put each question on an index card, and we'll place it in the box. Some questions should be fun, some serious, etc. But the answers should give us insight into each other. Things like, "What would you do if you hit the lottery tomorrow?" or "If you were an animal, what kind would you be?" Then we'll write the answers in the journal. Or we can talk about it along the way. The possibilities are endless.

What'd you guys do over the holiday weekend? Dad took me to the Jersey Shore. I just sat on the beach and worked on *The Tarot According to You.* For each card, you record the personal experiences that come to mind and then compare it to the card's traditional interpretation so that you do more relevant and meaningful readings. It's soooo insightful! Oh, and I finally caught up on all the episodes of *Starting Over* that Lourdes taped for me (thank you!!!!!). Jackie, how was the camping trip?

Blessings,
Irena

Life is nothing but a dream, and if you create your life with love, your dream becomes a masterpiece of art. —Don Miguel Ruiz

TO: imokurnot@yahoo.com, LuLuLinda@aol.com, DreaminginCuban@juno.com
FROM: Hazel1985@hotmail.com
DATE: May 31, 2006 9:41 AM
SUBJECT: Re: re: Cali Here We Come!
ATTACHMENT: Gamba Adisa Playlist.doc

Irena, love your ideas and you can switch with me (and bring that tarot workbook on the trip). But why are we on the road so late anyway? We should have dinner earlier and call it a night. Party or just chill. When else are we going to have the chance to sample Iowa nightlife? RandMcNally.com says there's going to be a big carnival when we pass through there that we can check out.

As for en route entertainment, I attached the playlist. Anything in bold is something I don't have, so if you own it, bring it to lunch on Friday. And if you asked for something that's not on there, it's because someone made a point to say that they didn't want it. (Sorry, Jackie, just about every Snoop Dogg song you wanted qualifies as a narcocorrido, and Lourdes isn't trying to hear that stuff.)

I went to visit my father and grandmother. On Saturday Dad gave me a letter and made me promise to wait until the ride home to read it. It was so beautiful, people on the bus must've thought I was crazy, the way I was going back and forth between sobbing and laughing. Then on Sunday I went to St. Raymond's to put fresh flowers at my abuelita's grave. Monday was quiet and uneventful, which is just what I needed. Yes, Ruby was away at God knows where.

My ten o'clock's early so I gotta go. Jackie, I'll finish your thesis if you come over here and do this woman's extensions. She wants to look like Alicia Keys when she has less fuzz than a tennis ball.

CHF
Your Cruise (Control) Director

TO: Hazel1985@hotmail.com, DreaminginCuban@juno.com, imokurnot@yahoo.com
FROM: LuLuLinda@aol.com
DATE: May 31, 2006 5:13 PM
SUBJECT: Re: re: re: Cali Here We Come!

Chicas,

I'm so sorry I'm only writing now. As I was driving back from taking some photographs in Jackson Heights, I got into a tiny accident with a taxi. No se apuren! I'm perfectly fine. My SUV's another story. ☹ Just pray I can get it fixed by Friday.

Anyway, I agree with Hazel re: the schedule. Another thing . . . shouldn't we avoid driving during rush hour? IMHO, we should be more flexible in the schedule not only to allow for FUN but for delays, too. Que piensan?

Hazel, can you resend me the playlist in RTF? My Mac couldn't open it. Oh, and when we go shopping for your graduation dress tomorrow, bring the CDs and I'll upload them to my iPod.

If Denver's out of the way, por favor, no se preocupen. I'm going home in August anyway. Besides I think my mother's going to be at a technology conference that week, and my brother's away at camp.

Jackie, what's this about Snoop Dogg? ☹ No me dejen ser la unica en el viaje que no fuma! I pray the police don't stop us.

This weekend I took myself on a photography excursion to Jackson Heights, East Harlem, and Sunset Park since those are the neighborhoods with many Mexican immigrants. Except for my tiny accident, I had a fantastic weekend!

Un abrazo fuerte a todas,
Lourdes

TO: Hazel1985@hotmail.com, LuLuLinda@aol.com, DreaminginCuban@juno.com
FROM: imokurnot@yahoo.com
DATE: May 31, 2006 10:14 PM
SUBJECT: Re: re: re: re: Cali Here We Come!

A "tiny" accident put your SUV out of commission??? I'm glad you're OK, pero tu eres loca. Y una princesa tambien, driving to school when you're only two train stops away. BTW, you have to come to Soundview where Hazel and I grew up in the Bronx. I dropped in on my pops, and your people are everywhere, LOL!

Anyway, I really hope you can fix the SUV, but I'll see if Raul can hook us up with a backup ride. Just know it might be a rickshaw or go-cart or something like that so I'd hold off on firing up the iPod. Instead get some rest then focus on collecting the common necessities we all need so we don't have four irons, hair dryers, etc.

And don't worry. The po won't be able to catch me let alone stop me! Seriously, if we should get pulled over, I say we just give up the potheads and keep it movin'. Que piensas tu?

If we can make it to Denver, can we crash at your house, Lou? It'd save us some money and be a nice break from all the motels. No pressure. It's your house, your family won't be there, etc. Like I said, Denver's an unlikely stop anyway, but...

To accommodate you freakin' party animals, I made changes to the schedule:

9AM—11AM:	Me
11AM—1PM:	Lunch & Sightseeing
1PM—3PM:	Irena
3PM—5PM:	Lourdes
5PM—7PM:	Hazel
7PM—???:	PAR-TAY (and maybe a liquid supper)

Irena, can we do your ritual thing on the road instead of on the morning before we leave? Is your pops going to hook us up with some food? You haven't gotten back to us about that yet. He knows you're going, right?

Wil and I had a blast this weekend. For a moment there though, I panicked because we got off the Metro-North in the middle of nowhere, and the stop didn't even have a station—just a rickety bench with a slab of wood that read "Breakneck Ridge." I kid you not. I said, "Where the hell's this ridge, Wil? In Bust-Yo'-Ass Forest?" But we camped, hiked, and even went white-water rafting. I'm hooked! That's our next trip.

Almost done with my thesis. Once it's done, I'M OUT THIS MUTHA! See y'all at the Olympic Flame next Friday.

Peace,
Jackie

P.S. Hazel, if you take us somewhere we have to line dance or sing karaoke, I will leave your ass on I-80.

JACKIE

1783 Willis Avenue
South Bronx, NY
Thursday, June 1, 10:39 A.M.

I make it halfway down the staircase when Wil calls my name. I hope he's changed his mind. I rush back to his floor, taking the steps two at a time and getting a kick out of the thump of my boots as they hit the chipped marble.

The man stands in his doorway shirtless, dangling my sling bag from his hand. "You forgot this." If Wil's going to tease me like that, he'd *better* have changed his mind. I once overheard him tell Kharim, "Another cool thing about Jackie is that she never passes up some lovin' because she's afraid to sweat out her perm like Miss Sheila." He has no business parading half-naked around me if he has no intention of giving it up.

I reach for my bag and say, "Irena says when you leave something behind, it's 'cause you really don't want to go." When I lean in to kiss him, Wil slides his fingers up my neck and gently grips my hair. He knows what that does to me! I press against him, trying to ease my way back into his apartment for another round.

But Wil stands firm in the doorway and then pulls back from me. "Since when do you listen to Irena?" He reaches out to straighten the strap of my tank top. Then he spins me around, swats me on the ass, and gently shoves me back toward the staircase. "I'll see you tonight."

He ain't right, grabbing my hair and kissing me like that, and he damn well knows it. "Be that way." Then I force a smile because the last thing I need to do before leaving for Frisco is to fight with him. As I head down the stairs, I can hear Wil laugh before closing his apartment door.

And to think that if I had taken that capoeira class instead of the LSAT prep course, I never would have met him. With the money I had saved last year by buying used textbooks and packing lunch, I decided to treat myself to a class over the summer. I still like the kickboxing one I take at school, but I needed a new challenge. I always wanted to learn capoeira since it combines so many things I love—martial arts, dance, hip-hop—so I RSVPed for a trial class taught by this kick-ass *brasileña* I read about in the *Village Voice.* But while on the subway to Chelsea, I spotted an ad for an LSAT prep course. I thought, *Damn, Jackie, that's what you need to do. You may have excellent grades and respectable extracurricula, but without an LSAT score in the 170s, you can forget about getting into a top law school, let alone getting a scholarship.* If I'm going to be the Latina reincarnation of William Kunstler, I can't afford to rack up a hundred grand in student loans. So I nixed the class to go home and register for the LSAT prep course. And who's there teaching it but the finest brother I have ever seen.

Jesus, I am starting to think like Irena. For a fleeting second, I almost chalked up meeting Wil to fate. Fate, my black ass. It was justice. For the first time in my twenty-two years on this earth, being the smartest chick in the room—and unapologetic about it—paid off. I'd better watch it or next thing I'll be reading my horoscope, going to some *botánica* to have my cards read or some crazy shit like that. Irena would love that!

As much as I like Rena, I'm not going to get caught up in her New Age gaga even though I get why she needs to believe in it. At first, I didn't understand why she froze during the Take Back the Night speakout two years ago. But when Irena left the podium and told me she had the unshakable feeling that bastard rapist was in the crowd, I said, "Point the animal out, and let's neuter his ass." Bet anything that would've done a lot more for her "healing process" than this turn-the-other-cheek bullshit.

When I leave the building, I almost trip over a brick-colored Spalding. Just as I pick it up, the little black girl who lives on Wil's floor comes toward me, dragging a broken broomstick. What's her name? I only know her as Li'l Bit, which is the nickname Wil gave her.

So I say, "What's good, Li'l Bit?" I don't know much about her, but I like her lots, and I'm not a big fan of kids (or they of mine, let me not front). While the other girls on this block sit on the stoop fawning over their Barbie dolls, Li'l Bit's running the streets like her little ass is on fire.

I hear this ruckus around the corner so I step off the stoop and look up the block. The neighborhood kids are in the midst of a heated game of stickball. I used to love that game and was pretty damned good at it, too. I turn back to Li'l Bit, who's standing next to me now, staring down at her ashy knees. Used to have those, too. "Why aren't you playing with them?"

She just shrugs and holds her hand out for the ball. I give it to her and kneel down to tighten the laces on my boots. As I do, I watch Li'l Bit throw the ball against the building wall and swat it with her broomstick. The ball ricochets around the plaza, and I jump up to catch it before it flies in the street. Li'l Bit's all power, no technique, just like me before my pops gave me a few pointers.

"So that's why they don't let you play," I say as I walk back toward her. "You're too good for those scrubs." But Li'l Bit just shakes her head, snatches the ball from me, and fires it into the wall. "Then what? C'mon, kid, talk to me." But I already know because as I watch her chase the ball into the concrete flower bed, my stomach burns with the same humiliation it did when I was nine years old and the neighborhood kids wouldn't let me play with them.

Li'l Bit gets the ball and says, "They let Minerva play, and she sucks." She tosses the ball into the air and whacks it with her broomstick with a vengeful swing. "She's the scrub, not me."

The ball bounces off the wall right into my outstretched palm. "You need to hold the stick like this," I say. I walk behind Li'l Bit and correct her stance. "Open your feet more. Lift your arms a little higher. Okay, now swing from your hips." Li'l Bit pulls back her arms. "No, you're swinging from your shoulders." I place my hands on her shoulders to weigh them down a bit just the way my dad had done when teaching me how to swing. Pivoting at the waist, Li'l Bit whips the stick forward and slices the air. "There you go, that's it!" I say. "Let's get out of here before we break a window."

I take her hand and lead her into the street. At the other end of the block, I see the kids playing their game. Pointing at the manhole cover, I say, "Stand over there." As I walk up the street, I pull off my sling bag and search the crowd, wondering which ones are the bullies and what nasty things they called Li'l Bit. Did they call her Brillo Pad? *Bembe* Face? Or the one I really hate . . . *cocola.* The little snots I grew up with used to call me that because they were too ignorant to realize that being black didn't make me *not* Latina and that I understood every nasty word they were saying. And I schooled them to the fact the hard way.

Li'l Bit's African American and probably doesn't understand the Spanish insults. Not that she needs to. Regardless of what language they use, she knows they're saying some racist shit. The venom in their tones and sneers on their faces makes *bembe* just as clear as Brillo. Shit, the poor kid has it worse than I did really. If one of those little *brujas* calls her a *cocola,* and Li'l Bit delivers the fat lip she has coming to her like I did, the brat can always deny that she ever said it.

I make Minerva on sight. She has to be that vanilla princess leaning against that silver Infiniti, twirling her waist-length dirty blond hair around her finger when she's supposed to be defending the box scrawled in blue chalk on the ground in front of her. The other team must be stealing third left and right. For a moment there, I want to scare a little civility into her prissy behind and send a message to all the other brats that are messing with Li'l Bit.

But I check myself because Minerva reminds me of Hazel when we were kids. Hazel was much prettier though, and probably kinder, too. For all I know, Minerva's just as innocent as Hazel had been. Hazel had no control over the vicious extremes that other kids went to to impress her, and maybe Minerva doesn't either. I seriously doubt that shit though. I'll never get the human impulse to turn cruel in the face of beauty. You'd think the opposite. Isn't beauty supposed to inspire kindness, charity, and all that? But then again, here I am thinking about going after the kid like Russell Crowe would a bellhop. I stop myself, remembering one of the immutable laws of playground politics. Li'l Bit has to show and prove. It's not going to help her for my grown-up ass to fight her battle and antagonize the most popular girl on the block. If anything, that'll make things worse for her.

Instead I drop my bag onto the ground and turn around to face Li'l Bit. "Remember what I told you," I say as I wind up and pitch the ball to her. With perfect technique, she whacks the ball, and it launches past me and into the middle of the stickball game. The boys look at each other trying to determine which one of them hit it, and I smile at Li'l Bit with loads of pride. "That's it!"

Li'l Bit jogs over to me, and I run my hand across her hair. It's soft and fluffy, and her eyes just radiate . . . She's the cutest fuckin' thing! A smile a supermodel would forgo a year of Botox for . . . How can anybody be mean to her? "Don't you ever let some little playahaters chase you from where you want to be, you hear me?" I say. I know that's easier said than done, so I pull the broomstick out of her hands and add, "And if they try, you grab the stick like this . . ." But then I had a better idea. "No, this is what you do. You pick out the biggest kid—the biggest boy—and you take his big head like this." I hook my arm around Li'l Bit's head into a gentle headlock.

She starts a giggling fit but waits for more instructions. Then I remember where wrestling with boys got me, and I let her go. But I don't think that Doña Myra's little fable about St. Benedict's going to work here either, so I just say, "Go tell an adult or something." That's what I'm supposed to say even though I suspect that it's probably as useless advice today as it was thirteen years ago.

"No!" Li'l Bit whines. "Teach me wrestling." The kid's a pisser—I love that. She growls and throws her arms around my hips, and we both stumble as she tries to tackle me to the asphalt. I laugh as I brace myself and straighten up. Geez, Li'l Bit's already a good four six, and she's only nine. All arms and legs, too, just like me at that age. Maybe with all that height, she'll grow up to be the next Naomi Campbell or Tyra Banks. God knows I sure didn't.

I throw my sling over my shoulder and give her an apologetic smile. "Can't, kid. I have to go to school."

"School? Now? Why?"

"I have to return these library books and then pick up my graduation gown." Okay, I admit I get a kick out of her disappointment. Like I said, I'm not exactly Maria from *Sesame Street.* "Then I have to run some errands 'cause I'm going on a trip to San Francisco with my friends." After I make this trek to Fordham, I have to find myself a cheap white dress for the New York Latinas Against Domestic Violence Emergency Brides' March. No, scratch that. We're leaving on Friday morning now so that's one less thing to think about. But now that Lourdes wrecked her SUV beyond easy repair, I'll probably lose the rest of the afternoon cajoling Raul into lending me his Escalade for the road trip instead of that red sardine can he has the nerve to call a car.

"I wanna go!"

"Sure, when you graduate from college."

Li'l Bit pouts, "Who's gonna show me stuff when you're gone?"

"My boyfriend'll teach you some moves until I get back. Now go play. And remember what I said." Li'l Bit picks up her stick and barges into the stickball game as I walk back to the Ford Tempo (technically Raul's, essentially mine). I climb into the car, place my sling bag in the passenger seat, and peek into the rearview window for one last check on Li'l Bit. She menaces the boy who caught her ball with her broomstick until he gives it back. Atta girl.

Then I catch my own reflection in the mirror. I rake my fingers through my hair, which is a dark maze encircling my face. Why would Wil want to stick his hands in that nest, let alone actually do so? I reach into my bag for the new serum, pomade, or whatever the hell it was that Hazel gave me. Still I can't bring myself to open it. I never can. And forget about all that stuff Irena says about cutting your hair to change your karma. I don't want to become one of those chicks who refuses to leave the house without her "face on" and her hair "did." I refuse to succumb to those bullshit pressures. That would make me the biggest hypocrite. You can call me a lot of things, but never a hypocrite.

So I toss the tube out my window and tear out of the parking space.

HAZEL

255 West 21st Street
Chelsea, NY
Thursday, June 1, 11:10 A.M.

Even though I know she's in her office on campus, I grow increasingly nervous as I get closer to Geneva's apartment. I sent her an e-mail as late as possible last night, telling her that I was coming by this morning to get the rest of my things. I both hope and dread that she stayed home just to have a last chance to see me, since I doubt she's coming to my graduation. I made it clear that despite our breakup she was welcome to attend, but she gave me a weak maybe. "I have to grade papers, meet with the freelance publicist I hired to organize my book tour, finish my presentation for the conference . . ." And I don't doubt Geneva has all those things to do. She wouldn't create excuses to skip my graduation any more than she would cancel her office hours this morning. But I'm still unhappy about it because as valid as every item on her extensive to-do list may be, every single one is a poor excuse to punish me for ending our relationship.

Maybe it's my fault. I shouldn't have just invited Geneva to my graduation but actually made her feel obligated to be there. But if you have to do that to someone who supposedly loves you, what's the point? Then again, that hasn't stopped me from dropping reminders for my mother left and right. Circling the date in bright red marker on every calendar in the apartment, making sure she's within earshot when I talk to Jackie about it on the phone, asking her opinion about what kind of dress I should wear or how I should style my hair . . .

I even offered to take my mother shopping to buy her dress. My treat, of course. She used to love to take me shopping. We'd go to Main Street in Flushing and spend the whole day wandering in and out of the stores. Even though we couldn't afford much, we had so much fun trying on clothes and finding accessories. And when we did buy something, we made sure we matched. We were the Beautiful Flores girls.

Then I turned thirteen, my mother found out I was queer, and she shipped me to live with my paternal grandmother in the Bronx. Except for Thanksgiving and Christmas when my *abuelita* roasted *pernil* and cooked a large pot of *arroz con gandules*, I'd never see her. I'd call Ruby on Mother's Day, and she'd speak to me on my birthday (after *Abuelita* placed the call to her, no doubt), but that was it. She even stopped taking me along on her visits to my father upstate. Then my grandmother died the summer before I started college, and I had no choice but to move back in with Ruby.

I walk the three flights to Geneva's floor and let myself into her apartment. Except for a bowl and spoon in the sink, the place is immaculate as always. If it didn't already exist, the word *tidy* would've had to be invented just to describe Geneva. No other word suits her so perfectly, and no other person is a better example of what it means. If she were a straight white guy, she'd either be the CEO of a Fortune 500 company or a serial killer.

I wonder who is braiding Geneva's tidy hair. I last braided it in December. We had switched on the news on NY1 just as a group of transgender activists were rallying outside of City Hall. They were calling for the passage of SOGENDA—the Sexual Orientation and Gender Expression Non-Discrimination Act. Margarita Lopez, the first out lesbian to be elected to the City Council, had proposed the bill to expand the state law banning discrimination against gays, lesbians, and bisexual people to also protect transsexuals—be they pre-op, post-op, or non-op—drag kings and queens, cross-dressers, and basically anyone and everyone who challenged traditional gender roles. When the state gay rights bill, called just SONDA, was on the brink of getting passed back in late 2002, transgender folks protested, demanding a more inclusive amendment. The ol' gay guard had a fit, fearing that the Republican-controlled state legislature would use the protest as an excuse to torpedo the bill altogether. Well, that didn't happen. Surprisingly, the bill passed—but not before longtime hostilities among factions in New York's queer community flared to an all-new high. My relationship with Geneva was one of the hidden casualties.

"There they go again," Geneva said, pointing at Councilwoman Lopez, a petite butch from the Lower East Side with droplets of Boriquen clinging to the occasional word as she spoke in front of City Hall.

"Keep still," I said as I started a new braid at the center of her scalp. "If you ask me, they never should've been left out of the state law in the first place."

"They almost cost us SONDA."

"Well, they didn't. Hell, we owe transgender people. It's because of them we have a movement."

"Carmen, I don't need you to tell me my history."

"It's my history, too, Geneva, but we all forget sometimes that what could've been just another police raid on a gay bar sparked a movement thanks to a Puerto Rican drag queen from the Bronx."

"Ouch, Carmen!" Geneva's hand shot up to her scalp. "Take it easy."

"Sorry. I just have a big problem with affluent whites being the arbiters of queerness, that's all."

"This coming from the self-proclaimed bisexual femme who hangs out with no one but straight girls."

I grabbed my coat and stormed out of Geneva's apartment, leaving her looking like Susan Taylor on crack. When I got home, I found a message from Jackie asking me to call her. She and Wil had had another fight about Sheila, but the second she heard my voice, Jackie knew something was wrong. I tried to downplay my argument with Geneva, but she insisted I talk. As I told her what happened, I began to cry. "Geneva doesn't want a girlfriend," I said. "She wants a protégée. No, not even. She wants a fuckin' fan. Sometimes she makes me feel no different than a guy who treats me like a mindless dime piece." Jackie had been so quiet that I thought we might have been disconnected. "Jackie?"

"I'm here." Then she sighed. With that simplest of sounds, Jackie let me know that she heard what I had never said. As often as I complained about Geneva's superiority complex, I believed it was warranted. I could get a college degree, read the books, know the complete histories, wear the buttons, and attend the conferences, but I'd still be nothing more than the pretty yet semi-closeted, working-class hairstylist from Queens. "It's kind of like Booker T. versus W. E. B. DuBois all over again," said Jackie. "But you really want to know why Geneva got pissed at you? Not only did you beat her to the more progressive analysis, you got there from the heart and not your head." Then she started laughing. "I mean, your position leaves room for a straight tomboy like me. No wonder ol' girl's granny panties are in a knot."

I laughed so hard when she said that. And that was when I started to believe that perhaps Jackie and I were meant to be more than friends. Still I agonized for months before finally breaking up with Geneva. I had never been the gay girl who secretly pined for the straight girl. I've never been one to pine for anyone at all. I always got whoever I wanted, and too many I didn't, although that never stopped me from getting involved in the first place. Between my history with Jackie and her ongoing problems with Wil, I finally left Geneva, who apparently had never been left, and that's why she's intent on defying one of the most sacred yet unwritten tenets of lesbian relationships: Even when it ends, you must remain friends.

I head to the hallway closet and look for something to carry my stuff. When I find my old Fordham gym bag with the broken zipper, I take it into the bedroom. There I find the last of my things neatly assembled across the bed: a stack of my clothes including a few tops that actually belonged to Geneva; a small pile of mass market paperbacks that you deny buying let alone reading, and a few CDs; a wicker basket of my personal effects including a Lady Schick razor, several pairs of costume earrings, and even little samples of shampoo and lipstick. It hurts me so much to see my things laid out for me. I console myself with the observation that not only did Geneva allow me to keep a few things that were rightfully hers, but she also didn't return any gifts or cards that I had given her. I keep my eyes away from the wastebasket to protect myself from any devastating realizations to the contrary.

While I'm stuffing all my things into the gym bag, the intercom buzzes. I consider ignoring it. I mean, it can't be Geneva. Why would she ring her own buzzer? But curiosity gets the better of me. By the second buzz, I'm at the front door. "Who is it?"

"UPS."

I let the guy into the building and press my face against the peephole. Within a few seconds a brown uniform appears in my view so I open the door. He's a beauty, this one. "Hi."

By the way his eyes dilate, I can tell he doesn't think I'm too shabby myself. "How are you?" He hands me the computerized clipboard. "Sign on line seventeen, please."

I take the clipboard and sign while he lifts the medium-sized box at his feet. I step back so he can place it inside the apartment on the floor and then hand him the clipboard. He thanks me and gives me another quick once-over. I like that he's making an effort to be subtle and wonder how many women have dismissed him on sight because of his blue collar. Or should I say brown collar? "You look kind of young for a professor," he says.

"Oh, I'm not Professor Boyd." I almost add *I'm her girlfriend* but catch myself. Even if it were still true, that'd be mean to say, and he's done nothing to deserve that. And as far as I'm concerned, I'm not going to be single for long. "Thank you." I move to close the door to politely signal the end of the conversation. But I watch him as he makes his way toward the staircase, and I can't help myself. "That must be part of the job requirement," I say after him.

He stops and looks over his shoulder. "Excuse me?"

Not *What?* Not *Huh?* Not even *Whadyasay?* But *Excuse me.* He deserves some kindness for that.

"Having nice calves," I say. "All you UPS guys have them. Must be part of the job requirement." He blushes and thanks me.

"You're welcome." Then I wave good-bye and close the door before things go too far. It really isn't so hard to put a smile on someone's face, so I can't understand why more people won't bother.

I grab the box and lug it over to the coffee table. I read the return address. With her book coming out in a few weeks, Geneva's press is on a tear. These must be her personal copies of the book. I'm tempted to rip open the box and take one for myself. Would she mind? After all, I practically co-wrote the thing. Not that I did a lick of writing. But I read drafts and gave her feedback. Geneva ran ideas by me, and I gave her my honest opinions, and whenever I wasn't feeling particularly vulnerable, challenged them, helping her strengthen her arguments. I understood when Geneva had found momentum in a tough chapter and didn't want to stop to catch the movie we had planned to see, and I readily forgave her when she completely forgot our lunch plans, agreeing to meet with her editor at a café in SoHo while I sat waiting for her at Ruby Foo's in Times Square.

I decide against helping myself to a copy of her book. At this point in our relationship, I have no clue if Geneva would mind or not, but it really doesn't matter. Not only should she give me a copy, she should write a personal note and sign it. But I can't ask her do that. She has to do it without any prodding from me or it means nothing.

So I take the broken gym bag full of my things, hang the keys on the rack by the door, and let myself out of Geneva's apartment for the last time.

LOURDES

Ansonia Hotel at
73rd & Broadway
Upper West Side, NY
Thursday, June 1, 4:32 P.M.

As many times as I've admired it, I can't help but look at the banner once more before I pack it. I drape it across the pebble suede duffel opened across my canopy bed. *Dios, perdóname* for being so proud of this beautiful work of art.

When the idea came to me last spring, I posted flyers in the art department.

Social Justice Organization
Seeks to Commission
Gifted Art Student
to create a banner to support an important cause
Pay $300.00.
E-mail Samples ASAP to Lourdes at LuLuLinda@aol.com

As I tacked up the last flyer and stepped back to reread it, I flirted with the idea of taking it down and making the banner myself. But I had to be realistic. I didn't have the time to do that, but I did have the money to make it happen.

I received a few great samples, but Roberta's were nothing less than divine. We hit it off from our first meeting, and she welcomed my suggestions. She especially liked it when I said, "Paint the *t* in *Catholics* as a cross." Roberta also turned the *o* in *Choice* into the woman symbol. Now why hadn't I thought of that? Roberta's brilliance filled me with pride and envy—that's two deadly sins from one act of charity!—so I paid her an extra fifty dollars.

It really surprised me when I unveiled the banner at the next meeting and some of the older women complained that I had no right spending that kind of money without the group's approval. I assured them that the banner was my gift to the organization and that I didn't expect them to reimburse me. Still they said *que todavía yo encomendaba un buen santo* because the point remained that I shouldn't have commissioned the banner without first consulting the other members. The ringleader of the naysayers said, "We might have wanted input into the design." But at the Roe v. Wade anniversary rally that January, all the other women's organizations praised the Catholics for Choice banner and asked where they might get one.

In fact, Roberta sent me an e-card to thank me for hiring her to create the banner. "Yesterday, about six organizations asked me for my contact info, and some are huge nonprofits with multimillion-dollar budgets," she wrote. "If only half of them follow through with projects for me, I can quit one of my jobs this summer and have time for my art without worrying about my rent. *¡Gracias, hermana!*"

I fold the Catholics for Choice banner, lay it in my suitcase, and then stuff it with all I have, trying to suppress the envy that has overtaken my pride. I don't like being jealous of Roberta, especially when there's no reason to be. I have my own visual talents. If I cultivated them, I probably could make a living as a photographer. But unless I change my major, being pre-med demands all the labs I can stand.

I glance at my Vacheron watch. If I hurry, I can make it to the registrar before it closes for the day. I grab my purse, race out of the apartment, and hail a yellow cab on Broadway. During the ride I pray for many things. To make it to the registrar before it closes. To not lose my nerve before I get there. To get to the registrar alive because the cabbie is darting in and out of traffic *como si estuviera loco.* To get my SUV fixed before we leave for San Francisco because Jackie drives just like him!

I arrive at the registrar ten minutes to closing and ask the woman behind the counter for a Change of Major form. She hands it to me, and I rush to complete it. I check that I'll be a junior in the fall, and under *Current Academic Information,* I write *Biology* in the space marked *Major.* Despite my mother's "urging" (the word I use *porque no quiero faltarle el respeto*), I had yet to declare a minor or concentration because I couldn't bear any more science courses. It's not that I find the sciences difficult or uninteresting. I've just lost my childhood passion for them. Besides, being a pre-med biology major challenges me enough without the additional pressure of accumulating more credits in another science for a minor.

But now I consider minoring in a science as a compromise with my mother. Last semester when Mamá called me in the middle of midterms to ask about my minor, in desperation I said to her, "So much of what I'm learning contradicts what the Church has taught me." *¡Qué escándalo!* God must be good because He didn't strike me down that second, since my anxiety had nothing to do with the evolution–creationism debate. I pleaded with my mother to let me attend college in New York so I could see the exhibits on Museum Mile, discuss art and politics in the sidewalk cafés in the Village, photograph the immigrant communities in the outer boroughs, and . . . Okay, hunt for the latest fashions on Fifth Avenue. Instead I spent most of my time with my face in a petri dish and not even the Paula Dorf eye cream with vitamin K that Hazel recommended could heal the dark circle under my right eye from boring into that microscope.

"Nonsense, Lourdes," *Mamá me dijo.* "There are many Christian doctors, and clearly some if not most of your professors must be practicing Catholics or they wouldn't be teaching at a Jesuit university. Speak with them about how they reconcile the contradictions. Hold on for a moment, Lourdes . . ." After a few moments, she returned to the telephone and said, "Why don't you take this course on intelligent design?"

"Intelligent design?" For a fleeting second of wishful thinking, I thought my mother had suggested I take a fashion course, and I almost dropped to my knees to thank God. But of course, I quickly remembered that if Fordham offered such a course, I would have discovered it *eons* ago. She had to have been talking about a computer course of some kind. "Mamá, I don't think I can handle another hard science—"

"It's a philosophy course," she said over the rustling of pages. "No, it's a theology course. *This course provides an overview of topics in apologetics in intelligent design, moral relativism . . .*"

My mother in Colorado was reading from a hard copy of my course catalog. If God were *that* good, He would have taken me right there. *Dios, perdóname.* I didn't mean that. "I thought you were saying I should take a computer class."

"That's an excellent idea! Everything is becoming computerized in one form or other, and the health care industry's no exception," Mamá says. "It'll serve you well to minor in computer science and learn how to use a computer to do something other than write a paper or shop on the Internet. In fact, I'll probably need your help at the company when you come home in August. Have you booked your flight yet?"

My pen is at the line that reads *New Academic Information—Major,* but my courage is fading. I reach into my purse for my phone and pray that Irena's home. I should have ignored her and given her a cell phone for her birthday.

"Hello?"

"It's Lourdes. I'm at the registrar."

Irena immediately understands the significance of my call and starts to coach me. "Okay, how far along are you?"

"I wrote in what I wanted to change it from." My breathing grows heavier, and my heart races. "Now I'm at the part where I have to fill in what I want to change it to."

"The other day when you were showing me the camera you bought for the trip and explaining to me all the different features, I wished you could've heard yourself, Lou," says Irena. "Just talking about it makes you so happy. Imagine if you did it. You have to go through with this."

"Ay, yo no sé . . ."

"What's Jackie always telling you?"

"That I'm nobody's doctor."

"And she's right. You're an artist. A photographer. And remember when Hazel said it'd be cool if you two went into business together?"

Claro que recuerdo. "She would do people's hair and makeup, and I would take their portraits." I'm convinced that fantasizing about working with Hazel when I should've been studying cost me an A in physics. I was more than satisfied with the B, but when my mother sees it, *se va enfurecer.* I envision walking into my house in Aurora and finding my mother standing in the living room, fuming until the report card in her hand bursts into flames. I make a note to myself to get a change of address form, too, since my mother insists on opening my mail, especially if it comes from the school. *"Ay, Irena, no puedo."*

"Yes, you can! Lourdes, you are going to change your major from biology to visual arts, go into business with Hazel, and have a charity shoot for my clients at the women's center."

"I am?"

"Yes, you are! And from that shoot, both Hazel and you will have some before-and-after shots for your portfolios to attract paying clients. But first you're going to introduce women who've been told that they're ugly and weak to their true essence. To their beauty and power."

I'm so excited by that idea, my heart catches fire. "*Sí, sí, sí* . . . I love it! I'll do it!"

The clerk behind the counter says, "Miss, if you're going to hand that in . . . We close in five minutes."

"Irena, I have to finish this before they close. Let me call you back."

"Okay."

"*¡Gracias!*"

"De nada!"

Under the section titled *New Academic Information* and in the line next to *Major,* I scrawl *Visual Arts.* Then I become confused. Do I declare photography as my minor or my concentration? I hope the woman behind the counter can assist me with this so I can finalize this today. Just as I raise my hand to gain her attention, my cell phone rings. I flip open the phone and wedge it between my ear and shoulder. "*Sí, sí, sí,* I have the form in my hand as I speak—"

"What form?"

"Mamá!" I rush to cover my surprise by asking for her blessing. "*La bendición.*"

"*Que Dios te bendiga, m'ija.* What form?" I take too long to answer. "Lourdes, what's wrong?" Of course, my mother sounds more annoyed than concerned.

"*Todo está bien.* Everything's fine, Mamá." Just like my mother to call me at this precise moment. Sometimes I wonder if she installed some kind of surveillance equipment in the jewelry she gives me. I even pick up the diamond crucifix hanging from my neck and inspect it for a tiny camera. "I was coming to the campus, and I promised my friend I'd pick up a form for her." Inspired by my own lie, I decide to test the waters. "She wants to change her major. From biology to photography."

My mother scoffs into the phone. "Do her parents know that she's throwing away their money?"

The woman behind the counter eyes me, and I drift away from the desk so that she cannot hear me. "Mamá, that's such a judgmental thing to say."

"No, it's truthful. You do not spend four years and tens of thousands of dollars to learn how to take pictures. Photography's a hobby not a career." *What about Tina Modotti or Gordon Parks or Jacob Riis?* But my mother wouldn't recognize any of those names even though she cuts a hefty check to the Denver Art Museum as one of the charitable donations she makes every December. Besides, if I launch into a list of successful photographers, I risk betraying myself. "Which friend is this?"

"Irena."

"*Ay, la pobrecita.* Every time I hear about some young woman getting raped on campus, I think of her, and it's all I can do to keep from putting you on the first plane back home. That could have been you, Lourdes. Now you understand why I didn't want you living in campus housing?"

"Yes, Mamá." I don't bother to remind her that except for when she stays with me during exams, Irena commutes to school from Jersey City, and that the rape occurred off campus. The last thing I should do is paint New York City like Batman's Gotham. Besides I never wanted to live in a dormitory anyway. Jackie can call me *una princesa* all she wants—sharing a bathroom and eating cafeteria food were aspects of the college experience I always intended to skip.

Lucky for me that during our trip to New York in my senior year of high school to visit Fordham, my mother fell in love with the Ansonia's beaux arts architecture. She said it reminded her of the second honeymoon she and Papá took to Paris the year before he died. I boasted that the Ansonia was the first air-conditioned building in New York City and that all the apartments were soundproof. Later I gave her an article I clipped about the photography exhibit about the building presented by the Municipal Art Society on its hundredth anniversary. I fought the urge to highlight the name of some of its famous residents—Igor Stravinsky, Theodore Dreiser, Jack Dempsey—since they were all artists or entertainers of some sort. And of course, I made sure my scissors took a wrong turn at the brief reference to the infamous Plato's Retreat, once located in the apartment-hotel's basement after the Continental Baths vacated (which served as many as one thousand gay men around the clock) and before the AIDS epidemic forced the city to shut it down.

"*Mira, nena,* when is your flight home?" my mother asks. No lie comes quickly enough for me to reply. "Lourdes, don't tell me you still haven't booked your flight."

I flash back to when I was ten years old and forced my parents to buy five books of raffle tickets for my Catholic school's fundraiser because I had waited too long to tell them I had to sell them. "Between studying for my exams, and writing my papers, and interviewing people to sublease my apartment—"

"Lourdes, I thought I told you to forget about that subleasing nonsense. I'd much rather continue paying your rent while you're home for the summer than having some stranger live in your apartment."

"Why pay all that rent when I'm not going to be here?" I mean it even though I only plan to spend August in Aurora. After all, that nine-hundred-square-foot one-bedroom apartment at the Ansonia costs Mamá $3,100 every month. Just because I can't bring myself to give it up doesn't mean I don't feel bad about it sometimes.

"Well, what's the point of my paying that kind of rent so you can live in a nice place in a decent neighborhood to let *quien sea* sublease it. Do you know how much damage a person can do in two months?" I try to defend my ability to judge potential subtenants, but Mamá continues. "If you really wanted to save me money, you would've booked your ticket after Easter."

"I was waiting to see if I got into this special program." The fib lands in my imagination like the dove that delivers the olive branch to Noah after the flood. "It's a two-week intensive between Fordham and St. Luke's–Roosevelt Hospital. Like a simulation of medical school. We're going to shadow the medical students, doing rotations, going to lectures *y todo.*" Too impressed with my own creativity, I dance to the rhythm of the details as they come to me even as the woman behind the desk rolls her eyes and shuts off her computer. "They're even going to keep us awake for thirty-six hours at a time!" *Me voy al infierno, lo sé.* Satan himself just made my bed, flicked a quarter on it, and left a mint on my pillow.

"Like a boot camp," my mother says with an unmistakable tone of approval.

"*¡Exactamente!* The selection process was so competitive, Mamá, but I got in." I almost add, *Do you know how good this is going to look on my medical school applications?* But with that thought alone, the guilt finally hits.

"That's going to look wonderful on your medical school applications," Mamá says. "I'm so proud of you, LuLu. I know your father's looking down on you right now, and he's proud of you, too."

No, Mamá, St. Peter and Michael the Archangel are holding Papá back. "He's proud of all of us, Mamá." I take the form off the counter, fold it, and walk out of the registrar. "As soon as the program's done, I'll be on the first flight to Denver."

"Just book your flight on the Internet today, and e-mail me your itinerary."

"I'm going straight home to do that right now. *La bendición.*"

"*Que Dios te bendiga.*"

I drop my cell phone into my purse along with the change-of-major form. I'm supposed to call Irena, but I just can't. I'm done with lying for the day.

IRENA

Above La Habanita
de Rodriguez Bodega
Jersey City, NJ
Thursday, June 1, 7:14 P.M.

I promised my co-workers at the women's center that I would finish these signs for the emergency march and drop them off before I left for Frisco, but ever since I found the letters my father's been hiding from me, I can't regain my concentration. I just sit on the sticky linoleum of our living room floor, tracing the same line on the poster even though the ink has run dry in virtually all my markers. The air in here's like soup because we can't afford air-conditioning, and downstairs in front of our bodega, someone is blasting "Gasolina" from his car as if one summer without that vulgar reggaeton song was too much to freakin' ask.

C'mon, Irena, concentrate. You're leaving for Frisco on the same day as the march, so these posters are the only contribution you can make. Block out the noise, forget about Dad and the letters, and finish these posters. Do it for Olga.

Last week a young bank teller named Olga Tamayo was shot to death by her estranged husband. She had fled to Jackson Heights, Queens, from Colombia to escape his violence, only for him to follow and kill her eight months later. Every year on September 26, my center and other antiviolence organizations join NYLADV in a march from the Dominican Women's Development Center in Washington Heights to the First Spanish Baptist Church in East Harlem to mark the anniversary of the murder of Gladys Ricart, who was gunned down by her abusive ex-boyfriend as she posed for photos in her tiara and gown hours before her wedding. NY-LADV called for a similar, emergency march in Olga's name when her husband's defense attorney argued that the charges against him be reduced from murder to manslaughter because his was a "crime of passion." On Friday our coalition plans to march down Roosevelt Avenue from the bank, where twenty-three-year-old Olga was shot while replenishing deposit slips at the customer counter, to the offices of her murderer's defender. And just as we do during the Annual Brides' March in Gladys Ricart's memory, the women will wear wedding gowns or white dresses while our male allies dress in black.

So focus, Irena. This is an important event. Finish these signs. DOMESTIC VIOLENCE = CRIME ~~OF PASSION~~. The lines through OF PASSION are too faint, and I had wanted to strike through the thick black letters with a broad red slash. But as soon as I pulled the cap off the permanent marker, I knew the pen had run dry when my nose didn't sting from the toluene.

I learned about that deceptive toxin the hard way. Twelve years ago I sat in this very same spot creating a Mother's Day Card to send to my mom in Cuba. I had surrounded myself with all the supplies I needed to create my masterpiece—scissors, glue, construction paper, glitter, and markers. I congratulated myself on being a big girl, having graduated from crayons to markers. But the pungent aroma of the toluene was so seductive, my enthusiasm for my art project turned into an obsession with sniffing my Magic Markers. Even though I had never huffed before—I mean, at seven years old I didn't even know what I was doing had a name—I sensed that what I was doing was naughty. And I didn't care.

According to the doctor at the Emergency Pediatrics Center at Beth Israel, it only took minutes of inhaling the fumes to trigger the worst asthma attack I ever had. She gave my dad a Spanish brochure about the dangers of inhalant abuse. The child psychologist who had interviewed me assured him that I was an innocent, healthy girl who stumbled into huffing over nothing more than childish hedonism. Still Dad wasted no time in removing every possible temptation from my reach. Until this day, he keeps all the aerosol sprays and cleaning agents on high shelves, while he stacks the dishes and cups along with pots and pans in the cabinets under the sink. Even though I barely read Spanish, I still have that brochure stashed in the files beneath my bed. It became the first item in my now extensive collection of health information and resources, collected from fairs, downloaded from the Internet, and photocopied from self-help books, all meticulously filed and cross-referenced on my computer with a hard copy of the database placed in a three-ring binder on my shelf. What else would you expect from someone who has Virgo in her twelfth house?

So I tossed the defective red pen into the trash can and headed to the closet in the hallway where Dad keeps the markers he uses to draw announcements of his weekly sales to post in the bodega's window. He prefers to keep his "art" supplies at home because he's afraid that the neighborhood graffiti artists might try to break into the store for them. As much as I want to call out his paranoia, I hold my tongue because I don't want to provoke one of his lectures about how I don't focus enough on my studies, wasting time on politics like my mother and running around *con esa negra loca.* Imagine my embarrassment when I asked Jackie what that meant! I don't know what bothers me more—his overt attacks on Mom and her activities in Cuba or his subtly racist digs at Jackie. But nothing feels worse than the fact that I have yet to tell my father how Jackie and I became friends in the first place.

But that's beside the point because Dad's been keeping something just as important from me, too. I go into the hallway closet to search for the markers, and when I don't find any in the buckets of tools, gadgets, and whatever on the floor, I drag a chair from the kitchen so I can climb on it and search the top shelf. That's when I discover the stack of old shoe boxes flush against the back wall. The last box had once belonged to a pair of Buster Browns Dad bought me for Easter Sunday when I was seven. I intuitively knew there were no markers in that particular box but that I still had to open it.

Dad and I came to the United States when I was three. To learn anything about my father's life in Cuba, I had to creep into the kitchen and eavesdrop on his tipsy conversations with the guys he invited over to play dominoes or watch the Yankees, trying to make sense with my limited understanding of Spanish by listening as intensely to his pauses and cadences as I did his words. I'd hear the echoes of his loneliness beneath his conflicting rants against Castro's intransigence and the U.S. embargo. He would talk about my mother with loving words but an angry tone. Sometimes Dad would even quote her letters, one moment bragging about denying her requests to see him and the next admiring her refusals to accept his offer of financial assistance. I had my own letters from Mom stashed away in my journals, although for some unknown reason I had not heard from her in over six months. So even though I knew I was not supposed to look through the boxes I found in the closet, that was exactly why I did.

The more I sift through the yellowing report cards and discolored Polaroids, my resentment grows toward Dad's convoluted sentimentality. If these things were important enough to save, why didn't he store them in an album where we could flip through them together? Why did he force me to scour through a dusty box behind his back like a criminal?

And then I find the first letter addressed to me written by Yadira Arroyo Suárez de Rodriguez and postmarked from Cuba slightly after Three Kings Day. The envelope had been ripped diagonally through the center. When I pull out and unfold the neatly scribed sheet, something falls out and into my lap—a pin of the Cuban flag with a banner that reads CENTENARIO across the top. Just what I had asked Mom to send me this past Christmas.

Mi querida hija, the letter starts. *Estoy escribiendo en español como me pedistes.* Lourdes gave me that great suggestion. *Pero quiero que tú me escribes in English so I can learn from you and practice my English, too, ok?*

Finding that letter fills me with a mixture of elation and rage. For over six months I believed my mother stopped writing me back because I had asked if I could visit her next summer. But the truth is that Dad just stopped giving me Mom's letters. I tuck the pin into the front pocket of my jeans and search through the other envelopes until I find three more letters from my mother addressed to me. One of them even includes a picture of the three of us right after I was born. Every time my father sees Cameron Diaz on television, he jokes, *"Allí esta la madre tuya."* I just roll my eyes because supposedly I'm the spitting image of my mother, and I look nothing like Cameron Diaz. I mean, I have blond hair and blue eyes and white skin and, okay, I'm pretty skinny, too, but the resemblance ends there. I'm barely five two, and no one confuses me for Anglo. At least, not other Latinos. Not that I know of. But one thing is true. I see my mother in this picture, and today I look almost exactly like Mom did then.

I return to the living room, park myself on the floor, and read them. My Spanish may be weak, but I understand that not only does my Mom want more than anything for me to come visit her in Cuba, she hopes that I can convince Dad to come with me, too. And she asks me to write her about the women's conference I'm attending in San Francisco. When she didn't hear from me in a while, she gave me the benefit of the doubt, writing that she understood that I had many things to juggle—helping my father at the bodega, volunteering at the women's center, and pursuing my college degree. Mom writes that she loves me and misses me. And Dad, too.

But I have to confront him. When he walks in here, I'm going to stand up to him and show him the letters he hid from me. I'm going to demand an explanation, and I'll refuse to leave until I get it.

I sleepwalk through the rest of the picket signs until I hear the key in the front door. Soon my father's tall physique fills the archway to the living room. "Irena?" When I rehearsed the scene in my head, I pounced on him waving the letters in his face. Instead I grab a blue marker and begin to outline the letters just to avoid his eyes. Dad walks over to stand behind me and reads over my shoulder. Then he just huffs.

"What's that supposed to mean?" Not that I need him to say anything since I've heard it all before. I recap the marker and shove it back into its cardboard box, feeling more disgusted with my inability to speak my mind than my father's disdain for my activism. "A man kills his wife, and that's all you can do?" Why can't I say more? Why can't I say what I need to say? If I can't stand up for my own convictions, how am I going to expose his lies? And when will I ever be free to reveal my own secret?

"*¿Qué tú quieres que yo diga?*" my father says. That's what he always says, and I'm sooo tired of it. "It's terrible. He should spend the rest of his life in jail then burn in hell." Dad eases into the lounge chair and pulls out a pack of cigarettes from his breast pocket. "Harrassing his lawyer won't guarantee that."

"Never mind," I say, and start to gather my markers and posters.

"*¿Y qué te pasa, m'ija?*" He thinks I'm upset with his smoking, so he stuffs the cigarette box back into his pocket. Even though he had given me the master bedroom and took the living room as "his" room, he tries not to smoke in front of me, because of my asthma. Ordinarily, I appreciate it but not right now.

"Nothing." I hobble out of the living room with all my things and a heaping mix of anger, shame, and guilt. "Nothing at all."

IRENA

The Olympic Flame
Upper West Side, NY
Friday, June 2, 12:03 P.M.

"Rena, you're nineteen years old," Jackie says. "You're old enough to decide how you want to spend your summer, whether it's driving across the country with your friends or visiting the mother you haven't seen in sixteen years."

"I know that." I just stare into my untouched glass of tap water. Yuck! "But I have to live with my father."

"I live with my pops, too."

Opportunities to tease Jackie are rare, so I can't let this one slip by. "Technically. Today. Tomorrow?"

"Oh, shut up. I'm not moving in with Wil." A frown flickers across her face as she grabs a piece of bread from the basket and tears it in half. "But that's a good example right there. I got sick and tired of telling my father I was staying with Hazel when I was spending the night at Wil's. I mean, what am I? Sixteen? No, I'm gonna be twenty-two in August. And Pops has met Wil, and he likes him, so why front? Just because I'm no Halle Berry doesn't mean I'm a fuckin' virgin."

I sigh as Jackie pops the bread into her mouth. "I wish you wouldn't say things like that."

"Don't be getting all Lourdes on me."

"Not the cursing."

Jackie shoves the other half of the bread into her mouth and washes it down with that yucky tap water. "What'd I say?"

She truly has no idea what I'm talking about. Is it because she's a poor listener or because she has bought into this myth that she's unattractive? "The whole Halle Berry thing."

"That? Big deal. It's true." Lourdes rushes into the diner, and I slide to the end of the booth so she can squeeze in next to me. After we greet each other, Jackie asks, "Did Irena tell you about her father and the letters?"

Lourdes's almond eyes open, and she turns to me. *"Sí, sí, sí. ¿Y qué tú vas hacer, Irena?"*

It takes me a few seconds to figure out that Lourdes is asking me what I'm going to do. "I don't know, but Jackie says I should confront him."

"I'm not saying get all up in his face," Jackie says. "But you have to tell him that you found the letters. And you should tell him that you're going to Frisco with us with or without his permission. And fuck it. While you're at it, tell him you're going to Cuba to see your mother next summer, too." She folds her toned arms across the table as if to finalize the matter.

"It's not that easy, Jackie," Lourdes says. She puts her hand over mine. "But if you do talk to him and things go bad—"

"Which they won't."

"—you can always stay with me for however long you need to."

I sigh again. Lately it seems to be the only way I can breathe. I know sighing is another form of emotional release, like crying or even yawning, but it doesn't suffice these days. It's too small for how I feel. "I wish I was graduating, too. I don't think I can stand to live at home for another two years."

Lourdes nods with empathy. "I love my mother, but if I had to go back home for the entire summer, *me muero.*" Thank the Goddess, I still have Lourdes for the next two years. If she were graduating, too, I don't know . . .

Jackie glances at her watch and peers through the window as people stroll by on Broadway. "Where the hell's Hazel? Her and her freakin' fashionable lateness. We have to be at rehearsal in less than an hour."

Always on cue, Hazel sashays into the diner with her graduation gown covered in cleaners' plastic and slung over her shoulder. She wears a gauzy sundress that accentuates her curves. As she makes her way down the aisle to our booth, every male head in the diner turns. I wonder if all that unwanted attention ever makes Hazel wish she were average.

"Don't start, Jackie," she says, raising her hand. "I left on time, but the cleaners took forever to find my gown."

Jackie slides to the end of the booth as Hazel hangs her gown on the hook. "You're supposed to factor in time for unforeseen shit like that," Jackie says, but she's obviously teasing. "What'd you bring that for anyway? Why're you dressed like that? It's just a rehearsal." As Jackie eyes Hazel's dress, Lourdes and I exchange amused glances because we know what's about to ensue.

"Didn't you read the letter? You were supposed to bring the gown and wear an outfit similar to the one you're going to wear at graduation." Hazel sits beside Jackie and sneers at her T-shirt and cargo pants. Jackie pivots and pinches the collar of her shirt so Hazel can read it. I love Jackie's T-shirts. This one says *Just Because You Have One Doesn't Mean You Hafta Be One.* But Hazel groans, "No, you did not."

Jackie winks at Lourdes and me. "This one's for Dean Ellison. Never let it be said I won't dress for a man. If it's, like, mad hot, I'm going to graduation in my cut-offs and my tank top that says *You Say I'm a Bitch Like It's a Bad Thing.* What the hell? It's a special occasion, right?"

"Or how about the one that says *I'd Play with Boys, But Where's the Challenge?*" I say, suggesting my personal favorite in Jackie's collection.

Lourdes and I laugh, and I can see Hazel's fighting the urge to join us. "I feel so sorry for Wil."

"Wil doesn't care. Know what he told me last night? The only reason he didn't skip his law school graduation was to not disappoint his moms."

Hazel points a finger at Jackie, and like always her manicure is perfect. How does she do that herself? When I try to polish my own nails, they always look like a kindergartner got to them. "That's exactly what you're gonna do to your poor father if you show up in one of your smart-ass T-shirts and Daisy Dukes," she says.

"Excuse me, I said cut-offs not Daisy Dukes," Jackie said, wagging a finger back at Hazel. Her nails are ragged but clean. "I do not wear shit like that, and you know it."

Hazel grabs Jackie's hand and inspects her fingertips. "Damn, girl, you should at least let me do your nails."

"Yeah, I know." But Jackie snatches her hand away from Hazel and jams it under her thigh. She says that now, but she probably won't sit still long enough for Hazel to give her a manicure.

Our waitress, Carolina, returns with two more glasses of that nasty tap water and places them before Lourdes and Hazel. "*¿Cómo puedo servirles?*" Hazel grabs Jackie's menu and flips to the breakfast fare.

"*Quiero los huevos rancheros con chorizo y un café, . . .*" says Lourdes. So she wants eggs. How she wants them I don't know. And I'm pretty sure *chorizo* is sausage. At least that's what Mexicans call them. What do we call them again? Oh, it doesn't matter, because I sure as hell am not going to order any pork.

"*. . . con un poquito de miel y cacao,*" Carolina says, completing Lourdes's order. I fight the urge to cheat by looking for *ranchero* on the menu.

"*Sí, sí, si. Gracias.*"

"Yeah, breakfast sounds good," Jackie says. "I'll have two eggs scrambled well, sausage, and an espresso please."

"No home fries, right?"

Jackie reconsiders her usual order. "You know what, Carolina? Bring on the carbs! I is a graduate." Carolina laughs, then turns to Hazel, who's still deliberating, so she nods at me to give her my order.

Okay, I'm going to do this. "*Por favor, quiero una tortilla . . . ,*" I say.

"Uh, oh." Lourdes giggles, and Hazel nudges Jackie to quit teasing me.

"*. . . tortilla sin . . . sin . . .* Damn, how do you say *yolk* in Spanish?"

Carolina smiles. "*Yema. Una tortilla sin yema.* You want an egg-white omelette."

"No, Carolina, in Spanish." My friends laugh, but I don't mind. I feel like a child in a very good way. "*Quiero una tortilla sin yema y una tostada de trigo sin . . . sin . . .*" Jackie's dying to jump in and tell me what to say. "No, don't tell me!"

"*Pero, nena,* Hazel and I gotta be at the school in forty-five minutes, and Carolina has other customers, and you know, a life outside of here."

"*¡Mantequilla!*" Yes! I pump my fist in the air. "*Quiero una tostada de trigo sin mantequilla.*"

Jackie, Hazel, and Lourdes burst into applause, and I fake a curtsy. "That's not for you, Snow White," says Jackie. "We're applauding Carolina for surviving your damn order." But nothing she says can take away my pride, especially since the shine in her eyes tells me she's proud of me, too.

Carolina asks, "*¿Y para beber?*"

"Is the orange juice fresh-squeezed?"

"No, *m'ija,* I'm sorry."

"You ask that every time we come here, Rena, and the answer's always the same."

"Okay. I'll just have water. Bottled, please!"

Carolina turns to Hazel, who says, "I've got it narrowed down between the French toast and the waffles." She always has it narrowed down between the French toast and the waffles. Or the waffles and the pancakes. Or the pancakes and the French toast. So Hazel's only narrowed it down to stacks, but that's progress for her!

"Carolina, just bring her the pancakes so you can get home to your kids at a decent hour," says Jackie.

Hazel swats her with the menu, then looks up at Carolina. "I'll have the pancakes." Of course. Carolina scribbles down her order, collects our menus, and leaves the table. Or more like flees.

"We need to tip her extra good," Jackie says. Lourdes reaches for her Prada shoulder bag. "Can we eat first?"

Hazel pats my hand. "Did you bring your cards?"

I reach into my hemp bag. "I bought a new deck just for the trip." Jackie and Lourdes groan as I pull out my Tarot of the Orishas. I've only owned them for a week, and they're already my favorite deck of the nine I own so far. I thought Lourdes might be impressed with the illustrations painted in hues of brown, blue, and green, but she is trying hard to ignore them.

"Give us a reading." Hazel clears the water glasses and breadbasket to make room for the cards.

"Oh, hell no," Jackie says. "You know I'm not into that mess." Lourdes inches away from me, grabs the crucifix of her rosary, and makes the sign of the cross. Does she really have to do that? "Put those away, Witchy Poo."

I start to place the cards back into my bag when Hazel grabs my hand. "Later for them. Read me."

So ignoring the grimaces passing between Jackie and Lourdes, I shuffle the deck. "Since you guys are in a hurry, I'll just do the quick, three-card spread. What do you want to know?"

Hazel cuts the deck and hands them back to me so I can shuffle them again. "Am I going to get what I want out of this trip?"

I stop shuffling. "It's really not supposed to be a yes-or-no type question."

"But that's what I want to know," she says. She cuts the deck and hands it back to me. Jackie snickers while Lourdes mumbles a plea to the Virgin Mary. "Enough, you two," says Hazel.

"Really." I give the deck one last shuffle. "What will Hazel gain from this trip?" I lay three cards down across the table and explain what each card represents. "Past, present, future." As I turn over the first card, Jackie slightly shifts forward while Lourdes peeks from the corner of her eye. The first card's upside down and features the Couple as they stand on a beach.

Hazel looks at the card. "That's my past?" Then she laughs. "I guess it's kinda right. It'd be more accurate if it were two women."

I wish I had thought of that sooner. What a cool graduation present for Hazel that would've been! "You know, I bet they do have tarot cards for lesbians."

"*Ay, Dios mío,*" mutters Lourdes.

Jackie squints and scoffs at the cards. "Okay, she's completely naked, but he's rockin' a loincloth. What's that about?"

"Ignore her, Irena."

I turn over the second card, revealing the brazen Outcast carrying his bag and holding a flower between his teeth. Then I turn over the last card and find Iku the skeleton with her cape and sickle. Lourdes gasps and makes another freakin' sign of the cross.

Jackie points to the card and yells, "What the fuck is that?" Before I can explain, she grabs the card and thrusts it into Hazel's face. "This says there's death in your future, Hazel. I don't know whether to freak out or say no shit, Sherlock."

Now Hazel gives me this worried look. "It doesn't literally mean death," I explain. "It means change. Usually."

"Usually?"

"Calm down. Forget about all those stupid horror movies you've seen. You don't interpret a card just by its face, and even then its face carries multiple possible meanings."

"Then how do you know which meaning is the right interpretation?" asks Hazel. At least she's trying to understand. "How do you know if the card means death or change or something else?"

"First, you have to consider whether it's upright or reversed. Then you have to interpret its position. Not just where it falls in the layout but also where it lands in relation to the other cards in the spread." I take the Iku card from Jackie's hand, replace it at the end of the row, and contemplate it for a few seconds. "In your recent past, there was much love but also jealousy. Crises."

"How recent is recent?"

Jackie throws her hands up in the air. "Are you gonna let the girl do the reading or what?" She's getting into it!

"Hello, this is my reading. You didn't want one, remember, so stop trying to bogart mine."

"*¡Por favor!*" says Lourdes. "Finish this already!"

"Like I said, in your recent past you were surrounded both by love and jealousy. But now you're in a tough space. A confusing place. Like you can kinda go either way. Be contradictory things at the same time. Playful but uneasy. Hypersensitive yet insensitive."

"Okay, this can't be her recent past," says Jackie, "because she was like that even when were kids. And people were always jealous of you."

"But what about the love? No, it couldn't be that far into the past."

"Wasn't Geneva the jealous type?"

Hazel hesitates then looks at me. "So what does it say about my future?"

"That this confusing transition will come to a resolution," I reply. "Things'll change."

"Hell, I could've told you that," says Jackie. "Except that part about her going either way. She's been doing that since we were thirteen." Hazel flips Jackie the bird, which makes Lourdes loosen her grip on her crucifix and finally crack a smile. Thank the Goddess for that.

So I continue the reading. "Notice how all the cards are principal cards."

Jackie glances over the spread. "You mean no suits?" She's genuinely taking an interest in it!

"Yeah, in a regular deck of cards you have hearts, spades, and whatever. The tarot of the orishas uses the elements—water, earth, fire, and air. Anyway, the secondary cards in a deck usually represent things that are within your control. So when you have a spread that consists mostly of principal cards like this one, that suggests that whatever's going to happen is pretty much out of your hands." I look at Hazel, whose eyes appear russet in the sharp light of the diner. "It's gonna be what it's gonna be."

Hazel sits back and folds her arms across her chest. Lourdes must also sense her discomfort because she says, "*Te lo dije.* She's upset. Are you happy now, Irena?"

Jackie sweeps up the cards up with one hand and hands them to me. "Do one for yourself now."

I can't do that. I mean, it's okay if you want to use the cards to explore an issue. Each of us already has any answers we may need, and the cards are one tool that enables us to tap into our intuition to uncover those answers. But Jackie means that she wants me to use the cards to predict my future because she has a narrow and misinformed view of the tarot. "You're really not supposed to do that."

"Bullshit. Every once in a while even Lourdes prays for herself. Right, Lou?"

"I'm doing it this very second being surrounded *con toda esta brujería!*"

"It is not *bru . . . bru . . .*" Oh, fuck it. "It's not witchcraft!" I look to Hazel for support.

"At least she's using the tarot of the orishas."

It's a weak defense, but I'll take it. "Yeah, this isn't a European deck like the Rider-Waite deck."

Lourdes huffs as she jiggles her crucifix. "Is that the one by that Satanist Aleister Crowley?"

"Satanist?" Jackie props herself on one leg, leaning farther across the table toward me. "I'm not feelin' any of this shit, but if women want to worship the moon and pray to goddesses and all that, I'm cool with that. I understand what that's about and to each her own or whatever. But I'm telling you, white boys and New Age don't mix." Hazel laughs, but Lourdes and I glare at her, although for very different reasons, I'm sure. "Seriously, New Age white boys tend to be just a bunch of freaks trying to find another way to dominate people. What's-his-face doesn't have to be a Satanist for me to know that much is true."

"Look, I'm not into Aleister Crowley either—"

"You shouldn't be into *ése satanista . . .*"

Lourdes shudders, and I wonder why I'm bothering. "By Satanist, you mean devil-worshipper, and that's not what he was."

"He called himself the Great Beast!" Lourdes yells, and that's something she never does. Hazel shushes her, and she lowers her voice into an intense whisper. "That's from the book of Revelations." Jackie starts to chant the score to *The Omen,* but Lourdes shoots her a dirty look.

Okay, by the worst accounts, the man was an egomaniacal pervert, but if I concede that to Lourdes, it's a wrap. "He was just baiting the conservative Christians of his time by throwing their accusations back into their faces. They regarded anything and everything outside their dogma as Satanism to justify the burning of witches." Lourdes puts her hands over her ears, and I give up. I don't understand why she's so freaked out by all this when she's supposed to be as liberal as a churchgoing Catholic can be.

"See what I mean? One white boy wilds out and the rest of 'em use that as an excuse to set a bunch of women on fire," Jackie says, reaching for her glass of water and taking a big gulp. "Bet you most of them were sisters, too." Her righteousness makes Hazel laugh even harder.

"The point is," I say, waving my Orisha deck, "this particular deck is based on what our ancestors believed."

Jackie nods. "Yeah, before the Spanish came and rammed Christianity down their throats." Hazel's laughter turns into applause.

Lourdes can't be angry at that, since those are the facts. Still she tries to wave Hazel quiet. "*My* ancestors didn't believe in this."

"Oops, that's true, Jackie. You keep forgetting Lou's not *caribeña*."

Jackie smirks at Hazel. "I didn't forget shit." Then she looks at Lourdes with a mischievous glint in her eye. "I know damn well that the Aztecs didn't practice *santería* or *vodú* or *candomblé*. A little bloodletting here, a little self-mutilation there, that was more their thing. Right, Lou?"

"Very funny, Jacqueline."

"How do you know you descended from Aztecs anyway?"

"I don't. For all I know I might be Mayan. Or Incan."

"And I was Nefertiti in a past life." Even I have to laugh at that. I actually believe in reincarnation, although I have yet to try past life regression. That's next after my Reiki training. "C'mon, Lourdes, you really think the transatlantic slave trade just skipped over Aztlan? I've seen the hair on your neck curl when you sweat. Your great-great-great-great-great grandpapi was probably a black slave in Veracruz."

"*¡Ay, déjame quieta ya!*" Lourdes once told me that her family on either side is from Mexico City, but I guess her knowledge of her lineage ends there.

Jackie must be satisfied that she has annoyed Lourdes enough because she decides to play nice. "Maybe you descended from someone cool like Yagna."

For a few seconds, Lourdes ignores Jackie, but she can't deny the possibility of greatness. "Who's Yagna?"

"The leader of a rebel slave community that kicked Spanish colonial butt up and down the mountains of Veracruz in the early 1600s. When the Spaniards realized that they couldn't beat 'em, they met with Yagna and he negotiated for the rebels to have their own settlement. Which was named after him." Lourdes's eyes just sparkle, so Jackie has completed her good deed for the day. "I'll forward you some links I found on the Web."

"*Sí, sí, sí.*"

"Go 'head, Irena. Read Jackie."

I shuffle the cards and tentatively hand them to Jackie. She grabs them and haphazardly cuts them across the table. "What's your question?"

"Do I get through this trip without killing one of you bitches?"

"*Ay, Dios mío.*"

"Same as mine," Hazel says. "What will Jackie get out of this trip?"

So I lay out three cards across the table, then turn over each in the same order. The first card reveals the Three of Air, depicting birds of prey as they swoop down on their unsuspecting victim. The next card is the Eight of Water and features a massive octopus wrapping its tentacles around a ship. The last card unveils the Five of Earth that shows a white goat falling into an active volcano while bats swarm the fiery opening. They're all reversed, so I have to take a few moments to ponder their meaning.

Jackie gapes at the imagery, which I must admit is quite daunting. "What the hell? . . ."

"It's not as bad as it looks," I assure her. I point to the Three of Air and interpret it. "Past transgressions are just that. In the past. Not that healing's been easy for you. The memories still hurt even though the violations are behind you." Everyone is listening to my every word, so I have to choose them carefully. I shift my finger to the grappling octopus on the Eight of Water card. "Now's the time for reflection and to let those old hurts go once and for all."

Hazel clasps her hands on the table in front of her. "What does all that mean for Jackie's future? Like these are all secondary cards. So does that mean Jackie's fate is within her control?"

Jackie sinks into her corner of the booth. "Ya think?"

"Jackie needs to embrace her own truth," I say, trying to look her in her sloe eyes. "No one else can hurt you more than you yourself, so don't become the victim of your own deeds." I take a last glance at the cards and add, "You can even make up for lost ground. It won't be easy. But it's not impossible if you're honest with yourself about what really matters to you. The only thing that stands between you and what you really want is your ability to admit to yourself that you want it. And that you deserve to have whatever it is that you desire."

Carolina arrives with our breakfasts and sets them on the table as we sit in silence. Even when she leaves, no one begins to eat. Then Jackie grabs a fork and jabs a sausage link. "In other words, whatever's not bullshit is common sense." She wedges the link into her mouth and tears off its end. "See, Lourdes," Jackie shrugs as she chews. "No big deal."

HAZEL
Lincoln Center
Upper West Side, NY
Friday, June 2, 2:07 P.M.

After graduation rehearsal, I convince Jackie to chill with me for a little while in the park. She buys herself a chocolate ice cream cone, I light up a cigarette, and we sit at the edge of the fountain across from Lincoln Center.

"Did you see Dean Ellison's face when he saw my outfit?" she asks with a smug grin.

"You're so bad." I watch her as she slides her tongue across a stream of chocolate that has dripped down her sugar cone.

Jackie catches me staring at her and gives a nervous laugh. "What?"

I'm tempted to tell her, but instead I say, "Please tell me you're going to dress appropriately for graduation."

"I'm going to dress appropriately for graduation."

"You did not just lie to my face like that!"

"Hey, you told me to tell you what you wanted to hear, so I did. Don't blame it on me if what you want to hear isn't true." Jackie flicks her tongue over the top of the scoop. "So what's really bothering you? Is your mom acting up again?"

I had been complaining for weeks that my mother had been acting as if no significant changes were happening in my life. Like when I tried to show her the dress that Lourdes bought for me as a graduation present and asked if I could borrow a suitcase for the trip, she just grunted and left the room. "She wouldn't be my mother if she weren't acting up," I say. Then I take Jackie's cone, help myself to a lick of ice cream, and pass it back to her. I can taste a hint of peach from her lip balm. "But that's not it."

"So what's bugging you?"

"Who said anything's bugging me?" I take a drag of my cigarette and quickly learn that chocolate and nicotine don't mix. "I just want my best friend to myself for a while. Between finishing school and preparing for this road trip, we haven't spent any time together, and I miss you."

Jackie smiles at me. "I miss you, too, Haze." She puts her arm around me. "But we're gonna make up for lost time on this trip, you'll see." Suddenly, Jackie drops her arm and takes a bite out of her cone. "You're still mad at me for inviting Lourdes and Irena on this trip, aren't you?"

"No." I was never angry—I really like Lourdes and Irena—just disappointed. I had always wanted this trip to be just for the two of us even before I came to admit that my feelings for Jackie had changed. From the day we met, it has always been just the two of us. So when Geneva sent me the announcement for the Gamba Adisa conference for women student activists, I forwarded it to Jackie with the note *A graduation present to ourselves?* After getting the e-mail, she immediately called me and yelled into my ear, "Road trip!" Only later in the conversation did I realize that she had forwarded the e-mail to Irena who forwarded it to Lourdes who called Jackie and suggested that the four of us drive to and from the conference in her SUV.

"Lourdes and Irena aren't even graduating," I said during one of the rare breaks in Jackie's brainstorming. "They're just finishing their sophomore year."

"So?" Jackie continued to ramble off our to-do list in preparation for the trip, and I had no response because none existed. No rational one anyway. The fact that Lourdes and Irena were juniors was no reason to take issue with Jackie's inviting them to go with us. Chances are they would've heard about the conference anyway and gone on their own. I would have preferred that. For me that telephone call officially marked our transformation into a foursome. When I was honest with myself, I realized that I really wouldn't have minded had I not fallen for Jackie and seen this trip as the perfect opportunity to convince her that we should take our friendship to another level.

As oblivious as I chose to be to our evolving quartet, I actually started it. Jackie and I remained pretty inseparable during our first years at Fordham, enrolling in the same sections of required courses, meeting for lunch several times per week, and things like that. By our junior year, I worried that we were drifting apart. Although we touched base every day by telephone and e-mail, days would go by when we would not see each other. One day Jackie e-mailed me saying she wanted to get involved in some kind of student activity, but shopping for a group had proved frustrating. "I was the only Latina at the Black Student Union meeting, the only *morena* in the Hispanic Student Alliance, the only sister in any of the women's groups who would bring up race . . . The prelaw society is dominated by white guys vying to be the next great liberal statesman. I probably should just get involved with a group off campus."

I sympathized with Jackie even though I hadn't tried nearly so hard as she did to find a place I could call my own on campus. Three meetings of the Gay Student Network, and I called it quits. At my first meeting, I suggested we join the campaign to convict the man who shot the teenage girl he was harassing on the street because she told him, "I'm a lesbian, so leave me alone." Making vague allusions to the Central Park Jogger case, the white members didn't want to touch it. One person gave me a strange look and asked, "Isn't the defendant Hispanic?"

"Well, so was the victim."

As if to bring the discussion to an end, the chair said, "And she wasn't truly a lesbian."

"Even more reason." The other people of color backed me up, but we were outvoted by the majority after debating it for over a half hour.

Meeting Number Two, and the "Of Color Caucus"—as Jackie refers to the people of color in any predominantly white group—is down to an African American guy named Tim, and me. Someone circulates a contact sheet for a study group she wants to start, and the first title is one of those stupid books about black men who are "on the down low." Neither Tim nor I sign up, and she disrupts the meeting to probe why and push us to reconsider. She goes on about wanting "diversity" and "authenticity" in the group.

"I just don't see how we're going to understand this phenomenon if neither of you is there to share your perspective." Never mind that Tim makes Richard Simmons look like a closet case, and that I'm not African American or male. Tim mutters that he's overextended. Instead of following his lead, I joke, "Don't waste your time. You already have all the information about being on the down low you need. I mean, haven't white men been having sex with each other behind their wives' backs for centuries?" No one laughed.

As Jackie predicted, by the third meeting, I'm LSS—Last Sister Standing. We finally decide to focus on AIDS, agreeing that the issue had lost its sense of urgency. While I'd rather rally for a cure, I hold my tongue when we decide to charter a bus to D.C. to lobby for more and better drug cocktails, even though I know my father will never have access to them in prison. Then we move on to the idea of doing some prevention education, and someone brings up the tension between the queer kids that hang out at the Chelsea Piers (virtually all of color and homeless) and the neighborhood's longtime residents (overwhelmingly white and middle-class). Apparently, some of the kids are acting out—making lots of noise, littering the streets, and even having sex in the foyers and alleys of people's homes, so the adults are pressuring the police to rein in the kids with little regard to the indiscriminate harassment and violence that may ensue. We all lament how tragic it is to see queer folks fighting one another, but I slam the lid on my own coffin when I say that I don't think that this qualifies as a gay issue. Only one other person agrees with me saying, "I doubt that all the residents who are complaining are gay. Some must be straight. It's an intergenerational conflict."

I responded, "True, but it's mostly about class. Even more so than race although it's about that, too." Folks who sympathize with the adults pounce on me as if I accused them personally of being racist. I try to explain that I just find it ironic that the same people who fled to the West Village as queer or questioning teens now wanted to deny that safe haven to the next generation. "And isn't it even more ironic that wealthy white gays want to create satellites of the Village in places like Harlem and Washington Heights even if it means displacing low-income people of color from the homes they had all the years affluent people of any race or sexual orientation refused to step foot in them?" I ask. "Like I'm all for gay marriage in principle, but why is securing the privilege to contribute to the American divorce rate so high on our list of priorities? Why are we trying so damned hard to emulate middle-class straight life?" Then they all hated me.

Through blinding tears of frustration, I fired off to Jackie a massive e-mail that night ranting about the GSN meeting. She wrote me back a two-line reply. *Girl, you done stood up in a roomful of white gay folks and questioned the sanctity of marriage . . . You know you can't go back, right?* I laughed so hard that I almost spilled my lukewarm coffee all over my keyboard.

Even though it was almost three in the morning, I picked up the telephone and called her. After we commiserated a bit more over the GSN, I asked about her search. She said, "For a while I thought about joining an off-campus organization, but most of the ones that really interest me are in Brooklyn, and I just can't afford to add another leg onto my commute." I sighed with relief because if Jackie joined a group outside of Fordham, I could have forgotten about seeing her. "I think that instead of pledging allegiance to one single group on campus, I'll just volunteer for a particular activity or event. Like Take Back the Night."

I loved the idea and went to the next planning committee meeting. There she volunteered to organize the program and before I could do the same, she pretty much pimped me to the outreach task force, which meant networking with other campus groups in the TBN coalition as well as generating a big turnout on the actual day of the event. That's how I met Lourdes. I did a brief presentation at her monthly Catholics for Choice meeting about the event. At the end of my spiel, Lourdes came up afterwards and asked, "Where did you get that cool pocketbook?"

"You won't believe it." I smiled. "Tar-jay!"

Lourdes and I met Irena in the cafeteria while doing outreach for the event. Irena volunteered to help organize the rally, and Jackie raved and ranted about her for weeks. "You know what Snowflake brought to the meeting tonight?" she once told me as we walked from the school to the subway. "Sage! She lit it up and ran around the room waving it over everyone's head."

"It's a Native American practice," I explained. "It's supposed to be purifying, I think."

"Purifying my ass! Two security guards barged into the room and started interrogating us. They thought we were smoking some kind of new, strange weed in there." Jackie then gave a transitory sigh as she always did when switching from complaining to complimenting Irena. "Let me shut up. Rena's the only one on the entire committee who consistently does what she says she's going to do when she says she's going to do it."

"Besides you."

"Exactly."

Irena took to following Jackie, and although Jackie sometimes grumbled about her new blond shadow, I knew she liked having a protégée of sorts.

Jackie finishes her cone and says, "I tell you what, Haze. Let's make a point during the trip to find some time to ourselves. Just the two of us."

"That's going to be hard," I say, even though my heart pounds at the thought. "How do we explain to Irena and Lourdes why we're excluding them?"

"We don't make it so obvious that it warrants explaining, silly!" Jackie brushes crumbs off her cargo pants. "Like we just get up earlier and go have breakfast or something like that. Besides there'll probably be times when they'd like to go off on their own together. They're practically roommates." She stands up and walks over to the trash can to discard her napkin. When Jackie sits down again, she sits so close to me, our thighs touch. Then I feel her hand on the small of my back. "Next week we're starting a new phase in our lives, and I want us to do it together. You know what I mean?"

Of course, I do. At least, I hope I do.

LOURDES

Bluestockings
Lower East Side, Manhattan
Saturday, June 3, 1:02 P.M.

Although I've never been to this bookstore, I easily find Irena because the place is both small and neat. She sits on the floor at the end of an island bookcase, one open book balanced across her knees and a stack of more next to her. "Hi! Did you find what you were looking for?"

"Hey, Lou." Still holding the book she's reading, Irena stands to give me a hug and peck me on the cheek. "Yeah, but now I'm wondering if I should get Jackie something else. I think I've narrowed it down to these two." She reaches down for one of the books on the stack. "I'm going to get her either this—" With her left hand, Irena holds up a softcover copy of *Women Who Run with the Wolves.* "—Or this." In her right she carries a hardcover book with a handsome light-skinned black man with glasses called *Why I Love Black Women.* "What do you think?"

I don't know what to say. "Well, what is it about those two books that you think Jackie will like?"

"Well, I know she likes the work of Michael Eric Dyson . . ."

"*Pues . . .*"

"But just the other day Jackie was ranting about the whole celebrity intellectual thing. You know, how too many of our best thinkers are trying to go the Dr. Phil way. I think that this might be one of those kind of books."

When is Jackie not ranting about something? We love her

rants so long as she refrains from drive-by tirades. Most of the time anyway. "I don't see what's so wrong with smart and conscientious people doing things that enable them to reach a wider audience," I say. "More power to them."

"But cultural accessibility should not and does not have to be at the cost of intellectual rigor."

Ay, no puedo. I have no doubt that Irena genuinely agrees with Jackie of her own accord. But those are Jackie's words coming out of her mouth right now. The only thing missing are the curses.

I take *Why I Love Black Women* from Irena. *El profesor es guapísimo.* I wonder if he loves Latinas, too. Then I stop that train of thought to think like Jackie. "She may ask why is *he* on the cover if this book is a so-called valentine to black women. I mean, it's obvious to me why he's on the cover, but you know how Jackie is."

Irena grabs the book from me. "You're terrible."

"Why you say that?" She doesn't answer me, so I say, "Let's be honest, Irena. Jackie ordinarily wouldn't read something like *Women Who Run with the Wolves.* You can't give it to her, because it's something you would read."

She puts *Why I Love Black Women* back on the shelf. "This might not be something Jackie would buy herself, but I truly think if she gave it a chance, she'd really like it." Irena heads to the front to pay. She laughs as she picks up a bumper sticker at the register. "Okay, I have to get this, too." The bumper sticker says *Divas Don't Yield.* Irena hands it to the cashier and reaches into her hemp tote bag for her wallet. "Don't let me forget. I have to get our journal and the offering box." Irena hands the cashier a few bills. "Aren't you getting anything?"

"Not here. First, I want to go to the West Village and then Union Square. Don't worry. I'll put us in a cab." We leave Bluestockings, and I hail a cab. "I found this wonderful heart rate monitor for Jackie. It also has a stopwatch and alarm, and it keeps track of your calories, too. And for Hazel, I saw the cutest little pride ring. It has the six stones of the rainbow—ruby, topaz, citrine, emerald, sapphire, and amethyst—set in a fourteen-karat gold band." The second I say it, I wish I had not. I don't want Irena to start about gemstones, chakras *y toda esa brujería* that she's into.

No quiero que empezemos a discutir. To change the subject, I ask, "What are you going to get her?"

Irena shrugs as if she doesn't know, but then says, "A CD."

"*¡Perfecto!* Hazel loves music. Do you know what kind of CD?"

Again, she hesitates to answer only to say, "I wanted to get her the latest by Sweet Honey in the Rock—"

"She adores them! So do I." Then I remember something. "*¡Ay, Irena!* I think the PBS documentary about them is out on DVD. Why don't you get her that?"

"Because it's almost thirty dollars, Lourdes."

"So let's go in on it together."

Irena throws up her hands. "But you're going to get her the pride ring!"

"But I haven't bought it yet so I can help you buy her the DVD." *¿Porqué ella se puso tan enojada?* "Is it my imagination or are you angry?"

"I'm not angry." *Claro que sí que está enojada,* but I say nothing. "Look, I really want Hazel to have a gift from me. Something that *I* thought about, and that *I* chose specifically for Hazel out of *my* own personal appreciation for the friendship she has given *me* the way I did with Jackie's present. But I can't afford fourteen-karat jewelry and high-tech exercise gadgets, okay?"

"Okay. I'm sorry."

I tell the cab to stop in front of a bank, and we head to the ATM. I stick my card into the machine and punch in my PIN. I lean into the screen for a better view because the balance looks strange. My Catholics for Choice group finally cashed my pledge, but for some reason, Mamá's transfer is much less this month than it usually is. Then I remember. Since she expects that I will be home for the summer, she only deposited enough to cover my rent and utilities for the months of July and August.

Suddenly, Irena straightens up. "Hey! How did your mother react when you told her that you changed your major?"

"Oh, I haven't told her yet." I request a bit less cash than I had planned. I almost confess that I didn't even change my major so I have nothing to tell my mother. But then that will lead to questions I don't want to answer and advice I don't want to follow.

I did not doubt Jackie when she told Irena at our first Olympic Flame meeting that if she didn't tell her father she was going on the road trip, she wouldn't let her come. "Sorry for the tough love, Rena," she said, not sounding a bit sorry at all. "No way am I driving cross-country with you behind your father's back. I refuse to take on that responsibility or chance. And that's some juvenile s---t anyway."

So, Irena finally told her dad that she was going on the trip. She's so much braver than I.

All I want to do now is spend some money. "*Pues,*" I say to Irena as I head to the bank exit. "We have some shopping to do."

JACKIE

1783 Willis Avenue
South Bronx, NY
Monday, June 5, 1:14 P.M.

Just as I send my senior thesis to the printer, Sheila calls. Ordinarily, I wouldn't have picked up the phone. Even though I practically live with the man, I still don't feel right about answering Wil's phone, especially when he's not home. He teases me, saying, "It's usually one of your girls looking for you anyway." I tell him to stop exaggerating, but I like that he's so comfortable with me in his apartment.

I say hello, then hear a click.

Who does Sheila think she's fooling? I know that bitch's click anywhere. And just like I suspect, she calls back. "Hello!" I bark into the telephone.

"May I speak to Wil?"

"Wil's *unavailable,*" I say, stressing every syllable. "Would you like to leave a message for him?"

"Is this Jackie?"

"Yes, *Sheila.*" I'll be damned if I play secretary to relay her messages. What if Wil doesn't call her back, and she tries to say it's because I'm blocking her. "How 'bout I hang up so you can call back and leave your message for him on the answering machine?" Before I can congratulate my evolved self for making a rare appearance and handling things, my true nature kicks her in the ass and says, "Because I'm headed out the door right now to turn in this last paper so I can graduate."

I feel a flash of shame because I know it's such a messed-up thing to say. Wil's told me about Sheila's insecurities about never finishing college, and I once sympathized with her. Then she started using Eric to manipulate her way back into Wil's life, so fuck that. She's got a son. I've got a BA. We're freakin' even as far as I'm concerned.

"No, I'll just call again later." I swear, I can see Sheila sitting there, tossing her honey blond weave and winking a green eye at herself in the mirror. She thinks she's so smooth, but I refuse to let her faze me.

"Well, you do that." I slam the telephone down. It takes my all to not hit *69 and give the bitch a piece of my mind. But I don't want to be that kind of woman. I know all the bizarre shit that women stoop to because they fear their man is cheating on them—Jesus, the stories Hazel would tell me about her mother—and Hazel and I vowed to each other that we would never let someone drive us to such desperate extremes.

I have a few hours before my thesis deadline, and all I want to do is take a long nap. Wil wants to take me to Camaradas in El Barrio tonight to celebrate my finishing this paper and his landing the job with that entertainment firm. After spending the past week skipping the gym and lounging around in my Fordham sweats, I can't show up looking like Carrot Top in blackface. Especially since I'll be off soon to Frisco with Hazel and the gals for two weeks. I have to take good care of Wil before I leave. Not just to thank him for putting up with my ornery ass for the past few weeks but also to Sheila-proof him before I go.

But Sheila has me wired, and I lie on Wil's bed waiting for her to call back and leave her message. She doesn't. That's because she knows that I'm here. Waiting and listening, that's what she thinks. Later for that insecure trick. I'm still here because I wrote the hell out of that paper, and my ass is exhausted.

I don't care if he doesn't like my politics, that Negro-con Ellison better give me my A. My arguments are on point, and I back them up lovely. Even on our first date over a year ago, I told Wil that for my senior thesis I wanted to compare the ongoing romanticization of white radicals of the sixties like the Weather Underground with the continued vilification of activists of color of the same time like the Black Panthers and the Puerto Rican *independistas.* He joked, "Are you really trying to graduate?" but I could tell that I had impressed him.

Reminiscing about that night—the great conversation, the amazing food, the intense sexual energy—must have relaxed me enough to finally snooze because about an hour later the phone rings and wakes me up. Thinking it's Wil calling to check in, I leap on it. "Hello?" Just another pause quickly followed by a click. It's that heifer, I just know it! I slam down the phone, leap out of the bed, and walk over to the computer to pull together my thesis. The phone rings again, and I hesitate for a moment but then answer it. "Hello!" No response but no click either. "Hello?" I hear some music in the background and press the phone against my ear so I can make it out.

Do you know he begged to stay with me? He wasn't man enough for me.

This bitch is on some other shit, calling me to play some Toni Braxton song over the telephone! The way Sheila keeps jocking Wil, it's obvious that he dumped her. Not man enough for her, my black ass. That's why she's started calling here every other day with *Eric needs you to do this* and *Eric wants you to do that.*

Oh, I'ma fix her but good. I hang up the cordless but take it with me into the living room as I tear through Wil's CDs until I find *Plantation Lullabies.* I shove the disc into the player, forward to the third track, and blast the volume. I dial *69 and hold the telephone right next to the speaker as the entire song plays.

Boyfriend, boyfriend, yes, I had your boyfriend. If that's your boyfriend, he wasn't last night.

By the time the song ends and I place the telephone to my ear, I hear nothing but that annoying buzz. I hang up and go back into the bedroom. I sing along with Me'Shell Ndegéocello as I pack my thesis into a large manila envelope. *Boyfriend, boyfriend, yes, I had your boyfriend.* The telephone rings again, but this time I ignore it. The machine plays Wil's greeting then beeps.

"Jackie!" Wil yells. "Jackie, turn that shit down and pick up the phone!"

I rush over to it. "Hello?"

"Girl, what the hell you doing with the music on so damned loud?"

He was the one who just called? "Someone was playing with the phone, and I just wanted to give 'em a taste of their own medicine." Damn!

"Playing with the phone?"

"Yeah, calling to not say anything but playing music in the background."

"I called a few minutes ago to ask you to meet me at the restaurant. Maybe a car rolled by when you picked up. . . . Jackie, can you hear me?"

"Barely." I bet Sheila blew up his cell phone before he called me.

The line cracks. "Just meet me at Camaradas at six. Jackie, can you hear me?"

"Yeah, yeah, yeah," I say, and I hang up. To hell with Sheila, and Eric. To hell with Wil, too. I have a thesis to turn in.

"Mami, breakfast's ready!" Even though the frying pan squeaks with cleanliness, I squeeze another glob of liquid detergent onto the raggedy washcloth. The radio DJ plays a Gloria Estefan ballad from the eighties. At least it's the weekend, and I don't have to endure that disgusting morning show hosted by those two idiots who stop their sexist banter only long enough to take homophobic shots at their callers. I've quit trying to explain to Mami why I hate that show, resigning myself to the fact that the very things I find offensive, my mother thinks are hilarious. And I just don't want to fight with her with my college graduation today and road trip around the corner.

"C'mon, Mami!"

I hear Mami's *chancletas* shuffle against the gray concrete floor toward the kitchen. Just as I place the last pan into the dish rack and shut off the water, she appears in the doorway in the same T-shirt and leggings she wore to bed.

"You're not dressed yet?" The fuzzy ringlets that drip from Mami's head toward her shoulders make me gasp. "You took the rollers out, didn't you?"

Mami shrugs and reaches for a mug on the shelf above the sink. "I had to. They hurt. I couldn't sleep."

I block her hand. "I put your coffee on the table."

My mother avoids my gaze as she opens the refrigerator. "*Coño,* we're out of milk."

"The milk's on the table, too," I say. Mami peeks over the refrigerator door like I might lie about that. She closes the door and shuffles toward the kitchen table, where I put her plate of scrambled eggs and buttered toast. Mami slides the plate away from her and pulls a half-empty pack of Newports from her breast pocket. She pats her lap then hips, realizing she has no other pockets and therefore no lighter. "Give me," I say. I take the cigarette from my mother and light it on the stove, taking a drag myself before handing it back to her. Then I finally ask, "You're going, right?" Mami takes a drag, then searches for something to catch the ashes. I yank an ashtray out of the dish rack and slam it on the table. "You are coming to my graduation, aren't you?"

"Carmen, you know I have to go visit your father." She grabs the carton and pours some milk into her coffee.

"They have visiting hours every day, Mami," I say. But she stands up and flees into the living room so I follow her. She's standing by my salon chair in the corner of the room, grabbing stray rollers and dropping them into a plastic shoebox.

"You complain that you don't want me to touch your things," she says, "but I'm tired of my home looking like this. I want my living room back, Carmen. Now that you're graduating, you better be thinking about getting a job at a real salon."

"And moving out," I finish her sentence.

Mami pauses but then resumes picking up rollers and pins and tossing them in the box with a fury. "I didn't say that."

Like she has to. I don't get this woman. Every time I talk about moving out, my mother gets quiet as if she really doesn't want me to leave. But the other 350-some odd days of the year, she acts as if she can barely stand to be in the same room with me.

I yank the box from her hand and drop it into the salon chair. "I told you the prison was never going to let him out just for my graduation, Mami." Jackie warned me about that, but I still wrote my letters, and I know my father put in the request. Hell, even Mami scrawled out a three-page handwritten appeal on yellow legal paper. Not that I have any illusions that she was motivated more by the possibility of our family being reunited for my college graduation than the chance of seeing my father beyond barbed wire.

Mami finally looks at me and places her hands on my cheeks and reaches up to kiss my forehead. I hate it. I hate that I need her affection so desperately. She never gives it to me, and when she does, it never comes from a mother's selfless desire to affirm her daughter. And I hate being the spitting image of her because our resemblance scares me. What if, in addition to the copper hair and hazel eyes, I inherit her life? I don't want to be another beautiful woman who can have almost anyone she wants only to fall irreversibly in love with the one person who she can never have. "*M'ija,* your father's counting on me to . . ."

I brush my mother's hands off my face. "Papi would do anything to be at my graduation, so don't go using him as an excuse not to go." I push past her and take off the robe I put on to protect my graduation dress while I cooked breakfast and washed the dishes. With my makeup already done, I could've slept later and left long ago. What a fool I am to hope that my mother would finally come through for me on this of all days. I fling the robe over the salon chair, grab my purse, cap, and gown off the couch, and head for the door.

"*¡Consentida!*"

"Spoiled?" I halted and spun around. "How the fuck am I spoiled?"

"*Tú eres una malcriada. Tu abuela—*"

I take a few steps toward Mami and yell, "Don't you dare talk about my grandmother. You have no right to criticize the way she raised me. You never should've sent me to live with her, and yet I probably wouldn't be graduating from college today if not for her. Don't you say another word about my grandmother." I head back to the door. This argument has become so clichéd, Mami can have it by herself.

"I did the best I could," my mother says.

"Yeah, well, your best sucked."

I slam the door behind me and storm down the block. I know my grandmother and my father are with me in spirit today. And Lourdes, Irena, and, most important, Jackie will be at my graduation. All the love I need is waiting for me at Lincoln Center.

JACKIE

Damrosch Park at
Lincoln Center
Upper West Side, NY
Saturday, June 10, 11:33 A.M.

This damn cap won't stay on this freakin' hive. Where are my father and brother? I keep looking for them in this sea of suits and gowns and can't find them.

A breeze whisks my cap off my head and sends it sailing to the grass. Hazel must have stabbed my scalp with a dozen bobby pins, and this damn thing still won't stay on my head. Just as I bend over to pick up the cap, an impeccable French manicure swoops in and beats me to it. I look up, and there's the diva herself. I may not be able to find Pops and Raul yet, but I've finally found family.

Hazel takes my hand and inspects my nails. Of course, the rushed manicure she gave me before the ceremony is already a smudged mess. Even though I warned her not to bother, I still feel a little bad that I wasn't more careful with her craftsmanship. Then Hazel says, "I told you. You should've stayed over last night so I could do your hair."

I just stick my tongue out at her, then open my arms. Hazel rushes into them, and we hug and jump like a pair of silly teenagers. I pull away to look into Hazel's eyes. "Girl, I ain't gonna lie," I say. "If it weren't for you, I might not have made it." Hazel grins and is about to respond when I feel this warm rush swoop in behind me and lift me in the air. I try not to show it, but I love it when Wil does that.

"Congratulations, honey," he says, and he pecks me on the

temple. "I'm so proud of you." He sets me down and reaches for Hazel. "You, too, Hazel."

My heart aches as I watch Hazel relent to Wil's embrace. He's a sweetheart, and they get along just fine, but Wil's not family. Not to Hazel. I scan over my classmates as they hug their tearful mothers and grin shyly for their proud fathers' cameras, and I know my own family is looking for me. But it kills me that no one is here for Hazel.

"So, Haze, you gonna come with us to City Island, right?" It's a rhetorical question really. Of course Hazel will come. She always does.

"I was up pretty late last night," she says. "Doing my hair, preparing for the trip . . . I'm really tired."

"You still have to eat," says Wil. "Come celebrate with us and then we'll give you a ride home."

"That's really sweet, but what I need more than food is a nap."

I guess the attendance of loving friends is no substitute for the presence of your parents. Not that if my own mother were to reappear this very second, I would care. Unless the bitch had a good story about being kidnapped and held captive somewhere for the past nine years, I'd just send her to hell.

"Okay, don't come to City Island, but don't even think about blowing off Lourdes's party tonight," I say. "We're both the guests of honor or whatever so if I have to do the whole toast, cake, speech thing by myself, I'm going to Frisco without your ass."

"Yes, please save us from one of her speeches," Wil says. I jab him in the arm, and my freakin' graduation cap falls off again. I scramble for it, but Wil snatches it up and keeps it out of my reach.

"Don't play." I lunge for the cap. "I must look like a fuckin' tarantula."

"Don't talk about my girlfriend like that." Wil gathers me into his arms and kisses me. I don't want to embarrass Hazel—God knows I've logged in many hours as the fifth wheel—but the man's too delicious to resist.

"I'll see you guys later," Hazel says. Before I can pull away from Wil and stop her, she's disappeared into the surrounding current of graduates and relatives.

IRENA

Damrosch Park at
Lincoln Center
Upper West Side, NY
Saturday, June 10, 11:36 A.M.

As I lean my back against the willow tree, I scrape the soft bark with my nails, then glance at my amethyst bead watch. Lourdes has been chatting up some graduates from her Catholics for Choice group for the past ten minutes. I want to go find Jackie and Hazel before they leave. Especially Hazel. I want to invite her along with us as Lourdes and I run errands for tonight's party.

Finally, an impatient relative drags away Lourdes's friend, but Wil's friend Kharim is waiting right behind her. "Hey, you two." He kisses Lourdes on the cheek and pats me on the shoulder. Does he know? I bet he can feel me bristle at his touch, but as terrible as it makes me feel, I can't help it.

So what if he volunteers at the women's center. He just started there, and I barely know him. So what if he is Wil's best friend? Would Kharim be volunteering at the center if he had not found out that I was working there? How predatory is that! We really don't need him, since those orders of protection he files for the clients aren't worth the paper they're printed on anyway. How's the center supposed to be a safe haven for the women with male volunteers milling about? My first day back from San Francisco, I'm going to raise that very issue.

I can't believe Lourdes. She's tossing her hair and batting her eyes at Kharim like she's interested in him. Okay, Irena, why does that bother you? What do you care? Why does your chest feel so tight? I pride myself on being self-aware, so I hate when I cannot attribute a physical reaction to its proper emotion. Sometimes the inability to identify my feelings causes more discomfort than the feelings themselves. Despite some stressful situations, I haven't had an asthma attack since the incident, and I'm convinced that naming the emotion threatening an attack is powerful enough to ward it off. So far I've been right. But right now Lourdes is flirting with Kharim, and it bothers the hell out of me because my lungs feel like stretching rubber bands, and I can't figure out why. As much as I try not to use it, I reach into my hemp bag for my inhaler and pump some medicine into my mouth.

"Are you all right, Irena?" Kharim asks.

"Yeah. The pollen." What a great excuse to leave! I turn to Lourdes. "I think we—"

"I've got asthma, too," Kharim interrupts me. "So does Jackie's brother."

"I know." Just like a man to cut me off. "About Raul, I mean."

"Really?" Lourdes says, "*Yo nunca supe eso.*"

Kharim nods at Lourdes but keeps his eyes on me. I like it and hate it all at once. My chest tightens, and I suck in another dose of medicine. "What do you take?"

I swallow. "Albuterol."

"I used to take fluticasone as a kid, but then I started playing football so I wanted to stop taking it because—"

"It's a steroid."

"Exactly."

"Irena hates that inhaler," says Lourdes. "She's into alternative treatments. That's why she does yoga and takes all these vitamins." I glare at Lourdes, who's oblivious, of course. Why was she telling him that? Is she matchmaking or cockblocking?

"See that's why I need to go on this trip to Frisco with y'all," says Kharim. " 'Cause a brother's trying to learn more about healing himself."

"Sorry, K, no boys allowed," Lourdes says. There she goes, grazing her hand down his arm.

"But I'm not a boy."

Great, now she's giggling. "That's true."

"And all you powerful sisters in one vehicle? I don't know. You might need an objective yet sensitive man to mediate."

Lourdes laughs and tosses her hair. I run my fingers through my own, wishing for once I hadn't chopped it all off last year. It's taken forever just to reach my shoulders. I still believe that when a woman cuts her hair, she changes her karma, but I cut my hair three days too late and six inches too short. "Even if we did need a man on this trip," Lourdes says, "why should he be you?"

" 'Cause . . ." Kharim reaches for an explanation. "Y'all need a *K*?"

"What?"

Kharim counts off on his fingers. "*H,* Hazel; *I,* Irena; *J,* Jackie; and *L,* Lourdes. Y'all missing a *K.* Now do you really want to drive three thousand miles across the country and back without a *K*? I strongly advise against it."

Lourdes and Kharim laugh like he's Dave Chappelle or something. I say, "Well, Hazel's not an *H,* anyway."

They stop. "I'm sorry?"

"She's really a *C* because *Hazel*'s a nickname . . ." I feel as stupid as I sound.

Kharim's smile fades as my hint sinks in. "Right, right," he says, shoving his hands in his pocket like a bashful schoolboy. "Hazel's real name is Carmen. Anyway, I'ma let y'all go 'cause I know the pollen's starting to bother you, and I should go find Jackie and Wil and Carmen and them anyway."

He forces a grin when he says *Carmen,* and my heart plummets into my stomach. So he's not as funny as Dave Chappelle. That gives me no license to be such a bitch. But I can't bring myself to say anything else.

Lourdes speaks for me. "But you're coming to my party tonight, right?"

"No doubt." Kharim gives Lourdes another kiss on the cheek and backs away a few steps before he gives me a small wave like I might swing at him for doing just that. "Bye, Irena."

"Bye." But he doesn't wait for me to reply before he turns and heads toward the plaza.

"He's such a sweetheart," says Lourdes. "And he really likes you."

Her eyes are on me like weights. "I know." Lourdes takes my hand and leads me through the sea of maroon satin as we look for Jackie and Hazel.

HAZEL

62nd Street &
Amsterdam Avenue
Upper West Side, NY
Saturday, June 10, 11:44 A.M.

I tear off my cap and gown and make my way through the clusters of well-dressed bodies across the marble plaza. I finally reach Broadway, sling my gown over my arm, and try to hail a cab. My good looks aren't worth shit today because one, two, three, four, five, six drivers passed by me, preferring to pick up graduates who are still in their gowns and surrounded by their relatives. I should've tagged along with Jackie and her family. Now, for the second time today, I have to endure a long subway ride by myself. Just as I climb back on the curb and head toward the train station, I hear a familiar horn honk at me.

"Carmen!" I spin around as Geneva reverses her navy Toyota Corolla. It puts a smile on my face not just to see her face but also because she's annoying the hell out of a yellow swarm of cabbies vying for families seeking rides.

I hurry to the passenger window and notice Geneva's new goddess braids. And to think, she declined my offer to do them before we left for San Francisco as if it's some tiny gesture to spend six hours on my feet braiding hair and cramping my hands free of charge. No, Geneva probably turned me down because we argued the last time I did her hair, and I ran out on the woman, leaving her hair half done. Or maybe because I made the offer the last time I was at Geneva's apartment to collect the rest of the things I had littered there over the past year. Geneva should've just swallowed her pride and let me do her braids because whoever did them didn't wind them as tight as they should be.

"Do you need a ride?" Geneva's only halfway through her offer when I throw open the door and pop into the passenger seat. She pulls away from the curb and into the middle of the flock of cabs that had just done the same. "Where are you headed?"

"Home. I have to get ready for Lourdes's party tonight. I'll probably end up crashing there. Which means I should pack an overnight bag." I finally smile. Everything I'm saying is true or could be. "So who did your hair?" It doesn't look bad; it's just not going to last her very long. "It looks really good."

"I just walked into some place around the corner from my old block," says Geneva with a dismissive wave of her hand. "It took all damned day. I swear she lost two hours just gossiping with the other stylists."

I laugh. "The gossip is the best part, especially if it's about people from around the way. You should've just sat back and enjoyed it."

"I have neither time for nor interest in such foolishness."

"Geneva, you can't walk into any beauty parlor in the 'hood expecting to breeze in and out," I say. "You have to pay for that convenience, subsidizing those ridiculous Manhattan rents for the privilege of making an appointment someplace in Midtown. That is, if you can find someone who can braid hair in Midtown."

"I'm going to do exactly that because time is money."

Geneva just gave me another variation of the ultimate reason why as attracted as I am to her, I could never imagine spending my life with her. I love that Geneva takes herself seriously, but I shudder when she insists that I take myself the same way. I respected the way Geneva sits at her computer every payday and promptly pays her bills through electronic checking, but I also always resented the faces Geneva made whenever I refused to answer the phone because I knew the credit company was at the other end. As much as Geneva nagged me about giving discounts to the old women in my mother's building wanting touch-ups, I know secretly she admired my generosity and wished she had as much faith as I did in the universe's reciprocity to keep me afloat. The very things we like about each other make us impossible together.

Geneva smiles and cocks her head backward. "Look in the backseat."

I find a maroon tote bag with a matte satin finish that perfectly matches my graduation gown. "You didn't . . ." I reach for it and place it on my lap. I leaf through the white tissue paper until I come across a six-by-four-inch gift box. The unusual shape makes me nervous. I hope Geneva didn't get me a piece of jewelry like a bracelet or necklace.

"Are you going to open it or what?"

"It's enough that you came to my graduation, Geneva."

"In that case, I can send it right back." She reaches for the box, and I yank it away. Geneva laughs, and then so do I. "Open it then."

I peel back the lid, then unravel more white tissue paper. Sitting on a bed of cotton is a pair of Mehaz styling shears. They're so beautiful! Twenty-five teeth of Japanese stainless steel. I run my fingers along the removable finger rest and then slip them into the contoured rings, parting the shears with a fluid ease. As Geneva pulls onto the Fifty-ninth Street Bridge, the blades gleam in the rays of the early afternoon sun. They had to cost at least a hundred and fifty bucks.

"If you already have a pair . . ."

"No, I don't. I mean, yeah, I have a bunch of styling shears, but nothing like these. It'll be a while before I can afford to splurge on a pair like these."

Geneva pulls into the middle line of the clogged bridge. "Trust me, I know."

I bet she knows. I can see Geneva, searching the Internet for an impressive yet professional gift. She probably came across the Mehaz brand after considerable research to determine if the name promised high quality. Then she saw the broad range of prices, grew frustrated trying to understand the features that determined the differences, and settled for a pair square in the middle of the scale. She didn't buy me the cheapest pair in the line, but she didn't order the most expensive either, and knowing Geneva like I do, affordability was the least of her criteria when making that decision.

I rewrap the shears into the tissue paper and place them back in the box. "I love them, Geneva." The box doesn't fit into my purse so I remove the shears again and stuff them into my purse, leaving the box on my lap. "Thank you." I throw my arms around Geneva's neck and plant a firm kiss on her cheek.

"I'm driving now, stop it. So that big guy I saw with Jackie. That her boyfriend?" I just smirk at her. We didn't have to go on a double date for Geneva to know exactly who the man was. "He's cute," she says when I ignore her. "For a guy."

"Whatever."

"You're making a mistake, Carmen."

I turn to face Geneva. "I don't want to fight about this with you anymore. Is this why you came to my graduation? To give the dead horse one last kick in the head?"

"I know you think I can't be objective, but listen to me. I'm not saying this for my own sake." Geneva reaches for the hand in my lap and holds it in her own, and I try to remember one time in the year that we were together when she ever did that while we were driving. "I've been where you're heading, Carmen. I was the same age you were when it happened, and I got hurt really bad. She broke my heart, and I lost my friend. I hate to break it to you, but when it comes to love, you have to stick to your own kind."

Stick to my own kind? Where did that come from? I've heard that before but where? Throughout the years, I've heard it all. Get off the fence. Choose a side. Pick a team. But stick to my own kind? Sounds like some crap my mother would say. But Mami can't stand it when I have a girlfriend, and as far as race goes, she wouldn't care if my partner's orange so long as he's a he. Stick to my own kind? Stick to my own kind. Wait a minute . . . stick to my own kind!

I burst into a laughter so loud, the Corolla suddenly feels crowded. I catch the frown on Geneva's face and tried to regain my composure, but her displeasure only makes the lyric now bouncing in my head that more hilarious. "I'm sorry, Geneva," I gasp between laughs, "but when an African American lesbian professor tries to give romantic advice to her girly Puerto Rican ex by quoting *West Side Story* . . ." The idea seems even more ludicrous given the somber reality of the situation. I start to sing, surprised that I still know the words. *"Forget that girl and find another. One of your own kind! Stick to your own kind!"*

"Carmen, stop it."

". . . A girl like that will give you sorrow. You'll meet another girl tomorrow . . ." I just can't get enough of the ironic perfection of that particular line so I stop singing, doubling over in laughter.

"I said, stop it!"

"One of your own kind! Stick to your own kind."

Geneva slams her fist onto the horn and holds it there so it blares like a car alarm. "Shut up or get out."

I remember who Geneva is. She's the anal retentive, proudly stoic control freak who cried when I told her it was over. But Geneva's also that thirty-six-year-old academic who had fallen in love only twice in her life and just admitted to the second woman to break her heart that the first woman to do so was straight. The Geneva who swallows her pride to attend my graduation, knowing that my own mother had no intention of going and that celebrating with Jackie with Wil by my side was no celebration at all.

I start to apologize to Geneva when she says, "You know what, Carmen? You're right. We're not meant for each other, but neither are you and Jackie. With that attitude, I can't imagine who is, so don't call me when Jackie—"

I swing open the car door and leap out of the car. The gift box for the styling shears tumbles out of my lap and onto the asphalt.

"Carmen!"

Leaving the car door ajar and the empty gift box on the concrete, I race down the Queensboro Bridge as a din of car horns blare after me.

IRENA

Grove Street PATH Station

Jersey City, NJ

Friday, June 16, 8:06 A.M.

"This train's going to New York City."

On top of everything else that went wrong this morning, I cannot miss this train. I bound up the staircase, rattling the wheels of my travel bag against the steps. My pocketbook slips off my shoulder, but I have to ignore it and let it dangle from my elbow.

"Next stop on this train is Pavonia Newport. Watch the closing doors."

The second I dart onto the train, the doors close immediately behind me. A Latino man about forty nudges his friend, points at me then laughs. "Yo, she just leaped on the train like O. J. in that commercial!" His friend shakes his head, whether out of embarrassment or agreement I can't tell. How dare he even mention that wife-battering murderer so casually, let alone compare me to him? What moron remembers that stupid ad but conveniently forgets the Trial of the Nineties? I yank my bag to the opposite end of the car, and the second the train stops in Pavonia, I'm moving to the next one.

As I flop onto an empty bench, I catch my tear-streaked reflection in the train's window. I reach into my bag for a packet of moistened towelettes and wipe my face clean. I hope the redness in my eyes fade by the time I get to Lourdes's place. At least, I'll be there on time.

I'm still clutching the pin. My mother's pin—now my pin—of

the Cuban flag glistens under the sunlight filtered through the train window. With two fingers, I tweeze out the threads from my torn shirt. Since I have on a tank top underneath my shirt, I start to unbutton it. But then the two men at the front of the car erupt into rowdy laughter, and I decide to wait until I get to Lourdes's. Instead, I tack the pin to my other collar tip and reached into my bag for that stupid asthma pump.

I can still feel my father's grip on my left shoulder while his other fist tightens around the pin and yanks. Although I had torn away from his grip, Dad still managed to loosen the pin from my collar. I had grabbed my bag and had run out the door and halfway around the corner when I heard the pin fall onto the ground. Abandoning my bag in the middle of the sidewalk, I raced back, dropped on all fours and searched frantically for it. Just as I found it, Dad had turned the corner. "Irena, I'm sorry," he cried. "Come back. *M'ija, no vayas así.*"

But I just grabbed the pin, got my bag, and ran and ran and ran. I didn't stop until I reached the train station. I just couldn't. I had to catch this train into New York City. I couldn't be late for this trip, even though I know Hazel and Lourdes would never let Jackie follow through on her threats to leave without any late-comers. Most of all, I couldn't miss this train, because I knew if I did, I'd go back home. And if I went back, they'd surely go to San Francisco without me. And if they left without me, then my rare and impulsive act of defiance would be for nothing.

But I didn't miss the train, so I don't want to think anymore about my fight with my father. He never dwells on our fights, so why should I? Our fights sit with me for days, and sometimes they make me so nauseated, I don't want to make the commute to school. But Dad never misses a day at the bodega so . . .

Oh, shit! I forgot the food. I banged my head against the window. Jackie's going to have a fit. Shit, shit, shit! In my desperate attempt to escape one harangue, I just guaranteed myself another. Shit!

I finally stick the inhaler into my mouth and give myself a fast pump of medication. As quickly as I did this, several other passengers notice me, including the two men in the front of the car. Why the hell are they checking me so much? I swear if they follow me when I switch cars at Pavonia, I'm going straight for the conductor!

I shove the pump back into my bag with such decisiveness, I knock it off my lap, spilling a few things, including my journal and some of its loose contents onto the floor—photos, letters, cards, and other things I hadn't yet attached to the pages. Shit! I bend down to scoop up my mementos when a young man across from me reaches down to assist me.

"No, no, no, it's okay," I say. Goddess, I hope I don't sound frightened. "I got it, thank you." He drops an ivory envelope and pulls back into his seat, crossing his leg over his knee and drawing his arms to his chest. Dammit, I offended him. I didn't mean to. I just didn't want a stranger touching my personal effects. "Thank you, though. Thank you." I repeat that over and over again until I return to my own seat and drop the pile on the one next to me.

I take the ivory envelope off the top and read the return address. San Francisco State University. I pull back the flap to retrieve the workshop registration form I should have completed weeks ago while waiting for my friends to tell me which ones they planned to take. Jackie and Hazel probably had forgotten all about it amidst the graduation hoopla, and Lourdes . . . well, she's always busy—okay, flaky's more like it, but I'm not judging, just accepting—so it's not like I actually expected her to respond to my e-mail anyway.

I skim the directions to find out how many I can choose. Of the over two dozen workshops available, I have three choices. I make two selections immediately, checking *Rediscovering Women-Centered Spirituality* as well as *Women's Ways of Healing.* In addition to the caucus for queer women of color, Hazel'll probably join me for at least one of them, and I can probably convince Lourdes to try the second one. I know better than to try to get Jackie to attend either workshop, and besides she volunteered to lead a self-defense workshop in exchange for free admission into the conference. Still, before this trip's over, I have to get Jackie into a healing circle, sweat lodge, or something!

As I scan the list of options to make my third choice, I feel overwhelmed with their number and quality. *Lest We Forget: Recommitting to the Battle against HIV/AIDS. No Turning Back: Preserving Reproductive Rights in Reactionary Times. Awakening the Sleeping Giant: Maximizing Women's Electoral Power.* Should I deepen my knowledge and build connections with women in a familiar area or explore a new topic? Jackie's been pressuring me to register for her self-defense workshop, but after skimping this past semester to save for this trip and openly defying my father to take it, I don't want to waste a minute of it on fighting.

When I reach the end of the list, I notice the last workshop offered has two sections. *The Silent Epidemic: Fighting Rape. Section A for Counselors. Section B for Survivors.* I pull a pen out of my hemp pocketbook and check the box next to the workshop title. Which section should I attend? My pen just hovers between the two choices as I wait for my inner voice to guide my selection.

The two men at the head of the car laugh raucously over something one of them has said. And I just snap my head up and glare at them. Yuck! *Ignore them, Irena.* I turn back and try to focus on the registration form on my lap.

The Silent Epidemic: Fighting Rape. Section A for Counselors. Section B for Survivors. My inner voice faintly tells me which one to choose, but I just can't bring myself to do it.

"This is the PATH train to Penn Station, New York City. The next stop is Hoboken. Hoboken, New Jersey."

Here's my chance to move. I wedge the registration form inside my journal, scoop up my pile of stationery, and stuff everything into my bag. I grab my travel bag and make my way to the nearest exit.

"Getting off already?" says one of the men at the front of the car.

Mind your own fuckin' business, I want to scream. *I'm not here for your goddamn amusement.* The train pulls into the station and comes to a stop. The second the door opens, I hustle out onto the platform and toward the preceding car.

"Have a nice trip," he calls through the doors closing behind me.

Only when I settle into the next car do I dare respond to him. "Fuck off." And even that I just mumble under my breath.

Astoria Houses

Astoria, NY

Friday, June 16, 8:19 A.M.

TO: Hazel1985@hotmail.com
FROM: gboyd@fordham.edu
DATE: June 15, 2006 10:00 PM
SUBJECT: Re: I'm Sorry

Dear Carmen,

Sorry it took so long to get back to you, but I'm just getting your e-mail now. I'm actually in San Francisco already and have been for a few days. Since I'm presenting at the conference, they paid for my flight out here. I asked if they could fly me out a little earlier and so here I am.

I appreciate and accept your apology. You probably expect me to apologize in return, but I honestly cannot do that. I stand by what I said to you. I said it to you because I love you, and I don't want to see you get hurt. I'm realizing now that I cannot protect you. Some lessons you have to learn on your own. All I can do is offer my shoulder to lean on when you do.

Even though you've heard me speak a thousand times, I do hope you'll come to my panel at the conference. But I'll understand if you feel that you cannot be there. In any event, please drive safely.

Geneva I. Boyd, Ph.D.
Professor of Sociology
Fordham University
Women's Studies Program
113 W. 60 St.
New York, N.Y. 10023

JACKIE

1783 Willis Avenue
South Bronx, NY
Friday, June 16, 6:17 A.M.

The aroma of bacon coaxes me out of sleep. I enjoy a nice stretch and a deep yawn, then roll over to look at the alarm clock. Then I slide over to Wil's side of the bed nuzzling my face into his pillow and inhaling his scent. No metrosexual, my man. His pillow smells of nothing but masculine cleanliness.

I spot the stack of DVDs next to the alarm clock and give myself a mental pat on the back. Good call letting Wil pick that Eddie Murphy bomb. I learned early in our relationship that bad rentals lead to great sex, so I encourage him to select one turkey after the next. Eventually, I revealed my secret when Wil asked me how I wanted to spend our first Valentine's Day.

"Maybe ice-skating at Rock Center or one of those moonlight cruises around Manhattan," he said.

I pretended to give his suggestion much thought, but then I said, "Or we could just try to re-create your mom's glazed ham and rent *Gigli.*" Wil immediately caught my drift, smart guy that he is.

The bedroom door swings open, and Wil carries in a tray piled with bacon, eggs, and toast. I sit up and yank the comforter aside. "If I didn't know any better, I'd think this was a bribe to keep me from going on the road trip."

Wil sets the tray over my lap, eases in next to me and feeds me a strip of bacon. "Then don't know better." Before I can respond, he adds, "Yeah, yeah, yeah, it's a sista thing. You mean six hours on a plane isn't long enough for y'all to bond?"

I reach for a piece of toast. "Aw, you even cut the bread into little diagonals. *¡Qué lindo!*"

"C'mon, Jackie."

"We've got August," I say. That's when we're going to spend the week in the Bahamas. Just the two of us. Our first vacation together and my twenty-second birthday celebration.

"August? See, I got your number now."

I swallow the forkful of scrambled eggs I just shoved into my mouth. "Do you?"

"This trip isn't about girls on the road. It's about boys on the side." I just laugh then slap my hand over my mouth, hoping Wil didn't catch a mouthful. "You just tryin' to make a brother suffer. Wonder and worry. Miss you and all that. Admit it."

See, when Wil talks about the trip that way, I never know how to take him. What if he's only testing me to see how much I wanted him with nothing more at stake than his ego? And if he means what he says about missing me and all, well, just exactly how much did that really mean?

"Look, I gotta be out of here by eight," I say. "Do you want to spend our last hour and half together fighting or fucking?"

Wil holds out his palms like the dishes on a scale. "Fight. Fuck. Fight. Fuck." I lean over and nibble on his ear. "Wait, I haven't decided yet." I poke him in the side, and he laughs. Then Wil lifts the tray, places it on the floor, and straddles me. He pushes the bottom of his John Jay sweatshirt off my belly and plants a kiss below my navel. I raise my arms, and he helps me pull the sweatshirt over my head and tosses it on the floor. As Wil descends on me, the telephone rings.

"You should get that," I say. I don't know if I mean it. After all, the man's sucking on my nipple, something he does so well.

"Later."

Then I realize it might be one of the girls trying to reach me. Some drama always manages to occur with either Hazel or Irena. I bet anything Irena doesn't come through with the food for some reason or another. If levelheaded Lourdes didn't have my back, I don't think we could have ever made this trip happen.

The ringing continues, and I give Wil a little slap on the back of the head. Instead of answering that annoying phone, he takes it as a cue to float over to my other breast. "C'mon, Wil!"

Finally, he reaches for the telephone and rests his head on my chest as he puts the receiver to his ear. " 'Lo." I feel his shoulders stiffen just before he pulls up and rolls away from me. "What's up?" Now he's off the bed and on his feet.

Fuckin' Sheila. I slash the air across my throat. *Cut that bitch off now.*

Wil turns away from me. "Yeah, I can do that. But I can't stay for the whole game. Fine, put him on and I'll explain it to him."

I've had enough of this shit. I scamper toward the end of the bed and flail over the edge as I reach for the sweatshirt. I snatch it and yank it over my head when I feel Wil's hand clamp on my ankle. This man is not grabbing at me while he's on the phone with that kid. "Hey, Li'l Man, how you doing?" he says to Eric. Li'l Man, Li'l Bit . . . what, he can't remember your name if you're under twelve years old? I tug my leg, but he refuses to let go of me. "Yeah, but just so you know, I can't stay for the whole game."

"Let. The fuck. Go."

"That's Jackie, she says hi." He gives me those pleading eyes. "Eric says hi."

Not if his mother is hovering behind him he didn't. The harder I wriggle, the tighter Wil grips my ankle. I swear I'm going to kick him. But then I spot the DVD cases and reach for the stack.

Wil's eyes fly open. "Don't you dare! . . . Not you, Eric. Jackie thinks she's funny."

I grab the top case and fling it at him. It misses his head by a yard, and he still has not let go of my freakin' leg. In fact, he anchors the receiver between his head and shoulder then latches on to my ankle with both hands.

"Because I start my new job on Monday, that's why, so I have a lot to do this weekend."

I keep yanking my leg while I grab another DVD case and fire it at Wil. This one sails straight for his grill so he jerks his hands up to block his face. My leg ricochets toward my shoulder, launching me off the bed and onto the floor. "Oh, sh . . . Eric, hold on." Wil finally drops the phone on the bed and runs to where I'm sprawled across the floor feeling like an idiot. "Jackie, are you all right?" He offers me his hand.

I slap it away and jump to my feet. "Do I look fuckin' all right?"

"C'mon, honey, don't talk like that when I got the kid on the telephone."

You know what? I think. *I don't want to talk to you at all.* Instead I scoop up my clothes and march out of the bedroom. The last thing I hear before slamming the bathroom door is Wil say to Eric, "Well, maybe I can stay for a little while."

I'm so furious, my shower's turning into a bloodbath. I brush my teeth so hard, I spit blood and the mouthwash sears my tongue and gums. Then I rub myself with the washcloth until my skin feels like it might catch fire. Finally, I attack my hair with Hazel's counsel echoing in my head. *Make sure the water's warm 'cause hot water makes it dry. Only shampoo your scalp and never mind what the bottle says—only apply shampoo once. And use your fingertips not your nails.* Still I scrape my fingers across my scalp, then rake the shampoo through the ends. Then I pour a massive glob of conditioner directly onto my hair, spike the wide-toothed comb Hazel gave me into my crown and try to yank it toward the ends. *Detangle your hair from the ends up and be gentle!* I tug until I feel a stab of pain in my scalp. "Fuck!" I just fling the comb across the shower and jam the water off.

I step out, dry off, and force this mass into a lumpy ponytail. I really don't care how I look. I just want to get the hell out of here and on the road. When I walk into the kitchen, Wil has breakfast waiting for me on the table. Ignoring him and his trifling peace offering, I head straight for my bags by the apartment door.

"Look, Jackie, Sheila's car is in the shop so she asked me to take Eric to his ball game this afternoon. That's all."

"Right. Her car's suddenly in the shop. At seven in the goddamn morning."

"Stop this already. You're not competing with Eric. Or Sheila."

"Because they're a packaged deal." Even Kharim tells him this, and he's Wil's oldest and closest friend. If Wil won't listen to him, what shot do I have? I can't lie to myself anymore that Wil continues to see Eric because he doesn't get this. At this point, he must do it because he does get it. I throw open the apartment door and drag my bag into the hallway.

Wil stands up and makes his way toward me. He seems as desperate as I am to put an end to this argument so I try one last time. "He's not even your son, Wil," I say. "Let him go." I've never asked him to do that. I've hinted, implied, insinuated . . . everything but ask him bluntly to just walk away from Eric. I haven't wanted to do that, because I know what it means to Wil to have a relationship with Eric. I know that he has an attachment to the kid, but it's deeper than that for Wil. Sheila knows that, too, and that's why she's trying to take advantage, and that's why Wil has to let Eric go. If she respected our relationship, I would never ask him to do this. But she doesn't, and I have no choice. If he doesn't do this, then he doesn't respect our relationship any more than she does, and they deserve each other, and I need to bow out gracefully. Well, maybe not gracefully, but I'll be damned if I stay with Wil until one day he runs out on me to do something for Eric only to come back that night with Sheila's perfume all over him. I'm not going out like that. "You have to let Eric go."

"Please don't ask me to do that," he says. "You can't ask me to do that."

My answer to that is to grab my suitcase and head for the stairwell. In his bare feet, Wil trails me, reaching for my bag. "Let me help you with that."

"I don't need your fuckin' help."

"You can't leave until we settle this, Jackie. Your friends can wait."

"I'm not putting my friends on hold while you play Cosby." I like Wil's mother, but I'm tired of paying for her decisions. She was on such a mission to find a father figure for Wil, it never occurred to her that allowing him to get attached to her boyfriend of the moment might actually do her son more harm than good. I have no doubts his mother had nothing but the best intentions, but now Wil refuses to stop posing as Eric's father, feeding both

Eric and Sheila's hopeless fantasy that Wil just might actually marry her, and fucking up our relationship by making me doubt just how hopeless that fantasy really is.

"There's nothing for *we* to settle. This is *your* problem. *You* settle it." Before he can answer, I start back down the steps.

Wil folds his arms across his chest. "You're going away for two weeks, and you're going to leave me like this? Fine, Jackie, I'm done chasing you. And I might not be here when you get back."

Then he turns to walk back into his apartment. "You must have me confused with Sheila 'cause I'm not fuckin'—" The slam of the apartment door cuts me off. "—coming back."

LOURDES

Blessed Sacrament Church
Upper West Side, NY
Friday, June 16, 8:38 A.M.

I sit in the last pew watching the other parishioners file into the aisle. My head's still reeling from Monsignor Casey's sermon. At first his words spoke to me, reminding us to live the seven works of mercy as a way to redeem the Church in this time of scrutiny. I admire the monsignor's courageous refusal to trivialize the allegations of sexual abuse. *Que Dios lo bendiga.* He's right. The future of the Catholic Church—its effectiveness and credibility—now lies not in the political stances of its leadership but in the everyday acts of its members. But then Monsignor Casey shreds me to bits by condemning my every good deed.

"So I say to you, my children, bring your neighbors to Christ by upholding His word in the conscious and faithful decisions you make in your everyday lives," he said. "Express not hatred to the young woman at the abortionist's office, but like Christ show her compassion and give her counsel so that she decides not to murder her unborn child. Commit no violence to the young man who fornicates with members of his own sex, but like Christ protect him from danger so that he seeks the treatment he needs to choose a lifestyle that gives glory unto God. Isolate not the atheist who fights to remove the name of God from this great nation's Pledge of Allegiance or to erase His miraculous creation from the teachings of our children, but like Christ spread the gospel of the Lord through your words and deeds to your children so that through their enlightened innocence he may see the righteousness that is God and amend his ways."

After a sermon like that, I'm too ashamed to receive Holy Communion this morning. *Pero a la misma vez,* I hardly think of any of my friends as sinners. Now I'll never understand Hazel's attraction to other women, but I've fixed her up a few times and have even gone on several double dates with her, and it's just really difficult for me to believe that Hazel's sexual orientation is a matter of choice. *Ay, no sé, pero* it's almost as if men are too captivated with Hazel's physical beauty to spark her interest the way an unrequited crush on another woman always seems to. Like when Hazel "fell" for Carolina at the Olympic Flame. *¡Qué preciosa se puso!* She found everything Carolina did endearing, from the way she tucked her hair behind her ear just before she scribbled down an order to the extra dip she added after filling a cup of coffee. When Hazel likes a woman, she appreciates the littlest things about her and for that matter everything else feminine in the world. No wonder I found that heavenly Gucci clutch while window-shopping with Hazel right after she met Geneva. The best thing I ever discovered while shopping with Hazel when she was dating a man *fueron esas botas horribles.* Even the *viejita* running the church's winter clothing drive turned up her wrinkled nose at them when I came to my senses and tried to donate them.

And I can't judge Jackie without feeling like a major hypocrite. She drinks beer, curses like a mechanic, and has premarital sex (and probably all at once) whenever she feels like it. Every time I feel even slightly critical of her wanton behavior, envy taps me on the shoulder and yells in my ear, "*¡Te cogí!*" I don't want to drink beer or curse like a mechanic, but I did confide in Jackie that I truly didn't want to wait until I was married to have sex. Then I made the mistake of telling her what I hoped my first time would be like: I spared no details from the rose petals in the bubble bath to the exquisite pleasure of graceful penetration. Jackie snickered, patted my knee, and said, "Okay, Lou, you need to give up those Harlequin romances. I mean, if you're not even trying to, like, practice with a dildo or something, the one thing you better count on in addition to Godiva chocolates and Neruda poetry is pain."

To make up for horrifying me, Jackie proceeded to tell me about the first orgasm she had with a man so I chose to focus on that. And she gave me a vibrator for Christmas which I never dared to take out of the box! While I can never do most of the things that Jackie does *Dios sí lo sabe* that I certainly want to. God help me, I don't know what I envy more—Jackie's fantastic sex life (which seemed only to intensify since she met Wil) or her ability to enjoy it without a single concern about eternal hellfire.

And even though Irena has become my closest friend, I have such a hard time tolerating her astrology charts and tarot cards. Reiki, yoga, chakras . . . all her lectures on alternative healing and holistic medicine, I can handle. Sometimes, I can even appreciate the naturalness of it all, and much of it is quite compatible with Catholicism. After all, didn't Jesus heal with his hands? But more than any of the others, Irena has inspired me—or at least has tried—to change my major from pre-med to visual art.

I resurrected when I met Jackie, Hazel, and Irena while organizing the Take Back the Night rally during my first year at Fordham. At the TBN organizing meetings, Hazel always brought great music and sang along like an angel. Jackie kept us in stitches with her imitations of professors and sharp observations on anything and everything. And Irena informed and inspired us with the articles she photocopied and stories she told. When I am with those three, I truly feel like a crusader for social justice yet never feel guilty for celebrating the small things that give us hope. A great song, a hilarious joke, a dear friend.

I watch the parishioners trail away from the altar back to their pews to pray, and I reconsider taking Communion. All the things that truly mattered, I still believe. The Mystery of Faith says *Christ has died, Christ has risen, Christ will come again.* Not *Life begins at conception.* Or *Homosexuality is abnormal.* I deserve to take Communion!

So I stand up, amble out of the pew, and join the line. I look forward to tipping back my head, closing my eyes, and feeling God's hand gently touch my bottom lip as I became one with His Son.

My turn is next. The monsignor raises the wafer above my head and says, "The body of Christ."

I take a deep breath and say, "Amen." Then I make the Sign of the Cross and head back to my pew. After taking a quick glance at my watch, I notice that I have only fifteen minutes to get back to my apartment or else the ever-punctual Irena might arrive before I do. I rush to the door. At first, I hope that no one notices that I'm leaving before the conclusion of Mass, but once I dip my fingers in the holy water by the door, I let it go.

IRENA

Gristedes at West 91st Street
Upper West Side, NY
Friday, June 16, 10:36 A.M.

"We don't need those!" I grab the package of Oreos from Lourdes and place it back on the shelf.

"Says who?" says Hazel.

"I say." Did everyone forget that I'm in charge of groceries? No matter that I fought with Dad and didn't bring the food as planned. Thank the Goddess, Jackie let it slide. But then Lourdes went and overpacked, so we barely had enough room in the car for our clothes, never mind groceries. We lost an hour unpacking Lourdes's silly gadgets, and now here we are in this stupid expensive supermarket.

"C'mon, they're reduced fat."

"And they're almost five dollars." I steer the cart around Lourdes and Hazel and head for the checkout. "Have you guys forgotten that we're almost two hours behind schedule?"

"You should've called me," says Lourdes. Through the corner of my eye, I catch her as she grabs the cookies and winks at Hazel. "I have an account here. I could've gone online and placed the order for you. Then all we would've had to do is pick them up on our way out of town."

And we would have a cart full of junk that wouldn't have fit in the car anyway with all your gizmos. "Coulda woulda shoulda." I park my cart behind a middle-aged blonde wearing a Ralph Lauren jogging suit and ignoring her wailing toddler. The poor little girl's hollering and shaking a crumbling piece of melba toast in her tiny fist like Norma Rae would a picket sign.

Hazel whispers, "Bet she wants an Oreo." And of course, Lourdes giggles.

I shoot them a dirty look, then look at my watch. "Jackie's gonna be so pissed."

"*¿Y dónde está ella?*"

"Looking for a pay phone."

"Why?"

"Who knows?" Hazel moves away from us toward the magazine rack.

Just as I'm about to ask her what's going on, my turn comes to pile our groceries onto the conveyor belt. A bag of yellow bananas. A bag of Doritos. A can of unsalted almonds. A package of assorted Hershey's Minatures. These two have thwarted my every attempt to make healthy choices.

"Jackie could've just used my phone," says Lourdes, who now stands next to Hazel by the magazine rack and is flipping through a copy of *InStyle* with her idol Salma Hayek on the cover. "Why didn't she just ask me?"

"She probably wanted some privacy."

Hazel peers over Lourdes's shoulder while holding a *Cosmopolitan* magazine with Jennifer Lopez on the cover. "She's beautiful and talented and all, but I don't know . . . Something about her strikes me as phony."

Lourdes presses the open magazine to her chest as if to protect Salma. "How could you say that?"

"When I hear her talk about social issues and politics and stuff, Salma says all the right things, but the way she says it—" Hazel circles her hands in the air as if to conjure the right words. "—I don't know. She just comes off like she's so above it all. Like we're so lucky that a woman of her status cares about these things."

Lourdes huffs. "This coming from a J.Lo fan."

"Hey, I never said I was a J.Lo fan," says Hazel. "I just said I'd do her."

"*Virgen, dame paciencia.*" Lourdes grabs the *Cosmopolitan* from Hazel's hand and slaps it back onto the magazine rack. "Salma

Hayek is involved in the fight against domestic violence. She spoke out against the war in Iraq. She creates opportunities for other Latinos in Hollywood. What has Jennifer Lopez ever done for anyone besides herself?"

"Didn't she perform on the remake of *What's Going On?* Wasn't that to raise money to fight AIDS in Africa?"

"*Por favor.* That was for her own benefit, too. To promote the myth that she's a singer!" I got to give Lourdes that one. But then I remember hearing something about Jennifer Lopez making a donation to a children's hospital after Hurricane Katrina. But if I get into this, we'll never get out of here.

"Okay, Lou, don't you think that's a tad bit . . . un-Christlike?"

I've never been a Christian but I feel myself becoming more un-Christlike by the second. "Let's go!"

They turn to look at me. Hazel says, "Who died and made you Jackie?"

"I'm sorry. I just need a hand here. I mean, it's the least you can do after you loaded up the cart with all this stuff."

"C'mon, Hazel. She's right."

"Just start bagging the stuff for me," I say as I place the last few items onto the conveyor belt. "Please."

Hazel and Lourdes ease past me to the end of the belt. The cashier scans the last package. "That'll be $237.09."

Shit! I don't have to count the money everyone gave me to know that we're short. Way short. I say, "We're going to have to put some stuff back." The cashier sucks her teeth, and my cheeks start to tingle. This probably never happens in Gristedes.

Now Lourdes is searching her wallet for her credit card. "I'll take care of it."

"No, Lou, that's not fair. It's not like we all agreed to buy everything here." Had it been up to me, half the things never would have left the shelves. I need to be more assertive.

"*No se preocupen.*" Lourdes offers the card to the cashier, who leaps on it as if it were a gift for her.

"She said don't worry," Hazel translates for me.

"I know what she said. It's just not fair for her to pay for everything. We can't let her do that, Hazel."

"What's taking you guys so fuckin' long?" Jackie blows over to where Hazel is bagging the groceries. Either the Upper West Side has no working pay phones or her telephone call did not go well.

I glance at Lourdes and catch her cringing. What did Lourdes care if all these bourgie people heard Jackie curse? Then I remember. *They're her neighbors.* "Are we going on this trip or what?" says Jackie. She doesn't sound as if she's cracking the whip. She sounds as if she's looking for a reason to abandon the trip. This is not like Jackie, and I have no idea what's going on with her. All I know is that turning back is so not an option for me.

"Just pay the woman, Lou," says Hazel, and I quit protesting. Lourdes motions for the cashier to proceed with the transaction. She nods and swipes the card through the reader.

Jackie grabs three bags and heads toward the exit. "Hope we can get all this shit in the car." I snatch four bags of produce and follow her. If Hazel and Lourdes want bags of canned junk, let them carry it.

HAZEL

West Side Highway
near 158th Street
Upper West Side, NY
Friday, June 16, 10:57 A.M.

As we coast north on Riverside Drive, I turn up the volume on the radio and sing along with Beyoncé. In the backseat, Lourdes and Irena continue the Salma versus Jennifer debate. Jackie's eyes are fixed on the asphalt before us. The closer we get to the bridge, the looser I feel, but this knot in my stomach won't unravel until we cross that tollbooth. I'm worried that at any moment Jackie's going to spin this car around and speed back to the Bronx.

"Now that she's done *Frida,* she should stay away from all those spitfire roles," says Irena.

"But that's what Hollywood pays for. Then Salma takes that Hollywood money and makes movies like *In the Time of the Butterflies,*" Lourdes said. "What does Jennifer do with her Hollywood money? She plans another wedding."

Okay, I have to defend La Lo here. "Hey, she wanted to play Frida Kahlo, too, now."

"Jennifer probably didn't even know who Frida Kahlo was until she heard Salma wanted to make a movie about her."

I shrug, then glance at Jackie, who just sighs and pulls into the left lane. With her eyes on the road and her mind on Wil, Jackie's missing out on one of her favorite pastimes—J.Lo bashing. I reach into my pocketbook and pull out my cigarettes.

"C'mon, Lourdes, that's not a fair thing to say," says Irena. "And didn't Jennifer take a break from all those big Hollywood movies to work with Gregory Nava on one about the disappearances in Juarez?" She's so nonjudgmental. And optimistic, too. At least about other people's ability to evolve from their dramas. Irena thinks there's nothing wrong with J.Lo that a period of celibacy and ongoing co-counseling sessions won't fix. She sticks her face between the two front seats. "You gonna smoke that in here?" she asks me.

I totally forgot about Irena's asthma, but I really need this cigarette. I don't get why breathing in secondhand tobacco can irritate her condition yet actually inhaling cannabis helps it. She explained it to me once, but I can't remember. I look at Irena's little face, and with that angular jaw, pasty skin, and blue eyes, she reminds me of a sugar cube with sky blue sprinkles. "Just this one time," I say. "I promise to keep it out of the window."

"Guess one's not gonna kill me." She sighs, leans back into her seat.

"Thanks, sweetie."

"Jackie, what's wrong?" Lourdes asks. She's been babbling about Salma Hayek for the past half hour, but just my luck she would notice Jackie's silence at that moment.

"Should've made a telephone call," she says.

"Call when we stop for lunch," I say.

"You can use my new phone." Lourdes reaches into her Coach and pulls out a handheld computer with a nubby antenna. "*¡Hace todo!* I can play MP3s, access the Internet . . ."

Lourdes eagerly passes her latest toy to Jackie, who looks at it in wonder. "It's gonna be years before I can afford something cool like this." She darts her thumb across the keypad, and digit by digit Wil's number pops across the screen

The knot in my stomach tightens, and I take a deep pull on my cigarette. "Last thing we need right now is for you to get stopped for talking on a cell while driving."

"I'll pull over."

"There's no place to do that here." And I'm not just saying that either.

Jackie stops dialing and drops the telephone in her lap. "I'm not trying to fuck with these state troopers. Guess I'm going to have to wait until we cross the bridge."

"I think so."

Jackie chooses the upper level of the George Washington Bridge, and I feel my stomach relax. The sun reigns over the sky as a few sailboats slice white streaks across the murky Hudson River. As we coast across the bridge, I look in the rearview mirror to watch the landscape of New York City shrink. Underneath the slopes of green leaves and reddish bricks, the North Bronx never looked so pretty.

"Fuck." I turn forward as Jackie slows the Tempo. A blanket of cars unfurls in front of us, and Jackie slows the Tempo to a crawl. "Guess everyone's trying to get out of the city this weekend."

Jackie grabs Lourdes's telephone and unlatches her safety belt. "Since we're just sitting here . . ."

"Jackie, no! We can start moving any minute now." But she ignores me and bounds out of the car, pressing the phone to her ear. I undo my own belt and open the door.

Irena sucks her teeth. "Where are you going?" Sometime she acts like such a kid.

I think quickly and reach for my pocketbook. "I'm gonna smoke a cigarette."

"But you just had one."

I just slam the door and then lean against it. I pretend to search for my lighter while I strain to catch Jackie's conversation as she paces beside the Tempo.

"It's a simple question, Wil, so why don't you just answer it?" I find the lighter and start to flick. "Wil, you there? Can you hear me? Wil!" No sooner does my lighter burst into a tiny flame when Jackie mutters a few curses and storms back toward the car. "Let's go."

So I close the lighter, drop it into my pocketbook, and jump into the car. Jackie yanks the belt across her chest and jams the key into the buckle. "You okay?" I ask her.

"*¿Y qué pasó?*" asks Lourdes.

"Don't worry about it." Then Jackie punches the dashboard and says, "You know what? Forget him!" She looks into the rearview mirror at Irena. "Forget your father." Then she looks at me. "And forget your mother. Fuck all of 'em."

"Jackie!"

I know Jackie curses too much, but Lourdes should be used to it by now and besides, she shouldn't be such a schoolmarm. "She's right, Lourdes," I tell her. "This trip is supposed to be about *las hermanas.*"

"*Y solamente las hermanas,*" says Jackie.

Lourdes catches on, and three of us say, "*¡Y nada más que las hermanas!*"

Poor Irena looks confused, of course. I hate when we forget that Irena doesn't really speak Spanish even though she takes it every semester. It's bad enough the girl looks like a miniature version of Cameron Diaz, although she hates to hear that. It doesn't flatter Irena one bit to be likened to the highest paid Latina in Hollywood—a likable and gorgeous model-turned-actress at that.

I reach behind me to squeeze Irena's knee. "Don't worry, Rena. You're gonna pick up a lot of Spanish on this trip." And I make a vow to myself to stop trying to sneak smokes in the car.

"Starting right now," says Jackie. "Hazel, hook us up. And no Gloria Estefan shit either."

So I reach for the CD case at my feet. "What do you have against Gloria Estefan?"

"Nothing. I just don't want to hear a happily married woman who makes gazillions of dollars every year singing any sappy ballads about you-can-beat-me-cheat-me-mistreat-me-just-come-back-and-repeat-me." She reaches into her back pocket for a few bills to pay the toll. "The only ballads Gloria Estefan should ever sing is something like 'Love Is a House . . . And It's in My Name.' "

Finally, a laugh the four of us can share, and the cars ahead begin to move, I slip a CD into the player, and La India's voice fills the Tempo. Jackie hates to sing, but she belts right along with Lourdes and me.

Dicen que soy
Tu manzana envenenada
Dicen que soy
El titanic de tu alma

I peek through the rearview mirror and see Irena grinning as she stumbles over every other word. I glance at Lourdes, who's looking at her the same way I am. Lou and I catch eyes and smile at one another, telepathically agreeing how adorable Irena is. But she's not as adorable as Jackie, who's singing with more passion than skill, and I feel her leaving her self-consciousness and Wil miles behind us. The knot in my stomach melts, and I turn up the volume.

Finally, we are on our way.

When you die and go to heaven, what is the first thing you will say to God? I don't know what I'd say. I think I'd be in too much awe to speak so give me ideas. ☺—LB

Chile, you better work them wings! (I figure that even though I've made it in, I'd still have a little kissing up to do.)–CHF

You're so much prettier in person.—IR

Where the @#$% you've been?—JA

This is what I get for presuming that you are all going to heaven—smart alecky answers? Never mind. ¡Olvídenlo!—LB

Lourdes, you're not serious, are you? Are you really mad? Because my answer was pretty much sincere.—IR

I'm sorry, Lourdes. Didn't mean to offend you at all. Seriously, my first words to God when I arrive in heaven probably will be, "Where's my grandmother?"–CHF

C'mon, Lou! Eternal Paradise is the hottest nightclub in the universe, and you're the biggest star, and the three of us are your entourage. If any of us get past the celestial velvet rope, it's only going to be because we know YOU! (Admit it . . . you're smiling right now, aren't you?)—JA

LOURDES

Interstate 80
Parsippany, NJ
Friday, June 16, 11:45 A.M.

Yo lo supe pero no dije nada. The Tempo conks out the second we hit Parsippany. If I hadn't crashed my SUV, we would not be driving *esta lata con ruedas,* so I suggest we rent a minivan. But they won't hear of it even though I make it clear that I would pay for it.

So we cross the toll bridge, merge onto Interstate 80, and drive for about twenty-five miles, when the hood begins to smoke. While Jackie pulls over, I call directory assistance for the closest repair shop with a tow truck. No one teases me about my telephone now. The tow truck arrives, and a brawny guy with baked skin and a blond ponytail hops out.

"It's the upper radiator hose," says Jackie. "I'd fix it myself, but I don't have what I need."

"When I'm done hitching up, just hop into the cab, and I'll take you over to the shop."

"There're four of us though," says Irena.

"I can't take all of you with me. Only got room for one other person. You're gonna have to call a cab or a friend or something."

"It doesn't make sense to have someone come pick us up," says Hazel. "Is it so bad that we can't keep going?"

"Aw, it'll only take about a half hour to fix it."

Jackie throws her hands up. "We haven't gotten out of the

damned tristate area, and we've already blown our budget for this fuckin' trip."

I offer to pay for the cab. Before anyone can argue with me, I wave for the tow truck driver's attention. "Would you happen to know a car service we can call?"

He dips into his lapel pocket and pulls out a card. "My friends own this company. Tell 'im Jesse sent you, and they'll take good care of you."

Jackie takes the card and motions for the four of us to huddle around her. "Okay, so I'll ride in the truck with Hulk Hogan, and you guys follow us in the cab."

"Why can't we all go together?" asked Irena. "I don't like the idea of us being separated."

"Rena, he's only got room for one person in the truck."

"Then let's wait until the cab gets here so we can follow you guys to the repair shop."

"No can do," says Jesse as he releases the coupler locking device.

"You were not listening to our conversation."

"Couldn't help it," Jesse says, crossing his thick biceps across his massive chest. "And, no, Hulk Hogan can't wait."

"Thought you said these guys were your friends."

"Yeah, but I don't work for my friends," says Jesse. "I work for an ogre who always seems to know just how long it should take to find a car and haul it back, no matter where it breaks down."

"Look, we're just four gals looking for some harmless adventure and finding nothing but trouble," Hazel says, eyelashes batting and lips pouting. "We lose our van, leave behind schedule, and now this. On top of everything, please don't separate us."

I rush over to them. "You sure you can't wait for us even for a little while?" I say, waving a twenty-dollar bill in Jesse's face.

Without taking his eyes off Hazel, Jesse snaps up the bill and stuffs it in his pocket. "I think I can do a solid for you, ladies."

Jesse heads back to the truck. Jackie hands me the card for the cab company and says, "You call the cab, and I'm going to hitch a ride with Jon Cena here."

"Jon Cena!" Jesse yells. "Now that's the f---in' man!"

Jackie laughs. "Ain't he though?" And she and Jesse get in the truck, gabbing about wrestling as if they've known each other for years.

About twenty minutes later, a maroon cab with a black stripe arrives, and the driver has a passenger in the front seat beside him. "Hey, ladies, I'm Marv, and this is my buddy Rob." Marv's slimy with a dated fade, but Rob's kind of cute with dark spiky hair and a cleft in his chin.

Rob turns in his seat and looks at me through the security glass. "Where are you from?"

"Me?" After a few embarrassing moments, I always make sure a cute guy's question is for me and not Hazel. To her credit, once she realizes I've caught his interest, she always steps back.

"Si, *tu.*" It drives Irena crazy, but if a cute *blanquito* wants to flirt with me in my own language, I'm all ears and eyelashes.

"Oh, oh, oh!" Suddenly, Irena is bouncing in her seat and pointing out of the window like a child passing Toys R Us. We look out the window and read a handmade sign:

YOU'RE ONLY 1 MILE AWAY
FROM THE PARSIPPANY FLEA MARKET.

"Is that flea market far from the repair shop, do you know?" she asks Rob.

"It's right across the road."

Irena claps. "Why don't we go check it out? You know, while we wait for them to fix the car."

Hazel says, "Cool with me."

¡Ay, no! No one loves a bargain more than I do, but reclaiming other people's junk? *No me interesa.* "Remember what Jackie said. We're way behind schedule and budget."

"Well, we can't go anywhere until they fix the car, and no one says we have to spend any money." Irena sinks into the seat and sulks. "It's just something fun to do to pass the time." *La basura de una mujer,* I guess.

"Look, if we can get Jackie to go, I say why not?" says Hazel.

"*Pues . . .*" Satisfied with Hazel's suggestion, I turn back to Rob because Jackie will never agree to go to that silly *mercandillo.*

IRENA

Meineke Car Care Center,
Route 46
Parsippany, NJ
Friday, June 16, 12:18 P.M.

When the mechanic tells Jackie it'll take at least an hour to fix the whatever-you-call-it, I tell her about the flea market. Even though she says, "Sure, let's spend money we don't have on more crap we don't need," I can tell she's open to the idea. The idea of sitting in this garage for an hour is already making Jackie fidget.

"We might find something useful," I say.

Lourdes says, "Like another car maybe?" I thought she'd jump at the chance to shop! And let's face it, she's the only one out of the four of us who never has to give money a second thought. She just wants to stay behind with that guy from the cab who isn't all that. I hate it when white guys scam on Latinas, especially when they try to speak Spanish to us as if we just got off the boat. How offensive! Like Jackie always says, "That shit never made me buy a chicken from Frank Perdue, you think it's going to work for you?"

Hazel has my back though, so Jackie agrees to go. She asks Lourdes to give her cell phone number to the mechanic so he can call us when the car's ready. After taking some snacks from the car, we make our way across the road to the flea market. On the way there, I tell Lourdes, "Thank God you have a phone!" And that makes her smile so I think we're cool.

But within minutes I wish she would have just stayed behind at the shop. I take her to the clothing section, but she refuses to look at anything. And people are selling name brand stuff there, too!

Anne Klein, Donna Karan, Cole Haan . . . They call this a freakin' flea market? It's an outdoor outlet. If I wanted this shit—which I don't even if I could afford it—I'd just go to the galleria in Secaucus. Still Lourdes turns her nose up and makes some comment in Spanish about other people's *trapos.*

I take her to the book section, same thing. So I decide I'm just going to see what I want to see whether or not it interests Lourdes. I mean, I don't want to be bitchy, but she's being bratty. But I can't change her, right? I can only change my reaction to her.

So I go over to the jewelry section and find a woman selling the most beautiful gemstones. I wish I had saved more spending money for this trip because I would love to buy a crystal for each of us and place it in our ritual box. Definitely a moonstone for Hazel because I sense her third chakra is close to depletion. She's usually so vibrant, but she's struggling with something. And medicating herself with more nicotine than ever! No matter how much she smiles and sings, I feel this ache emanating from her that stems from fear. I pick up the moonstone, clasp it in my palm, and visualize Hazel. She's afraid of losing something. No, it's someone. She's afraid of being rejected by someone, and so she's projecting a false self. It's probably Jackie. I myself am anxious about what will become of our friendship after this trip, so I can only imagine how Hazel feels. A moonstone would be perfect for her. Not only would it alleviate her stress and anxiety by keeping her from becoming overwhelmed by her feelings, it would enhance her perception and allow her to open herself to new beginnings whatever they may bring.

I put the down the moonstone because the polished jade of a chrysoprase stone calls to me. This would be for Jackie. Her fourth chakra's a mess. She'd never admit it, but her heart is broken and has been for a very long time. Long before she met Wil. If anything, she won't allow herself to love him, because she hasn't even begun to love herself. While working with the chrysoprase, I would ask her to repeat an affirmation. Something like, "I release the past and free myself to love in the present." Like that's going to happen. I return the chrysoprase to its place on the velvet-lined table.

Of course, the second I pick up a cluster of pyrite, Lourdes reappears. "*¡Vámonos!*"

I can't resist the urge to test both Lourdes's knowledge and patience. "The Aztecs used to make mirrors out of this to divine the future." I hold the pyrite up to her face for a closer look.

She says, "*Por favor,* that's not real gold." Before I can tell her that I'm well aware of that, Lourdes grabs the pyrite and bites into it.

"What are you doing?" I snatch back the pyrite and look over my shoulder. Thank the Goddess that the saleswoman is too busy explaining the properties of an amethyst bracelet (like my watch) to another customer to catch Lourdes sinking her teeth into her merchandise.

"*Tú ves.*" Lourdes points at the golden flecks the stone left on her fingertips. "That would never happen with gold. Not only is gold much heavier, it's more orangey. This might as well be tin." Then she spins on her heel and starts to walk away from me. "*Irena, vente,*" she calls over her shoulder. "It's time to meet Jackie and Hazel."

"They don't call it fool's gold for nothing," I say. I put the pyrite where I found it and take the woman's business card from the plastic display case on the table. "Perfect for you," I mutter under my breath. *Open up that third eye and narrow mind, Lou.*

We head to the area where the food vendors have their stands and patio tables and chairs have been set up so shoppers can eat. Lourdes and I first spot Hazel, who's pulling a sundress over her tank top, then Jackie, who sits at a table sifting through a shoe box. When we arrive, Hazel reaches under the skirt, yanks down her shorts, and steps out of them. I mean, she doesn't flash anything, but sometimes that girl is too bold! Hazel models the dress for Jackie, who just throws a nod at her and turns back to these palm-sized cards in her hands. Hazel glares at Jackie then turns to Lourdes and me. "What do you think?" she asks as she pirouettes for us. "Ten bucks."

"Cool," I say, and Lourdes gives her the thumbs-up. The dress is a bit snug on her and too long although Hazel can always hem it. She can still get away with it, but I actually think the sundress would look better on Jackie. If she would ever wear something like that.

We all turn to Jackie, who is too absorbed with her cards to notice. She reaches into the shoe box for another handful and sorts through them quickly, adding some to the fan in her hand and tossing the rest back into the box. On the table amidst the snacks Jackie and Hazel have spread out, I see the bag of carrot sticks. As I reach for it and look for the hummus, I ask Jackie, "What you got there?" Lourdes sits besides me across from Jackie and opens the box of Oreos she snuck into our cart at Gristedes.

Hazel takes a seat next to Jackie. "Some lady sold her a box of old baseball cards for five bucks, and she found a Norberto Clemente card—"

"Roberto Clemente!" Jackie corrects her. "Get it right."

"Anyway, it's supposed to be worth a lot of money."

Of course, Lourdes takes interest. Without asking Jackie's permission, she grabs the box and starts to look through the cards. The sense of entitlement on that girl! She pulls out a card and says, "What about this one? Is it worth anything? He's cute."

Jackie snatches the card out of her hand, throws it back into the box and then takes the box from Lourdes.

I lean forward to get a better look at the card. "I don't know anything about sports, but he reminds me of . . . what's his name? Sammy Sosa!" Then I start to get that feeling. I take a chance and ask Jackie, "Can I see it?"

She seems happy that someone's taking her seriously and holds out the card to me. "Yeah, he does kinda look like Sammy Sosa." But before I can take the card, however, Jackie whisks it away. "Clean your hands first!"

Even though I only ate a few carrot sticks, I take a napkin and wipe my hands. Jackie finally hands me the card, and the feeling grows stronger. When I visualize that feeling, I see a crystal shot glass filled with seltzer water percolating in the center of my chest. I stare at Roberto as Jackie describes the value of the card and the significance of the man on it. "That's a 1956 Topps of the first Puerto Rican—the first Latino even—inducted into Major League Baseball's Hall of Fame. He won twelve Golden Gloves, four Batting Crowns—"

"So, Jackie, is the card worth a lot?" asks Lourdes.

"At least a hundred and fifty dollars."

"*¡No me digas!* That much for a baseball card?"

"It's in excellent condition so possibly more. All the cards in this box are in pretty good shape, but the rest of these players were bums. At least I've never heard of them, and I know my baseball."

I flip over the card and read his birthday—August 18. That's Jackie's birthday, too. This makes her proud. She wants to point it out but holds her tongue because she's afraid to come off like a starstruck teenager. With that thought, Roberto's face flashes across my third eye. It looks as it is on the baseball card against the backdrop of a baseball field. Then this outdoor background blossoms into this beautiful shade of emerald. Suddenly, Roberto's face dissolves into a dark spot that blinks then disappears as if he were on television just as the power goes out. I look at Jackie over the card. "He died suddenly, didn't he?"

"You read about him somewhere," says Jackie. Before I can respond, she snatches the card from me and tucks it into her fanny pack. "Everybody knows that Roberto Clemente died in a plane crash on his way to bring aid to earthquake victims in Nicaragua."

Hazel steps into her shorts and pulls up her zipper.

"Where he had a mistress," she says.

She yanks the sundress over her head and folds it. "C'mon, Jackie, you know how these ball players are."

I start to speak, but Jackie gives me the Hand. "You've said enough, Miss Cleo." Then she jumps to her feet and grabs the shoe box.

"Jackie, stop. Sit. Eat," Hazel orders her. "You know how you get when you don't eat."

"I'll meet you back at the shop." And she storms off like she always does when her feelings come too close to the surface.

Lourdes jumps up and shoves one last cookie into her mouth. As she rolls the top of the Oreo package, she says, "It'd help if you would stop it with all that psychic stuff."

I'm not psychic nor did I ever say I was, I want to scream.

Hazel puts her arm around my shoulder. "Jackie's just cranky 'cause we're really behind schedule," she says. "The faster we get back on the road, the farther we get away from New York, the calmer she'll be." I know Hazel's speaking for herself, but since I've said enough, I stay quiet.

JACKIE

Interstate 80
Hazleton, PA
Friday, June 16, 1:16 P.M.

The Brewers are spanking the Yanks 10 to 2, but truth is, I lost interest in this game since we entered Pennsylvania. People think I'm loud and opinionated, but that doesn't mean I never want to be quiet. Between Irena's psychic *mierda,* Hazel's smart-ass remarks, and Lourdes's *ay, no puedos,* I've had my fill of girl talk for a while. I mean, no one's talking right now, because of what happened at the flea market, and that's fine with me.

I didn't even want to go to that flea market, but it beat staying at the shop with those silly white boys. They wanted to tag along, and Lourdes was fixing to invite them, too, but Irena would've freaked had I not nixed that shit. I only went to the damned flea market to keep them in check. No way in hell can I let those three go off on a shopping spree, wasting more of their money and our time. For that we might as well have picked up the car and gone home.

The farther south we drive, the weaker the radio signal gets. Eventually, the static starts to work my nerves so I shut off the radio altogether. But I don't put on any music, because I need some more quiet. For once I have some damned luck, because Hazel's staring out the window at the roadside shrubbery, Lourdes is sleeping, and Irena's scribbling away in her journal.

Freakin' Wil. He says, "I know Sheila's using Eric to get back with me, and that's precisely why you should trust me." But she has no respect for our relationship—or her son, for that matter, foisting him on a man who's not his father for her own selfish ends! I do like Eric, and I don't want to begrudge the kid a father figure, but am I just supposed to sit by while Ms. Fabulaxer plays her games?

And yet I hate being this way. I don't like feeling like this. Least of all now when there isn't a damned thing I could do even if I had any clue what that is. But Wil didn't answer the phone even though I had just left his place. When he finally answered, and I asked him where he was, he told me that I had no business monitoring his comings and goings after leaving him the way I did. "If that's why you're calling, don't bother," Wil said. Then he hung up on me! And I still tried to call him a few times while roaming through the flea market, right until I came across the woman selling the baseball cards. So it's not like I didn't try to make things right before I went too far.

But I can't go back now. The one thing that scares me more than losing Wil is going to desperate extremes to keep him. If Wil wants to use our fight as an excuse to fall into bed with Vanessa Williams, Jr., and be her baby's daddy, there's nothing I can do about it from I-80. And if he'd do something like that because I refuse to be a *cabrona* in the making, I'm better off without him.

We need some gal music—now. I pop in some good ol' Mary J. *Don't need no hateration holleratin' / in this dance for me.*

Of course, Hazel jumps right in and blows Mary out the water. Then Irena and Lourdes are into it, and fuck it, I join in, too, even though I can't sing for shit.

What is one stereotype about your community that sometimes you secretly wish were true? You can define community any way you want, but feel free to surprise us by not choosing the obvious. For example, with all the damned gentrification happening in New York, I like the fact that everyone still believes that the Bronx is a hellhole full of criminals, junkies, and welfare cheats. It keeps our rent down.—JA

Hmmm . . . keeps "our" rent down? Jackie, you didn't move in with Wil and not tell us, did you? ☺ The one stereotype about Cubans that I wish was true is that we have the U.S. government in our pocket. If this Cuban ever had that kind of influence, the rest of my kin would have me locked up!—IR

I wish queer folks were on a recruitment drive. Each and every one of you would be at the top of my prospect list. When not annoying, straight people can be downright boring! Not that any of you are boring or annoying, but the rest of your kind . . . do I really have to explain this?—CHF

God forgive me, but some days I wish I had an "inner chola" I could unleash on the racists who assume that I'm a waitress or nanny or something.—LB

Every woman has an inner chola, but our histories have forced most Latinas to be in better touch with ours. Mine's named Alize. I bet you think there's nothing "inner" about my chola, but trust me, she would do things I'd never do.

Alize will cut you. Lou, the next time you deal with some moron who assumes you crossed the border for the honor of serving him, remind him that while your ancestors were building empires, his were picking toe cheese with their teeth without bending over!—JA

Jackie, you are too funny!—CHF

I want to believe I have an inner chola, and that I just haven't met her yet. Or maybe she's the one who shows up to all the marches and rallies. This reminds me of Fried Green Tomatoes! TOWANDA!!!—IR

OK, Irena, you couldn't get any whiter than that?—JA

Ignore Jackie, Irena. Not only does she have Fried Green Tomatoes on DVD, she has the *book* and has read it at least THREE times.—CHF

I know. She forgot that she lent it to me. I still have it. —IR

You got me that time! Now give me back my shit!—JA

Por favor, no cursing in the journal!—LB

Interstate 80
West Middlesex, PA
Friday, June 16, 7:22 P.M.

We're almost in Ohio before I finally have Jackie to myself. Not completely to myself obviously, because Irena and Lourdes are in the backseat. But Lou's asleep again. That woman could sleep through a monster truck rally. Irena's trying to catch some Z's, but she can't seem to get comfortable. She's curled up in the corner with her head against the door. Shoes off, eyes closed. I hope Irena conks out soon because Jackie looks like she wants to doze off, too.

I'm wired from the soda I had when we stopped for gas. To make up time and get to Cleveland on schedule, we all agreed to keep going. But if I hadn't jumped into the driver's seat while Jackie paid for the gas, she never would've given up the wheel. She drove right through Irena's turn, and Lourdes was too ready to let Jackie drive through hers, as well. And she wonders why Jackie calls her princess.

For a while there I was afraid that we might get claustrophobic and jump down each other's throats again, especially when Irena broke out *The Little Book of Stupid Questions.* "Which one of the Brady sisters would be most likely to have gotten pregnant as a teen?"

"Jan, obviously," Jackie said.

"What do you mean *Jan, obviously*?" I said. "Marcia's the boy-crazy one."

Irena agreed with me. "Marcia was sooooo male-identified!"

But Jackie's explanation made sense. "Jan had all those middle-child issues. She would've gotten knocked up just to get attention. If they had tabloid talk shows back then, Jan would've been on Maury Povich talking about *I want a baby, Maury, 'cause I need someone to love me unconditionally.* What do you think, Lourdes?"

Lourdes shocked all of us. "I have no idea. I never watched it." We couldn't believe it. She had never watched *The Brady Bunch!* I even sang the entire theme song to her. *Here's the story of a lovely lady . . .* Nothing. She didn't know or care about the words.

"We're talking one of the biggest shows of the seventies," says Jackie.

Lourdes just shrugs. "I didn't come here until '92. *¿Y no me llevan dos años?* You weren't even born until '85, so how did you watch it?"

"No one, I mean, no one grows up in the United States and has never seen *The Brady Bunch.* I didn't even have cable growing up, which I'm sure you did. I watched reruns after school on one of the local channels."

"Me, too," said Irena.

"I heard about the show," said Lourdes, "*pero nunca lo vi.*"

"So how did you learn to speak English so well?"

"Through this nifty little invention called books."

"Give it to her, Jackie," I said. "How else would she come across a word like *nifty?*"

"Bull, Lou! You did not learn to speak English as well as you do by chillin' with Berlitz. Especially if you taught yourself as you claim."

For sure I thought Jackie and Lourdes were headed for a fight, but then Lou said, "Okay, I never missed an episode of *The Cosby Show.*" We all laughed because it explained a hell of a lot more than her proficiency in English.

To keep us on this lighthearted track, I asked, "So which one of the Huxtable sisters do you think would've gotten pregnant and secretly would have had an abortion?"

Jackie and Lourdes yelled, "Denise!" But I said Vanessa. Then we all looked at Irena.

"Rudy."

"Rudy?"

"She was a teenager of the nineties." We all had to agree. In fact, I recently saw her on the cover of *King* in ruffled panties beside the headline *Rudy's Got Milk* or something like that.

But for the past half hour no one has said a word, and the silence is driving me insane. I just want some conversation while I drive. So I reach over to tug at Jackie's hair. She swipes at my hand. "Stay up and keep me company."

"I'm tired." But Jackie turns her head away from the window and toward me, and I appreciate that.

So I start singing this lullaby. I don't even know where I learned it and why it came to me. The words just float from me.

Duerme, duerme, negrita
Que tu mamá está en el campo, negrita.

"My mother used to sing me to sleep with that song," Jackie says. "Even on the night she bounced."

When we were kids, Jackie always climbed up the fire escape and tapped at my window when she wanted to see me. No matter what hour or weather, she never used the front door. So when I answered the front door that night to find Jackie standing there, I immediately knew something was wrong. She rushed inside my grandmother's apartment.

"Mami's missing, and Papi won't call the police," she yelled. "She's out there somewhere in trouble, but he won't do anything." I knew exactly how Jackie felt. How many times my father didn't come home for days at a time, and my mother did nothing except wait?

We went into my room and planned to cut school the next day and search for Jackie's mom. So many times we overheard her mother on the telephone complain about her overseer of a boss, recounting proudly how she sassed him about this or called him out on that. Jackie was convinced that he had something to do with her mother's disappearance, and it didn't take long for her to convince me, too. So we planned to put on our uniforms, grab our schoolbags, and meet in front of the building the next day as we did every school day. Instead of taking the bus to school, however, we would jump on the downtown subway and head to the Lower East Side. We would interview the other seamstresses and maybe even confront their boss if necessary.

While still a bit anxious, Jackie seemed much better than when she had appeared in my grandmother's doorway, and I felt I had done something for my best friend. My one true friend. Not like the girls at Holy Cross or Scanlan High School who only wanted to be my friend because I drew boys. Not like the kids back in Queens who pretended not to know what was obvious to the entire neighborhood—my father was a dope fiend, and my mother didn't have the guts to leave him. The least they could have done was to acknowledge my situation and offer me some compassion. They didn't have to ignore me. My mother was doing a fine job of that without their help. And when I moved to the Bronx, Jackie was the only one who bothered to ask me what brought me to live with my grandmother. I told her that my father was too sick for my mother to take care of us both, which to this day still strikes me as true even if only euphemistically speaking.

A few minutes after Jackie left, my grandmother came into my room. She sat on my bed and asked me to join her. Then in her ever gentle voice, she told me that she overheard our scheme and prohibited me from cutting school the next day. I could never lie to my grandmother, so I said, "But I have to help Jackie find her mother."

"*Carmencita, nada malo le pasó a la mamá de Jackie,*" she said. "*Ella no quería quedarse casada.*"

I couldn't understand it. What did she mean that Amaia no longer wanted to be married? Especially to a nice-looking and hardworking man like Raul, Sr. To this day my mother pines for my father—a recovering heroin addict serving fifteen years to life who could've infected her with HIV—even when Papi told Ruby that she should move on with her life and divorce him! And even if Amaia did have problems with Raul, what kind of mother just leaves her two children? Then again, not too long after my father went to prison, Ruby shipped me off to the Bronx to live with my grandmother, which is when I met Jackie. Now that I'm an adult, I realize that her selfish move was probably the best motherly impulse she ever had toward me. But how could Jackie's mom, Amaia, walk away so easily from being a mother just because she no longer wanted to be a wife? But I understood why Jackie had to believe that her mom left against her will.

So in midverse I stop singing the lullaby and that unnerving silence returns. Then Jackie says, "She was sitting on my bed singing, and I pretended that I wanted her to stop, like I was all embarrassed. You know, I was fourteen, too grown for that shit and all that. But the truth is I liked it. I should have known something was up 'cause she hadn't sung that song to me since I was five years old. After all those years, she comes into my room, tucks me in bed, then sings me to sleep. Then she picked up her suitcase and tipped out the door."

Suddenly, Irena asks, "When are we going to do the ritual?" I hear the hesitancy in her voice, and I wonder if she has overheard our conversation. At first, I find it an odd time for Irena to ask about that. Then again, it seems like her timing is perfect.

I look at Jackie, who rolls her eyes. She has no use for Irena's New Age practices, but I hope she bites her tongue. Of course, Lourdes hates it, too. Which commandment does it break? Thou shalt not take on a false idol, I think.

Now Jackie sits up and looks into the rearview mirror at Irena's reflection, and she has this timid expression on her face, bracing for Jackie's no. Instead Jackie says, "How 'bout Illinois?" Then her voice lifts. "At the point where the time zone changes. I mean, I don't know if that has any special meaning or whatever—you tell me."

Irena's face lights up. "That's an awesome idea!"

"Won't be until tomorrow night though."

"No, that's okay." She's really into it, which is a relief because if Irena had her way, we would never have left New York without first doing the ritual. "That would be perfect if we could do it."

Jackie smiles at the mirror and then curls back into her seat. The silence comes back, but it no longer bothers me. Then Jackie pokes me in the knee. "You gonna keep singing or what?" I reach over to stroke her hair as I drive and sing:

Te va a traer codornices para ti.
Te va a traer muchas cosas para ti.
Te va a traer carne de cerdo para ti.
Te va a traer muchas cosas para ti

Lourdes joins me. It's so cool she knows the song! Sometimes without meaning to we exclude her by making cultural references she doesn't understand. Most times it's not American pop culture that trips us up as much as the assumptions Jackie, Irena, and I make because we're Caribbean.

Y si la negra no se duerme,
Viene el diablo blanco y ¡zas!
Le come la patita
Yacapumba, yacapumba, acapumba . . .

Irena whispers to Lourdes, "What's it mean?"

I keep singing while Lourdes explains. "It's a lullaby. Cuban, I think, but it's sung throughout Latin America. To get her child to sleep, the mother is promising to work hard to give him the world. At the same time, she's hinting at how overworked and underpaid she is."

"So *el diablo blanco*? That means 'white devil,' right? Is that her boss?"

"I think so. She's singing to him, 'Little Black One, go to sleep or the White Devil will come and—zap!—eat your foot."

Irena just stares at Lourdes, and I stop singing again. Irena always insists that she's white but not White which means that the rest of us have no idea how she's going to take a comment like that. Oh, shit!

Then Irena breaks into a grin. "Wow, a pro-labor lullaby. How cool is that! Teach it to me."

And now we're all singing.

We had arrived in Cleveland so late, we made no attempt to have a night on the town. Fine by me. Especially since we still had fun writing, reading, and reacting to the entries in our collective journal before turning in. I'm so heartened that the gals are making an effort to maintain it. With Lourdes's picture and the other souvenirs we collect, it's going to look awesome! If it were up to me, every night we'd break bread at a healthy yet affordable café in our host city then go back to our motel to bond by writing in our journal, sharing our stories, and getting beauty tips from Hazel.

When Hazel sees the WELCOME TO CHICAGO sign, she pulls right off the highway at the next exit ramp and onto the grass.

"C'mon, not here," says Jackie.

"*Ay, no,*" Lourdes agrees.

"We promised Irena we would do this once and for all, and this is as good a place as any," says Hazel. "If we don't do it now, let's face it, it's not going to happen, and that's not fair to Rena. When we're done, we can get right back on the interstate from here, then find our motel."

Hazel, Lourdes, and I climb out of the Tempo and look around at pretty much nothing. This interstate's not at all like we expected. It's plain and flat. The trees may be thick or sparse, but we drive for miles and see nothing but the same road ahead and sky above. Depending on the hour and the city, there aren't many other cars on the road with us. I actually thank the Goddess for that because I rarely drive and nothing unnerves me like having a big truck or speeding SUV in the next lane.

"Oh, all right," Jackie says as she opens her car door and steps out. "She said she wanted to do it somewhere near nature, and I guess this is as much nature we're going to find off the I-80 in Chi Town." Okay, why are folks talking about me as if I'm not standing here? Jackie walks across the grass for a few yards, unknots the sweatshirt wrapped around her waist, lays it on the ground, and sits on it. Ordinarily, I'd be afraid to stop here in the middle of nowhere. It's not exactly a rest stop or even an emergency parking spot. What if the other cars exiting the interstate won't let us back on the road? What if to get back on I-80, we actually have to circle all over the place and we eventually get lost? What if someone sees us here and decides to pull over to bother us? But Jackie doesn't seem to think we're in any danger, and I trust her. I know we're safe because we're all together.

The rest of us join Jackie on the ground. I sit across from her, and Hazel and Lourdes are on either side of me. We form a diamond and lean our respective flashlights on our pocketbooks in front of us. In the center of our diamond, I place the offering box and reach for Lourdes's and Hazel's hands and close my eyes. I take a deep breath as I tune into the highway bustling next to us. The occasional beam from a passing headlight or the honk of a truck comforts me. I feel like civilization is giving us our space yet reminding us that it's not too far away if we need it.

I start the ritual with the statement of purpose I had written and memorized. "In Africa, the words *Gamba Adisa* means 'Warrior: She Who Makes Her Meaning Clear.' It can mean both to make your position known to others or to become self-aware of your own significance in this lifetime. As individuals and as a community, we undertake this physical and spiritual journey both to understand our purpose and to share it with others, expanding the sisterhood we have created, dedicated to healing ourselves, our communities, and our world. We take this moment to evoke the names of our warrior foremothers who have preceded us on this path and have transcended. Let us call their names and invite their spirits into the cipher to guide and protect us as we follow our personal and common paths." I start the evocation by naming the only woman who fought alongside Che Guevara in Bolivia. "Haydee Tamara Bunke Bider aka Tania la Guerrillera." Did I pronounce that right?

"Audre Lorde, June Jordan, and Sylvia Rivera," says Hazel. Of course, she would name Audre, who at one point took on the name Gamba Adisa. I considered starting the evocation with her name, but I left it for Hazel because of the particular importance of Audre's life and work to the lesbian community. But who's Sylvia Rivera? Oh, I think that's the drag queen who sparked the riot at Stonewall. Later I'll ask Hazel to be sure.

"Frida Kahlo," says Lourdes. Of course!

Jackie fires off a string of names without taking a breath. "Gloria Anzaldua, Antonia Pantoja, Harriet Tubman, Fannie Lou Hamer . . ."

"*¡La Malinche!*" Lourdes blurts out. Okay, this is not, like, a competition. And she had to throw in a controversial one, too! I guess I should feel thankful that Jackie's too busy snickering to make Lourdes defend her contribution. I bet anything, though, that Jackie's eyes are open. And then I hear Hazel giggle, and I know she's peeking, too.

I squeeze Hazel's hand, and she knocks it off, so I continue. "Now let each one of us state a personal intention that we take with us into this collective journey and ask our sisters to support."

A long pause occurs. Just as I'm about to model what I meant by intention, Hazel speaks. "To find love." I like her intention. It's at once specific and universal. We all want love yet have different understandings of how it would look in our lives at any given point and time.

Lourdes quickly adds, "To learn something new." Eh. Isn't that a given? Okay, Irena, don't be so judgemental.

The long pause returns as I wait for Jackie to precede me. Just when I think I have to speak to push forward the process, she says, "To release fear."

Excellent! I say, "To experience both as individuals and a group each thing that my sisters have intended." Gee, I hope nobody thinks I was using my role as facilitator to one-up everyone.

Now it's time to proceed to the closing pledge and presentation of our gifts to the group. "We pledge to be each other's personal sanctuary for the remainder of this journey. Now to symbolize this pledge, each of us will make an offering to her sisters."

I open my eyes and look at Lourdes. When I do rituals like this at the center, I usually save the skeptics for last so the other women can model the process for them, but since Lourdes didn't fuss when Hazel pulled over, I say, "Lourdes, why don't you start?"

Everyone opens their eyes, too, and Lourdes seems touched that I asked her to go first. She takes an envelope and drops it in the ritual box I brought. Hazel grabs the envelope, takes out the pictures, and flips through the first few. In the picture, Hazel holds a picket sign that says WOMEN UNITE! TAKE BACK THE NIGHT! I made that sign!

They're all photographs from the Take Back the Night march and rally two years ago. Not only was it the first rally I'd ever been to, it's the reason why the four of us met. I try to smile and acknowledge the significance of the event for all of us and honor it as the blessing it was. But it's hard. Real hard.

Hazel senses my mixed emotions because she jokes, "It's a miracle Lou and I didn't scare you away." She gives Lourdes a slight pinch in the shoulder. "Remember how we started arguing in front of Irena about whether men should be allowed to participate?"

"Really?" says Jackie, who apparently had never heard this.

"Well, I did ask them," I say. Hazel was handing out the flyers in the cafeteria. I recognized her as the girl I always saw with Jackie, so I took a flyer and read it. *Take Back the Night is an annual event that seeks to bring awareness to and the end of violence against women.* Before I finished reading the flyer, I asked Hazel, "Do men participate?"

"No!" Just then Lourdes came up to Hazel and asked her for more flyers because she had run out. While dividing her stack of flyers in two and giving half to Lourdes, Hazel said to me, "The purpose of the march is for women to claim our right to walk the streets at any time without the threat of being harassed or violated. If guys marched with us, it kind of defeats the purpose."

Lourdes interrupted, "The purpose of the march is to put an end to sexual assault, and men are victims of it, too."

"C'mon, Lou. It's not like men are getting raped, harassed, or abused at the same rate as women. We're specifically trying to address *male* sexual violence against *women.*"

"Well, any man *que tiene los cojones* to publicly associate himself with a bunch of angry women who have taken over the streets should be welcomed with open arms."

They just went back and forth as if I wasn't standing there, and I knew I had to participate in this event. I even signed up for the speakout that Jackie was emceeing. I had never met her, but I had seen her on campus, and she had always fascinated me. I wanted to be more like her.

Lourdes says, "Hazel, show Irena the one I took of her during the speakout."

Hazel finds a picture of me standing at the podium. To be honest, it shocks me to see it. The camera didn't pick up the tears on my face or the lump in my throat. It couldn't capture the quivering in my voice as I try to speak, but it all comes back to me. I understand intellectually that I should be proud of myself for trying. That even if I eventually could not get out the words, the fact that I went up to the podium and stood before all those people was enough to break the silence about what happened to me. Although I failed to speak that day, I should still feel like a survivor. But that burning in the pit of my belly as I stare at the picture is the way I feel shame, and that's what I feel now.

Then I notice the other pair of hands in the photo. One rests on my shoulder as the other adjusts the microphone, bringing it towards my lips. The fingers are brown and long, athletic yet feminine. When I couldn't finish my remarks and began to cry, Jackie came up to the podium and told the crowd, "Give her a big hand, because by just coming up here, this brave sister has made a statement." And the crowd applauded and cheered as if I had given the speech of the century.

"My turn!" Hazel reaches into her pocketbook and pulls out a pair of styling shears. The silver shines like new, and I hope she didn't buy them just for the ritual. The point was to share something meaningful to us with the others, and how meaningful can something be if you run out and buy it only days earlier? I thought I made that clear, but I'm not sure, so I say nothing about it. Hazel places the styling shears in the box and says, "Women come to me and say, Make me beautiful. Well, to me, all of you already are beautiful." And then she looks at Jackie. "Just the way you are."

And because Jackie has difficulty accepting compliments, she says, "Aaawww!"

Hazel snatches the shears out of the box. "First chance I get, I'm gunning for those split ends." How that's helpful, I don't know, but sometimes I can't say anything to Hazel about how to deal with Jackie. They've been best friends since junior high, so who understands Jackie better than Hazel? Although I do think Jackie should let Hazel trim her hair. She would know how to bring out Jackie's natural beauty. But ever since Jackie got a peek at Wil's ex-girlfriend when she first dropped off her son for a visit, she has something to prove. Jackie tries so hard to be the antithesis of Sheila, sometimes she overcompensates for the fact that she can never look like her anyway. Ironically, I think that sometimes makes her more like Sheila—the jealous and insecure Sheila that Wil eventually left—than she realizes!

Hazel reaches for a lock of Jackie's hair. "Chop, chop, chop!"

Jackie backs away from her. "*Ni lo pienses.*" Which I know means *Don't even fuckin' think about it.* She says it so often, it's become a mantra. Bad, bad, bad. That's another thing I hope to work with her on this trip. Replace all that negativity with affirmations.

"*No lo voy a pensar,*" says Hazel. "*¡Lo v'acer!*"

"C'mon, you guys. Get serious." To get them back on track, I better model the appropriate behavior. I reach into my jeans pocket for the tiny pin of the Cuban flag. I hold it in my outstretched palm so everyone can see it before I let it drop into the hope chest. "My mother sent me this pin along with the letter where she explained why she stayed in Cuba when my father left for the States. And why she allowed him to take me with him." One day I'll read the letter to them—I'll share all of them—but for some reason, I want to keep them to myself for a while. These letters are the only way I have to connect to my mother, and I guess I want to share only so much of her. Like I want to be sure she's truly mine before I expose her to the others. I don't know where this comes from, but it's how I feel, so I won't question it—I'll just honor it. "That despite all the challenges, she still believed in the revolution. But with the embargo making it difficult for me to get the medication I needed, she wanted to be a good mother, which meant placing my interests before her own. That meant letting Dad take me with him when he left."

I stare at the pin as it lies in the box on top of the photograph of me at the podium at Take Back the Night with Jackie's hand on my shoulder, I feel compelled to reveal something else. "My father noticed that I was wearing the pin as I was leaving. We were already fighting about my going on this trip. Then he saw the pin, and that's how he found out that I had discovered the letters, because I hadn't told him yet."

Everyone sighs. Now they understand what happened yesterday morning. "So what'd you do?" asks Jackie.

"I stood up to him!" My voice echoes slightly in the air. Its strength surprises even me, and I wonder which emotion is the source of this energy. Is it my anger at Dad for refusing to let me think for myself and sabotaging my attempts to have a relationship with my mother? Or is it guilt for leaving on this trip without making some kind of peace with him, no matter how tenuous? I realize that I started on this tangent because for the longest time Jackie has been telling me to stand up to him, and I finally had. I want her to reaffirm that I did the right thing despite the lack of closure. I need Jackie to be proud of me the way she is of Lourdes for changing her major. Maybe even more so. "I told him that not only was I driving to San Francisco with you guys, but that next summer I'm going to Cuba. I'm going to visit my mother and see what it's like there for myself."

"*¿Y qué te dijo?*"

My father had not said anything. He saw the pin on my collar and lunged for it. I tried to jump out of his reach, but he already had gotten a hold of it. I know in my heart that he only wanted to take the pin away from me because it hurt him so much to see it. The pin symbolized so many more things to him than it does to me, all of them painful. Still he should not have grabbed me. He may be my father, and I may have defied him, but he had no right to take anything from me, least of all anything on my body. The fact that Dad still doesn't know what happened to me during my first semester at Fordham is no excuse. But he's a good man. He has never beaten me. I counsel women to name the violence in their lives no matter how trivial it may seem, but even from my friends I want to protect my father.

All I say is, "Your turn, Jackie," and hope that they give me the space I'm requesting even if I'm not asking for it explicitly.

Thank the Goddess, Jackie reaches into her fanny pack and pulls out a piece of folded paper. "Okay, y'all have to bear with me 'cause you know this is not my thing." She unfolds the paper, revealing a photocopy of a page in a book with a chunk highlighted in fluorescent yellow. "This is an excerpt from *Women Who Run with the Wolves.*" I just gave her that book! Not only did she actually read it, she liked it. I sit there and grin so hard, my face hurts.

And Jackie smiles back at me. "I mean, if you had to give me New Age gaga for a graduation present, at least you represented." She paused to squint at me. "Clarissa Pinkola Estes is a Latina, right?"

I just can't be mad at her. "Yes."

"Cool. Anyway, I thought the stories were dope. In fact, I even went to the bookstore looking for other books by her. Wil was with me . . ." I wonder if anyone else catches the hint of sadness on her face when she mentions his name. It strikes hard but immediately fades like a gunshot into the air.

"Anyway, I memorized this." To me that's the biggest gift of all. For Jackie to take the time to do that? Of course, she did it to please me. She places the paper in the box, closes her eyes, and recites the lines.

> Healthy wolves and healthy women share certain psychic characteristics. Keen sensing. Playful spirit. A heightened capacity for devotion. Wolves and women are relational

> by nature, inquiring, possessed of great endurance and strength. They are deeply intuitive, intensely concerned with their young, their mate and their pack.

This is the perfect way to close the ritual. I close my own eyes and reach for Hazel's and Lourdes's hands. I mouth the words along with Jackie's voice because, I, too, have committed this particular passage to memory.

> They are experienced at adapting to constantly changing circumstances. They are fiercely stalwart. And very brave.

And I swear to the Goddess, at that precise moment somewhere out there, a wolf howls. Lourdes insists it's the wind, and Jackie agrees, reminding us that we're in Chicago, where the wind is so fierce they call it the Hawk. But I know what I know, and sometimes knowing has to be enough to let it go.

What phrase do you wish people would say more often? Call me corny, but my vote goes to, "I love you." If everyone had to say that at least once every day—and mean it—I think it could really change the world.—CHF

That's a beautiful sentiment, but I think before many people can get to "I love you," they have to become comfortable saying, "I'm sorry."—IR

Irena, that is certainly true in the U.S., but I wouldn't necessarily assume that is the case around the world. Se que me van a molestar, but even before we can get to "I love you," we have to learn to say "Thank you." Maybe if we said, "Thank you" more often, we'd have to say "I'm sorry" less often.—LB

It's all good. But I'm not going to front. The single phrase that I don't think people say ANYWHERE near enough that would have MAJOR ramifications for the U.S. and indeed THE WORLD is more simple and practical than any of those, and that's, JACKIE, YOU ARE ABSOLUTELY RIGHT!

JACKIE, YOU ARE ABSOLUTELY RIGHT!—CHF

JACKIE, YOU ARE ABSOLUTELY RIGHT! LOL!—IR

¡Tu absolutamente tienes razón, loca!—LB

LOURDES

Interstate 80
Chicago, IL
Saturday, June 17, 8:24 P.M.

We spend some time just chatting, looking through the other photos I have so far, writing in our travel journals, and teasing one another about what we've written. We talk about the places we have been before this trip, and it shocks everyone that I have not been all over the world, let alone the United States. They think I'm so rich when at best my family is upper middle class, thanks to my father's financial savvy and generous estate. Coming into a modest fortune at the age of fifteen because your father works himself to death and then your mother picks up where he left off is hardly the way to become rich. I keep this to myself because we are getting along wonderfully, and I don't want to bring down the mood. But every once in a while I have to challenge this prevailing notion that I'm the Mexican Carolina Bacardi!

"With the exception of Paris, London, and Mexico, of course, I really haven't been anywhere," I say.

Jackie nudges Irena. "You hear her?" *Y se burla de mí.* "With the exception of Paris, London, Mexico, Venus, Oz, and Neverland, why, I've never left Tara."

"Leave her alone, Jackie," says Hazel.

"I'm just saying . . ." Jackie turns back to me. "Lou, you shouldn't be embarrassed that you've had opportunities to travel. What other places in the U.S. have you seen? I've never been out of the tristate area until now."

"Me, too," says Hazel.

"Ditto," adds Irena.

I count off the cities on my fingers. "Besides New York and Denver, I've been to Orlando—"

"Disney World!" the other three yell in unison.

"—and Los Angeles to visit some cousins I have there. That's really it." And this is the reason why I am so eager for a new urban experience. I've read about the exquisite architecture of downtown Chicago and want to see just how men have built a metropolis over a river. I only hope that I have enough light to take some amazing photographs.

And being in Chicago without my mother's knowledge reminds me of how I even came to explore Denver. When my father died right after I started high school, I grieved through quiet rebellion while my brother Oscar acted out by neglecting his schoolwork and abandoning his extracurricular activities. When my mother took over my father's company, she hired Valería, whose priority quickly became to rein in my brother and maintain the house. So even though I had always been forbidden to go into Denver by myself, I began to tell Valería that I wanted to go to the mall. Of course, she thought I meant the Aurora Mall and would drive me to the Foley's. The second I saw her silver Honda Civic turn the corner, I jumped on the first bus to the Sixteenth Street Mall in LoDo. Those clandestine trips gave me my first hunger for big cities, and by the time Valería caught me, I had already outgrown Denver and had set my sights on New York City.

Although I have so much left of New York City to explore, after two years of being mostly confined to Manhattan's West Side, I am ready to give Chicago the chance to excite me. I nonchalantly look at my watch and ask, "*¿Y cuándo nos vamos?*"

Finally, we pick ourselves off the ground and head back to the car.

"I'll race you!" Jackie says. *¡Ay, no!* But off Jackie and Irena go while Hazel and I take our sweet time.

When Hazel and I reach the car, Jackie's drinking bottled water while Irena's trying to catch her breath. *Empiezo a apurarme.* It always bothers me when Irena exerts herself in any way.

"For someone who's so health conscious, why're you so winded? Don't you work out?" asks Jackie. "My brother's asthmatic, too, and he's in that gym every other morning." Her words sound critical, but I hear the concern in her voice.

"So am I," Irena says. "I mean, I don't go to the gym, but I practice yoga three times a week at the center."

"Uh-uh, girlfriend. That's not gonna cut it." *Pues* maybe *that's* a bit judgmental even if Jackie means well. "You also have to do some kind of aerobics at least three times per week. When we get back, I'm taking to you to my kickboxing class."

"Only if you promise not to kill me." I elbow Hazel, and we smile at each other. We all know Jackie would never spar with Irena, so as *not* to kill her. *Un puñazo a la cara, y adios, Irena.* No matter how much Jackie teases her, she has a soft spot for Irena. Oddly, that's the precise reason she teases her so much.

Pero esa pobre negra has a knack for putting her foot in her mouth. She says to Irena, "Don't worry about me, but you'll be glad to know how to kickbox if some day you're walking down the street and some jerk gets out of line." Irena gives a slight cough, and if it weren't for that, I wonder if Jackie would have even noticed her faux pas. But in addition to that knack for putting her foot in her mouth, *gracias a Dios* that Jackie also has a gift for making people laugh. She grabs Irena in a headlock and yells, "*¡Lucha libre!*" Irena bursts into giggles, and Hazel and I both sigh with relief.

"When are we going to stop and do something fun?" Hazel asks. When we reached Cleveland last night, we barely had the energy to climb the steps to our motel room. Except for a quick stop at the drugstore, we went straight to our room, ordered takeout, and called it an early night. "Let's go dancing!"

"Can't," Jackie says."

"*¿Y por qué no?* I bet we can find a great club here." Maybe I can make some new friends in Chicago. Even though the Mexican population in the Big Apple is growing, I spend so much time in Manhattan, I rarely see them. That is, if you don't include the busboys at any given Midtown restaurant or the custodial workers at

Fordham. Of course, there's Lucía and Rocio from my Catholics for Choice group, but they're *women.*

"We may be back on schedule, but we're still over budget," says Jackie. "And unlike you, I didn't pack Copacabana wear." Patience is a virtue, and one must be unusually virtuous to be friends with Jackie. But she can be reasoned with—it's one of the qualities I like most about her. It's one way that Jackie and I are alike and different from Hazel and Irena. So I try to think of something assertive yet nonconfrontational to say.

"I don't care where we go so long as we do something fun," I say. "I read that the bars here are open until four in the morning. Drinks on me!"

Hazel points at Jackie as she's on her way to the driver's side and says, "I'm telling you right now, I'm not spending this entire trip jumping between cheap motels and that tin can Raul fooled you into thinking was a car." She smashes her half-smoked cigarette under her sandal, throws open the car door, and dips inside.

Jackie turns to look at me as if to ask *¿Y qué pasa con ella?* When we get into the car, she says, "We're not going to spend every night in a motel. We're going to crash at Lou's house, and she's going to show us Denver."

¡Ay, Dios mio, ayúdame! I never said anything like that. Before I can respond, Hazel says, "I'm not stopping or staying anywhere in f---kin' Colorado. In your lovely state, gays and lesbians cannot file discrimination cases. I refuse to spend a single cent there."

Jackie laughs, "You won't have to. Lou's gonna hook us up with food, lodging, and even a round of drinks. Right, Lou?"

"Remember I'm from Aurora, not Denver."

"Are they far apart?"

"Far enough," I lie. "You know I would want nothing more than to bring you to my house, introduce you to my family, have Valería make you a home-cooked meal . . . But going to Aurora is really going to take us out of our way. And if Hazel's uncomfortable about Colorado . . ."

Did Hazel just suck her teeth? I'm the one trying to get her on a Chicago dance floor and keep her out of Colorado. Why all of a sudden is she upset with me? "*¿Y qué te pasa?*"

"*¡Nada!*" she practically spits into the rearview mirror.

I say nothing because I deserve the attitude even though Hazel doesn't know what I'm up to. But the Devil sure knows. He just ran me a bath in a cauldron of scalding water.

HAZEL

Super 8 Motel

Joliet, IL

Saturday, June 17, 8:51 P.M.

When I realize that Jackie reserved a room for us in a motel off the highway in Joliet instead of in Chicago, I become more pissed. I know she was thinking about money—it's probably a bit cheaper to stay here than close to the downtown nightlife—but that doesn't matter to me. When we were planning this trip, Jackie was as excited about staying in Chicago as everyone else was. At one of our planning meetings at the Olympic Flame, I laid out the options I researched, offering something for everyone. Lourdes said she wanted to take photos of the sculptures in Grant Park and do some shopping on Michigan Avenue. Irena mentioned going to the zoo in Lincoln Park, and I didn't have the heart to tell her that it'd probably be closed by the time we got to Chicago. Jackie joked about going to a Cubs game at Wrigley Field wearing a Mets jersey.

I didn't care what we did so long as at one point we visited the Japanese Garden at the Botanical Gardens. I had read it was one of the most romantic places in Chicago. Of course, I didn't tell anyone that. Since I would be the driver on duty when we arrived, I was just going to find a way to get Jackie there and tell her how I felt when the moment was right.

Now she doesn't want to go anywhere. Why? Probably out of some twisted loyalty to Wil. As if having a man prohibits her from going dancing with her girlfriends. Jackie's becoming the kind of woman she swore she would never be when she got involved with a man. And over a man she doesn't trust to be faithful to her—and with good reason.

I pull into the motel parking lot, and we all climb out with our respective things without saying a word. Okay, so the place seems nice for only sixty bucks per night. It's a two-story Tudor in a quiet neighborhood right off the highway. Lourdes makes a point to beat us to the registration desk and plop down her credit card on the counter. After we check in and find our room, Jackie finally says, "Look, if you guys want to go out, go ahead. Take the car. I don't care, but I'm staying here."

"Me, too," says Irena.

Holding the guest manual open in her hands, Lourdes gives me a hopeful look. "*¿Y qué quieres hacer?* It says here we're only thirty-five miles from downtown Chicago, ten minutes away from the riverboat casinos and the Rialto Theater, fourteen minutes away from . . ."

"Let's check out Cabrini Green," I say. Jackie gives me a nasty look. I turn away from her to unpack my nightshirt.

But Lourdes lights up. "Is that Chicago's version of Tavern on the Green?"

"Cabrini Green's the toughest housing project in the freakin' country, Lou," says Jackie, as much annoyed with Lourdes's gullibility as she is with my sarcasm. I head toward the bathroom with my toiletries and pj's, and she blocks my path. "Don't fuck with her because you're pissed at me."

I step around Jackie, walk into the bathroom, and slam the door behind me. Still I overhear Lourdes say, "I'll go! If Hazel really wants to see what it's like, *me voy con ella.*" I can hear her voice quaver with false bravado. "You think it'll be okay to bring my camera?"

"No!" Irena yells.

"Lourdes, drop it. No one's going anywhere tonight." Then Jackie raises her voice more than loud enough for me to hear through the bathroom door. "Hazel's just being a drama queen."

I turn on the water to drown out all of them. When I finish in the bathroom, Jackie takes her turn. Now she wears an extra large T-shirt that says *Not Perfect . . . But So Close It Scares Me.* The quote is pure Jackie but clearly not the size. She must have bought it for Wil just to steal it from him. She avoids looking me in the eye and slams the bathroom door behind her.

Irena has already changed into capri-length pajama bottoms and a tank top with a glittery unicorn that reads *Capricorn.* She sits cross-legged on the double bed she'll share with Lourdes, skimming through our travel journal. Holding out until the last possible minute, however, Lourdes remains dressed from head to toe. But she takes one look at my nightshirt and finally resigns herself to a night in. "Is it okay if I go into the bathroom next?" she asks Irena.

"Sure." Then Irena crawls across the bed toward me with the journal. "We're not keeping this up as we should. Now's a good time to write something."

She tries to hand it to me, but I resist. "C'mon, Irena . . ."

"Please. Anything. Answer one of the questions or even write about how you're feeling now." The look on Irena's face tells me that she would actually prefer that I purge my funky mood and the reason behind it onto the page. But that's the last thing I should do even if I want to.

Still I take the journal from her, then let myself on the balcony for a smoke. I sit out there and read what we've already written. Some of the entries make me laugh aloud, making me feel even sadder at the same time. I turn to a fresh page and scrawl a new question across the top. This is the farthest I go in revealing what's going on with me at this time.

I don't know how long I stay out there, but when I go back into the room, the lights are out and everyone is in bed. I place the journal on the chair by the door and slip into bed next to Jackie. She's still awake. After all the nights we've shared a bed, throughout the years I don't have to see her face to know whether she's asleep or awake. I can feel her eyes staring into my back. Does she ever look at my silhouette at night the way I have hers? Did Jackie ever have dreams about us kissing, like the ones I have? If I were to reach over and graze my fingers across the small of her back, would she draw away or melt into me?

Even though I have not said any one of these things to Jackie, I find myself asking her, "So?"

Jackie exhales. She always exhales before giving in to me. I start to smile before she even says it. "So where do you want to go tomorrow night?" I turn around and grin at her. "Besides that?"

I suck my teeth at her and whirl around. Jackie pokes me in the back, and I bounce as far on my side of the bed as I can go.

"Hazel!" She jabs me again. "We can do that at home."

"But we never do."

"But we could."

"If it were up to me, we'd go every night."

"I know!" As if that were such a terrible thing. I can't remember the last time we went dancing. It has to be before she met Wil. He's the first to admit that he can't dance, but even when I was dating Kharim, Wil refused to double with us when we went to the Copa. Not that K was the Bronx's answer to Usher, but at least he was willing to try. We couldn't even get Wil to do the Electric Slide at the graduation party that Lourdes threw for us. Hell, even she got the hang of it!

It boggles my mind because Jackie likes to dance, and for such a butchy gal, she's the ultimate femme on the dance floor. Both her parents could dance their asses off, and they certainly passed on their ability to their kids. I dated Jackie's brother Raul for as long as I did because the way that boy swung his hips when we salsaed always made me forget what a lousy fuck he was—in and out of bed. And he still doesn't have a thing on his sister. Dancing is the only physical activity where Jackie's feminine side bursts through with a vengeance . . . as far as I know, and I want to know so much more.

But as much as Jackie likes to dance, she hates going to clubs. She calls them meat markets with soundtracks. The guys swarm me the second we walk through the door. Having never been desperate for a man's attention, I would never sentence my homegirl to a night of pocketbook-watching duty like some *pendejas.* But I go to have fun, so I pull Jackie onto the dance floor, and we salsa together as if no one else is in the room. Then the *sucios* start to mind Jackie as much as they do me, and it bothers me more than when they ignored her. They hound her to dance, and because I haven't got half the energy she does, I watch the pocketbooks while Jackie trips the light fantastic with one guy after the other. They try to chat her up but are lucky if they get a monosyllabic answer to their questions. Jackie really socks it to 'em when they ask for her number. She says no. No apologies. No explanations. Just no. They ask why, and Jackie tells them, "I don't want to see you again." Now some of them become desperate and try to foist their numbers on her, but Jackie's just not one of those girls who plays nice with the male ego. She hands the number right back and says, "Isn't it better this way? You don't want me to take this like I'm interested, just to never call you. Give it to someone who really wants it. Or someone who'll pretend to want it, if that's what you're into. Thanks for the dance."

The first time Jackie did that, I ragged on her, but she insisted that she wasn't doing it to mess with them. "Men complain that either women don't know what we want, or that when we do know, we still want to make 'em guess," she said. "I'm just being honest with these guys. In fact, I'm probably being more honest with them than they are with me. How many of them really intend to call me?"

"Well, why would they ask if they didn't want to see you again?"

"Either they think I'm easy or assume that I expect them to ask for it. Either way it's all sport to them. That's why I hate these fuckin' places."

"And your telling them to keep their numbers instead of graciously accepting them and throwing them away when you get home isn't?"

"Hazel, I'm not doing it on some bitchfit. If I were, I'd have no problem admitting it to you. But I swear, I'm not trying to give them a taste of their own medicine. All I'm doing is being as honest as everyone claims they want everyone else to be."

"Okay, but can you enjoy it a little less?" I said. But secretly I was fascinated. Jackie's zealousness for honesty has always been something I admired.

But now I'm mad at her for refusing to go dancing tonight.

Wil's starting to be a bad influence on her. I inch away from her until I'm a millimeter away from falling out the damned bed and onto the stiff, beige carpet.

"Okay, we'll go dancing when we get back home." If she mentions bringing Wil, God help me . . . "But can't you choose something else to do tomorrow night? Whatever it is, I'll be down. I promise."

If tomorrow you met your soul mate—the person who you knew instantaneously was compatible with you in every way—intellectually, emotionally, spiritually, sexually—but this person was a woman, would you be able to be with her?—CHF

I'm pretty sure I could be. Your soul mate is your soul mate. I believe everyone has one, but not everyone finds her (or him) in this life. If you're one of the lucky ones to find yours, and there's no major barriers to keep you apart (like she isn't married to someone else), you'd be foolish to not be together. As far as I'm concerned, homophobia is not a good enough reason to not be together. I'm not saying it'd be easy for me. My father wouldn't be happy, but I'd like to think he would come around, and he's really the only person in my own life that I'd be concerned about. I know my friends would support me. ☺—IR

Yo no se. I'd like to say yes, but I really don't know. I honestly don't believe my soul mate is a woman. I like men too much, and I didn't choose to be heterosexual. It's just the way I am.—LB

Somebody's defensive. Anyway, I don't believe in soul mates, period. There's no single person who can make you happy. There's more than one person out there you can be perfectly happy with if you're both willing to put in the work. Look at all the people who marry the love of their lives, lose them when they die, yet eventually find someone else who makes them just as happy. But to answer the question, if it turned out that I met some woman who rocked my world, yes, I'd have no problem being with her. Life's too short, and everyone thinks I'm gay anyway. Why not?—JA

I am not defensive! All I meant is that since I happen to be straight, I doubt my soul mate could be a woman. That's all. —LB

I hate to say it, Lourdes, but yes, you are being defensive!—IR

Don't mind them, Lourdes. You answered my question, and your answer is no. And that's perfectly fine because you're being honest. I can respect that.—CHF

I didn't say no. I said I didn't know. There's a difference. It's one of those situations where you really can't say until you're in it. Hazel, on one hand you say sexual orientation is not a choice, but then you ask if we would choose to be with a woman. I didn't choose to be straight so, no, I don't think I would "choose" to be with a woman.—LB

Hey, it's not fair to jump on Hazel for asking the question. I knew. Jackie knew, too. And we're both straight.—IR

Let's settle this. One, Lourdes is gay. Two, she just doesn't know it. Three, if and when her soul mate sashays into her life and sweeps Lourdes off her feet with a swipe of her American Express platinum card, we won't know it either so let's stop arguing about it.—JA

Wait. She has a platinum AMEX? If Hazel had said that in the first place, this whole discussion could have been avoided. I don't think my mother could shun a daughter-in-law with credit that good.—LB

IRENA

The Chop Shop
Des Moines, IA
Sunday, June 18, 7:35 P.M.

I can't believe we're in this stupid bar-lounge-whatever, and I can tell Jackie sure as hell doesn't want to be here either. But at some point last night, she promised Hazel that she could choose what we were going to do tonight, and I'm so upset. No one person should be calling the shots on this trip, but these two got together and cut a deal. This is why I wanted to rent a car instead of taking Lourdes's SUV or Jackie's brother's car. Not that I would think anyone would purposefully try to use the car to control the itinerary, but it happens. And it did. Jackie and Hazel got into an argument last night because Jackie thinks she can drive single-handedly three thousand miles without eating, sleeping, or pissing, while Hazel wants to jump out the car every hour on the hour, talking about, "Where's the party?"

So minutes after we have this amazing bonding experience last night, they're arguing over going dancing in Chicago. And I see both sides. On the one hand, I don't want to freakin' go dancing. I don't even do it at home. On the other hand, you've seen one Super 8 Motel, you've seen them all. I start to mediate between them, but Lourdes tells me to let them work it out.

When I wake up this morning, they're all giggles and smiles so I think everything's cool. Jackie checks our itinerary and says, "Next stop, Des Moines." We reach Iowa, and it's nothing like I had imagined. I expected it to be miles upon miles of brown farmland, but there we were rolling up and down these green hills.

We stop to eat at a sidewalk café in Iowa City, which is the first college town I have ever seen outside of a movie. The four of us stand out a little bit, but I won't assume it's a race thing. When the first person nodded at me and said, "Hi," I thought maybe she confused me with someone she knew. The third time it happens, I realize, hey, these folks are genuinely friendly. I mean, it works my nerves when people, especially other Latinos, learn that I'm Cuban and assume I'm some rich *gusano* who spends all my free time plotting Castro's assassination, so where do I come off making assumptions about these people? Iowa may not be the most diverse state in the union, but that doesn't automatically render the folks here bigoted hillbillies. And Hazel always draws attention just because she's so beautiful. Sure, Jackie's dark-skinned, but I can't put the occasional stare on that as much as the fact that she's five nine and tied her hair this morning in a ponytail so her hair's sprouting up from her crown like a black velvet satellite dish. Now Lourdes is pretty in her own right and has an indigenous look that lets her blend in in certain neighborhoods in New York City, but what sets her apart anywhere are her stylish clothes and chic accessories. I mean, I have on a pair of jeans, ten-dollar *chancletas,* and a Fordham university T-shirt; Hazel wears a black skort with a matching sleeveless vest and mules; and Jackie throws on beige cargo pants, white basketball sneakers, and a man's undershirt. (I refuse to call it that awful name. Who comes up with this shit, and why do people repeat it without a second thought?)

But Lourdes dons this blinding white, strapless sundress and leather slides. With heels, no less! Of course, she also has a matching handbag and her Givenchy sunglasses. Folks are pointing at her, wondering if she's Eva Longoria or something. No wonder she's so excited when Jackie and Hazel finally break the news that we're going out tonight. She's already dressed for it!

We could at least do a little research, get some suggestions from our server at the café, and come to a group decision. But Hazel's on some spontaneity kick, and we walk into a random spot. So here we sit in this lounge-bar-tavern with loud rock music that Twyla Tharp couldn't dance to, and the menu has not a single thing that I can eat.

"Sausage, ham, pork . . ." I read to Jackie while Hazel and Lourdes primp in the ladies' room. "Where are the vegetables? I thought this was a big potato state."

Jackie laughs. "That's Idaho, Rena."

"Oh."

"I'm going try these boneless pork chops that are supposed to be the rage here."

"Yuck."

"Okay, Irena, so far you've been really good about not being one of those righteous vegetarians. Don't start now. Have some corn on the cob."

"I guess." But I'm not feeling all that hungry anymore. I search the crowd for Hazel and Lourdes. No wonder they haven't come back yet from the ladies' room. They're at the bar flirting with two guys. "How can they do that?"

"Word, at least bring us our drinks first."

But that's not what I meant, and Jackie knows it. "Who flirts with strange men anywhere, let alone at a bar in a town you've never been before?"

"It happens. All the time. Without drama." Jackie takes a deep breath. "You know, Rena, I think it's time you started dating again."

She can't be serious. "Here?"

"You act like I just told you to go the bar and pick up a stranger."

"Well . . ."

"Look, I'm not talking about anything romantic, let alone sexual. All I'm saying is make new friends. Male friends. You don't have to go out alone with them either. Go out in groups. Hey, maybe one day you can go out with me, Wil, and Kharim. C'mon, don't you think K's a nice guy?"

First of all, I don't have any male friends. Maybe I haven't had a lot of experiences with men, but I have enough to know that the term *male friend* is an oxymoron. A figment of the neo-feminist imagination. A mythical creature from the land that breeds gargoyles, dragons, and trolls. In the best scenario, a male friend is someone who suppresses his sexual interest in a woman because she has set her boundaries and made it clear that she intends to enforce them.

"For your information, your Mr. Nice Guy was flirting with Lourdes at your graduation."

Jackie shakes her head. "No. I think I know Kharim, and I definitely know Lourdes. *She* was flirting with him, but he likes you."

"He doesn't even know me!"

"You kidding me? K sees you all the time at the women's center. If anything, he knows the best things about you."

My face begins to burn. "You didn't tell him, did you?"

"No! Irena, I would never put your personal business out there, and I'd kick anyone's ass who did. But Kharim knows what you do at the center, so you have to accept that he at least suspects. And you know what, Irena? He still wants to know you better." I just pick at my cuticles until Jackie sighs and asks, "Rena, where do you see yourself in, say, ten years?"

Thank the Goddess! She sensed my discomfort and changed the subject. This I can talk about as I think about it so much. I look up and say, "At minimum, I want to get an MSW. But I'm thinking I'd like to get a doctorate if I can find a program that will let me study both western and eastern traditions . . ."

"I'm sure that exists somewhere," says Jackie. "And eventually do you want to have your own practice?"

"Yeah, but that would be just a means to an end, you know. 'Cause my real dream is to start my own center. See, I'd start by creating my own practice where I would work with people like . . ." I'm thinking people like Lourdes. Not because she has issues or anything like that. I mean, she does. We all do. What I mean is that Lourdes has money and can afford to pay for the range of services I want to provide. But I don't mention Lourdes because I don't want Jackie to misunderstand.

". . . You'd work with rich folks like Lourdes," Jackie says. We both laugh. "I'm not kidding though. I mean, Lourdes isn't crazy. She's got her shit like anybody else except the difference is she has enough money to deny it or deal with it." We laugh again, and it feels so good that Jackie understands me perfectly without my explaining a thing. Then she says. "So you'd use the money you'd make off the rich folks to start your center."

"Exactly! Why shouldn't poor women have access to things like yoga and Reiki? They probably need it most of all."

"True."

"And they could really own these techniques they would learn at my center. Not my center! It'd be their center. They'd come and learn the techniques for themselves. Not only could they do them at home whenever they needed it—"

"—They could teach other women. Their family, their friends—"

"—neighbors, co-workers, whoever they want!"

"I think that's dope. And anything I can do to support you, name it. Maybe I can help you incorporate and get your tax exempt status."

"I'd love that!" Then Jackie gets serious on me. "What's wrong?"

"But what about personally, Irena? Ten years from now do you see yourself married?" I fold my arms across my chest, and Jackie leans against the booth. "Okay, maybe not married, but do you see yourself in a relationship?"

I can't believe she's saying this to me. *Jackie* is saying *this* to *me.* I feel . . . betrayed. On top of that, I know in my head that I shouldn't feel that way yet I still do. "I don't need a man to make me feel complete."

"Absolutely not!" She sounds offended, and I wish I can take back what I said. "But there's nothing wrong with *wanting* to have someone special in your life, you know."

"Nothing wrong with not wanting it either."

"Really?"

"Yes."

"There's never anything wrong with not wanting that ever?"

"It's not like I'm alone in the world. I have my family. Friends. Clients."

"You honestly believe that?"

"I'm someone special enough."

Jackie folds her hands and props them under her chin. "Can't argue with that." She sighs and leans against the back of her seat. "You really want to get outta here, don't you?"

"Yeah, I do. I'd hate to be . . ."

"I'm with you on this one, Snow White. I stick out in this joint like a raisin in a bowl of farina." Jackie gets up, finishes her glass of water, and grabs her fanny pack from behind the chair. I watch as she heads to the bar. Hazel and Lourdes are not going to like this, but for once I can live with being a little selfish.

HAZEL
Iowa State Fairgrounds
Des Moines, IA
Sunday, June 18, 8:06 P.M.

When Jackie approaches Lourdes and me at the bar and insists that we leave, I don't question. After our last fight and her concession, I assume that she has a good reason. One look at Irena's face, and I know. If she's not comfortable, I have no problem leaving the Chop Shop and finding somewhere else to go. Lourdes is another story, but she has no choice.

But our recreation tonight is still my choice, so when I notice the carnival sign, I say, "There." I had forgotten all about it even though I had mentioned it.

"There what?" asks Jackie.

"The carnival. That's what I want to do tonight." I give Jackie a look that makes it clear I won't take no for an answer. I glance in the rearview mirror into the backseat. Lourdes is cool with it, and Irena's just ecstatic.

But Jackie says, "You're yanking my chain, right?"

"I'd never do that to you, bitch," I say, and then I laugh.

Jackie crosses her eyes at me but then shifts into the right lane. She pulls off the interstate and drives toward the carnival. As we pull into the parking lot and step out of the Tempo, I catch the smell of pretzels and popcorn. The lights from the rides and games brighten the purpling horizon. A group of teenagers runs by us, shrieking with laughter, and in the distance I hear the Corrs's "Breathless." *The daylight's fading slowly, but time with you is standing still* . . . Irena jumps up and down and points at the sky. "Look, guys!" We all gaze upward in time to catch a burst of red, white, and blue fireworks explode into the sky and then fall down toward the rainbow of plastic tents. I glance at Jackie, thinking that the spontaneous detour to this carnival may be more romantic than any Japanese garden. But my heart sinks because she doesn't look game for either romance or adventure, and I know who this scene has brought to Jackie's mind.

At least Lou's over leaving the bar because she giggles something at Irena, then hooks her arm through hers. As they walk toward the ticket booth, I put my own arm through Jackie's as we follow. Irena looks over her shoulder and says, "I hope they have one of those giant roulette wheels where the pressure from spinning keeps you pinned to the cage thingy."

"It's the same force that pushes you against the door when Jackie rips around a corner," Lourdes says. "Or more accurately, the door hits you."

"Leave me out of your science lesson, Lou."

Lourdes just shoos at Jackie and continues. "The gravitational force that holds you in place during a typical ride is usually four times the force of gravity. If it were ten times, you'd pass out."

"How much to kill you?"

"Jackie!"

Lourdes takes it in stride. "Fourteen, I think."

"This is why high schools should have more field trips," I say. "I might have done better in physics if we had gone to Great Adventure. I needed something to make the material more interesting and fun."

"You needed for Kerry Devers to be transferred to another class, that's what you needed."

I tug at her arm. "Jackie, why are you always putting me on blast?" But I'm glad she's getting into the conversation, especially since we're on this topic. We join the end of the ticket line.

"Kerry?" Irena asks. "Guy or gal?"

"Gal."

"If our physics teacher had taken us to Great Adventure,"

Jackie says, "Hazel would have tried to finger Kerry on the water slide." Irena laughs, and Lourdes cringes.

"Actually, I would've done her like Rosario Dawson did that basketball player in *He Got Game* on the ferris wheel, but let's not quibble."

The line moves forward, and Lourdes uses this as an excuse to turn her back on the conversation. Okay, Jackie and I can be a bit crude sometimes, but there's a tad bit of homophobia going on here. But Lourdes is only human, and she's usually pretty cool. I mean, she wouldn't be our friend let alone travel across the country with us if she weren't. But every once in a while her traditional Catholic thing kicks in and along with it comes the slightest hope that my occasional penchant for boys becomes a lasting preference. We sure do have a hell of a time with them at the clubs.

Jackie taps Lourdes on the shoulder and asks, "Lou, you mind if I borrow your telephone?" That can only mean one thing, and I hope my resentment isn't obvious.

Lourdes reaches into her purse and hands Jackie her telephone. Jackie gives me her cash and says, "Get my tickets, and I'll catch up to you in a few minutes."

I start to pursue her when Irena steps in front of me. "I know you guys are super close, but maybe you should give her a little privacy. You know she can't loosen up until she smooths things over with Wil." All I can do is nod and fidget as we watch Jackie walk toward the concession stands as she dials the number. Although she's out of earshot, Irena coaches her. "C'mon, girl. Just swallow your pride and tell him how you feel."

"*¡Ay, sí!*" Lourdes turns from the ticket window and stuffs a bunch of tickets into Irena's hand.

Irena looks perplexed. "How much do I owe you?"

"My treat." Then she hands me twice as many tickets for Jackie and myself. "*No se preocupen.*" Lourdes hooks one arm through Irena's and one through mine and says, "Let's see if they have Irena's ride."

I wriggle loose from her. "You guys go ahead," I say. "I'm going to stay with Jackie." Then I glance at my watch. "How 'bout we meet at the bumper cars in an hour?" Before they can confirm, I break into a jog in an effort to catch up to Jackie.

"What if they don't have bumper cars?" I hear Irena call after me. "Where do we meet then?"

I slow down just enough to turn around. "C'mon, Irena, there's no such thing as a carnival without bumper cars."

I spot Jackie just as she reaches a pretzel stand. Now that I see her, I hang back a bit to watch her. She still has Lourdes's telephone to her ear as she places her order. By the time the lanky teenager in the striped ball cap squeezes mustard on her pretzel and hands it to her, Jackie has turned off Lourdes's phone and placed it in her fanny pack. She grabs some extra napkins, takes the pretzel from the vendor, and walks a few feet away from the booth. She doesn't look for us at all. She just wanders a few feet, folding back the cellophane paper around her pretzel and licking mustard off her fingers. Then she just stops and lowers herself to the grass, and even though I have no specific memory of seeing her like this, it feels so familiar. It's like Jackie's thirteen again.

As I expected, Jackie pulls out Lourdes's telephone and dials one more time. I start to approach her, and just as I reach her, she ends the call and puts the telephone back into her fanny pack. I sit down on the ground across from Jackie, swipe some mustard off her pretzel, and lick it off my fingers. "Not home?"

Jackie shakes her head. "He's there. All the guys are there. Watching the ball game."

I neither know nor care which sport she's talking about. "So what'd he say?"

"Who is this? Stop playing with the phone. I'm gonna tell your mother." At first, I'm relieved that they haven't spoken. If Wil has not realized that Jackie's the phantom at the other end of the line, he doesn't deserve her. But that thought makes me hurt for her. "Why don't you tell him it's you, *pendeja?*" But we both know why, and Jackie just offers me some of her pretzel. I tear off a piece. "He probably knows it's you." Which makes him a big jerk if he just doesn't call her out and make her talk to him.

"Maybe he thinks it's Sheila."

"When has that drama queen ever called Wil and not chewed his ear off?"

"True."

"This pretzel's pretty good."

"I had to see if they were anything like the ones in New York." Jackie finally takes a bite and then shrugs. "It's a'ight."

"Well, there're no pretzels like the ones in New York."

"No pretzels, no frankfurters, no pizza, there's nothing like the ones in New York."

But that doesn't stop me from reaching for Jackie's pretzel and taking a bite out of it. I know she doesn't mind. We've been picking at each other's plates for years. Jackie doesn't share her food with anyone but me. And now Wil. "You'd think he'd know damn well it's you calling."

"Yeah, well, the guys are over there watching the game and making a racket as usual," Jackie says smiling as she imagines the scene at Wil's.

What if she eventually connects with him, and he finally tells her what she wants to hear? I have to tell Jackie what Wil won't, and I have to do it soon.

I grab the pretzel, haul myself off the ground, and offer her my hand. "Let's go find some boys to pick on."

Jackie grins and takes my hand. "Best idea you've had all trip."

JACKIE

Iowa State Fairgrounds

Des Moines, IA

Sunday, June 18, 8:13 P.M.

I need to get active and shake off these ill feelings, so Hazel and I walk past the rides and head toward the game booths. I see one where you win prizes by knocking down puppets. We draw closer, and the fuckin' puppets have witch doctors painted on them! This is the new millennium . . . you'd think we can finally learn to have some fun without resorting to racist imagery? At the very least we can level the playing field. Like how 'bout we throw baseballs at puppets painted like Dr. Phil for kicks.

Hazel knows me too well. The second I start toward the booth, she says, "Don't go over there giving that poor girl a hard time," referring to the teenager operating the booth. "She's not responsible for that."

"I know." Before we get to the booth, some local guys beat us to it. Something's off about them, I don't know why, but they just set off my instincts in a bad way.

Three of them wear casual gear—sports jerseys or T-shirts, jeans, sneakers—but the last guy in the foursome is wearing a suit with a tie and everything. Who comes to a carnival in a suit? That would make him stick out if he were alone, but he's with these other guys who look like they just came from a sports bar. They remind me of that matching game on *Sesame Street. Three of these things belong together . . . Can you guess which one of these doesn't belong here?* I even start to whistle the song as I walk over to the booth.

I pick out the leader in a snap. He resembles the guy in the suit except he's taller, thinner, and dressed in a red and white Iowa State Cyclones jersey. As a rule, I don't check for white guys, but every rule has its exception, and this guy looks like a younger version of the actor at the top of my list of exceptions to the No White Boys rule—Cole Hauser. Wil hates the flick *Pitch Black* as much and for the same reasons as I love it. He tries to get under my skin when I watch it, making wisecracks about the homoerotic chemistry between Vin and Cole, but he doesn't fool me. Wil knows damned well that when those two are on screen together—especially when Johns and Riddick are in the ship's cabin gibing at each and talking about, "Remember how this moment could've gone and didn't"—I'm thinking Jackie sandwich.

One of the other guys has caught Hazel's eye because she slips her arm through mine and says, "Let's teach those mucho machos something." That's Hazelese for, "He's cute enough for me to let him think he stands a chance."

We get to the booth, and the scene there's kind of pathetic. Pretty Fly for a White Guy and the fella in the suit are taking turns lobbing balls at those racist puppets. Every time Pretty Fly pitches, a puppet goes down with a resounding clang, and all his boys start hollering and slapping high-fives like the man's Randy Johnson or some shit. Meanwhile, every time the guy in the suit pitches, he misses the puppet by a yard, and the members of the peanut gallery either cackle at him or call him all kinds of fag. It's pretty disgusting. Even though I feel for the kid, a part of me wants to smack him upside the head and say, "Why are you bothering, son? Not only are you out of your league, you should be proud of it! Make some friends a little higher up the food chain." I'm witnessing a rare case of a white man struck with a severe case of internalized oppression. How else do you explain why he would subject himself to this ridicule for the approval of such obvious morons?

Irena and I debate this all the time, and I wish she were here to see this case study in action. She thinks that it's impossible for a white man to experience any kind of IO unless he identifies with some marginalized group—like if he's gay or poor or something like. But I say not only is it possible, there's no more dangerous occurrence of IO than when it strikes a white guy who has every advantage in our society. When people of color—or PoCs, as I like to say—subscribe to racist beliefs about ourselves, the results are gang violence, teen pregnancy, substance abuse, and all those terrible things that eat our communities alive from the inside out. But for the most part, we do the worst damage to ourselves, and because of the way our public institutions work, or more like don't work, these problems ironically remain contained epidemics.

But what happens when you tell someone that by virtue of his race and sex he should be running the world, and he wakes up to find himself as alienated and broke as all the colored folks who are supposed to be doing his bidding? You get Columbine, Jonesboro, and Santee. You get militia groups. You get Timothy McVeigh and Jeffrey Dahmer. When left untreated to fester to its worst extremes, White Boy IO leaks out of the burbs and fucks up all of us.

Even though I have just so much sympathy for Suit Boy, I always have to side with the underdog. Hazel and I walk up the booth, and of course, the peanut gallery notices us because she's a hottie, and I'm a darky. I pull out a dollar and slap it on the counter. The girl operating the booth reaches beneath the counter, comes up with three balls, and hands them to me. I don't pitch right away though. Instead I watch Pretty Fly and Suit Boy finish their round. The closer I look, the more obvious it is to me that they're brothers.

Now that his audience consists of women, Pretty Fly plunks down three bucks, and the girl gives him an entire basket of balls. Now while he's winding up he's singing that stupid witch doctor song: *Ooh eeh ooh ahah, ting tang wallawallabingbang.* Everyone laughs except for me, Hazel, Suit Boy, and Booth Girl. Glad to know there are some folks in this town with a social conscience. In fact, Suit Boy says, "As if the puppets weren't racist enough."

I say to Hazel, "You can say that again," and of course, she nods.

None of the guys heard me, because one of them yells at Suit Boy, "School's out, dude."

Another goes, "Shut the fuck up, Jimmy. That PC shit's for fags."

Time for a gut check. I appreciate Jimmy's attempts to check his friends, but sometimes you can't send a Suit Boy to do a sister's job.

I grab my balls, step around Jimmy, and stand next to Pretty Fly. And he is Pretty Fly. So much that I'm starting to find the *ting tang wallawallabingbang* kind of endearing, so I have to give *myself* a gut check, thinking about all of my shaman ancestors who were maligned, even slaughtered by so-called Christians and scientists who might've looked just like this character.

He sees that I'm watching him, and really starts to ham it up. *I told the witch doctor you didn't love me true.* Ya got that shit right, buddy. Not that I think the dude's flirting with me. I know better than to think that. I learned long ago that an interest in me in no way means a man desires my interest in him. Or what he perceives to be my interest in him. Or what he misconstrues to be my interest. Anyway, Pretty Fly strikes down a puppet, and without really looking at me, he picks up another ball, winds up, and says, "Anyone ever tell you that you look like Pam Grier?"

"Never." But maybe that's only because I, like, don't.

He knocks down another puppet, and this time he stops to look at me. "Can I call you Foxy Brown?"

"No."

"So what should I call you?"

I almost say *Nunya.* As in *None of your business.* But now I have a plan, and I bat my eyes, or do something with my eyelashes that I hope comes across to him as batting my eyes. How does Hazel do that shit? "Jackie."

But before I can seize control of the situation, Pretty Fly says, "You see! Perfect. Can I call you Jackie Brown then?"

"No."

But the guy refuses to let me intimidate him. "What's your last name?" He picks up another ball, fires it at the puppet, and down it goes. "Can I guess?" This is too delicious to resist, so I smile and nod. I expect the usual—Williams, Jones, Lee. Instead he says, "Lawrence? Griffin? Harvey?" And even though there's about seven hundred nautical miles between his guess and the right answer, I'm impressed that he went for common but not obvious surnames. His friends laugh, and I quickly realize what a *pendeja* I am. "Murphy? Rock?"

That motherfucker's naming black comics.

And how would his friends know to laugh if he's not done this kind of thing before? It's not like they're reading cue cards. Lemmings can't read.

I have to set him straight but keep my cool. "Try Alvarado."

He stops in midswing and looks at me, "That's Spanish, isn't it?" I just nod, and he grins. "Alvarado. That's pretty. Pretty name, pretty girl." He throws the ball, and hits the last puppet but not hard enough to make it fall. Instead of teasing him about his streak coming to an end, his boys actually groan with disappointment. What kind of sick little fraternity these guys have going here? Probably the kind where the initiation activities include inventing nasty one-syllable words to describe vaginas, menacing gay men in public places, and participating in circle jerks. Maybe except for that kid Jimmy. He seems okay. "I love Spanish women."

Then get your ass to Spain. I look over my shoulder at Hazel, and she's standing there with Jimmy. They're whispering in each other's ear. I want to ask them what the hell they're bonding over, but first things first.

I take one of my baseballs off the counter and take a step back. Booth Girl resets the pyramid of puppets for me. I glance at the ringleader, and I say, "And what's your name, badass?"

He smiles at me. "Brian."

"Brian?" I look at Hazel, and she winks at me. She always knows where I'm headed. "Nice name. Solid name."

"Damn right."

"Is that Brian with an *i* or with a *y*?"

"You kidding me?" He laughs, and all his friends join in even though they have no freakin' clue what he thinks is so funny. I know what has his jockstrap in a twirl, but they sure as hell don't. "Do I look like one of those metrosexuals?" Look, I'm no fan of them either, but since my brother apsires to be one (although he's four tax brackets and a dozen zip codes away from joining Derek Jeter and Jason Sehorn at Labrecque's for a lemongrass scalp treatment), I don't appreciate this Neanderthal making them out to sound like a step above pedophiles. It's not their fault they've fallen victim to Madison Avenue's latest conspiracy—making heterosexual males as equally insecure about the way they look, feel, and smell as they do gay men and straight women so they'll spend money hand over fist in search of perfection in a five-ounce tube. "It's Brian with a fuckin' *i*."

"Brian with a fuckin' *i*." I wind up and pitch the ball. It slams into the puppet at the center of the pyramid. I grab the next ball and wind up again. "*B . . .*" I fire the second ball, and down goes the next puppet. "*R . . .*" When I take the third ball, the girl operating the booth dives under the counter and comes up with a basket full of them. Hazel picks up the basket and stands besides me. She hands me the balls as I finish spelling out Mr. All-American's nice, solid name while taking down a puppet with each letter. "Fuckin' *I . . . A . . . N . . .*" Even though I run out of letters, I fire one baseball after the other. *Clang, clang, clang,* the puppets collapse with a rhythm that makes me want to dance, but I check myself. I've already stolen the guy's thunder, so no need to stoop to his level of immaturity and break out into a musical number.

Hazel leans her elbow on my shoulder. "Jackie, how do you say *Brian* in Spanish?"

I pretend to give it some thought. I look at Brian, who stands in front of his boys, his bulging forearms locked across his wide chest. "You don't."

IRENA

Iowa State Fairgrounds

Des Moines, IA

Sunday, June 18, 8:42 P.M.

Each ride requires four to five tickets to enter, so within a half hour, Lourdes and I run out. "There's a ticket booth over there," she says, pulling on my wrist. "I'll buy us some more."

But I dig my heels into the ground. "Let's go find Jackie and Hazel first." Not only do I not like us being separated, I'm not comfortable with Lourdes paying for all my rides. "Not to mention I'm starving. Let's go find the others and then get something to eat. I didn't have anything to eat at the bar."

"*Ni yo tampoco,*" Lourdes says, obviously unhappy to be reminded how Jackie ushered us out of the Chop Shop in midflirt. "Let's eat first, and then we'll go find Jackie and Hazel."

I figure I have to compromise, so I agree and we follow the salty scent of popcorn and pretzels to the booths that sell food. Lourdes and I get on line, and I read the menu. Hamburgers, hot dogs, French fries, cheese nachos, onion rings, pizza . . . Crap upon junk. Yuck! My stomach growls more from frustration than hunger.

"Nothing you like?" Lourdes guesses. I shake my head. "So are you just not going to eat until we leave here?"

"I don't know."

She points to the menu, "*Mira, tienen* chicken nuggets. You still eat chicken, don't you?"

I do. Fish, too. But I'm trying to give up both. "Eventually, I want to become a vegan."

Lourdes snickers. "Not on this trip."

I realize she's right, and I have to laugh. "I guess I can have some chicken nuggets." They're going to be breaded and fried, but I'll just peel off the skin like I used to do the ones in the McDonald's Happy Meals my father used to buy me.

When we reach the counter, Lourdes says, "I want chicken nuggets, a hot dog, nachos, a diet Coke . . ." She turns to me and says, "Water, right?" Before I can answer, she turns back to the cashier and says, "And a large bottle of water." Then before I can find my wallet in my bag, she whips out two twenties and slaps them on the counter. The woman is like Annie Oakley with her cash, shooting from the hip as if she carried her bills in a holster!

"Here," I say, thrusting my ten-dollar bill toward her.

She waves me away. "No, no, no."

"Yes, Lourdes. Take it."

"*Te dije que no.*" The cashier piles our junk food onto a plastic brown tray and goes to get our beverages.

"You already paid for all the rides."

"*No te preocupes.*" The cashier returns with my bottled water and Lourdes's cola and plunks them on the tray. She rings up the order and looks up to find a brown fist with two twenties and a white fist with a single ten in her poor face. Her eyes dart between us. "Irena, put that away. You're confusing her."

But I stand my ground. "The nuggets and water are a separate order." The cashier sucks her teeth as she already has rung up everything at one time.

Lourdes elbows her way in front of me. "No, they're not. Don't listen to her." Since the order is under twenty dollars, the cashier sides with Lourdes and takes a bill from her hand. Then she gives her the change, which Lourdes immediately drops into the jar with an index card with *Tips* scrawled in marker and taped to its front.

The least I can do is carry the tray, so I slide it off the counter and start toward the tables. Lourdes catches up to me, clutching two straws, some plastic utensils, and a batch of napkins.

We find an empty table that's not too dirty, and I set down the tray. Before her butt hits the bench, Lourdes stuffs two nachos into her mouth, and then she washes it down with a sip of soda.

I pick up a nugget. I pinch it and realize that it has no skin to peel. The amount of freakin' grease they must have used to make the damned breadcrumbs stick to it! I can forget about fantasizing that this was an organically farmed chicken who passed gently in her sleep.

She picks up her hot dog and sinks her teeth into it. I can't believe it when my mouth starts to water. I must be really hungry because hot dogs are the worst of all junk food. They're nothing but elastic tubes of mechanically separated meat and sodium fillers. I wonder if I can find a soy hot dog anywhere in Des Moines. Then Lourdes claps her hands together and leans forward. "*Pues vamos a chismear.*"

"Let's what?"

"Gossip!"

"Oh."

"Is it me, or is there something weird going on between Jackie and Hazel?"

I don't like to gossip, least of all about my friends. It's so spiritually incorrect. But I suspected something before we even left New York, and I've felt burdened by my suspicions. I'm happy not to be the only one to notice something, so maybe Lourdes and I can figure it out before it deteriorates. "Well, Jackie's having her usual problem with Wil, but it seems like it's coming to a head," I say. "And for some reason, Hazel is not as sympathetic as she usually is."

"She must be tired of telling Jackie to leave him."

"She shouldn't leave him!" Wil and Jackie are perfect for each other. He needs a woman who's materially independent and doesn't look at him like an ATM with a penis. She needs a man who's emotionally mature and won't treat her like a breathing Kewpie doll. Those two need each other because they love each other and not the other way around. That's the way it should be. Before Lourdes can protest, I find myself saying, "If Jackie and Wil break up, it's going to be awkward for you and Kharim."

Did I just say that? Where did that come from? Lourdes can't believe it either. "Nothing's going on between Kharim and me."

"Didn't seem like it at the graduation."

Lourdes gives me a devilish smile. "*Tú eres celosa.*" I give her a blank stare, and she translates in singsong. "You're jealous."

Goddess forbid! "Jealousy is such a useless emotion."

Lourdes rolls her eyes at me. "You shouldn't be. I like K, but only as a friend. Which is not the way he likes you."

"No!" When did these three caucus and decide to launch this campaign to match up Kharim and me? Who's idea was this? Probably Jackie's.

The thought of Jackie sparks that warm sensation in my chest, and an image flashes before my eyes. I see Jackie and Hazel tied back-to-back like witches at a stake. A group of faceless men surround and menace them. One of the men breaks forward and tries to help them, but the others seize him and push him back into the crowd. Just as the men are closing in on Jackie and Hazel, the image vanishes, replaced by Lourdes's palm waving in my face and jingling her gold bangles.

"Irena, I'm only teasing you," she says. "You're looking at me as if I just—"

"Look, forget about it." I shove a nugget into my mouth as if I need to fuel up for battle. "Let's just finish and find Jackie and Hazel."

Lourdes looks hurt. "*Está bien.*" She thinks I don't want to talk to her anymore, and I feel so bad about that. But not as bad as I do when I replay the image in my head. The four of us need to come together again now.

HAZEL

Iowa State Fairgrounds

Des Moines, IA

Sunday, June 18, 9:09 P.M.

We don't find Lourdes and Irena right away, but Jackie and I have a blast. Heights give me the chills, but almost all the rides lift you high in the air, and as far as Jackie's concerned, the higher, the better. But she's my girl, and I ride with her even when she runs toward the Zipper, which is exactly what it sounds like. Jackie and I barely fit in the cage, which has no other restraints than the lap bar on the door. Before I notice the rungs, the ride starts and the main boom launchs forward, spinning the cage on its own axis and tossing us like kernels in a popcorn maker. We both scream ourselves hoarse and slam our hands against the walls of the car, except I sound like Sarah Michelle Gellar in one of her horror flicks while Jackie flails around like Elizabeth Berkeley in the pool scene in *Showgirls.* Too bad I'm too terrified to be turned on or jealous that she's having the time of her life while I'm imagining the mesh on the cage window giving way and the two of us hurtling to our deaths.

The ride ends, and we tumble out of the cage. Jackie brims with adrenaline, and feeling my sandals on the earth and seeing her so carefree makes my terror evaporate, and this amorous surge fills me. Jackie notices my expression because she brushes my hair off my face and asks, "Haze, you okay?"

"Let's go find the Ferris wheel."

She sighs with relief that I'm neither ill or angry. "Okay, but let's find the bathroom first."

The bathoom is actually a row of Porta Pottis, and each has a line of two dozen people desperate enough to subject themselves to the guaranteed unsavoriness. "I think I can wait until we get back to the hotel," I say.

"Damn, I wish I could. Look, why don't you wait for me over there?" She points to an arcade game a few yards away. I agree, and she takes off to join the queue.

I arrive at the booth, which is one of those games where you take a pistol and shoot water into a rotating head. At the top of the head is a balloon, and the more water you get into the head, the bigger the balloon gets. The first person to burst the balloon wins the prize. I get to the booth just as a group of teenagers finish playing, so it's just me and the tubby game operator, who's too engrossed in his books to notice me. On his left knee, he balances a spiral notebook and pen. On the other, he has a yellow book called *The Weekend Novelist.* Just as I'm about to ask him what his novel-in-progress is about, Jimmy appears by my side. "Hey, Glen. How's the book going?"

Glen looks up and reaches across the counter to shake Jimmy's hand. "Nowhere, man." He piles one book on top of the other and puts them both aside in frustration. With his pudgy arms now by his side, I can read Glen's T-shirt. It has a giant catfish across his "breasts" above the words *National Fishing Week.* "Wrote myself into a corner, and I just can't get out of it."

"That sucks." Jimmy looks over to me. "Glen's got this great idea to write a modern-day version of—"

"Don't tell her, man!"

"He's afraid someone's going to steal his idea."

"Damn right, I'm afraid. It's one hell of an idea. Pardon my French, miss."

"Consider your French pardoned, sir."

Glen blushes, and Jimmy introduces us. Then he places a dollar on the counter so we can play the game. I look at my choices and select the water pistol behind the fox. Jimmy chooses the horse on my right. Glen clicks a switch and the game starts to buzz; then a bell rings. Water shoots out of our pistols and the animal heads start to rotate. Jimmy starts yelling like he's been possessed by the spirit of Marion Rambo. He must've inspired me because I start yodeling like Xena, the Warrior Princess. The two of us are crouched behind these water pistols, firing and screaming like we're Butch and Sundance. I'm not a yeller, and I never have been (that's right, not even in bed), but now I feel what I'm missing and I'm not the least bit self-conscious about it, because how can I seem silly when I'm not the only one doing it? For the first time, I notice the block of tension that sits low in my belly, and my screams are causing it to shift and disintegrate. I scream even louder as if to scare away my tension.

Then the bell rings, and the buzz of the game fades. Jimmy turns to Glen and says, "Why'd you shut off the game, man?" My shooting technique amounted to all intensity, no aim as hardly any water landed in the fox's mouth, and the blue balloon over its head just flops there like one of Raul's balls. "Neither of us has won yet." When Jimmy says this, I look over at his horse and realize that he's just as lousy a shot as I am.

Glen shakes his head. "C'mon now. Look at this place." Jimmy and I look at each other and then at the booth. We never got water into the horse or fox but had managed to get it all over the other animals, the floor, the back wall, and some of the prize teddy bears hanging from a beam, spared from the cold stream by plastic bags. "I can't in good conscience let y'all empty the river until you figure out a winner."

I turn to Jimmy, and he shrugs. Then the three of us start to laugh. I catch Jimmy staring at me from the corner of my eye, and for that I returned the attention. "What do you do when you're not emptying the river?" I ask Jimmy. He reaches into his lapel pocket and pulls out a business card. "You sell cars."

Jimmy nods. "What about you?"

"I'm a hair stylist. In New York."

"Oh." He sounds disappointed. While I'm not surprised, I'm still flattered. "What brings you to Des Moines?"

"We're just passing through on our way to California."

"Oh." Then Jimmy says, "My brother's going to be disappointed. He's got a crush on your friend."

"Yeah, I could tell by the way he was yanking at her pigtails."

"No!" Jimmy says, "Jackie's the one who tripped Brian and knocked his books out of his hand."

He laughs, but I can't bring myself to join him. "Well, I don't know if you want to tell him this or not, but Jackie's spoken for."

"Really?" Jimmy's gray eyes open with surprise. "Sure could've fooled me." He stares for a moment at his feet; then he rejoins my gaze. "What about you? Do you have a boyfriend?"

"No, but I'm hoping to connect with someone special on this trip." Then I turn to Glen and ask, "Are there any games in this place that don't require athletic ability?"

"Better stick to the rides."

"How about the bumper cars?" Jimmy suggests. I take in his wrinkled suit and undone tie, and I can't imagine him tearing corners and slamming into other drivers. He wants to impress me. How sweet. Jackie wants to ride the bumper cars, too, but I doubt that she would want Jimmy to tag along with us. Especially since he's obviously taken a liking to me. Maybe a little male attention is just what I need to feel Jackie out before I make my big confession. Get her mind off Wil and on me. I don't know if she'll experience the kind of jealousy I want, but anything that makes her feel threatened over me can't hurt my cause.

So I tell Jimmy, "Let me get my friend, and we'll meet you over there."

JACKIE

Iowa State Fairgrounds
Des Moines, IA
Sunday, June 18, 9:31 P.M.

I climb into a purple car, but Hazel hangs back. "What're you waiting on?" I say. "Get in."

She jams her hands on her hips. "Last time I got into a bumper car with you, I ended up with a bloody nose."

Hazel has to let some shit go. "*¡Coño!* You still not over that? That was, like, five years ago when I didn't know how to drive."

"You still don't know how to drive." Before I can offer a few choice words, she looks past me and starts waving. "Jimmy!"

"Jimmy?" Who the fuck's Jimmy? I turn around and Suit Guy is headed our way in a yellow car. "Oh, so you and he are boys now?"

Hazel ignores me. I love Hazel. She truly is the sister I never had with all the fuckin' aggravation that entails. One reason why I can't live with the girl though is her annoying tendency to pick up strays. Particularly those of the three-legged variety. Can't she tell this guy is crushing on her? Of course she can tell. That's precisely why she's encouraging him to tail us all around the park. If Hazel gets into his car, I swear I'm calling it out.

"I need a girl to ride, ride, ride . . ." Now here drives up Brian in a white car, and Hazel jumps back to avoid being hit. "I need a girl who's mine oh mine . . ." Brian eyes me and pats the seat next to him. How many songs has Usher cut since that corny track? I'm tempted to serenade him back with the last cut on the Cree Summer album Irena plays when she's driving. *Curious white boy, when am I gonna meet your mama?*

Without a word to him, or Hazel for that matter, I drive off. When I turn the corner, I catch Hazel shooing Jimmy to the passenger side of his car. If she has to ride with him, at least she's insisting on driving. The girl hasn't totally lost her senses.

The ride starts, and I decide to have my fun. When I reach them though, Hazel and Jimmy are still situating themselves so I knock the hell out of two skinny girls who probably got their learner's permits yesterday. Finally, Hazel and Jimmy latch their seat belts, so I move in for the kill. She's not out of their spot two seconds when I let them have it. They fly into the rail, and as I drive past them, I cackle and give them the finger. I expect Jimmy to get his nuts in a bind, since guys hate to be outdone by gals period, let alone in situations they presume to be their domain. But to my surprise, Jimmy's laughing harder than Hazel. I respect that about him and hope to have another chance to show it by hitting them again.

Behind me I hear a guy yell, "I got her, I got her!" I look behind me. Brian's gunning for me.

Hazel says, "Jackie, watch out!"

Jimmy nudges her. "Hey, whose team are you on?" God, if he only knew how many times Hazel's been asked *that.*

Brian's gaining on me. I slow down to let him get close enough to hit me. Just as he's about to ram into me, I swerve to the side, and he goes crashing into a pile of unused bumper cars. He bangs the steering wheel and curses. So I drive back to Brian and say, "You're so cute when you're angry."

I zip around and immediately wish I had been a better sport because blocking my path is a mess of giggly teenagers. "Move, move, move!" I think I can squeeze between this kid's green car and the island bumper so I go for it. But then the dork shifts, trapping me between his car and the island. "C'mon, c'mon, c'mon!" I can feel Brian on my neck as if he were in the car with me. The kid finally steers out of my freakin' way, but before I can jam on the gas, Brian crashes into me. My car lurches forward, and my body follows, flopping like a rag doll. I regain control of myself and look for Brian. He actually looks concerned, but I smile at him to let him know I'm fine.

Then I look for Hazel and Jimmy and spot them across the floor. She looks ferocious, but I don't know why. The skinny non-driving chicks are sailing toward them. "Hazel!" But it's too late. *Las flacas* slam into them, and Hazel and Jimmy fly into a cluster of broken bumper cars. He laughs, but Hazel's out of it. Jimmy takes over, attempting to steer them out of the pile without much luck.

It sucks to spend most of the ride entangled in a knot of cars, but the only thing I can do is find Brian for some payback. But when I find him, he's ricocheting toward Hazel and Jimmy. The floor's buzzing with fair game, and he's going after them when they're trapped? I don't believe it until Brian fires his car into them. Jimmy catches him and has a chance to brace himself, but before he can warn Hazel, Brian slams his car into theirs and her head whips like a bobble doll. What a dirty fuckin' hit! That bastard has to pay.

I jam on the gas and race for Brian. He coasts around Hazel and Jimmy without so much as a, "Y'all okay?" And this time Jimmy's not laughing as he tries to steer them out of the corner and off to the side to safety while Hazel rubs her neck. Meanwhile, Brian zips in and out of the other drivers without so much as a bump at the easy targets. He wants a challenge. He's looking for me? I've got something for his ass.

Luckily, I maneuver my car behind Brian before he can spot me amidst the crowd of drivers. It'd be mad sweet for him to look over his shoulder just to see me rushing him like a bull toward a red cape. But there's another gang of knuckleheads who can barely walk let alone drive clustered in the middle of the track so if I strike now, I'll jack myself up, too. The ride's about to end, and this is my last chance to put Brian in check. Fuck it. He hurt my girl. He's going down even if I have to go down with him.

So as Brian searches the crowd for me, I zoom toward him. When I'm inches from his bumper, I blow smooches at him as if he were a puppy. Just as he turns and we catch eye, *slam!* We both careen into the knot of idiots. I lurch forward, and my safety belt cuts against my shoulder. If you want to win, you have to play through the pain. I shift to reverse and let the car sail back a few feet. Then I jam into drive and slam into Brian again. Now he grabs his neck in pain, and I take that as a sign that he can stand one more hit. I pull back a few feet again, stomp the gas, and *slam!* The buzz of the electricity fades to silence, and I undo my belt, stumble out of my car, and go to check on Hazel.

LOURDES

Iowa State Fairgrounds
Des Moines, IA
Sunday, June 18, 9:42 P.M.

Irena drags me to the bumper cars as if we were fleeing a fire. When we arrive, we see Hazel in a car with a guy. *¡Qué chévere!* I mean, he's not for me, but maybe he has a friend who is. "You see, Irena," I say, "Hazel's right there."

"But where's Jackie?"

"*Ahí está ahora.*" Jackie runs to Hazel's car. Behind her is this gorgeous guy in a football jersey with the sexiest limp. He puts a hand on Jackie's shoulder, and she slaps it away.

Irena points. "I told you something was wrong."

I hate to agree with her, but this scene makes me uncomfortable. Then it gets worse. Jackie yells at the guy, and Hazel and her friend climb out of their car and try to mediate. The handsome guy plants his hand over his heart as if Jackie's breaking it. Instead of being softened by his gesture, Jackie grows more irate. She curses at him then grabs Hazel's hand and drags her our way.

When Jackie reaches us, she barks, "We're out of here now."

"Okay," Irena says, and she grabs my hand and yanks at me, too. This time I don't argue. As we rush to the parking lot, I look over my shoulder. *¡Ay, Dios mío!* They're following us! They've been joined by other guys, and they're following us and saying these terrible things.

"Oh, I get it now. They're a bunch of dykes."

"Jimmy sure can pick 'em."

"What do you call a group of dykes anyway, Jimmers? There's a school of fish . . ."

"A colony of beavers."

"How 'bout a pack of b-----s?" They're saying all these nasty things about Jackie and Hazel being lesbians; They sound as if they want to do something about it. Jackie and Hazel hear them, but are too busy blaming one another to turn their attention to where it belongs.

"Was it necessary for you to dis him like that?" says Hazel.

"Was it f----in' necessary for you to bother with them in the first place?"

"Me? What about what you did to him at the game booth—"

"I put his ass in check, and he got the hint. You're the one who went looking for Jimmy while I was in the bathroom. For what reason, I don't freakin' know!"

Jimmy hears his name and runs toward them, his friends hissing him and calling him all kinds of names. He says, "I'm really sorry about this." And I know by the way that Irena clings to me that she's thinking what I'm thinking. Is he apologizing for what they are doing or what they are about to do? I don't know how someone sensitive enough to apologize would hang out *con esos animales* in the first place.

Jackie and Hazel ignore him, preferring to continue going at each other as *los idiotas* behind us yell catfight, catfight, catfight! Jimmy tells them to shut up and the gang of them cackle like warlocks. If I had a weapon on me, I would use it. I don't know whether to thank God for that or not.

"You're wrong, Hazel," says Jackie. "You led this poor little white boy on." And Jimmy's standing right there! His face turns red as if Jackie had called him a cracker or *un gringo.* Hazel's need for attention may have gotten us into this ugly situation, but Jackie has no right to attack him like that. She has no business attacking anyone right now except the ones who are attacking us! *Dios te salve María, llena eres de gracia . . .*

Irena trembles and whispers to Jackie, "What are we going to do?" She looks over her shoulder at the men trailing and catcalling us.

Jackie clutches Irena's arm. "Stop freakin' turning around, for starters."

"Ouch!" I'm about to give Jackie a piece of my mind when this guilty look overtakes her face. She immediately lets Irena go and puts her arm around her. "You know I'd never let anything happen to you. No one messes with you on my watch, right?"

Irena wipes her eyes like a child. She is still frightened, but she believes Jackie. She always believes in Jackie *y no sé por qué.* I want to believe in her, too, but I cannot. I believe in only one person.

Padre nuestro que estás en los cielos, santificado sea tu nombre . . .

The short walk to the parking lot takes a decade, and we finally climb into the Tempo. I continue to pray even though I know it annoys Jackie. *Dios ayudame,* she had better not say a thing to me. I'm doing the only thing I can to make things better. God help her if she criticizes me now *porque no soy más que humana,* and if anyone can see us safely through this trouble, it's God.

Jackie revs up the engine, her eyes fixed on Brian and his friends as they continue to approach us. *¿Y qué pasa con esos malditos?* Are they so hateful that they would do something while we're in the car? Are they going to block our path? Throw something at us?

Jackie says, "I swear to God, I'll f---in' run them over." Oh, now she evokes Him. *Padre, perdoname,* but if they do come over here, I pray she has the guts to do as she threatens. Whatever happens then, Lord, is in your hands.

Jackie flashes the high beams at Brian and his gang, and they recoil *como los vampiros que son.* They make a left and head toward a minivan. Jackie cuts off the engine, and Hazel yells, "Let's go already!"

With a calmness so sudden, it's eerie, Jackie says, "Let them leave first."

"*Chica, ¿tú eres loca? ¡Vámonos!*"

"Jackie, please let's just go," begs Hazel.

"She's right," says Irena, "It's safer to wait." *Dios mío,* this is no time for another one of her "visions."

"Of all the ridiculous . . . We really should . . ."

"We should what, Hazel? Lead them back to the only place we freakin' know in this town? Take them straight to our motel? Where there might be no one in the parking lot to help us when we get there? At least there's a s---tload of other people here." Even though no one argues with her anymore, she adds, "I know what I'm f---in' doing."

A dark minivan rolls by, seeping the heavy bass of metal rap music and the devilish laughter of young men. But we can't see inside of it. Hazel says what everyone is thinking. "Was that them?"

Jackie says, "I can't tell." Oh, now she doesn't know everything!

"Por favor, vámonos."

She finally starts the engine and pulls out of our parking spot toward the exit. We reach the street and drive in an unbearable silence. I make the Sign of the Cross and say, *"Gracias a Dios,"* but no one responds. I wonder what my mother would think if she knew I was traveling with a group of heathens.

A harsh light beams into the Tempo. I turn and see the dark minivan on our bumper. But Jackie refuses to speed up saying, "Back the f--- up off me."

Then as if the driver heard her, the minivan veers around us. It sidles besides us, and the window slowly rolls down. All of us look *y ahí está una viejita* wearing a hideous yellow plastic visor that she must have won at one of the carnival arcade games. Her radio is now playing something Motownish, and she's staring us down like some kind of *chola* in a bad gangster film, even though she's old enough to owe King Tut a nickel. *¡Ay, Dios, ayudame por favor . . . I'm starting to think like Jackie!*

"If she's in such a rush, let her drive around me." The old woman says something, but we cannot hear her, because Jackie's window is closed. Jackie jabs a button, and the window starts to fall. "What the f--- you said?"

"Jackie!"

"She's staring me down like I'm cramping her steelo! I don't care if she's as old as dirt." Jackie turns back to la *viejita* and yells, "Keep it movin'!" Then she mutters under her breath, "Old b---h."

Now this time Irena says, "Jackie!"

La viejita lets out a stream of curses I have not heard since

Jackie talked us into sneaking into that horrific Quentin Tarantino movie. (I truly believed then and still believe *que Dios me castigó* with all that filthy language and gory violence for committing theft of service. I had nightmares for the rest of the week.) Then *esa vieja sucia* gives us her middle finger and drives off like there's a Winston cup waiting for her at the end of the road.

Jackie screams after her, "Shoulda done that in the first place," and calls her the Spanish p-word. Not that one. Or that one. And she wouldn't use that one either because that's a Mexican term, and she's *caribeña.* I mean the word that refers to hair down there. That word.

"*¡Mira, qué fresca!*" And for once I don't mean *esa negra malcriada* behind the wheel but the little old lady in the minivan. "I can't believe she did that."

Then Irena starts to giggle. "I hope I'm like that when I'm her age." And then she laughs so hard, her blue eyes disappear into tiny slits of joy. I start to laugh, too, more from nerves at first. And then Jackie starts, and the three of us chuckle and chatter about what happened. I say, "Jackie's already like that."

"I know," she agrees. "I'll be lucky if someone doesn't kill me before I can get to that age."

Only then I notice that Hazel's not laughing with us. Instead she's staring hard ahead even though there's nothing to see but the white markings in the road.

Irena notices, too. "Maybe when we get back to the motel, we should do a healing circle."

"I'm not doing anything when we get back to the hotel except getting in my bed and going to sleep," Jackie says.

Finally, we agree on something.

I usually don't care when someone's pissed at me, but I hate it when Hazel's upset with me. With the exception of my father and brother, whose tempers make me look like Mother Teresa, she's the only person I know who can weather my storms. I even scare Wil sometimes (or so he claims), but I'm trying not to think about him right now. But Hazel usually enjoys the show, so if I pissed her off, I have to wonder if I've gone too far.

But to be honest, I have no idea why Hazel's angry at all, let alone at me. What's there to be mad about? It'd better not be-cause I disrupted her flow with that white boy. When she got her flirt on in the wrong place at the wrong time with the wrong fuckin' person, I got us out of there without anyone getting hurt.

And it's not the first time either. Although it's never gone this far, if I had a dollar for every time I had to give a lesson on how to respect a woman's boundaries to one of Hazel's overzealous suit-ors, we'd be driving to Frisco in my Dodge Magnum with chrome rims instead of this giant Spam can on wheels.

When we arrive at the motel, Hazel holds me back and tells Rena and Lou to go ahead. She's still upset, but the edge is off.

"The last time some guy called us dykes, you had a lot to say," Hazel says. She tries hard to suppress it, but I hear the edge creep back into her voice.

She's angry because I didn't rip Brian a second asshole for calling us dykes?

If there's one thing I hate worse than Hazel being angry with me, it's my getting angry at her. But I can't help myself. She has me more confused than a U.S. marine searching for WMDs in Iraq. "Wait a minute. Hold up. Hit pause. First, you're pissed because I say something to that moron. Now you're mad because I *didn't* say something. What gives, Hazel?"

"I just want to know what's so different this time. And don't tell me they were in a group or it was nighttime or any BS like that. That was true from jump, and it didn't stop you from showing up Brian every chance you had."

"You know what I want to know? I want to know why for someone who's so out, who said that this trip was about the sistas, who insisted that we stop here so we homegirls could have fun together, you gravitated to the boys so quickly?"

"Please. Where do you come off going there with me? You're the one who should've just strapped Wil to the roof the car and brought him along with us."

"Oh, you want to make this about me?"

"It is about you, Jackie!" Okay, I didn't start this scene, but now that it's under way, I'm going to finish it. I live by the credo *Don't start none won't be none,* and ordinarily I couldn't give a half damn about losing my cool in public, but we've imported enough drama into this poor town. All we need is the manager of the motel to throw us out because the guests are bitching about the loud black chick in the parking lot.

So I start to walk away from Hazel to the staircase leading to our room. She trails me, and I say over my shoulder, "Why didn't *you* say something?"

"Why should I be the only one?"

"Then why're you only mad at me?" But she's right though. Checking those bastards should not have been Hazel's sole responsibility just because she's the one who's queer. When those guys started with their homophobic crap, everyone who heard it and didn't like it should have spoken up about it. "I always gotta defend myself," I say. "I gotta defend you. I gotta defend every-fuckin'-body. When I'm doing all this defending, who the hell's got my back?"

I reach our room, and before I can jam my card key into the slot, the door swings open. Lourdes stands behind it looking mortified. Irena's sitting on the bed with her legs crossed and her hands over her face and goddammit, she's crying! Why is she freakin' crying? So what if Hazel and I are fighting? Real friends do that sometimes. It'd do Irena and Lou's friendship some good to go at each other every once in a while. If the girl's so big on the four of us bonding and getting closer and whatnot, she needs to wake up and smell the friction.

Hazel says, "Don't front like I've never been there for you, Jackie."

I lose it because I don't exactly remember it that way. It never bothered me back then because I truly believed that Hazel did have my back. But for her to say now that she stepped up for me the same way I always have for her because she thinks I slacked off this time? I'm not fuckin' having it. "Yeah, all after the fact. Back in my room or on the train, it'd be, 'Fuck them, Jackie. Those ignorant bastards. Racist idiots.' Blah, blah, blah, after it all went down. But when they were in my face calling me Brillo pad or tar baby or some shit like that, you would stand there and say what? Nothing, Hazel. You'd say absolutely nothing."

I put my hands on my hips and wait for Hazel to respond. Her mouth gapes like a fish, and now she looks like she's about to cry, too. I don't want Hazel to cry. I don't mean to make anyone cry, least of all my best friend.

Just as I'm about to deliver a ridiculously overdue forget-about-it, Hazel says, "If I never said anything . . ." Again, the edge fades from her voice, but so does the soft look in her eyes. Hazel folds her arms across her chest. "Well . . . you'd say all that'd have to be said."

Yeah, that's it. That explains everything. Now we're all Kool and the Gang. "Whatever, Hazel." I go into the bathroom, slamming the door and locking it behind me. I stop the tub and run the hot water. I'm staying in here as long as I feel like it, and if they need to take a leak before I'm through, let them go to the lobby. I don't want to hear from anybody for the rest of night.

HAZEL

Roadway Inn

Des Moines, IA

Monday, June 19, 8:26 A.M.

I haven't slept much, and try as she may to hide it by keeping her back to me, I know Jackie hasn't either. This is how connected we are. From when we were kids until this day, if I'm wide awake staring at the shadows on the ceiling, I know that Jackie is lying on her side watching the headlights of passing cars flash across the wall.

Even when I came out to her, and we didn't speak for two weeks. We were fourteen and had snuck downtown to the Village. We were strolling around Astor Place and came upon the Hetrick-Martin Institute, where there's a high school for queer kids. In front of the building stood a group of girls, most of them sporting baggy jeans, short hair in bright colors, and an array of body jewelry. But there was one girl in that crowd who looked no different than the kind you might see in a hip-hop video. She had dark hair that flowed down her back, flawless makeup, and long, polished nails. Jackie noticed her and whispered in my ear, "Look, Hazel. That's the gay school. But see that girl with the Baby Phat T-shirt and the matching Tims? She's, like, a black version of you."

Without a second thought, I said, "She could be me."

Jackie slowed down. "What do you mean by that?" I quickly recognized that I had gotten too comfortable and transparent. I said nothing, but Jackie pressed, "You're not gay! I mean, you like guys, don't you?"

This moment had crept up on me, and the time to protest convincingly had expired. It always flashes by in these instances, and the irony of that never ceases to amaze me. Silence is supposed to be a shield for those in the closet, and yet in those moments when one's sexuality is questioned without warning, mere seconds of silence can prove so telling as to be quite damning. It exposes the very thing you wish to hide. I recognized this at a young age, so I chose to be as honest with Jackie as I had been to myself at that point. "Sometimes."

Now Jackie completely stopped walking. "Sometimes what? Sometimes you like a guy when there's a guy worth liking? Or sometimes you like a guy when you're not, like, checking out other girls?"

"Both, okay!" I yelled. And because I wanted blood, I said. "But not you, so don't worry about it."

Funny how we still went home together, even if in total silence. We headed to the Astor Place station, took the hour-long ride to the Bronx, and walked the three blocks from our neighborhood station without ever separating or saying a single word to each other. Jackie went to her apartment, and I went to mine. I tossed and turned all night, and I know she did, too. I had nightmares about Jackie leading the taunts at school once she divulged my secret to everyone, and I imagined that she had nightmares that someone would catch me making a pass at her and spread the rumor that she was gay, too.

For two weeks we didn't speak to one another, but when classmates noticed and asked what had happened between us, neither of us revealed the truth. I'd say to the girls, "We had a fight, that's all," and Jackie would tell them, "Mind your fuckin' business." After the first week, Jackie appeared at my window. I let her into my room but made her do all the talking. She came prepared with a long speech, apologizing for her reaction to my news. "You gotta understand, Hazel . . . I've got enough problems without people thinking I'm like you. I mean, in that way. But it's not your fault that people are stupid, and I'm just sorry that I got caught up in their stupidity. I shouldn't have done that, especially since I kinda know what it feels like." I immediately forgave Jackie, but I didn't let her know it. I held out for another week, and she proved her sincerity, going to and from school with me, inviting me over to do homework, and eventually punching Whatsername in the mouth for calling me a stuck-up bitch because for the third time I said I couldn't go shopping on Fordham Road with her one Saturday. That particular weekend my *abuelita* was taking me upstate to visit my father, and I didn't want anyone to know that he was in prison. To this day, Jackie swears that fight wasn't the reason she got kicked out of Scanlan, but I know it is and still feel guilty about it.

Lourdes snores ever so lightly, and I wonder if Jackie's plotting to throw it in her ladylike face at the opportune moment. Irena fidgets, probably more from unresolved tension than the sound of Lourdes's snoozing. I'm glad someone is getting some sleep, and I hope Lourdes is getting enough for all of us. She may have to do more driving than she anticipated.

At about half past eight in the morning, I slip out of the bed. As I make my way to the bathroom, I hear Jackie rolling over into another position. I look over my shoulder, and once again she has her back to me. I wait to see if she will look over her shoulder at me, but Jackie just exhales and falls still. I guess we can forget about hitting the road at nine A.M. sharp today.

I tiptoe into the bathroom, feeling the cold tile beneath the balls of my feet. I close the door quietly, unbutton my nightshirt, and hang it on a hook behind the door. On the next hook hangs Lourdes's cosmetic bag, and I spot a bottle that looks familiar, so I take it out. It's an opened yet unused bottle of semipermanent hair color called Scarlet Radiance. Lourdes brought it along when I told her that I hoped one night we would have an old-fashioned slumber party and do each other's hair and nails. We probably would have been doing this last night if not for what happened at the carnival. No, if not for what happened *after* the carnival.

Before I can stop myself, I take the bottle and set it on the counter. Then I rummage through Irena's bag, hoping to find the box where we put our offerings during the ritual at the timeline. When I don't find it, I open the bathroom door and peek into the room. Everyone remains asleep. I scan the room for Irena's bag and spot it sitting at the foot of her bed. I hope no one catches me going through Irena's things wearing nothing but my panties. I find the little box, open it, and take out the styling shears that Geneva gave me as a graduation present and sneak back into the bathroom. I yank a towel off the rack and fill the sink with water.

I can never seem to stop at just changing my hair color or trimming my ends. It's always all or nothing. Before I know it, my hair that once hung right below my shoulders—honey blond, courtesy of Clairol's newest line—is all over the towel around my shoulders and on the bathroom floor. Seconds later I climb into the shower and dye my hair, which now barely grazes the place where my neck and shoulders meet.

And even though I have yet to put on my clothes, I make up my face with a detail I've neglected throughout the trip. Since we left New York, I've been content to throw on some sunscreen, put on one coat of mascara, and apply a nude colored lip gloss. But now I go the distance, applying concealer followed by foundation and powder.

I tweeze my already sparse eyebrows until I barely have any. As I do this, I chuckle because I remember the time Jackie and I went to see *Anaconda.* She keeps leaning over and whispering to me, "Something's wrong with Jennifer Lopez." I hush her because not only is she annoying everyone in the theater, she's dead wrong because La Lopez is nothing short of perfect. Jackie mutters, "I haven't figured it out, but something about her is off." I nudge Jackie with my elbow then put my finger to her lips. She broods but quiets down. Then just as Jennifer-as-Terri sets sail with her film crew down the river into the Amazon jungle, Jackie jolts forward in her seat, pointing at Jennifer and yelling, "She's got no eyebrows! Look at her, Hazel. I told you something was wrong with Jennifer. She's got no damned eyebrows." Someone in the back yells at her to shut the fuck up, and I fear this is the beginning of the end for Jackie and me. Instead she turns around and says, "Am I right though?" A brother to the left says, "Shit, she right, dawg!" And everyone takes a closer look at Jennifer. Slowly, everyone in the theater bursts out laughing, especially the kids who are too young to be watching a PG-13 movie.

After I tweeze my eyebrows, I fill them in with a dark pencil. Then I outline my lips with an equally dark liner and fill them in with an eggplant shade that I would tell any of my customers is much too dark for daytime, especially during the summer. When I change my look, I go by instinct. I can never seem to follow the rules when it comes to my own appearance. I don't know what leads me to a certain color even if it's last year's shade or, by all expert opinion, is wrong for me. Somehow I learned early on that I can feel satisfied with the results only if I follow my gut even when it rubs up against the codes of fashion.

But when I finish this makeover, I still feel an ache in my chest. I search my reflection for mistakes, but I find no feathers of lipstick or clumps of mascara. As usual, my application is flawless. For the first time in ages, the perfect results leave me empty. My only consolation is that it *is* perfect . . . even if I do look like Milla Jovovich in *Resident Evil.* Milla's a pretty girl. But her look's not mine.

Not up to removing the makeup and stuck with the hair color for at least six weeks, I open the bathroom door. Lourdes and Irena still sleep, but Jackie's up. She sits cross-legged above the covers with her fist pressed against her cheeks. Her head snaps back at my new look, but she says nothing about it.

"You want to go get some breakfast?" I ask.

"Okay."

She climbs out of the bed, grabs some clothes, and heads into the bathroom. While she showers, I fix the bed even though I know housekeeping would have done it, just to give myself something to do. I look through the visitor's guide on the desk to find some motel stationery so I can write a note to Lourdes and Irena. As I search, I learn that the motel offers a free continental breakfast but decide to keep that to myself. I prop the note against the alarm clock then I go outside for a smoke.

A few minutes later Jackie comes out of the room, and I follow her toward the car. "When's checkout time again?"

"Eleven." She glances at her watch. "We've got a little over an hour."

"Let's just stop at the first little diner we see."

"Yeah."

We get in the car, and Jackie puts on the radio and searches for a station. She hears "Star 102.5" and settles there. I almost laugh when the DJ introduces the latest from Green Day because I know with a name like "Star," Jackie was expecting to hear R&B. To my surprise, she doesn't change the channel. Not that it matters because seconds later, she spots a diner called Drake, which I guess is named for the nearby university.

The decor of the '50s-style diner is black and chrome beneath dim lighting. Jackie and I take a booth and look over our menus. I stick to the breakfast special, but Jackie opts for a portabella mushroom sandwich off the "Good for You" section. The waitress leaves, and we sit there in more silence, and I grow nervous. And the nervousness makes me nervous! Jackie and I are so close that I can't remember the last time we ever shared an awkward silence. Did we ever do awkward silences? This is not us.

So I say what is in my heart because that is us. "I don't know, Jackie. On the one hand, I still feel I was right to call out that you didn't speak up last night at the carnival. On the other hand, I totally heard what you said back at the motel. I don't know what that's about. I guess I have to think on it some more." I know Jackie has her theories, and I brace myself for an interruption, but she just makes tiny rips in her napkin as I speak. "I don't know," I say again. "I'm going to ask Irena to do some co-counseling with me, help me figure it out."

Jackie crumples the napkin and snickers. "You don't need to do any fuckin' co-counseling with Irena, Haze. We've been friends since junior high and know each other probably better than we know ourselves."

"So?"

"So what?"

"What happened last night?"

"What happened last night is that we both fucked up. I went too far, you didn't go far enough—" She stops to correct herself. "No, you went too far with the flirting, I went too far with . . ." Jackie flusters again. "Whatever. It doesn't matter."

"It doesn't?" I don't know whether to be bothered or relieved.

I would like nothing more than to put last night behind us, and a part of me cheers that she thinks it's as simple as doing just that. But a small part of me feels there's so much more to it, and as scared as I am to bring it to light, I'm even more afraid to let it lie, fester, and explode later without warning.

"No, it doesn't, because it's not the first time, and it won't be the last time." Before I can ask what she means exactly, Jackie barrels on. "What matters is that we get through it. Last night ain't shit compared to what you and I have been through together." Jackie starts to count the experiences as she rattles them off her memory. "My mom's running off, your dating my brother, your grandmother's passing . . ." I want her to stop. I know she just wants to list all the major life changes we've weathered together, but not only do I not want to think of those painful things, I hate the fact that most of the dramas she describes are mine. Jackie laughs, then says, "Hazel, if we can handle the *telenovela* episodes that life scripts for us, no way we can't deal with the stupid little things we do or don't do on any given day. All that matters is that—major drama or little snit—we stay girls."

I want that very much. I want more than that. And yet I still feel that for the first time in our lives, we're drifting apart rather than closer together.

"Eat, ma," Jackie says, pointing at my eggs and fries. "We don't have a lot of time."

Bad enough Jackie and Hazel take off somewhere without us, but Lourdes is getting on my final nerve. She sleeps through the night like a baby as if nothing has happened. Then the first thing out of her mouth when she gets out of bed is, "*¡Ay, Dios mío!* Is it too much to ask to get into the bathroom before Hazel starts her skin care regimen?" That's so not the damned question! Hazel's not even here.

"We have to check out by eleven," I say. "Maybe we should just start packing everyone's stuff."

She wrinkles her nose at me like I farted. "You mean Jackie and Hazel's things, too?"

"Yeah, because we don't know where they are or if they're going to get back here in time." I grab the pajama pants and T-shirt Jackie wears to sleep and quickly fold it and carry it to her open bag on the floor. "If come eleven o'clock, they're not here, we'll just take our stuff into the lobby so management knows we're leaving soon and wait for Jackie and Hazel there. Hopefully, they won't charge us for another night." I stuff Jackie's bedclothes into her bag and then reach for Hazel's nightshirt.

"I don't know how I feel about going through their things," says Lourdes. "I mean, I wouldn't like it if someone touched my things, even to help me pack."

You need help packing because you have so much goddamned

stuff! I want to snap. *You brought more shit than the rest of us put together.* But I let my actions do the talking. I walk into the bathroom and collect all our things except hers, of course, because *Dios* forbid or however you would say that in Spanish, anyone touch Lourdes's precious gadgets and expensive cosmetics. When I walk out the bathroom, she's splayed over the bed like Cleopatra on a chaise watching some priest on television. "*Mira, Irena,* they have Padre Albert in Iowa!"

"Who?"

"He's this wonderful priest." Despite myself I look at the television and this fairly young priest with a big smile and blue eyes counsels a mother and her teenager. "*Y cubano como tú,*" Lourdes adds. Oh, then I'll just race to the nearest church, won't I? And then she says, "Okay, I know I'm not supposed to say this, but he's sooo cute!"

"Yuck!" Just because I was never raised Catholic doesn't mean I think it's cool to harbor crushes on a priest. Scandalous enough that Lourdes finds him attractive, but she expresses it, too?

"*¡Qué gracioso!*"

I don't know what she means nor do I really care. My mind is on the tightening in my chest and the alarm clock, which reads 10:53. I reach into my pocketbook for that dreaded inhaler and take a hit of medication. As much as I hate this contraption, I'm glad that Jackie insisted that I bring it. And that reminds me that Lourdes might have a way to find them. "Can't you use your fancy GPF phone to find out where they are?"

"That's GPS, and I'm not Sydney Bristow, Irena. First of all, the telephone is here. Second, we would need—"

"If they don't get here in seven minutes, the motel's going to charge us for another night, and I just can't afford to spend any more than—"

"*Irena, cálmate, por favor.*" And then she reaches for her pocketbook. I expect her to take out her super phone but instead she pulls out her wallet.

"So help me, Lourdes, if you offer to pay, I'm going to smack you!"

"Excuse me?"

"I'm sorry. I didn't mean to say that. What I meant to say was could you please, please, please stop throwing your damned money around all the time!"

Lourdes pops up like a toy. "I do no such thing! I share it because I have it."

"And constantly remind the rest of us that we don't."

That second Jackie bursts into the room. "Hazel and I have breakfast for you two in the car." She stoops down and grabs as many bags as she can carry. "Let's go. We have to check out of here right now." She backs out the door, leaving it wide open.

I start to snatch up bags while Lourdes just stands there with her hands on her hips. "So is it that you're jealous of my wealth, Irena, or my generosity?"

I have to stop and respond to this ridiculousness. Dropping the bags at my feet, I look Lourdes in the eye. "Generosity? Try guilt. Why don'tcha just write a big ol' check to MALDEF or the National Council of Las Raices or whatever the hell it's called. Just get it out of your fuckin' system instead of spoiling the rest of us ad nauseum!"

"How dare you! Where do you come off—?"

"No, where do *you*—?"

From the parking lot, Jackie hollers, "Let's go *now*!"

Lourdes finally runs into the bathroom to finish the packing that she should have done first thing this morning. I take as many bags as I can and leave the rest for her. I waddle out on the balcony in time to bump into Hazel. When did she do that to her hair? "Let me get a few of those," she says. She slides two bags off my shoulder and takes another out of my hand and races back to the car. As I start to follow her, Lourdes appears behind me, lugging mostly her own shit. She says, "Look, Irena, if my offers make you uncomfortable—"

I stopped in my tracks and spun around. "Go 'head, say it. Pay you back. That's what you were going to say, right?"

"Don't put words in my mouth."

"How can I do that when there's no room with the platinum spoon ya got in there?" I hear Jackie chuckling at my zinger, and the adrenaline pumps through my veins. "That's what you want,

Lourdes? You got it! I'll repay every damned cent of my share of everything you've paid for. Ever!" From the corner of my eye, I see Jackie making her way up the staircase toward us. Knowing how much Lourdes hates strong language, I yell, "Every last fuckin' penny, I swear to God!"

Lourdes's light copper skin takes on a red undertone. "Fine."

"Fine." She tries to walk around me, but I block her path. "Irena, either keep walking or let me pass."

"*¡Ay, qué santita!*" Jackie always told me that I knew more Spanish than I thought, and that it'd probably take a moment of passion to prove it. "*Santa Lourdes la Virgen.*"

Lourdes jabs her finger in my face. "Don't you dare make fun of my faith!" Her nail is inches from my nose. I've gone too far, and she's about to go Crusades on my skinny ass.

"Enough, you two." Jackie grabs me by the shoulders, spins me around, and gives me a light shove toward the steps. I make sure she's between Lourdes and me before I turn my back because I genuinely fear that Lourdes might heave one of those designer handbags at my head. The last thing my underinsured behind needs is to fall down these motel steps and wind up in a hospital two thousand miles from home. The image of me in a hospital bed flashes before my eyes, and I freeze with panic. Hazel comes toward me. "Irena? Irena, are you all right."

My chest tightens, and I grip the banister. Now Jackie asks, "Rena, you okay?" I nod even though the terror courses through me. After all that has happened, I have to keep this to myself even though this is the most literal image I have ever seen. Why can't I see, like, lotto numbers?

I slowly make my way to the ground, reach into my pocketbook, and take another hit from my inhaler. "Shit, Irena!" Jackie picks up the bags I lay down. "I'll take these. You just get in the car."

"I'm okay." The fear begins to fade, and I inhale deeply. Once I realize that I can take deep breaths with no problem, I say, "Let's just get the hell out of here."

LOURDES

Kum and Go Gas Station

Des Moines, IA

Monday, June 19, 11:12 A.M.

When Jackie suggests that Hazel stop for gas, I know my chance is coming. If I had installed the GPS kit for my telephone, I would have whipped it out and told Hazel exactly where to find the nearest gas station. Since I can't do that, I make a to-do of calling home to check my messages, swinging my arm to the side toward Irena, and using my thumb to dial the number with slow and deliberate punches. Irena sniffs and turns her head to look out the window. So I make sure she hears me as I recite my voice mail number in Spanish.

I finish the area code when Jackie turns to look at me. "Lou?"

"*¿Qué?*"

She mouths *Grow up.* I give her a dirty look, but I stop dialing aloud. At least Irena didn't hear her.

After I finish dialing my number and password, I put my phone to my ear and wait. *You have three new messages.* The first is just a click—probably one of those telemarketing firms that use computers to dial. *¡Qué agravante!* But it's one of the occupational hazards of being a fashion bug. When you have all the charge cards and shop on the Internet as much as I do, you wind up on too many lists. I vow to buy myself a TeleZapper and erase the message.

The second message is from my bank. Because of the unusual number of out-of-state charges, the security department asks me to call them to confirm that all the charges I made since I left New York are authorized. I hit SAVE and continue to my third new message.

"Lourdes, llámame." I thank God that I had the foresight to revert back to my original greeting. As I packed for the trip, I had changed my outgoing message so that callers would know that I would be away for two weeks. But then I thought what if Mamá called me at the apartment while I was away, so I rerecorded my initial greeting. *"Es tu madre."* As if I wouldn't recognize her voice. *"I'm worried that I haven't heard from you. I want to know how the program is going. Surely, you can find a minute to call home and let me know that you're fine."*

I debate whether I should call. My mother's voice makes me homesick. So many times I sit alone in that big apartment, and I wonder if my entire family would move to New York City. Even Valería because she's family, too. I know it would never happen, and on most days, *qué tremendo alivio!*

I can't call home. Not just yet. We're too close to Colorado. My mother will interrogate me, and although I have had much practice evading her at home, lying to her while on the move is not something I think I can pull off. I play the entire conversation in my mind. Whether she grows suspicious or not, she'll ask questions until she corners me into an inconsistency. I'll confess that I'm on the road with my girlfriends, and she'll erupt like Dostero. Mamá may even force me to come home.

As I make my decision, Hazel pulls into a gas station. I turn off the phone, drop it into my pocketbook, and reach for my wallet. "Gas is on me." From the corner of my eye, I catch Irena mimicking me like a brat. *¡Malcriada!*

"It's better for you to pay inside rather than at the pump, Lou," says Jackie. "Even if you only buy twenty bucks' worth of gas, sometimes they authorize twice as much. Especially at these gas stations with lots of truck traffic." Hazel walks with me toward the cashier.

"*¿De veras?*" I ask Hazel, and she nods. "Why?"

"To prevent fraud," she says. "People using stolen credit cards to buy gas. Nobody's at the pump to check IDs or anything."

"Oh." Then Hazel looks over her shoulder, and I follow her gaze to the vending machines. I'm about to compliment her on her new look, but I get the feeling she'd rather that I ignore it. Jackie drops coins into a soda machine as Irena runs off at the mouth. Probably filling her in on our fight at the motel and making me out to be the villain. "*Chismosa.*"

"Like you're not dying to tell me your side of the story." We enter the convenience store. "So what happened?"

"*Ay, yo no sé. Ella se levantó muy agitada,* and the next thing I know, she's accusing me of flaunting my money just because I offer to pay for things." I search my pocketbook for my wallet and pull out my credit card. "Fill it up on pump four." I hand the clerk my card and turn back to Hazel.

"Accept it, Lou. Your homegirl's a closet socialist."

"She is not."

"She sure is. Just like Jackie except she'll tell anyone in a heartbeat there's no such thing as a free market. It's up to you and me to restore their faith in capitalism's ability to correct itself."

I hush Hazel. Even though she and I are with the majority on this particular issue, I don't want us to be overheard using any words that end in *ism* in this part of the country. These debates are perfect and safe for the Tempo, but not in public. "I don't have to do anything." I reach for the pen on the counter and wait for the clerk to return my card with the receipt.

Hazel rolls her eyes at me but lowers her voice, *gracias a Dios.* "What're you gonna do? Pretend the last two years never happened? Ignore Irena for the rest of the trip."

"She owes me an apology."

"Okay, but you owe her one, too."

"Why?"

"Because, Lourdes, even though you mean well . . ."

"What?"

"You do throw your money around."

Before I can challenge her to prove her accusation, the clerk says to me, "Miss, your card has been declined."

I think nothing of it. Sometimes I use it so much, the strip grows worn. "Try it again."

"I've already tried it twice. Do you have another card?"

Dios perdóname, but I snatch the card from her. As soon as I do, I apologize both for the mishap with the card and my rudeness. I hand her another credit card, and Hazel and I wait for it to process. This one is almost at its limit, but I should have enough to cover the gas. Three other drivers wait behind me, and my stomach sinks as the clerk wipes my new card with a concerned frown.

"I'm sorry, miss. Same problem. Would you like to pay another way?" She hands me back the useless card.

I stand there with my jaw on the floor, unable to speak. Hazel steps in front of me with her wallet open. "We'll pay cash."

Remembering my telephone messages helps me recover my voice. Because they didn't hear from me, my credit card company must have put a hold on my card. They did it for my own protection. There's no reason for me to be embarrassed, I tell myself. The only mistake I made was not to check my messages earlier and call my credit card company sooner. With all that had just occurred, who could blame me? "May I have my card back, please?"

"I'm sorry, miss, I've been directed to confiscate the card."

"But I can prove it's my card." I scurry through my wallet for my driver's license and hold it up to her. "See?"

She barely glances at my license. "Even so, miss, I can't give you back the card." She looks over my head at the lanky male driver behind me. "May I help the next customer?"

But as he tries to walk around me, I block his path. "Excuse me, but you're not finished serving me."

The entire line behind me groans like a symphony of walruses, and the clerk blinks nervously at me. "We're all squared away, miss. Your friend paid for the gas with cash."

"I know that. I saw that. I'm not blind."

Hazel grabs my arm. "Lourdes, let it go."

"I will not let it go. She has my credit card. I don't want to leave it here." I shake myself free from Hazel's grasp.

"You obviously can't use it, so—"

"One call to my credit company can clear up this whole thing."

"Okay, let's do it outside." Hazel takes my hand and pulls me out of the store.

As I punch keys and wait for a human, Jackie comes toward me. Holding two cans of soda in her hand, Irena climbs into the backseat of the car.

"What's going on?"

Hazel puts a finger to her lips. I want to walk away from them, but as much as I don't want any more witnesses to this nightmare, I stay put. I have nothing to hide. Nothing to be ashamed of. Finally, a customer service representative named Matt gets on the line. I give him my name and card number.

Jackie shakes her head in disbelief. "I don't know my card number by heart. That's how little I use it. Until graduation came, and I had to max it out."

"Me, too," says Hazel.

I hush them. Matt asks for my mother's maiden name. "Fernandez."

"I see here that a hold has been put on your card, Mrs. Becerra."

"That's Miss Becerra."

"I'm sorry. Miss Becerra."

"I've been traveling across the country and using my credit card. All those unusual charges you see are definitely mine."

"Okay, but just to be on the safe side, we like to go through each and every one to be sure that all of them are authorized."

Matt's voice is so soothing, and he has an endearing twang. With every word, I regain confidence in my ability to correct the situation. I'd rather not stand in the gas station and go through every single transaction, but it seems like I have no choice. "If you insist, Matt." I smile at Hazel and Jackie and motion for them to follow me. They shrug at each other and, for some unknown reason, they shake hands and join me as I head to the car. I get into the backseat, where Irena is scribbling in her journal so fast, she just might set the page on fire. Hazel and Jackie get into the car, and Hazel pulls away from the pump and parks off to the side.

"Your security is very important to us, Miss Becerra, so if you could bear with me, we'll verify all the charges and release that hold on your card, okay?"

"Wonderful."

"Let me just pull up the appropriate screen . . ."

Irena picks her head out of her book. "What are we waiting for?"

"When Lourdes resolves this, she's gotta go back in and get her card back from the clerk," says Hazel.

"They took her card away?" Jackie asks. "That's not good."

"Why would they take her card away?"

"That's what she's trying to figure out. Will y'all be patient, please?"

Matt returns to the line. "Miss Becerra, according to the notes on your account, we did not put a hold on it."

"But I just received a message saying to call this number, and it said that if you did not hear from me to verify that all the recent charges are legitimate, you would put a restriction on the card. Now I just attempted to pay for gas in Des Moines, and not only was my card declined—"

"Yes, if we had not heard from you within forty-eight hours of placing that call, we were absolutely going to put a restriction on your card. But we never did that because—"

"But my card was confiscated!" Irena has been avoiding me ever since we checked out of the motel, but now she cannot take her eyes off of me. Sitting in the car, I have no way to escape her gaze. No matter where I turn, there are two pairs of inquisitive eyes boring into me. Even when I look out of my window, I know Jackie can see me through the side mirror.

"Your card was confiscated, Miss Becerra, because it was reported stolen."

"Stolen? But I had it in my possession until a moment ago. Who would . . ." And then it hit me before Matt could even answer. I had used that card so much in the past two years, I'd completely forgotten that it wasn't really mine.

"Your mother reported the card stolen, and since she is the primary cardholder—"

I hang up on him, then blubber the next four words as if each cost me a thousand dollars. "I . . . have . . . no . . . money."

"Honey, don't cry," Hazel says.

"But I have no money!" I know my mother has cut off the other card, too.

"Hey, enough of that now," says Jackie. "You're going to make yourself sick, and we can't afford that, so knock it off." Then she crosses her eyes at me.

A short laugh sneaks out of me followed by a torrent of tears. They're going to ask me how this happened, and I'll have to confess that my mother has no idea that I'm on this trip at all. That will be far more embarrassing than getting caught fifteen hundred miles from home without a cent to my name.

"Aw, Lou, don't get like that," Jackie says. "You've always had our backs, so now we have yours. For real, stop crying. It's okay. We got you. We'll figure it out somehow."

Something cold presses against my thigh, making me flinch. Irena offers me one of the sodas she bought from the vending machine. I finally look into her face, and finally she's looking into mine, and I see tears pool in her eyes. "It's my fault. You paid for all that food that I was supposed to get us from Dad's bodega. I'm sorry."

This is not her fault, but I appreciate her gesture. I take the soda from her. "Me, too. And whatever you guys put out for me during the trip, I'll pay back as soon as we get back to New York."

"Don't worry about it," Hazel says.

Jackie agrees. "If we watch where we eat, we should be fine."

Then Irena sucks her teeth. "I want interest." She raises her soda can as if she were Groucho Marx twiddling his cigar. "Lots and lots of interest."

What is something normal that, if you did it, would shock everyone who knows you? I guess for me it would be to become an atheist.—LB

That's easy. Smoke. I'd scarf down a hamburger before I pick up a cigarette.—IR

Irena, you mean something besides pot, right? ☺ I'd have to say have kids. I can totally see myself getting married (it'd have to be to a woman though). But with the role model I've had, I'd be scared to death of becoming a mother.—CHF

Hazel, you took my answer and you need to stop frontin'! You don't want to have kids, because you're too vain to get pregnant, LOL. For me, getting married AND having kids would shock the hell out of everyone I know. Myself most of all.—JA

JACKIE

Interstate 80

Omaha, NE

Monday, June 19, 1:33 P.M.

Irena's at it again. The closer we get to Frisco, the more time she spends in that notebook of hers. That in and of itself doesn't bug me. It's when she pulls out those stupid tarot cards. She shuffles them, lays them across the backseat, and then records whatever she thinks they "say" into her notebook.

Lourdes hates it, too, but not for the same reason I do. She's on some second-commandment shit. Probably believes that reading tarot cards is a way of communicating with the dead or evoking the devil or some crazy shit. I don't believe that; that's not why it bothers me. The cards bug me because they're a crutch. It's dangerous for Irena to think that she can somehow predict the future with those things. That they can somehow help her foresee and change and otherwise control her fate.

But I know Irena's got more in her. The way she went off on Lourdes? I'm so damn proud of her. Probably been holding that back for the entire two years they've known each other. I bet all those things she told Lourdes back at the motel, she's vented in that journal time and again, but it did squat to dissipate her feelings. I never understood how writing in a journal helped a person quell demons. Isn't journaling about safekeeping? All you're doing is wallowing in all that negativity, storing it for prosperity or whatever. Best way to deal with funk is to air it out your system, not stash it away.

"You've been writing in that thing for over an hour," I say. "What are you going on and on about?"

Lourdes sniffles as if she detects the odor of Satan himself. "She's doing a travel forecast."

"A what?"

"Leave her alone, Jackie," says Hazel.

"All I'm doing is asking Irena what she's up to. Making conversation. If it's all that private, she just has to tell me to mind my own business." She really should be talking to us instead of squirreling away all her thoughts and feelings into that stupid notebook.

Irena hesitates, which tells me I'm going to love this shit. "Well, we've been experiencing so many issues along the way, I started wondering why. Is it our own compatibility? The places we're stopping? The route we're taking? And it's taking me so long to map it all out 'cause I have to take into account for four astrological signs, I didn't bring my ephemeris . . ."

Oh, yeah, I'm loving this shit. "You didn't bring your ephemer-what?"

"Ephemeris. It's a table that tells you the location of celestial bodies on . . ." Irena's voice trails.

The look on my face must be giving me away, but I'm not quite ready to quit feigning interest. I like to be informed before I dish out tough love. Otherwise, it's just abuse perpetrated for its own sake, and I'm really not helping her. "And just how is this map or forecast or whatever supposed to help us?"

"I figure if we can improve our compatibility by getting off this interstate, maybe take the back roads—"

"Wait, wait, wait," I interrupt her. The girl's trying to introduce her astrological mumbo jumbo into the itinerary that it took me hours to research. She's complaining about juggling four different zodiac signs and not having an ephemerwhatever when I had to figure out how many hours we realistically could make each day, by which days we should be in what city, where were the best places to stop for the night and things like that all within a budget and under a deadline! If Irena wants us to get along better and stop running into drama, all we have to do is stick to my plan *y ya*! I take a deep breath and say, "Irena, we can't get off I-80. This is the most efficient way to Frisco, and we have some time to make up because we didn't leave Des Moines until after eleven."

"I know, Jackie." Irena's hand jitters as she speaks. "It's just I'm starting to feel that the trip there's just as important as the conference. Maybe even more so, given all that's been happening to us."

"Ay, y ésta es una autopista muy fea."

I shoot Lourdes a look. I didn't build the freakin' I-80, so it's not my fault it isn't the most picturesque of highways. "Hazel, slow the hell down. I didn't say that for you to speed up."

"You of all people—"

"I'm serious. We're in Middle America now and can't afford to take any chances. Some Midwestern state trooper would just love to ambush a bunch of brown girls with New York plates."

"Could've stayed in Jersey for that," says Hazel. "Seriously, Jackie, you've been watching too many bad road trip movies. How the hell's some cop gonna ambush us out here? There's no place for him to hide."

"Are you sure about that?" I turn to Irena. "What do the stars have in store for me today? Is, like, Mars passing through my third house and shielding me from becoming a victim of racial profiling?"

Lourdes laughs and offers me a high-five, but Hazel says, "*Deja esa nena ya.* We've been driving for almost three hours, so next chance I get, I'm pulling off to the side so we can have lunch. We all need to get out of this car for a while."

Irena consults her notebook. "No, let's wait until the next major exit."

Lourdes pleads to God under her breath, and I give Hazel a *you see!* look. The girl's out of control with that shit, and we just keep indulging her. No more.

"Let's stop here right now."

"Jackie, we're practically in Omaha," says Hazel. "We'll stop when we get there, and then Irena can take over the wheel."

"No, Hazel, you were right. We have to make up time, and this is our chance to do it. Let's just stop now, make some sandwiches, and push through. Let's see if we can make it to Denver by tonight."

"Denver's at least nine hours from here, and it's almost two o'clock," Lourdes says. "We have to stop for the night way before Denver and push through Colorado tomorrow."

I'm beginning to suspect that nothing would please Lourdes more than if the entire state of Colorado disappeared off the map, but dealing with Irena is more important to me right now than dredging up whatever the hell she's hiding. One thing at a time. "We'll worry about that after we break. Hazel, pull over."

HAZEL

Interstate 80

Omaha, NE

Monday, June 19, 1:47 P.M.

When we came back from Drake's to find those two going at each other in the motel room, Jackie was thrilled. I told her that perhaps we were rubbing off on them too much, and she said, "Lou needed to be called out on that shit even if she does mean well. And Irena's finally standing up for herself." Then they regressed into kindergartners, and Jackie and I had to tag-team them. We shook on it and got to work, and all was cool. But ever since we left Des Moines, Jackie's been fixing for an opportunity to nudge Irena into this dance with anger. She won't be satisfied until the girl explodes. A part of me would love to see her scream at the top of her lungs or punch someone out. I just prefer it not be anyone on this trip!

But if Irena must go there, best she does so with Jackie.

Lourdes helps me lay out a blanket and unpack the cooler while Jackie pulls Irena aside to talk to her. We chitchat about how hot and dry it is, but we both have our eyes on them. Irena clutches her journal to her chest as if it were the Holy Grail while Jackie waves her arms every which way. Suddenly, Jackie latches on to the notebook. Although Irena resists, Jackie's much stronger than she is, and with little struggle, she wrestles the book away from her. I leap to my feet and head over there, Lourdes at my side.

"All I'm saying is you need to give this supernatural *porquería* a rest," Jackie says. She holds Irena's notebook above her head.

"*¡Ay, sí!*" Lourdes chimes in.

"Fine, I won't bring it up anymore," Irena says. "How 'bout we compromise? Let's do a healing circle right now, and I promise I won't bring it up for the rest of the trip."

"Aren't you fuckin' listening to me? I'm so sick of this New Age *mierda*!"

"Okay, Jackie, I heard you. Give me back my journal." Irena grasps at it, but Jackie pulls it out of her reach. "You have your tools, I have mine."

"Tool? Did you just call this a tool? Irena, this is a crutch."

Irena lunges repeatedly for her notebook, but Jackie has six inches on her. It'd be comical if it weren't so ugly. Lourdes agrees with me because she says, "Jackie, give Irena back her book. This isn't funny."

"You're damn right this is not funny." Jackie flings the book several yards away from her into the grass. Not hard enough to damage the notebook or any of the keepsakes Irena has wedged inside of it to fall out. When Irena moves toward it, Jackie steps in front of her and blocks her path. Irena shifts to her left, then her right, but Jackie thwarts her at every turn.

"You narrow-minded bully!" screams Irena. Whoa! She's never lashed out at Jackie like that. Not just because she doesn't dare, but because she idolizes her so much.

I think Jackie's about to read her when instead she lights up as if Irena's surge of anger pumped electricity into her. "That's it, Irena!" she yells. She looks to Lourdes and me and says, "That's what I'm talking about." Jackie turns back to Irena and coaches her. "Stop being a victim, Irena, and stand up for yourself. Get tough."

It is exciting seeing Irena defend herself, so I get into it. "That's right, *nena*," I say. "Tell 'er about herself." But Lourdes just stands there, gripping her crucifix and mumbling what I'm sure is a prayer that I could recite along with her if I cared to listen to the words.

"I am tough!" yells Irena. "I couldn't be an activist if I weren't. I couldn't be a healer if I weren't tough. You think I could go into that center every day hearing one story of abuse and violence after the other if I weren't fuckin' tough?"

Jackie throws her arms in the air in an exaggerated shrug. "So fuckin' what?" I get what she's trying to do. At least, I think I do. "These women go to you and practically slit their wrists in front of you. Why would they do that? Why go to you? What makes you so special?" Jackie grabs Irena by the shoulders and gives her a shake. "You're just a scrawny college sophomore, so what qualifies you to listen to all those horror stories day in and day out and be of any fuckin' use to those women?" Irena shakes loose from Jackie's grip, and Jackie sees this and gets a crazed look in her eyes. "Don't fuckin' shrug me off."

"Leave me be, Jackie, please." Irena uses the back of her hand to wipe her runny nose.

"All that psycho babble about talking things out and processing issues and all that? It doesn't mean shit, Irena. You don't need to talk. What you need is to kick some ass, and get all that anger out." Jackie grabs Irena's hands, balls them into fists, and positions her hands in the air.

"This oughta be good," I say.

Lourdes says, "What're you doing?"

"Shut up, Lou. I know what I'm doing." Jackie gets into Irena's face. "Hit me, Rena. You pretend I'm that bastard, and you just go off!"

Irena drops her hands. "Jackie, please. This isn't my way." Jackie snatches her hands and lifts them up again. Irena struggles, flopping around like a rag doll.

"But it was his way, wasn't it, Irena?" Jackie screams into her face. "That's the whole fuckin' world's way. You want to stop being a goddamn victim? Throw your hands up!" Irena maintains her hands in the air but starts to sputter.

"Clock her good, Irena," I say.

Every once in a while, Jackie does turn that tough love on herself, and it can be more extreme than anything she might dish out for someone else. Irena and Lourdes probably don't know that, since she's not one to play masochist for an audience. Not even for me. I'm just acquainted with this side of her because I've known her for so long, and she can't hide from me if she even bothered to try. Jackie wants Irena to hit her not only to make Irena vent her suppressed anger but also to let Jackie endure some kind of punishment for any of her misdeeds on this trip.

I have to laugh. "Bitch deserves it, and she knows it. Pop her in the snout so we can have lunch and get back on the road."

"How can you find this funny?" Lourdes asks.

Her question offends me to no end. "How can you think for even a second that Jackie would actually hurt her?" The last thing Jackie wants to do is hurt Irena. She's doing this because she wants Irena to stop hurting.

"Why are you doing this to me?" Irena cries so hard that her little chest starts to heave.

"Because I know there's a fighter in that skinny little body of yours." Then Jackie does the last thing I ever thought she would do. She shoves Irena, her violent gesture betraying the tenderness in her voice. "Stop shackling her with that pseudo-spiritual-semi-psychological bullshit and let her out! Where the hell's Towanda?" Jackie shoves Irena again, and she stumbles backward. Irena clenches her fist. "That's it, girl. If you don't like it, make me stop."

"This is so barbaric," Lourdes says.

"Then you do something." The harshness in my voice surprises even me. "Otherwise, shut the hell up." Lourdes whirls around and storms back to the blanket. I turn back to Jackie and Irena. "That's not Jackie, Irena," I coach her. "That's every asshole who ever hurt a woman."

"No, I'm not." She shoves Irena so hard, she almost loses her balance. Jackie advances toward Irena, who curls her tiny white hands into pink fists even as she backs away from her. "I'm the son-of-bitch who hurt *her.* What are you going to do about it?"

She shoves Irena once more, and Irena bounds toward her. I shrink, too, hiding my face behind my raised arms as if Irena were coming at me. Lourdes is by my side again, clutching my arm and burying her face in my shoulder. I wait a few seconds for the hard crack of hand on flesh, but I hear nothing except a heartbreaking howl. When I drop my hands, I see Jackie standing over Irena, who has collapsed sobbing to her knees

"Did she hit you?"

"No."

"You didn't hit her, did you?"

"Of course not!" Jackie looks back at Irena, whose sobs consume her entire body. "Forget it, Irena. C'mon let's go."

With her head hung low in pain or shame, Irena tries to contain her sobbing and rise to her feet. She pitches her hands into the grass to steady herself, and her sobs turn into a dry cough. Just as Irena extends her hand for support, Jackie walks away from her back toward the car. I don't think she saw Irena's hand, and Irena assuming it would be there stumbled forward and back on the ground. Lourdes dashes to her, and I start to search for Irena's notebook.

Just as I find it, I look up to see Lourdes struggling to bring Irena to her feet as her coughs turn into heaves. "*Ay Dios mío*, I think she's having an asthma attack."

Irena nods, and I call for Jackie, who is halfway back to the car. "Get her inhaler!" Jackie runs to Irena's bag where she had left it beside our blanket on the ground. Unable to breathe, let alone speak, Irena shakes her head as she clings to Lourdes for support. "What's she trying to tell us?"

Lourdes attempts to translate. "You don't want the inhaler?" Irena shakes her head. "*¿Y qué hacemos?* Do you need us to take you to the doctor?" Irena nods, and it seems like the weight of her need weakens Lourdes's knees.

Jackie races back toward us. "Oh, my God, she's turning blue!"

Lourdes grabs her telephone and dials 9-1-1. "Where are we? What do I tell them?"

"There's no time for that." Before I know it, Jackie lifts Irena as if she were a firefighter and breaks into a run to the car.

Lourdes returns to her telephone. "I need to know where the nearest emergency room is near Omaha off Interstate-80. I don't know where we are exactly, just that we're practically in Omaha. No, we can't afford to wait until you get here, she's having an asthma attack!"

"Lourdes, just follow Jackie to the car," I say as I rush to pick up all our pocketbooks. "The sooner we get back on the interstate, the sooner we'll see a sign and can tell them where we are."

She nods once and runs back to the car. Juggling our pocketbooks and Irena's journal, I race toward the interstate, too. We have to leave everything else we've unpacked behind.

LOURDES

University of Nebraska
Medical Center
Omaha, NE
Monday, June 19, 3:56 P.M.

Hazel strokes my hair as I bury my face into her lap and cry. The words of Reverend Niemöller echo in my head. *First they came for the communists, and I didn't speak up because I wasn't a communist . . .* Although he was a Lutheran pastor who intially sided with Hitler, Reverend Niemöller has always been one of my heroes. Now the reverend's most famous saying haunts me. *Then they came for the Jews, and I didn't speak up because I wasn't a Jew . . .* How would I have felt if Jackie had snatched my rosary from me and refused to give it back? I should have stood up for Irena. I should have stopped Jackie. I should have forced Hazel to help me intervene. I should have done something.

Como si fuera una bruja, Hazel whispers in my ear, "There was nothing you could do, honey." I pull away from her, and she takes my chin in her hand. "None of this is your fault. We need you to calm down so you can help us figure out what to do next."

We are in so much trouble, I don't know what to do. *O most holy apostle, St. Jude, faithful servant and friend of Jesus, the church honors and invokes you universally, as the patron of hopeless cases, of things almost despaired of. Pray for me, I am so helpless and alone.* The one thing I had that might have been useful is sitting in a cashier drawer at a gas station off Interstate 80 in Des Moines, Iowa. I know it is no panacea, but money would be of great help right now. *Make use, I implore you, of that particular privilege given to you, to bring visible and speedy help where help is almost despaired of.* At a minimum, we need a place to stay. I cannot begin to think of Irena's hospital bill or the cost of her flight home. *Come to my assistance in this great need that I may receive the consolation and help of heaven in all my necessities, tribulations, and sufferings, particularly in helping my friends though Irena's medical emergency, and that I may praise God with you and all the elect forever.*

"We have to call Irena's father," I say. I reach into my purse for my telephone. "We have to tell him what happened to Irena, and maybe he can wire us some money."

"Excellent," says Hazel. "That's exactly how we need for you to start thinking." I dial Irena's home number and hand Hazel my telephone. She seems surprised, but I insist she take it. I refuse to be the one to tell Irena's father what happened to her and what brought on the attack. I stand up and walk away from her to let her know I mean it.

Hazel presses the telephone to her ear and waits. "There's no answer."

"*Pues dejes un mensaje.*"

Hazel clicks a button, ends the call, and thrusts the phone toward me. "I will not leave a message like that on the poor man's answering machine."

"You keep the phone," I say. "Keep trying."

"Do you have the number for her father's bodega?"

"I did, but Irena really didn't like it when I called her over there. Eventually, I stopped, so now I don't remember the number."

Irena practically moved in with me last semester. As we were on line at the registrar at the beginning of last semester, Irena was looking through the course catalog when a particular class caught her eye. "I love this school!" she said. "They're offering a course on social justice in the human service agency context." Then Irena groaned. "Forget it."

"*¿Porqué?*"

"It meets too late."

"*Dime en español.*" She had asked me to speak to her in Spanish and to push her to respond to me in Spanish. Otherwise, I would not have done that.

"El clase . . ."

"La," I corrected her. *"La clase."*

"La clase . . . how do you say *meet* again?"

"La clase se reúne . . ."

"La clase se reúne muy tarde."

I look over her shoulder at the course catalog. The class Irena wanted to take met from six to eight on Tuesdays and Thursdays. I personally did not find that so late even if Irena had to take catch the PATH train back to Jersey City. But I understand how Irena feels about her safety, so I tell her that if she wants to take the class, she can always stay with me. Irena was so happy, jumping and hugging me. She scheduled all of her classes on Tuesdays and Thursdays and stayed with me on those nights. At first, I worried that our spiritual practices would clash, but I actually enjoyed walking into the apartment to the smell of the incense she burned from time to time. It reminded me of my church in Aurora. Irena would light the incense in the hallway, then go into the study and meditate. Sometimes, inspired by her discipline, I would go into my room and pray. *Me hace mucha falta Irena.*

"Keep trying to reach her father," I say to Hazel. She reluctantly keeps my phone while I pace. *Dios me perdona, pero* Hazel's mother *es una sinvergüenza inútil* who would probably create more trouble than she would resolve. No sense in calling her. Jackie's father's an option, but I'm hesitant to suggest that just yet, since I know she feels terribly guilty as it is. Then the perfect solution comes to me. "Call Wil."

"What?"

"Call Jackie's boyfriend." Wil's support—financially and morally—is exactly what she needs at this time. *El es un hombre muy bueno.* No matter what happened between them before she left New York City, Wil would give Jackie whatever she needs if she weren't too proud to call him. So one of us has to do it, and it should be Hazel.

"If I call Wil, I'll wind up in the bed next to Irena."

"That's not funny, Hazel."

"I'm not trying to be funny."

And then I see the vulnerability in her eyes, and I realize that Irena's suspicions were right all along. But instead of feeling compassion for Hazel, God forgive me, I find myself becoming furious with her. "If you really loved Jackie, you would call Wil."

"Excuse me."

"*¡Virgen, dame paciencia!* Sisterly love is not that blind."

Hazel stands up. "I will not call Wil." But suddenly she reaches for her pocketbook where she left it on the floor. She scours through it and pulls out a business card. It reads *Truesdale & Sons New & Used Autos.* "I'll call Jimmy."

Jackie enters the waiting room. Where has she been? "Who are you calling?"

"Jimmy. He gave me his number. He's so sweet on me, he'll do anything to—"

Before she can finish speaking or dialing, Jackie grabs the telephone from her, *gracias a Dios.* For once I'm grateful for Jackie's "snatchiness." "Are you crazy?"

"Yes, she is."

"He's only three hours away, and I know he feels terrible about what happened . . ."

"Absolutely not! Hazel, what makes you think that man's going to come all the way over here to help a bunch of women he barely knows? Did it ever occur to you that since we left, his asshole brother might have done a number on him? Brian probably convinced him that you were just a lipstick lesbian toying with his feelings to get your butch girlfriend jealous. If he were to come over here, it wouldn't be with any good intentions. You don't know this man, Hazel, but you're going to trust him after all the shit that went down in Des Moines? You must be crazy."

"Totally," I say.

Jackie walks away from us, leans against the wall, and sinks to the floor. The three of us remain in place, silently avoiding each other's gaze. I start to reconsider. This is a time for family, and if it's too hard for Jackie but she gives me permission, I'll make the call to her father. Just as I start to ask for the telephone, Jackie begins to dial.

"Who are you calling?" Hazel and I both ask.

"I'm calling Wil," she says. "I'll just have him wire our vacation money."

¡Vaya! I'm so proud of Jackie right now. I honestly don't know what twisted reasoning motivated her to treat Irena the way she did, but at least she's taking responsibility for it. "I think that's the best thing to do." Now if only Irena would get better, I would feel completely at peace.

Then Hazel gasps. "Lourdes can call her mom!"

Jackie stops dialing and jumps to her feet. "Yeah, Lou, call your mother."

"No . . ." *Dios mío, esto no me esta pasando.* "It's better if you call Wil."

"How's it better for me to call someone in New York City than for you to call your mother when she's only . . . what'd you say? Nine hours away? She doesn't even have to come here. All she has to do is wire us some money."

"*¡Por favor baja la voz!*"

Jackie eyes me and then punches her thumbs into the keypad of my telephone, searching for my mother's number. "There." She finds it and shoves the telephone toward me.

I have no choice but to take it from her. I look at the display, and just my terrible luck, she dialed my mother's direct line. I put the telephone to my ear and pray that she's out of the office.

"Lourdes!"

"*Hola,* Mamá."

"It's about time you called." I turn my back on Jackie and Hazel, but they swarm around me like vultures on a corpse.

"Guess what, Mamá. I'm almost home."

"You are?"

"*¡Sí, sí, sí!*" With Jackie in front of me and Hazel behind me, I have nowhere to escape. "Some friends and I are on a road trip, and guess what? We're in Omaha!" My giddy tone makes Jackie suspicious, and I can only imagine the look on Hazel's face. I'm doing what I have to do, and if I'm successful, perhaps they'll be too relieved to give me a hard time over my little white lies.

"No me pedistes el permiso para pasar en ningún viaje." My mother's speaking so loudly, Jackie and Hazel can hear her every word as if she were in the room with us.

Jackie makes a face, and I hope it's because she wonders why my mother would think at my age I would need her permission to go on a trip rather than because she realizes that this is the first time she's heard about the trip at all. She nudges me. "Ask her. Tell her what happened and ask her."

"Who is that?"

"That's my friend Jackie." I try to turn away from her only to bump into Hazel, who has the same exact look on her face. "Mamá—"

"Jackie who? Wait, you need money. That's the only reason why I'm hearing from you, isn't it, Lourdes?"

"No, Mamá, we were going to surprise you—"

"What the fuck are you talkin' about?" Jackie yells. "For Christ's sakes, Lourdes, this is a medical emergency. Tell her what happened to Irena."

"Who is using that filthy language?"

I motion for Jackie to be quiet, but she grabs the telephone from me. "Hello, Mrs. Becerra? My name's Jacqueline Alvarado, and I'm a friend of your daughter. I'm sure she's mentioned me in passing . . . Oh . . . We went to Fordham together . . . Because I graduated, *ma'am*." She says *ma'am* with the same venom she would use to send her to hell, and my heart feels as if it is going to burst through my chest. "We were driving cross-country—there's four of us all together—when a friend of ours took ill . . . To attend a woman's conference in San Francisco . . . Because we were seeking adventure. Look, Mrs. Becerra, we're at the University of Nebraska's Medical Center in Omaha, and we wouldn't be calling you if we were not in serious need of money . . . You would have to ask your daughter that, *ma'am* . . ." Jackie hands me the telephone and pulls Hazel away.

I turn my back on them as Jackie relays my mother's end of the conversation to Hazel in furious whispers. "Mamá?"

"Lourdes, I order you to come home now."

"I can't leave my friends."

"You will if you want to help them."

"Then let me call you back once I've found a place for you to wire us the money. I'll rent another car and—"

"No, I refuse to send you another dime. *¿Querían ser Guevara y Granado?* Then let these so-called friends of yours get you to Aurora. Only if and when you arrive will I wire them any money." Before I can respond, my mother hangs up on me. Never in my entire life has she done such a thing.

I stand there in a daze with the telephone still pressed against my ear. Unsure of what to make of my silence, Hazel and Jackie inch toward me. When Jackie realizes that my mother is no longer on the line, she gently pulls the telephone away from me. "Lou? You okay? What'd she say?"

"She said she'll wire you the money if I go home." My mind leaps on all the reasons why I can't get to Aurora, but soon the gears already churning in Jackie's head drown out my excuses. She'll find a way to send me to Colorado, and Hazel will side with her. Even if my mother forbids me to return to Omaha, they'll continue without me, whether toward San Francisco or back to New York. This is the end of the line for me because there is no one left to speak for me.

IRENA

University of Nebraska
Medical Center
Omaha, NE
Monday, June 19, 7:59 P.M.

When I wake up, the first thing I notice is the brightness of the room. I think, *This is one ritzy motel. Jackie must have given in to Lourdes's complaints.* Des Moines taught me that if Lourdes is willing to run up her mother's credit card, who am I to say no? It wasn't like she wanted to check into the Radisson or Hilton while the rest of us stayed at the Motel 6. The universe sent me a very wealthy and generous friend. I have no business dismissing its blessing. With my stomach kicking with hunger pangs, I decide to ask Lourdes to treat me to some pancakes this morning. Wait, I can't. Lou is as broke as the rest of us now.

I turn to face her only to see the metal bar along the edge of my bed, and I remember I'm in a hospital. In Des Moines? No, Omaha. These sheets are stiff and make me itch. Who knows what kind of toxins they use to wash them? My body aches from inactivity, and I check under the sheets praying to the Goddess that I don't have any bedsores. Then my eyes scan the room until they find the clock. Almost eight? I look out the window again and realize that it's not dawn but dusk. How long have I been here?

I inch my way toward the edge of my bed, searching for my chart. I don't remember anything after the attack, and I want to know what happened and how they treated it. And where is everybody? I reach for the clipboard attached to the end of my bed and scan it until I hit a word that makes it all clear. Steroids! I must have had the mother of all asthma attacks.

"Fuck!" I drop the clipboard onto my lap and pat around me on the bed. When I find the button to summon the doctor, I jam it with all I have. "I can't believe this." Who the hell gave these pharmaceutical whores permission to pump the same drug in me that turns harmless geeks into raging hulks with severe cases of backne? Where are Hazel and Lourdes? And Jackie? She put me in here and now is nowhere to be found.

A dirty-blond woman in her forties wearing a stethoscope and lab coat rushes into my room. "Irena! Are you okay?"

"Are you my doctor?"

"Yes, I'm Dr. Taylor."

"Why was I prescribed a steroid?"

"First things first," she says as she takes hold of my wrist and examines the monitor next to my bed. "How do you feel?"

"Like crap." How the hell else am I supposed to feel?

Dr. Taylor gives me half a grin. "Can you be more specific?"

"I'm sorry, Dr. Taylor, I'm just so not cool with being prescribed steroids."

"We had no other choice, Irena. When your friends brought you in, we first tried to normalize your breathing with a stronger inhalant, and it had no effect. In fact, your attack grew more severe. So we ran some blood tests, and the results showed that you were at serious risk of respiratory failure."

"Really?" I start to feel a bit guilty for being so bratty. "Did I eventually lose consciousness?" I ask.

"We sedated and incubated you, and you spent the next few hours on a respirator," says Dr. Taylor. "We removed it when you came to early this evening." She puts on her stethoscope, motions for me to sit up, and then places it against my back. "Take a deep breath and hold it." I do as she asks. "Good."

I am almost afraid to ask the next question, but I do because I have to know. "Where are my friends?"

The doctor takes my chart and scribbles some notes across it. "They're here. Lorena? . . ."

"Lourdes."

"Yes, she's in the chapel. And I believe Jackie and Carmen may be in the atrium. I'll have the nurse find them for you."

"Okay." She asks me a few more questions about how I feel, takes some more notes, and then turns to leave. "Dr. Taylor, can I get off the steroids?"

"We'll see, Irena." Then she walks out the door. I wish I had stayed unconscious. I hate lying here feeling helpless with tubes coming out of me in every direction.

A few minutes later, Hazel rushes into the room. The sight of her makes me burst into tears. "Oh, honey, why're you crying?"

Even though I feel like a fool just thinking it, I blurt out, "I thought you guys went to Frisco without me."

Hazel laughs at me, which I'm totally cool with, and gives me a hug. "Irena, where should we call your dad?"

"No, you can't call Dad."

"Irena, you're in the hospital. How on earth are we not supposed to call him?"

"I'm okay now, Hazel. There's no need to worry him. Please don't call my father." While I am genuinely concerned about worrying him, I also hate the idea that the first time he hears from me while I'm on this trip is when I'm in trouble. I know it's petty and irrational and all that, but still that's how I feel. I tore out of the apartment and never looked back to prove to Dad that I was an adult and could come and go as I pleased. To call him now in a time of crisis makes me feel weak and childish and just . . . yuck! I mean, I have to take some responsibility for what happened, right? I chose to trust this woman and take a trip across the country with her only to learn the hard way that she is no friend to me. She may have put me in the hospital, but that's hardly a consolation when I was the one who placed her on a pedestal. And she's not even here. I can't bear to think about it anymore. "Please, please, please don't call Dad."

Hazel considers my plea. "We won't call your father."

"Thank you!"

"Because you are."

"Hazel!"

"Irena, all that energy you're spending on groveling you need to redirect into recuperating, okay? You have to get well enough for us to send you home."

"Send me home?" While they go on to the California? No way!

"Look, I refuse to discuss this with you now. When Jackie and Lourdes come up—"

"No!"

"No what?"

"I don't want to see Jackie." And I mean it. "Keep her away from me."

"Irena, she's on the edge over what happened to you."

"Tell her I said jump."

Hazel pouts. "I understand how you feel, but—"

"No, you don't understand how I feel. You want me to get better? Keep her away from me."

Hazel lets out a long sigh and then moves to a door in the room. She opens it up and pulls out my bag. Then she reaches in for my journal and lays it open across my lap. Over the span of two pages in bright red markers and hip-hop graffiti-like letters it says *Irena, I'm sorry.* "Jackie did that while we waited for you to come to earlier."

I glare at Hazel. I can't believe she allowed her to desecrate one of the most personal, even sacred, places I own. "First, she tries to steal my journal, and now's she's ruined it. Great. She's the one who needs to go home. Not me."

Hazel eyes cloud with sadness. She finds a pen on the night table next to my bed and hands it to me. "I guess you need this now more than ever." Hazel backs away from my bed toward the door. "I'm going to find the others and let them know that you're okay. I mean, that . . . Well, you know . . ."

As Hazel leaves, a young black woman in paisley hospital scrubs enters holding a tray with two white small cups on it. Her name tag reads SHONDA, and she seems only a few years older than I am. While one is a regular small paper cup, the other looks like the kind in which they wrap miniature muffins. The regular cup contains water while the smaller one holds two white pills. "Please tell me that's not more steroids."

Shonda just smiles at me and says, "If you really want me to . . ." And she picks up the cup of pills and offers it to me. She is so not open to negotiation.

I reluctantly take the cup. "When can I get off this stuff?" I close my eyes, throw my head back, and toss the pills down my throat. I swallow hard on the gross taste and reach for the cup of water.

"You'll have to ask the doctor about that, sweetie." After I drink the water, Shonda holds out her hand for the empty cup. She crumples it up along with the other cup and throws them in the wastebasket. "I read that stress can bring on an asthma attack, but I have never seen anything like this before." Shonda checks her watch with one hand while reaching for my chart with the other. "If I were you, I'd mind Dr. Taylor," she says as she documents the current dosage of medication. "I'll be back to check on you later, but if you need anything before then, just push this button right here."

"Thanks, Shonda." I watch her leave the room and reflect on what she said. Not about capitulating to steroid use, but that the doctor attributed my asthma attack to stress. At least someone tried to tell Dr. Taylor the truth. Probably Lourdes. I can forgive her for not intervening in my behalf. Hazel, too, although it'll take time. But I'll never forgive Jackie.

Jackie drives down West Dodge Road with the attention of a surgeon conducting a bypass. She's trying to hide it, but she took Irena's refusal to see her really hard. "I wouldn't want to see me either," Jackie said. Then she just shrugged and gave a halfhearted laugh.

I wait with Jackie while Lourdes follows the nurse upstairs to Irena's room. I bet Lourdes told Irena about her trip to Colorado tonight, and I doubt that made Irena think any better of Jackie even though I agreed that Lourdes should go. Once Lourdes got off the phone with her mother, the three of us discussed—more like argued over—our options. We finally decided that Jackie and I would find an inexpensive place to stay for a night or two while Lourdes took the train to Denver. And we made sure Lourdes called her mom in front of us to keep her honest. When Lourdes came back—or at least called us to tell us that she was not coming back—and Irena was ready for discharge, we would figure out how to get Irena on the first plane to Jersey and then drive ourselves home. Haunting me throughout our conversation are Lourdes's words, but, of course, I share nothing with Jackie about it.

When we are only a few blocks away from the hospital, the long strip of occasional mom-and-pop shops and gas stations gives way to a string of retail chains and franchise restaurants. Appleby's,

Kinko's, Best Buy, Old Navy, Borders . . . She eventually pulls into the parking lot of the Econo Lodge, and together we walk into the tiny lobby. Jackie tells the chubby blonde behind the desk, "Two adults." Only then does it sink in that with Irena in the hospital and Lourdes staying with her until her train leaves for Colorado tonight, Jackie and I are alone. This is not how I wanted this to happen.

"And how many nights will you be staying?" the woman asks.

Jackie shrugs. "One, maybe two." The woman hands her two key cards, and Jackie gives one to me. We climb back into the car to drive closer to and park in front of our ground-floor room. With the exception of Irena's bag and a duffel for Lourdes to take with her on the nine-hour train ride, Jackie and I carry all our luggage into the room.

As with most motel rooms, the lighting is dim and the carpet stiff. The room is pretty large though, with one king-sized bed taking up most of the space. It also has a microwave and small refrigerator. Jackie takes one look at the appliances, grabs the car keys, and starts to think aloud. "Yeah, that's a good idea. I'm going to go buy us some groceries so we can save money on food. Besides . . . no way Irena's going to be feeling that hospital food." She heads toward the door.

"Wait, I'll go with you," I say. Jackie turns to me, and I catch a hint of resignation gloss over her face. "What, you don't want me to go with you?"

"No offense, Haze, but I kinda want to be alone right now."

To run off and call Wil? I think, but I don't say anything. "I'm just going to buy us something for dinner, maybe some yogurts or whatever for breakfast, and then take Lourdes to the Amtrak station."

"Lourdes's train doesn't leave until ten thirty. What are you going to do until then? Where are you going to go?"

"Jesus, Hazel, I don't freakin' know, okay! I'll probably go back to the hospital for a while, and if Lourdes and Irena don't want anything to do with me, I'll figure something out."

My best friend is in the middle of a crisis, and she wants nothing to do with me. What the hell's going on here? I feel as if she's punishing me for what has happened. "Well, I want to go back to the hospital and be with Irena and Lourdes, too."

Jackie throws her hands up. "Fine, I'll go get us some food and come back for you, and we can go back to the hospital together." I glare at her, and she yells, "What? I have to bring the food back here to put it in the freakin'—" She stops in midsentence and throws open the front door. "Fuck this shit. I don't need this right now."

"Neither do I!" I heave my bag onto the bed and yank the zipper so hard, it's a wonder I don't break it. "As a matter of fact, don't come back to get me. I fuckin' need to be alone, too."

"Hey, this isn't showtime, drama queen!"

"Just go." I want to call her a choice name, too, but angry as I am at her, I can't bring myself to do it.

And Jackie already wants to undo the hurt she has caused me by calling me a drama queen because she says, "I'm coming back for you." She says that as if she's issuing an order. I am to wait here until she returns so we can go back to the hospital together. "Don't go nowhere," she says as she steps out the door.

I almost say that there's no place I can go without the car, but it's not true. We passed quite a few places within walking distance—at least to a New Yorker—where I can pass the time. Yet I hardly feel up to browsing at Borders or Best Buy. I just nod my head, and somewhat reassured that we have struck an unspoken truce, Jackie leaves.

Barely ten minutes pass before I climb the walls. And if I know Jackie, determined to have her alone time, she will drag her feet at the supermarket even though we have room and money for only a basketful of things, and then just drive aimlessly around the city until she feels good and ready to deal with the rest of us. That can take until Lourdes has to leave to catch her train.

So I check my pocket to be sure I have my key card and walk out of the motel room. I head back to West Dodge Road, make a right back toward the hospital, and just walk. This is one of those places where pedestrians are rare, so I take extra care to briskly cross the six-lane streets at the stoplights and watch my back as I wander into parking lots.

As I walk, I find myself thinking about Lourdes and what she said to me at the hospital when I suggested that I call Jimmy. If I had called him, I wonder what I would have said to him, if anything, before I had the audacity to ask him for money. Chances are I wouldn't have had to say much to him over the phone. He probably would have taken the three-hour drive to bring the money to me, probably forcing me to tell him the truth to his face. The man would deserve more than the proverbial "It's not you, it's me," although ironically that is the case here. Would I have revealed that despite the fact that sometimes I genuinely find a man attractive in some way, I truly am lesbian? Although for a long time, I did believe I was bisexual. If anything, breaking up with Geneva and wanting to approach Jackie—not just "another" woman, but someone who has been part of my life for a very long time—has proved to me just how much I love women in every way.

And it makes me realize just how much courage I need to tell Jackie how I feel about her because my profound and complete love for women scares me. Look how Jimmy's brother Brian reacted when Jackie would have nothing to do with him. That's how the world feels about women like me. The other night Brian proved what can happen to women who have no desire for men. Especially a relentless femme like me who never leaves the house without a full face of makeup and every hair in place.

No, my occasional attraction to men—which was never at once sexual and emotional—didn't make me bisexual at all. I was sexually attracted to Raul but emotionally drawn to Kharim. And Jimmy. But I never felt as completely connected to any of the men I have dated as I have to the women in my life. If anything, I had been using my one-dimensional interest in men to hide my lesbianism primarily from myself.

Damn. Gay and straight folks alike have given me so much flak about flitting between the two when the truth is people who are genuinely bisexual should have the biggest problem with me. People like me who really belong to one particular camp make it hard for those who can truly be drawn to either men or women—emotionally as well as sexually—to be accepted by everyone else. I owe bisexual people, and maybe even transgender folks, a huge apology of my own.

Speaking of apologies, I wonder if Jackie is in the supermarket now attempting to call Wil collect on a public telephone. How could she? Jackie cannot even talk to me about the situation, and I'm right here in the trenches with her. Surely, she's not going to call Wil now. She has too much pride.

I try to remember if the Kinko's I saw as we drove to the motel is within walking distance. No matter if it is because I'm on a mission. I'm clear now what's the right thing to do. Not that knowing makes me feel better. About fifteen minutes later I reach the Kinko's, find a computer station, and log in to my e-mail.

TO: BigBxWillie@yahoo.com
FROM: Hazel1985@hotmail.com
DATE: June 19, 2006 9:12 PM
SUBJECT: Stranded in Omaha

Hey, Wil,

Hope this message finds you well. Wish I could say the same about the four of us. Some things have gone down during this trip, and while we're all safe, Jackie needs you. I mean, I know you started a new job and things are tough between you, but if you can swing it, I really think you should fly here.

But I can't bring myself to keep the stakes that low. It's not true to how I feel. More importantly, it's not true to how Jackie feels. So I delete the last sentence and write:

I know you started a new job and things are tough between you, but if you truly love her, you will find a way to get here. That's how serious I think it is, and you know I of all people should know.

I decide to leave it to Jackie to explain to him what has happened when he calls. I feel like I am already doing too much, although I can't pinpoint why that is. I type in Lourdes's cell phone number as well as the number to our room at the Econo Lodge. Then I hit SEND.

JACKIE

Amtrak Station
Omaha, NE
Monday, June 19, 10:17 P.M.

I get back to the motel, and Hazel has disappeared. I put away the food, expecting her to walk through the door at any moment. She never does, and I wonder if I should call her on Lourdes's telephone. But then I think, fuck it. Hazel's fine. How far can she get on foot in this place? Okay, I'm a bit worried, but I have bigger things to attend to right now. I have to get Lourdes to the Amtrak station in time to catch her train to Denver. But Lou and I drive in silence, and I honestly have no idea who's not speaking to whom. I mean, Lourdes obviously is mad at me because I insist she go to Colorado, and ordinarily, I wouldn't blame her. What grown woman wants to run to her mother, hat in hand, begging for money?

But the truth is I'm pissed at Lourdes for lying all this time. To me and the gals, her family, all of us. What's so grown about that shit? I don't blame her moms for having a fit. And when did we ever give her the impression that we would dis her because . . . I don't even know why the hell she lied to us! Is it because Lourdes is ashamed of her homegirls from the 'hood? I have a hard time believing that and not just because I don't want to. Maybe it's her family she's ashamed of. Maybe her mom is a raging alcoholic and her brother Oscar makes bombs in their basement. I don't fuckin' know. I shouldn't be overanalyzing this situation anyway. Whatever's going on with Lou is her shit, and now she has to deal with it.

The station's easy to find. Not only are Shonda's directions perfect, but signs to the station appear everywhere. I pull into the parking lot, cut off the engine, and go inside the station to buy Lourdes's ticket.

"One adult to Denver, please," I say, even though I'm thinking of Lou as a spoiled brat. And a sneaky one, at that. I pull out my wallet, and coming face-to-face with my dwindling cash flow makes me really nervous.

"Round-trip?"

Jeez, now that we have to stay here in Omaha for God knows how long, buying a round-trip ticket is such a bad idea. Especially with Lou's moms threatening to forbid her to come back anyway. I could be wasting some desperately needed cash. But I can't ship Lourdes off to a seething parent without some plan of escape, can I? If Lourdes remains stranded in Denver because I wouldn't spring for a round-trip ticket, Irena's really going to hate me, if she doesn't already. On top of everything else, I can't have that on my tab, too.

"Yeah, one adult round-trip ticket to Denver." I hand over all the cash I have, save a final twenty-dollar bill. Fuck.

I get back to the car and hand Lourdes the ticket. Without looking at me or the ticket, she takes it and chucks it into her purse. "It's round-trip." Lourdes remains perfectly still, but now tears are cascading down her cheeks. I reach into my back pocket for the telephone card I bought for her on my grocery run and hand that to her as well. It was the least I could do, given that she's making a nine-hour trek to grovel to her overbearing mother for money and leaving her cell phone with us. But Lourdes is crying so hard, she can't even see that I have something else for her.

"I bought this calling card for you so you can reach us while you're on the move," I explain as I try to stuff the card into her fancy pocketbook. As I do, I jostle her crucifix, and it glows after catching the ray of light beaming from the streetlamp into the car. Once I had a rosary just like it, although mine obviously had plastic beads instead of diamonds. My mother had given it to me when I made my first Holy Communion. I reach out to touch Lourdes's crucifix, and she recoils from me as if I were going to hit her. Ouch. I may be a bitch, but I'm not a monster. "You want me to go with you, Lou?"

She looks at me for sincerity. I am sincere. I don't know how we'll swing it, but if Lourdes wants me to go home with her, I will. We can exchange the single round-trip ticket for two one-way tickets and figure it out from there. Or maybe I can get a refund, give the cash to Hazel so she can cab to and from the hospital to see Irena, and Lou and I can take the Tempo to Denver.

I know Lourdes wants me to go with her because she stays quiet for a very long time. She's thinking it's a lot to ask. It is, but I'll do it if she wants me to. But she has to ask. It's not for me to invite myself along even though it might do all of us some good if I just disappeared for a while. I'm done trying to be anywhere I'm not wanted. Finally Lourdes says, "If there's any chance of my mother giving me any money or coming back to Omaha, I can't take you with me."

"So Mamá doesn't like her LuLu Linda to play with *morenas*?" I say it to tease her and bring some levity to the situation. That's the main reason anyway.

"Don't you dare say anything about my mother!" Lourdes breaks down and sobs like a little girl.

I feel terrible. Am I destined to break down everyone on this godforsaken trip? I put my arm around Lourdes and say, "Hey, it's going to be okay. How bad can it get? She's going to yell at you. Guilt-trip you a bit. Maybe even threaten to cut you off. But you've got to stand your ground, Lou. You've got nothing to lose. No matter what you say or do, your mother's not going to stop loving you. It might as well be the real you."

"How can you be so sure?"

How can I be so sure? "Because my father still loves me, and we all know I'm not exactly La Lupita and shit." I finally get a laugh from her. "Pop and I will scream at each other until we're hoarse and then an hour later we're drinking Coronas and watching boxing on HBO. It's how we love each other." Lourdes nods like she understands. "Sure, you don't want me to come with you?"

"Unfortunately, my mother drinks Cordon Negro."

Like mother, like daughter, I guess. "Good choice." I almost add *if you can afford it,* but I know Irena would counsel me against that even though I'm only kidding.

"My father used to drink Cordon Negro. Then he died and my mother took over his company. Took over his wine, too, I guess. She never even liked wine."

The horn of the coming train startles us, and we both leap out of the car toward the platform. As we join the throng of people, I say, "Listen, when you tell your moms about us, you may wanna leave out a few details. Just for now. Like that Hazel's a lesbian."

"And that Irena's a witch."

"And that I'm . . . me."

Lourdes stops and puts down her overnight bag. She pulls her rosary beads over her head and hands them to me. "Watch them for me while I'm gone." Then she reconsiders. "No, promise me that you will use them."

"Aw, Lou . . ."

"I want you to pray for me. All of us, especially Irena. Promise me or I won't get on this train."

"Are you for real?"

"I'm dead serious."

Of all times to pull rank! I'd call her brilliant if I weren't on the receiving end of it. "Fine. Go before the train leaves without you and the point's moot." Lourdes grabs the handrail and pulls herself onto the first step. "Lou . . ." She stops to look over her shoulder at me. "Really, I promise. And if your moms goes ballistic and won't let you come back to us, just call me. No matter what she says, if you want to come back, we'll figure out a way to make it happen. Even if I have to drive all the way to Denver to get you myself. I promise you that, too."

Lourdes leaps off the step and back onto the platform. She throws her arms around me and squeezes hard. Then just as quickly as she hugs me, she spins around, leaps back up the steps, and disappears into the train to California via Denver, Colorado. And I can't help but think that as overbearing and angry as her mother may be, Lou's so lucky to have a mother who gives a shit about her.

LOURDES

California Zephyr

Lincoln, NE

Monday, June 19, 11:29 P.M.

Even though I close the curtain on my window, push back my seat as far as it will go, and pull the scratchy navy blanket over my head, I still cannot sleep. I should feel safer than my friends because I am going home. *Pero me siento mas vulnerable que nunca* because they have each other, and I am alone. I finally understand Irena's anxiety over separating during the course of the trip, and I wish I had asked Jackie to come with me.

I pray to God that when I arrive in Denver, Valería will be waiting for me. I need to see her before I face my mother. She is the only ally I have now, and perhaps she can help me convince my mother to help my friends and let me return to them. I actually feel a bit happy at the thought of seeing Valería, and I remember the night she found out about my first secret trips and how it changed our relationship.

I had told her I needed some art supplies for a class project, so Valería dropped me off in front of Archiver's at the Aurora Mall. That much had been true. I had to write a paper on a current event affecting Colorado for social studies class, and I had decided to support my thesis with pictures. "*No olvides,*" Valería warned me. "Your mother Big Dinner tonight. I pick you up *a las cinco* because I need you help."

The Big Dinner was my mother's attempt to woo new investors into the family business. Our home had been in an uproar for weeks as she planned this dinner. As my mother networked with everyone from the silver-haired moguls in their two-story town houses in Cherry Creek to the buzz-cut dot-comers at their lofts in LoDo, she had no idea that I was capturing the drug transactions and sex negotiations on Colfax Street or the tourists lining up to enter the U.S. Mint with the new Nikon Coolpix 990—my first digital camera—that I had asked for for Christmas. She whipped around the house saying, "We have to get this place ready for the Big Dinner. Oscar, for the last time, it is not Valería's job to pick your dirty clothes off the floor. Lourdes, I need you to help Valería in the kitchen."

I spent only twenty minutes in Archiver's—a warehouse of materials for those for whom scrapbooking is a religion—buying photo tape and corners for my exhibit and chatting with some friends from school, one of whom was picking up some things for her mother. Not really friends. These were the same girls who snubbed me on the first week of school, assuming that I was Valería's daughter and on scholarship. That is, until they heard me speak better English and saw me wear better accessories than they did. They invited me to go shopping with them, but I told them I had to head to Larimer Square. *Gracias a Dios,* they did not invite themselves along. Then I jumped on the 6 bus to downtown Denver to get what I needed most of all for my school assignment—the photographs.

I lost track of time and completely forgot about the Big Dinner. Valería searched the Aurora Mall for me until she ran into my classmates. They told her where I was, and she drove downtown to find me. Eventually, she found me sneaking a photograph of a homeless man sleeping on a bench in the promenade and wearing a sign that said *Bush-t!* Valería grabbed me and yanked me into the Civic and started to yell at me as she never had before.

"You know you no belong here," she said in Spanglish. "*En menos de una hora,* your mother be home with all those guests for the Big Dinner." My mother's plan was to take the potential new investors on a tour of the company and then bring them to our house for a lavish feast.

"*No me importa,*" I said. "*Y no te preocupes con lo que yo hago.*

Mamá's doing what she has to do. I'm doing what I have to do. So you just worry about whatever it is you have to do."

"*¡No me faltes el respeto, Lourdes!*"

It surprises me to this day to think about it because it is unlike me to disrespect my elders. But on that evening, I had had enough of my mother's wheeling and dealing, and I took it out on the only person available to me. "You're not my mother," I told Valería. "You're just her servant."

Before I knew it, four lithe fingers flash before my face and sting my lips. No one—not even my parents—had ever put their hands on me. I stared at Valería in disbelief, the faint smell of lemon-scented dishwashing liquid still lingering beneath my nose. Valería apologized over and over again for slapping me, and she begged me not to tell my mother and spare her job. I started to cry less from the pain of being hit and more from the realization that I fully deserved it, and the more Valería pleaded, the harder I cried.

When we arrived at my house, I know she expected me to run straight to the telephone to call my mother and tell her what had happened. Instead I went into the kitchen, where I saw that Valería had started to slice avocados for her unrivaled guacamole dip. I imagined her there cutting away with determination until she looked up and noticed that it was time to pick me up. So I placed my bags on the island in the kitchen—the tiny plastic bag from Archiver's and my leather camera bag—washed my hands, and then proceeded to finish slicing the rest of the avocados.

I stood by Valería's side for the rest of the night while my mother wooed the twelve potential investors. The Big Dinner went off without a hitch as we all played our roles without missing a beat. Even Oscar brilliantly performed the little perfect gentleman, and I'm sure in everyone's mind but especially my mother's vision, the future of the company. As I watched him in awe from across the dinner table, I wondered what magic Valería had worked on him. My mother probably still thinks proudly on that night of her first big yet successful risk as the fledgling head of our family business.

But I remember that night warmly as the one when Valería and I came to understand and began to love each other as surrogate mother and daughter. Without exchanging one more word about the incident in Denver, Valería and I forged a silent agreement: I would keep her secret, and she would keep mine. But she didn't keep my secret to protect her job, and I didn't keep hers to spare my freedom. She stopped being "the help" to me, and I was no longer the petulant brat to her. I started to assist Valería with her housekeeping chores so she could spend time with her own children, and she drove me to and from Denver as I wanted. We spent those times together in the laundry room or in her Civic getting to know each other and growing closer.

Maybe I should have told Valería about this trip. No, that was too big a secret to expect her to hide. If she had known and my mother had found out, I don't think any amount of begging on my part would have saved her job. With me out of the house and Oscar now a teenager, who knows what future Valería has in our home. My mother hired her without warning, and she may let her go in the same fashion. The very thought makes me shiver, and I pull the itchy blanket tighter around my head and body.

Or perhaps I should have called Valería instead of my mother. Not that I have any idea what she could have done to help me. I know she's saving as much money as possible for her son's college education. But I never could have asked her to lend me that money.

The best I can ask of Valería now is good advice and strong support to deal with my mother. And as much as it scares me to face Mamá, I feel good about the chance to see Valería whether she can help me or not. But not good enough to get any sleep.

IRENA

University of Nebraska
Medical Center
Omaha, NE
Tuesday, June 20, 12:04 A.M.

Dear Dad,

I hope this letter finds you in the very best of health and spirits. As for me, I could be in better health and spirits. I miss you so much, and I feel terrible about the way I left. So I'm writing you this letter in the hopes of starting the process of healing our relationship before I come home.

Please believe me when I say that I never meant to go through your personal stuff. I was looking in the closet for something I needed when I came across Mom's letters. But you never should have kept Mom's letters from me, Dad. They were my letters, addressed to me, and not for you to open and read, let alone hide from me.

I've been trying to understand why you would do something like that. At first, I thought it was because you discovered that I wanted to go to Cuba to see Mom, and seeing how you feel about Castro, you might have felt betrayed by me. At first, this made me feel so guilty because as badly as I want to see Mom, you're the most important person in the world to me. For the past sixteen years, you have been my father and mother. I love you so much, Dad. No matter how close Mom and I might become in the future, you'll always be my heart.

But then I started to feel really hurt and angry. Yes, I want to see Cuba for myself. I won't let anyone tell me what I should think and feel about my own birthplace, least of all people who refuse to go themselves even to see the loved ones they claim to be so concerned about. What I want most of all is to see my mother, and nobody's politics should have any bearing on a woman's relationship with her mother. I'm sorry, Dad, but that includes you, especially when that woman is your only child and her mother is a woman you still love. And since you've read my letters, you know that Mom still loves you. I understand that when Mom refused to come to the United States, you feel that she betrayed you. I used to think that Mom betrayed me by not insisting that I stay behind with her, but then she started to write me and explained why she did it. I understood and forgave her. Did you ever stop to consider that when you chose to leave Cuba, Mom may have felt that you betrayed her?

Remember the day that you gave me that first letter? I had just come back from registering for classes on my first day at college. I came into the bodega to help you and you handed me the letter. I asked you how did you get it and you said that a friend of yours got it from a friend in Miami who had gone to the island. I asked, "Did she write you, too?" and you said yes. You had a smile on your face and tears in your eyes. In fact, you were happy that she and I started to write each other regularly.

And then you changed, or so I thought. You begrudgingly gave me Mom's letters. When I asked if you had written to each other, you wouldn't answer. At first, I wondered if you were jealous of Mom. But it seemed so ridiculous. I heard from her every few months, and you were here every day with me. Now that I'm writing you this letter, I realized that you didn't change. You wouldn't have known that I wanted to go to Cuba if you had not read my letters, so something else had to compel you to do that. I understand now that I was the one who changed. I changed, and you didn't know why, and you thought you might find out if you read those letters.

Dad, something happened to me during my first semester in college that I never told you or Mom. Remember the night I told you I had to go back to the school to attend a dinner orientation for first-year students? I lied about that. The real orientation happened that afternoon. Afterward I met a guy who invited me to a party so I went back into the city to meet him. When he started leading me away from the campus, I became suspicious. But I wanted him to like me so I said nothing about it. I convinced myself that because I knew his name and where he went to school, I was safe.

He took me to a party in a ritzy building across the street from Central Park. Although he was a perfect gentleman throughout the evening, the entire night I had this scary feeling that something bad was going to happen. I didn't recognize anyone at the party from school, and he didn't introduce me to anyone. I dismissed it as nervousness that I would miss my train to Jersey City and you would find out that I went out on a date without your permission. When the time came that I had to leave to catch my train, he became angry with me, only to insist on taking me to the station. Again, I ignored my instincts and I followed him to a parking garage. Instead of getting on the West Side Highway, he pulled over and raped me. He then drove me to the PATH station on 14th Street as if nothing happened.

As you might remember, I didn't go to school for a week. I let you think that I had bad menstrual cramps. I couldn't tell you what happened to me, not because I thought you would be angry with or ashamed of me; I felt that I deserved it for defying you and had no right to burden you with my trauma. When I finally went to campus security to report what had happened to me, I found that this man had given me a false name. There was no student in the school enrolled by that name, and I could not find his picture among the ones they showed me of incoming students. The police believed that he was someone who came upon the outdoor orientation and seized an opportunity to find a victim. The minute they told me that I knew that I wasn't the first, and that because they would never find him, I wouldn't be the last.

So I threw myself into my classes and activism and distanced myself from you, and maybe that's why you started reading my letters. You saw that I had changed in such a way that you could no longer reach me, and you hoped to find some clue in those letters. But I never told Mom what happened to me either, so you never found out.

Although I truly believe I've done a lot to help myself over the last two years, it took this trip to understand how I continued to victimize myself all over again. One way was by keeping this a secret from you. That as much as I did my share as a volunteer at the women's center, I still thought of myself as a victim and lived in fear of being violated again. Only now have I been able to see myself as a survivor. A survivor who has family and friends who love me and will teach me how to live fearlessly again if I only let them. I am ready to do that.

So much more has happened on this trip, and I am sure much more will. I miss you so much and want to be able to share all the things I've learned with you when I get home. But I have to leave home in order to have things to share. Just know that no matter where I go, I take you with me, and that when I am ready, I will always come home if you will still have me.

Your loving daughter,
Irena

JACKIE

University of Nebraska
Medical Center
Omaha, NE
Tuesday, June 20, 12:17 A.M.

I'm going to lose my mind. Irena won't speak to me, Hazel's about to cut me off, and it'll be hours before Lourdes calls. Even if I could sleep, this chair's killing me. I've read through every magazine in this goddamned waiting room, and if I could reach that fuckin' television set, I'd probably rip it out the wall and throw it out the window.

The worst thing about it? I have no one to blame but myself. Lourdes sometimes wonders if she's going straight to hell for being friends with a wannabe astrologer and unapologetic lesbian. Now I bet she's asking herself why she let a nappy-headed she-devil cart her across the country at eighty-five miles per hour. If Lourdes truly believes in life after death, in either heaven or hell, never mind keeping company with idolaters and homosexuals, fraternizing with me is what she needs to reconsider.

I wouldn't blame a single one of them if they cut me off. Hazel included, even after all these years. Just jumped in the car and left my black ass right here in the Big O. From what Irena's nurse Shonda tells me, the black folks live in the north side of Omaha, and the Latinos live in the south, so my only real problem would be deciding where I should live. But that thought just makes me homesick for New York City where black and Latino folks live side by side, and I wouldn't have to choose.

I walk over to Hazel, who managed somehow to fall asleep in that chair. All I need is for her to lean until she conks herself on the armrest of the chair next to her, so another one of us can be laid up in the hospital. "Hazel?" I place my hand on her shoulder and shake her awake. "Why don't you go back to the hotel, hon?"

"I'm okay."

"Go sleep at the hotel," I said. "What are we renting a room for?" Hazel slowly pulls herself out of the chair, gives a short stretch, and then grimaces in pain as she presses her palm into the small of her back. "See, you need to lie down in a bed."

"You coming?"

"I'm going to stay here tonight." I reach into my pocket for the car keys and hand them to her. "Someone should stay with Irena, and it's not like I'm going to sleep anyway. Just let me have Lourdes's phone."

Hazel takes the keys and hands me the phone. She hugs me, and I really wish she would insist on staying. I pull away from her though, because she deserves a good night's sleep and some time away from me. "You need anything before I go?"

"Nah, I'm good. Thanks."

I walk Hazel to the elevator. When it arrives, she steps on and hits the button. As the door closes, Hazel says, "I love you."

I need to hear that. "Love you, too. See you tomorrow."

The doors close, and I head back to the waiting room. I sit there for a while doing nothing but counting my split ends. I glance at Lourdes's cell phone for the exact time. It's after midnight. Irena's probably asleep so I can go into her room and check her bag. I bet anything she has something to read in there.

I walk into Irena's room, expecting her to be asleep. But she's sitting up in her bed scribbling like a demon in her journal. My presence takes her aback for a second, and I freeze in place. She quickly goes back to ignoring me. Well, not only did I give her a lot to write about, thanks to me, she has some time to make up.

At some point today, Hazel braided her hair. Two thin pigtails sit on her shoulders and make Irena seem barely in her teens. Even though she looks adorable, I know she hates it. It annoys Irena when people think she's younger than she actually is. She never says why, but she doesn't have to. At least not to me. But it's just like Irena to let Hazel do her hair to make her feel better.

I walk over to her bed and sit on the edge. Her hair's not as straight or as blond as I always thought it was. Irena continues to ignore me, and I have to fight the urge to slide the elastic off one of her pigtails and unravel the braids. I bet it would glide through my fingertips. "You have such pretty hair." I take a deep breath then say, "I wish I had hair like yours. I know I'm not supposed to think like that, but . . ." I thought for sure that she'd respond to that, but Irena continues to write as if I'm not even there.

"In case you haven't noticed, we're not having any fun without you. I mean, you're in here and you're okay, but you're not. And you're probably thinking I mean teasing you about your tarot cards and whatnot, but that's not it. Ever since I put you in here, we've been eating a lot of *porquería* 'cause you're not around to encourage us to eat healthier. And you know all that greasy junk food's costing us a mint, right? And without you, we're obviously not doing any of the little bonding exercises either. Nobody has stepped up to, you know, document our trip the way you have in your journal." Irena fastens her grip on her journal like she's afraid I might try to take it away again. To assure her that I have nothing like that in mind, I pull myself off the bed and sit in the chair by the window.

"You're like our historian, Irena. And our peacekeeper and . . . well, don't tell Lourdes and Hazel I said this, but you're kind of like . . ." I struggle to find the words. "Okay, Lou and Hazel, they're the party girls, right. If they had their way, we'd be in a different nightclub every night tripping the light fantastic and shit. And you and me, we like to have fun, but that's not our scene. We're just as happy to dance on the bed to the radio in the motel room. Or hike in the sun or skip rocks across a lake.

"So I need us to be cool again. At least for whatever's left of this trip. You want to blow me off when we get back to New York City, I totally understand. But until then if you'll just have my back, I promise I'll quit teasing you. No more comments like Snow White and Glinda the Good Witch and shit like that, I swear. You want to cast your astrological charts or do a tarot card reading, I'll keep my big mouth shut, and I won't let Lourdes say anything either. And anytime you feel like you want to take me up on that punch in the head, go right ahead. You don't even have to give me a heads-up."

I have to laugh at my own stupid suggestion because I know it's the last thing Irena wants to hear. "I know what you really want. You want to get me into one of those healing circles or co-counseling sessions." I catch the slightest pause in her writing, and I know I'm on to something. "Okay, here's the deal, Irena. I understand the thinking behind it. Now I'm not saying I buy it, I'm just saying I understand it. The way you describe it, it actually sounds much cooler than paying some shrink out the ass for him to listen to you run your mouth just to say, 'Hmmm . . . interesting. How do you feel about that?' 'Muthafucka, what am I paying you for if after listening to me for an hour you have to ask me some simple shit like that?' " I realize that my rambling is losing her, so I get to the point. "Rena, I guess what I'm sayin' is if you can put what I did aside until we get home, I'll give your way a shot."

Irena finally stops writing and looks me in the face. She wants to know if I mean it. Even though I'm not one to say things I don't mean, she needs more than words from me now. How do I prove this to her?

I walk over to the bed and stand in front of her. She stares up at me, and I lean toward her. She flinches, and it kills me that I scare her. I kiss Irena on the forehead and then dash out the hallway. I find myself fighting tears because she has every reason to think I would hurt her. Those few moments by the highway undid any and every good I have ever done for her. Despite my intentions, have I ever done any good for Irena?

I have to do something major now to make things right between us. For all of us. And maybe that's just to find a way to leave them alone and get myself home.

I reach into my pocket for Lourdes's cell phone and dial the number I swore I never would when we left Des Moines. Bad enough I was blowing up the man's cell and home phones from Lourdes's number, taking advantage of the fact that he probably has no idea who would be calling him from this area code. At least, I left him alone at work. "May I speak to Wil Evans please? Well, is Kharim Freed available? No, just tell Mr. Evans that his girl . . . that Ms. Alvarado called, and that it's urgent he call me back at 303-555-9594 as soon as he can. Thank you."

Kinko's, West Dodge Road
Omaha, NE
Tuesday, June 20, 12:32 A.M.

On the way back to the motel, I stop at the Kinko's to check my e-mail. I hold my breath as I enter my e-mail address and password on the sign-in screen. My breathing stops when I see that I have a message from Wil. Not only did he respond to my e-mail from his new job, he copied Jackie on it.

TO: Hazel1985@hotmail.com
CC: imokurnot@yahoo.com
FROM: William.Evans@franklinassociates.com
DATE: June 20, 2006
SUBJECT: Re: Stranded in Omaha

Hazel,

Thanks for your e-mail. I really appreciate how you have Jackie's back and that you reached out to me in her time of need when she couldn't. We both know what that's about, but now that's neither here nor there.

Hopefully, Jackie won't give you a hard time about it since she should have called me herself first thing. And if she had, I would have been on the first plane out, no questions asked. But if she couldn't do that small thing, I really can't justify going to that extreme to help her.

Instead I'm wiring the money Jackie and I have been saving for our cruise in August. It should be at the Western Union in the Kmart on 144th Street. Below there's a link with all the info you need.

Do me one last favor, and don't let Jackie convince you that I did this because I don't love her. If anything, you let her know that I'm doing this precisely because I do love her. I love Jackie so much that I really can't allow her to put me through these changes anymore. Even though we saved this money together, I don't expect anyone to pay any of it back. Just consider it my parting gift.

Peace,
Wil

William D. Evans, J.D.
Attorney-at-Law
Franklin & Associates

I feel at once vindicated and sad. I made it clear that if he truly loved Jackie, he would find his way to Omaha to be with her in her time of need. Maybe he thought I was being the extremely loyal and melodramatic best friend or that Jackie knew I was sending him the e-mail, maybe even put me up to it. Regardless, Wil made a decision to not be here, throwing money at the problem when he should know that Jackie cannot buy what she needs at this time. So I feel justified in sending the e-mail and giving him an ultimatum, and most of all telling Jackie how I feel about her. On the other hand, my heart breaks for Jackie. I have to reveal how I came about the cash and convey to her that Wil essentially broke up with her via cyberspace. Even though that conversation is the perfect prologue to my most important confession, I am hardly looking forward to it. It will all be worth it, however, when Jackie realizes that I love her more than any man can, no matter how good he may seem.

I print out Wil's e-mail as well as the Western Union page he hyperlinked. Then I switch to MapQuest to get directions to the Kmart where I can pick up the money. Apparently, Wil took the time to find a matching address for the Econo Lodge number I gave him and research the closest Western Union location. He went to all that trouble to facilitate the wire transfer, but then he did not bother to call Jackie or even me to find out what happened.

I drive to the Kmart on 144th Street, and sure enough the cash is there. I consider calling him to let him know I retrieved the money and to thank him for it. I decide against it. He'll probably receive some kind of notification via e-mail from Western Union. Once I speak to Jackie, I'll head back to the copy center and send him an e-mail thanking him for the money. Depending on how things go with Jackie, I'll copy her on it the same way he did. Let Wil wonder where he stands with her, because despite what he wrote, his male ego will want to know. As for me, I can wait until I see Jackie tomorrow.

Union Station

Denver, CO

Tuesday, June 20, 7:30 A.M.

The train pulls into Union Station on schedule this morning. Before leaving the station, I head over to the ticket window. "Excuse me, can you tell me when is the last train to Omaha?"

The gentleman says, "Seven twenty-five P.M., gets there about five thirty the following morning."

"Thank you." For the first time since I called my mother from Omaha, I feel some hope. I have almost twelve hours to convince my mother to give me money and allow me to go back to Jackie, Hazel, and Irena.

I walk out to Wynkoop Street expecting to see Valería's silver Civic. To my surprise, Mamá herself picks me up in her black 325i sedan from Union Station. She glares at me, begins to dial a number on her cell phone, and then drives toward Aurora without saying a single word to me. "Marie? For once the train is on time, so I should make it into the office within the hour. I need you to assemble some material and have it on my desk when I get there." She rattles off a list of documents to her assistant then hangs up. Without giving me a second look, my mother punches the keypad on her phone several times and adjusts her headphones. "Gary? Roz." Roz? When did she change from *Rosa* to *Roz*? "You don't have to stand in for me at the meeting after all, but I still need you to prepare a few things."

Between the fourth and fifth call, I finally ask, "Why didn't you send Valería to get me?" If my mother is not going to speak to me, I don't understand why she came instead of sending her.

"With your brother away at camp, I sent Valería on vacation."

"Oh." She has never done that before. Then again, even though Oscar goes to camp every summer, I'm usually home, even after my first year of college.

I wait for my mother to say more—to interrogate me about this trip to San Francisco, ask me about what happened in Omaha, lecture me about being a spoiled and disrespectful *mentirosa . . . algo!* But she gets back on the cellular phone as if nothing out of the ordinary has happened, and I just fade into the black leather seat.

I reach over to turn on the stereo. "You're with the Kool Morning Krew on Kool 105 with mile-high hits of the sixties and seventies . . ." I turn down the volume so I can barely hear the opening chords of a Neil Diamond song. *Girl, you'll be a woman soon . . .*

"Lourdes, I'm on the phone!" My mother snaps off the radio. She didn't have to do that. I didn't have it on that loud. "Where was I, Gar?"

I spend the rest of the ride looking out my window to avoid any more glares and saying the Lord's Prayer to myself. We turn onto Colfax Avenue, and I can't help but smile as we drive by the Mexmall, the Azteca ranch market, *y la Carnicería la Perla*, and especially when we pass the Martin Luther King, Jr., public library, where I shared my first kiss with Truman Lee—a black Chickasaw boy—behind the magazine stand, and the Axum Ethiopian restaurant where I had my first meal that was neither Mexican nor American. I almost laugh out loud when I see the familiar graffiti of the Golden Arches trapped in the slashed circle under the red slogan *We're Not Lovin' It.* Obviously, the McMad Neighbors Against McDonald's are still waging their battle against the construction of a new restaurant between Krameria and Leyden Streets. I wish I had not left my camera in Omaha.

Then I become overwhelmed with homesickness even though we are only minutes away from our patio home in Windmill Creek Reserve. This is not the way to come home. I restart the Lord's Prayer. *Padre Nuestro que estás en los cielos, santificado sea tu Nombre . . .*

When she pulls into our driveway, I leap out the car and run to the doorway. When I reach the door I remember that I left my house keys in my apartment in New York City. So *como una boba* I have to wait for my mother to come open the door. She walks up the drive with her cellular phone to her ear and her keys dangling from her hand. Mamá scowls at me as she unlocks the door. I am halfway to her office, where her lashing and my pleading always take place, when I realize that she is not behind me. I jog back to the front door in time to see Mamá backing out of the driveway.

I run out of the house and to my mother's window. Again, she is on the cell phone speaking through the headset. I knock on the closed window and startle Mamá. She presses the MUTE button on her cellular phone and rolls down the window. "*¿Pero a dónde vas?*" I ask.

"What do you mean where am I going? To work."

"But aren't we going to talk about helping my friends stuck in Omaha?"

"Oh, we certainly are going to have a discussion about these so-called friends in Omaha when I come back tonight."

I panic because my mother never comes home from work before six. That is nowhere near the amount of begging time I need before I have to be at Union Station to catch the 7:25 train back to Omaha. Even Jesus had three hours in the garden before his Crucifixion! *Dios perdóname,* I know I am nothing like Jesus. If I were anything like him, I wouldn't be in the position that I'm in right now. *Te suplico que me perdones y me ayudes.* And not even for me, God, but for my friends. "Are you coming home from work early?"

"Why are you asking me such inane questions?"

I pause to choose the right words. "Because I know I owe you so many explanations, and I want us to have whatever time we need to talk things out and resolve everything before I have to catch the train back to Omaha."

My mother scoffs at me and says, "I will resolve everything for you right here and now in five seconds. You. Are. Not. Going. Back." She rolls up her window, whips backward out of our driveway, and screeches down the street, leaving me alone crying like an orphan.

JACKIE

Econo Lodge on
West Dodge Road
Omaha, NE
Tuesday, June 20, 9:16 A.M.

Lourdes finally calls this morning in tears to tell us that her mother forbids her to return to Omaha. I'm too pissed for her to even ask about money, but Lou swears that she will get some to us somehow. "And she won't give me any money," she says between sniffles. "But I'm going to get some to you, I promise."

"Lou, don't even worry about that. I put in a call to Wil, and I know he's going to come through for me." What a big lie. I won't know what that man's going to do or not until he does or doesn't do it! But with Irena already in the hospital and Lourdes within striking distance of a furious Latina mother, the last thing my conscience can bear is for Lou to cry herself into cardiac arrest.

Just then Hazel comes out of the shower and stands in front of me. She mouths to me *What?* and I mouth back *Wait.* Then I turn back to the phone and tell Lourdes, "We're going to be all right. You just worry about yourself."

"I'm going to figure out something and call you right back," says Lourdes. "*¡Te lo prometo!*"

And even though I have no idea how to make good on it, I reiterate my own promise. "Do you need me to come get you?" I'm scared to death that Lourdes might take me up on it, and yet I can't help myself. "Irena's looking good, and Hazel can just stay with her in the hospital." And that's all I know. Can I manage that nine-hour drive to Denver by myself? Where the hell do I spend the night if I can't? What am I going to do short of robbing Mrs. Becerra after practically kidnapping her daughter to get us both back to Omaha? No fuckin' clue.

"No, stay put. I have to handle this myself, and when I do, *te llamo otra vez.*" Before I can give Lourdes the you-go-girl she needs and deserves, she hangs up. I don't know, but I think good's going to come from Lou's trip home. I'm just not sure what good it is, and I guess that's why I still feel a bit messed up about sending her, especially by herself.

After I hang up the phone in our hotel room and bring Hazel up to speed, I say, "Look, I'm going to drop you off at the hospital and then make myself scarce for a few hours."

"Why?"

"Because I have to." Does Hazel really need me to explain this to her? Of all people, she should know.

"You're going to leave me with Irena while you go off and do whatever?"

"Hey, it's not like I'm off to take in a Huskers game. All that matters is that Irena's not alone, and that I leave her be. If that's what she needs to get better, so be it. I'm just sick of sitting in that hospital—"

"And I'm not."

Hazel has a point. I'm not being fair. "Okay, how 'bout this? I'll just take off for two, three hours, then come back. Then you can take the car and do the same."

She looks like she wants to argue with me yet doesn't know how. Hazel reaches into her suitcase, snatches some clothes, and yanks them on. We leave the hotel and drive to the hospital in complete silence. We've driven over twelve hundred freakin' miles, and those three and a half miles have been the longest of this godforsaken trip.

I drop off Hazel and just drive. I remember Shonda telling me that Latinos live on the south side. At the time, my head snapped because it never occurred to me that there could be enough Latinos in Omaha to constitute an entire "side of town." But now it seems like I lucked out on some information that I should put to use. So after driving east for about four miles, I make a right on a random street.

Only a minute or two later, I begin to see and hear things that feel more like home—a range of brown faces standing at a bus stop, a phrase of Spanish punctuating the air, the odor of beef grilling from a *taquería* . . . These are not my people and yet they are.

So I just roam around and decide to dip off onto the side streets. I circle blocks of one-and-a-half ranch houses in varying conditions with triangular roofs and no porches like you might see in a kid's picture book. So weird to be in a Latino 'hood without housing projects and tenement buildings, but maybe that's the Midwest for you. I end up in a more industrial area, where I see warehouses and boxcars amidst the homes and occasional auto repair garage and hardware store. Except for a car now and again, I see no one else on the street.

I decide to head back toward the main street. I sit at a red light when I catch a foursome of women reach the corner and cross the street. As they stroll by the Tempo, I can tell that they're *hermanas.* Two of them seem to be in their forties, maybe fifties. The third one holds a baby swaddled in a mint green blanket and appears to be in her late twenties. The last one looks to be a teenager. All of them dress simply in T-shirts and jeans with rubber-heeled sandals or dime-store sneakers. They speak casually among themselves in Spanish, and while I can't make out their words, I can pick up on their inflections. One of the older women is definitely *caribeña,* whereas the other sounds like she may be Mexican. The younger two—they look like they might be related—have round faces and angular features, and they listen on as their elders converse.

No one is behind me to honk me out of his way so even though the light turns green, I stall to watch where they are headed. In the distance, I see a three-story office building. I wait at the light until I see the foursome turn into the parking lot and walk toward the building entrance. The light is red again, but I look around and then run it. I pull into the small parking lot of the office building, cut the engine, and get out.

I don't know why I'm doing this. I mean, I could've parked on the main street where there were tons of pedestrian traffic and mom-and-pop shops to camouflage me. Maybe it's just me, but this building seems a bit out of place in this kind of area and because of that I want to check out what might be there.

I enter what seems to be a back entrance because there's not much to see but wall and floor. I look around for a directory and off to my right side I see a small glass door that reads *Latina Resource Center.* Of course, I gotta check this out.

So I walk through the door into a narrow corridor that serves as the reception area. Empty chairs lean against the wall, and on a small table sit a variety of health care resources in both Spanish and English. *Why you should breastfeed your baby. What to expect during menopause. How to speak to your children about drugs.* I snatch up one of every single brochure in each language. I know Irena already has tons of these at home and at the center, but that has never stopped her from adding to her collection. If she were here, she would pick them up, so I'm doing it for her.

Then I scan the posters on the wall, most of which are about domestic violence. My immediate favorite is a black-and-white poster of a round-faced Latina with long dark hair and a black eye with the slogan *La violencia no es parte de nuestra cultura.* Damn straight, it's not.

Irena and I had a long conversation about that once. We were sitting in the Olympic Flame, waiting for Lourdes and Hazel (as always) when she brought up a problem she was having at the women's center where she volunteers. She overheard two staff members discussing an "issue of cultural competency" to deal with domestic violence among their Latina clients.

"And they kept talking about how they needed to address *machismo. Machismo, machismo, machismo,*" Rena said in exaggerated gringo. "And the whole thing made me so uncomfortable, and I can't figure out why."

"White chicks?" I mean, isn't that the obvious fuckin' question?

"Yeah, but it can't be just that."

"No, you're right, it isn't just that. It's a lot more insidious," I said. "See, when you or I use the term *machismo,* it's just our word for 'sexism,' plain and simple. But when people outside the Latino community use it—and I'm not just talking white folks here 'cause I've heard black folks do it, too—they mean something more than that."

"What?"

"When they use the word *machismo,* they're envisioning this special Latin-style sexism that's unique to Latino men."

Irena put down her cup of chamomile tea. "There's no such thing. Sexism is sexism is sexism." She pouted. "Latino men are no better or worse than men from any other community."

"Exactly! But that's not their perception. They think that somehow sexism is more rampant or destructive in our culture just because we have this special name for it." I paused to take a sip of my hot chocolate. "Well, let's be real. Lots of Latinos think that, too. I mean, where did they get it from, right? So what'd you say to those staff people."

Irena shrugged. "I didn't say anything."

"Why not?"

"Because I'm just a volunteer, I wasn't part of the conversation—"

"Well, what the hell are you there for if you're not going to give them all you got to offer? It seems like they mean well but got it twisted. Straighten 'em out. If they're truly 'bout it, they'll appreciate it."

"I guess you're right."

"I'm totally fuckin' right." And Irena just laughed.

"Buen día. ¿Necesitás ayuda?"

I turn to the soft voice and see a middle-aged woman sporting a smart navy pantsuit and paisley scarf of multiple shades of purple. She has a shoulder-length bob and petite metal-framed glasses hanging from her neck. I say, "No, I'm okay. Just looking around." Then I remember to add, "But thank you."

She takes a few steps toward me. "Where are you from, if you don't mind my asking?"

Geez, this New York accent's like a brand on my ass. But she speaks to me as if she genuinely wants to help me and know who

I am. Like I could tell her I just escaped from the penitentiary, and it'd make no difference to her; if there's something I need that she can provide, she's going to fork it over, no questions asked. So I say as politely as I can, "I'm from New York . . . passing through on my way to California with some friends." I pause for a moment and then add, "One of my friends is sick, and I know she would've loved to have come here with me. She hopes to start a center like this in New York or New Jersey."

"Really? I'm from New Jersey," she says, walking to me until we are standing face-to-face. "Union City."

"*¿Cubana?*" She's gotta be. You don't get any more Cuban than that outside of Miami and the island itself!

She nods her head then squints at me. "*¿Dominicana?*"

"*Dominicana y puertorriqueña,*" I say.

"*¡Qué chévere!*" That's a first. As common as it's becoming in New York, you still tell people that you're Puerto Rican and Dominican, and they look at you as if you have three heads and ask you stupid things like which "side" you like more. I mean, maybe if my mom had left when I was much younger, I'd think of myself as Puerto Rican, but she didn't, and I saw the difference between our place and Hazel's grandmother's apartment. Sure, there were plenty of commonalities, but my birthday cake tasted different, the dance steps were different, and the precise wording of the warnings that preceded the dishrag as it flew toward my mouth were *definitely* different. I saw both the commonalities and differences in my house long enough to discern and appreciate them, and I felt really lucky until my moms bounced. "*¿De dónde?*"

"My dad's from Cabo Rojo, and my mother was from the Haina."

"Was?"

"Oh." I hadn't even noticed how I put that. "I mean, she's still alive. I think she's still alive, but she no longer lives with us." Christ, when did I get so loose-lipped about my personal business? "So is this a health clinic or . . ."

"We provide bilingual and bicultural advocacy, prevention, and crisis intervention services for the survivors of domestic violence and sexual abuse." She reaches toward the table, selects an

English brochure with the name of the center on it, and hands it to me.

"Really?" That's hot. "So you've got a lot of Latinos here in Omaha, huh?"

"About thirty thousand, which is almost eight percent of the city's population. In fact, Nebraska's one of the states with the fastest growing Latino population in the United States. Since the last census, our numbers have increased twenty-seven percent. Same thing in Iowa," she says, pointing east.

Damn, Toto, we're not in New York, Florida, Texas, or California anymore. "So where are they all coming from?" I ask.

"Most of them are Mexican, immigrants from Mexico and even migrants from California who come here to work in the meat-packing industry," she replies, motioning for me to follow her down the corridor. "But take our program director, Vanessa. She's Puerto Rican, born and raised here in Omaha. But we have a little bit of Latinos from everywhere—*salvadoreños, colombianos, venezolanos, ecuatrianos, panameños,* you name it, they're here." She leads me around the corner to a receptionist desk where a woman in her early twenties clacks away at a computer. "Julia, this young woman is visiting us from New York."

I offer the woman my hand. "My name's Jackie. Jackie Alvarado."

She swivels in her seat to offer me her hand, and I notice the purple ribbon pinned to her gleaming white collar. "Hi, I'm Julia."

I turn back to the kind older woman and extend my hand to her as well. She takes it and says, "I'm Cecilia Gardón, and welcome to the Latina Resource Center and to Omaha. Would you like to see the rest of our place?"

"I'd love to."

I follow her through a door and down another corridor. "It's small, with just a few offices, but we have a large meeting space where the women participate in workshops, take ESL class, and do arts and crafts. And there's a room and toys for their children, too." We end in an open space where we see a young woman in her thirties with a small Taino petroglyph hanging from a black cord around her neck. She must be Vanessa. She's drawn a food pyramid on a dry erase board on an easel and has asked the semicircle of women—including the foursome that lead me here—to tell her where the foods they usually prepare for their families belong. The women call out the staples of their diets—*arroz, frijoles, yuca, moto,* potatoes, plantains . . . No Atkins aficionados in this joint, except for a woman who I suspect is Argentine, and not just because of the extra trills in her *r*'s. Instead of mentioning different kinds of food, she's actually describing with passionate detail the multiple ways she cooks *bife.* If I ever had to move to Omaha, I know who my first friend would be.

La cubana waves to the group, and so do I. They smile and wave back at me as if they see me every day. The young girl I saw as part of the foursome whispers to the one holding the baby how much she likes my boots. I flash a grin at her before following *la cubana* into one last door with her name on it. CECILIA A. GARDÓN, PH.D.

The office is tiny or maybe it just seems so because it's filled to the ceiling with books, plaques, and replicas, both Latino and Christian. Many things catch my eye but nothing keeps my attention like her collection of drawings of Catholic saints popular among Latinos—Juan Diego, Teresa of Avila, Rosa of Lima, Martin de Porres, and even Benedict *el negro,* who was actually born and raised in Sicily to enslaved Africans. Despite all my Catholic schooling, I never saw a picture of a black saint until I stepped into Hazel's grandmother's apartment for the first time.

After I punched out Ralphie Muñoz for calling me a nigger, Doña Myra brought me upstairs. I expected her to reprimand me, maybe even punish me by throwing some chores at me or, much worse, force me to just sit there at the kitchen table with nothing to do. Instead she took me to her bedroom where she had a picture of St. Benedict tucked in the frame of her mirror over her dresser. She said to me in Spanish, "One day when he was working in the field, a neighbor started to call him names because he was black and his parents were slaves. A hermit came by and told the man, 'You taunt him now because he's a Negro, but it won't be long before you hear about his greatness.' " Doña Myra told me that St. Benedict was one of my patron saints, and that no matter what anyone might say about my blackness, he watched over me because God had destined for me to be great. The craziest thing about it? She didn't say, "And that's why you have to control your temper, you can't go around hitting people no matter how nasty they may be, blah, blah, blah." Doña Myra left it at that. She gave me a piece of homemade flan and a glass of milk and sent me back outside to play. I was eight years old. It was five years before Hazel came to live with her, and long before my own mother walked out. This is just one of the reasons why when she passed the summer before Hazel and I started college, it broke me up as if I had lost my own grandmother.

"Are you Catholic?" Cecilia asks, interrupting my thoughts, thank God.

"I was raised Catholic," I say. "I went to Catholic elementary school. I honestly can't say I'm still practicing, you know."

She nods, both sadly and accepting. I bet Cecilia hears that a lot. "So what is it that you do, Jackie?"

Besides drive people to the brink? "In the fall, I'm starting law school at NYU." Suddenly, I feel self-conscious and don't want to talk about myself. "I want to help my friend Irena start a center like this. You know, all the legal stuff."

"It's not very difficult at all. Just a bit time consuming," Cecilia says. Then she asks, "Is your friend Irena a law student, too?" She motions for me to have a seat.

I clear away a stack of reports on a chair and sit down across from her. "No, Irena's studying social work. We all go to Fordham. Well, I just graduated, but she's got two more years to go."

"I'm a social worker as well."

You know, there might actually be something to this synchronicity stuff that Rena talks about.

"*¿Por qué estas tan preocupada?*" Cecilia asks.

I guess I'm pretty obvious. But I don't want her to think it's about me, so I say, "I'm a little worried about my friend."

"Because she's sick."

"She's better now. It's just that . . ." I try to check myself, but I don't know, I feel at total ease with Cecilia. Here she is asking me questions that can lead to some pretty personal territory, and yet I don't feel the need to put up my guard, and that's not me. Maybe it's because she's a stranger I'll probably never see again. Maybe it's because I know that she has no idea what she's probing around. Maybe it's because it's really about Irena and not me, and if Irena were here, she'd take to Cecilia and bare her soul. "Irena's been through a lot in the past two years, and I'm really at a loss of how to help her. How do you counsel the counselor, you know. Especially someone like me."

"Someone like you?" Cecilia laughs as if the idea is ridiculous.

I laugh, too, pretending like I'm offended. Like who knows me better than myself so who is she to argue with me. "I'm not spiritual or sentimental and things like that. If anything, I guess I'm too in my head sometimes. I mean, nothing wrong with being brainy—"

"Absolutely not."

"But it's just not helpful when you have a friend who's in a lot of pain and in denial about it." I shift forward in my seat. "No, it's not denial. I can't say Irena's in denial. But she's just not really dealing with it either. I'm having a hard time articulating it."

Cecilia says, "I think you're doing just fine. It may help if you can tell me the primary issue that Irena's dealing with. If that's okay. Whatever you say here, stays here."

I think about it for a while. Would Irena mind? Certainly not several days ago anyway. Not at a place like this. So I finally say, "During her first year of college, Irena was raped on a date by a guy she just met."

Cecilia nods then asks, "And does she talk about it?"

"Yes and no," I answer immediately. "Irena talks, like, around it. So it seems like she's coping with it, but then . . . I don't know. It's like the whole issue is a big campfire, and Irena wants to walk around it. She gets close enough to it to feel a bit of the heat, hoping that you won't see that she's really scared of getting burned."

"And what would you rather she do?"

As fucked up as I realize it is now, I've gone this far and have to own up to it. "I want her to walk through it. I want Irena to walk right into the fire. I know damned well that she can't do it without getting burned, but it's what I would do. It's what would work for me, and so I want Irena to do it, too."

I brace for Cecilia's lecture about how it's not for me to say how Irena should handle her trauma. But Cecilia says, "You want Irena to walk through the fire because you have complete confidence that she can survive it."

"Exactly."

"And you would go through the fire with her."

"Absolutely!" Cecilia gets me. "I would totally go through it with her." But at that same moment I say that, I realize that maybe I haven't exactly made that clear to Irena. I thought I have, but maybe it just didn't transmit because of how I went about it. "I assumed that she would know that, but maybe that's been my mistake."

"Okay. Or maybe . . . Well, let me ask you this, Jackie. Has Irena watched you go through the fire yourself?" I want to say, of course, but something inside me won't let me. I mean, I think I have. But I'm not really sure. And Cecilia sees that because she says, "Have you—?"

"No, I've never been raped."

"That wasn't my question. And, yes, it's very important for Irena to connect with women who share her experience, but you don't have to go through what she did to help her," Cecilia says. "What I wanted to ask you was much simpler. Has Irena seen you walk through the fire—your own personal hellfire—get burned, and yet survive?"

"I don't know."

"Does she even know what it is?"

"I'm sorry—"

"You may not have been raped, but you have some idea of what Irena's hell is like. How much does she know about yours? See, Jackie, I have no doubts that Irena's fully aware of how much sympathy you have for her. What I'm wondering is how often have you allowed her to have sympathy for you?"

"Me? I don't know, Cecilia. I mean, how much does that matter when it's not about me anyway." C'mon now, isn't this where

I'm stuck? Isn't this where I fucked up? I tried to force Irena to deal with her problem my way. How am I supposed to help her by making her issue about me. Sounds pretty fuckin' selfish and more of the BS I've already been doing.

Cecilia's telephone beeps, and then Julia's voice comes over the speaker. "Dr. Gardón, I'm so sorry to interrupt you, but you asked me to remind you fifteen minutes before the Girls, Inc., meeting started."

Cecilia gently slaps her forehead with her palm. "*¡Ay, muchisimas gracias! Casi se me olvidó.*"

"That's what you have me here for," Julia sings before hanging up.

Cecilia looks at me and exhales. "Jackie, I am sorry that I have to end our conversation now. I have a meeting at the Girls, Inc., up the street with the other nonprofits that serve the women and girls in Omaha. Would you like to join me? I'm sure they wouldn't mind."

I really want to accept the invitation. And I really don't. I stand up and say, "Wow, I would've loved that, but I really should head back to the hospital."

"Hospital?"

Damn, I never mentioned that? Shit. "It's a long story, but Irena's there. We had an emergency, but she's fine now. I really wish she could've met you."

Cecilia opens her top desk drawer, pulls out a business card, and offers it to me. "Well, when she's better and if you have time, do bring her by. And if not, she can call or e-mail me any time with any questions." I take the card and put it in my back pocket. "And, of course, you can, too, Jackie."

"Thank you, Cecilia."

I pick up my brochures and accompany Cecilia to the parking lot. "The Girls, Inc., is only a short walk up the street, but after this I have to run a few errands." I walk her to her midnight blue Sunbird. Cecilia gives me a slight hug—not too familiar yet not so distant—encourages me to stay in touch, and gets into her car. I watch her drive off, reading her bumper stickers. On the left: *Let Cuba Live—End the Embargo.* And the right: *Because All Life Is*

Sacred—Catholics for Kerry. See, that's why you have to keep your electoral politics to buttons, but I'm certainly not mad at the good doctor.

I walk back to the Tempo and glance at the bumper sticker that Irena gave me: *Divas Don't Yield.* Sure haven't on this trip, and that's my fault, too. These are the kind of stops we should've planned to make, and Irena should've been here to see the center and meet Cecilia. Lourdes, too, for that matter, because they clearly have so much in common. Even Hazel would've gotten something out of coming here, because if I thought of her grandmother, then no way would the resemblance—at least in spirit—have gotten past her. The one person who didn't deserve to be here is the only one here. Maybe that's the reason why as I'm pulling out of the parking lot, I'm feeling both relieved and sad that my visit had to come to an end.

HAZEL

University of Nebraska
Medical Center
Omaha, NE
Tuesday, June 20, 12:22 P.M.

When Jackie returns to the hospital, she seems different. Her heart is still heavy and her mind is still preoccupied, but certainly not in the same way or for the same reason as when she left. At once, she strikes me as less restless yet much sadder. "Where'd you go?" I ask when she walks into the waiting room and sits down next to me.

"South Omaha. The Latino part of town. You should check it out."

"So what'd you see there? What'd you do? Any suggestions?"

Jackie shrugs. "I'll tell you about it later. Still thinking on it." She hands me the car keys. "How's Irena?"

"She's okay." Now I definitely know she found someplace or met someone. Of course, I'm very curious and hurt that she won't speak to me about it. What's the secret and why won't she share it with me? But I also know that it's futile to push Jackie at times like this. Even though learning that we now have a substantial amount of cash would put her at considerable ease, I can't tell her without explaining how I came about it, and something tells me that now is not the best time. "She's in there reading her books, journaling up a storm, and throwing every reason at Dr. Taylor to get her to stop prescribing the steroids."

Jackie smiles. "Do me a favor."

"Anything."

"Drop me off at the motel first." She stands up and starts toward the door. "I'm going to see if I can finally get some sleep and then come back and talk to Irena."

Clearly, Jackie's whereabouts this afternoon will be part of that conversation. "Okay."

"What?"

"Nothing. Let's go. I want to get out of here for a while, too."

"I hear that."

We walk out of the hospital and to the Tempo without saying much, and the ride to the Econo Lodge is just as quiet. I pull up to our room and ask, "Any word from Lourdes?"

"Nope. We should just accept that her mother's probably not going to let her come back. And we can certainly forget about getting any money from there."

I consider telling her about the money Wil wired, but I know she desperately needs to sleep. Whatever relief the influx of cash will bring will be outweighed by his refusal to come or even call. "You get some rest, honey. I'll be back in a few hours for you."

Jackie hands me Lourdes's phone. "Since I'm going to be here, you should take that."

I take the phone and place it on the passenger seat. "Okay."

I drive out of the motel parking lot and head south like she suggested. Before long the scenery changes from shopping centers and gas stations to storefronts and bus stops. I see why Jackie recommended I come here. As different as it is from the Bronx or Queens, it feels much more like home than anything we have seen on this trip thus far.

Lourdes's phone rings after I randomly turn on South Twenty-fourth Street. I hope it's Lourdes with some great news, but I don't pick it up. I don't know what the laws are here about driving while talking on a cell, but I prefer not to take any chances. The last thing I need is to get pulled over by a cop and slapped with a major fine or, even worse, get into a car accident because I'm distracted in an already unfamiliar environment. When he was teaching me how to drive, Jackie's father, Raul, said an accident is likely to occur when someone is new to the place where they're driving, not knowing when the next stop sign, legal turn, or oncoming traffic may appear. He also said never to doubt that even familiar territory can be treacherous because it's impossible to know if the person in the next car is the newcomer.

When I spot a parking space, I dip into it, turn off the car, and reach for the telephone. Whoever called did so from a New York City number I don't recognize and left a voice mail message. I see a key with an envelope icon on it and press it, hoping that the system doesn't ask me for a password.

You have one new message. To listen to your messages, press one. Funny, the second I do it, I know exactly who called before I even hear his voice. Still I can't bring myself to shut off the phone. I just have to hear what he has to say even though I'm clueless as to what good or bad news from him would be. *Lourdes, this is Wil. I still don't know what's going on with you four, but I hope you're all okay. I'm just returning Jackie's call, Hazel's e-mail . . . Tried the motel but there's no answer. Went online and saw that the money transferred was paid, and I guess I just want to be sure that it was by y'all because, like I said, I have no idea what's going on. I mean, Hazel said you were stranded so I just assumed what you need more than anything is money so . . . Okay, please have Jackie call me back. If she calls me at work, tell her to have the receptionist page me, and, well, I'll save all that for when she calls. Peace.*

I neither save nor delete the message but just shut the phone and put it in my pocketbook. Then I just start walking down the street with no idea where I want to go and how to get there. I debate whether to call Jackie and let her know that Wil called. I mean, I can't *not* tell her that he called although she never mentioned to me that she called him. He did say that she called him, didn't he? I don't know when she did it, but in addition to Lourdes's number, she probably gave him the number to Irena's room at the hospital as well as our room at the Econo Lodge. Instead of sleeping, Jackie is probably talking to Wil right now. They're having a fight, coming to an understanding, and falling for each other all over again. Jackie will bring up the trip they're taking to the Bahamas and Wil will ask her about the vacation money he wired when he got my e-mail. She'll realize that not only did I reach out to him behind her back, I failed to tell her when he responded. Our friendship will be irreparably damaged—and maybe mine with Lourdes and Irena, too, when Jackie tells them—if not over.

Only when I catch a little boy staring at me as he walks down the street holding his mother's hand do I realize that I'm crying hard enough for people to notice. I stop before a discount shop to check my reflection in the front window. I haven't bothered to wear makeup these past couple of days, and without eye shadow and lipstick of very particular colors, this scarlet hair color makes me look less like Milla Jovovich and more like Velma from *Scooby-Doo.*

I start walking again, determined to enter the first salon I see. Within seconds I spot a place across the street called Salon de Chelena. I jaywalk across the street and am inside the salon before I realize that there might be laws in Omaha against that, too.

Chelena's is brightly lit and very clean without seeming cold and sterile. Unlike the square salons that I'm accustomed to in my neighborhood, this one is like a long but wide corridor. While a few chairs line the wall to the left, most of the stations zigzag in a row down the middle of the salon with chairs alternating on each side. One stylist about my age blow-dries a teenage girl's hair while her friend sits in the next chair reading an article about Luis Miguel's latest exploits from *People en Español.* Another stylist in her early thirties on the other side of the row laughs at the gossip as she collects and sorts the bobby pins scattered across the tabletop of her station.

"*Hola,*" I say as I near them.

The two stylists look my way and give me warm smiles. The one who's unoccupied seems happy to have someone to help. "*Bienvenida, ¿y cómo te puedo ayudar?*"

I point to my hair and say, "*Hace como dos, tres dias desde que me cambié el color y ya me lo quiero quitar si es posible.*" Then I add more to myself than to anyone else, "A big, impulsive mistake."

The woman reaches out to take a strand of my hair and rub it between her two fingers. "Your hair is in excellent condition," she says with a moderate accent that I can't place. We both laugh at my discovery that she speaks English.

"Thank you. I do hair myself."

"Ah!" she says, smiling. "So you did it yourself at home?"

"Yeah, but I wish I hadn't gone with this color, and I know better than to try to change it myself. Especially since it's only been a few days. Please tell me you can fix it."

She puts her hand to her chin and ponders my request. "Well, at least your hair is healthy. Do you remember what kind of dye you used?"

"It was definitely semipermanent." Thank God for that. "And I want to go darker."

"Oh, okay," she says. "I don't have to tell you, that makes it much, much less risky than going lighter."

I don't realize it until I say it. "No, I want to get as close to my natural hair color as possible."

The stylist reaches across her station for a hair color guide in the frame of her mirror. On the grid of colors, she finds and points to my current one and says, "So you want to go from this to what, mama?"

It's been so long since I wore my hair naturally, I can't remember myself what shade of brown it actually is. And I can't bother to refer the poor woman to my eyebrows, because I dye them to match my hair.

The stylist senses my frustration and asks, "Maybe you have a picture? Your driver's license?"

No, that won't be of any help. And even if I had any of Lourdes's pictures on me, my hair would either be this color or whatever the hell I had before I left New York City. Then I remember that I just might have a picture in my wallet. I reach into my pocketbook for it and unfold it. I flip through the wallet-size photos that I've taken for granted. My little *abuelita* wearing a humongous corsage on her eightieth birthday. A roughly cut Polaroid of my father in his prison greens. Even a head-and-shoulder shot of my mother that my grandmother claims was taken while she was pregnant with me. And then I come across a high school graduation picture of Jackie and then one of the two of us together that my grandmother took. We're wearing our Catholic school uniforms and sitting on the stoop of our building. Jackie and I have our arms around each other and our cheeks pressed together.

"Aquí tengo un retrato perfecto." I pull the photograph out of its sleeve so that the stylist can get an accurate look at it. As I hand it to her, I say, "This is what I want to go back to."

LOURDES

6403 S. Blackhawk Way

Aurora, CO

Tuesday, June 20, 2:34 P.M.

After I hang up with Jackie, I cry myself to sleep only to wake up now. It takes me a moment to realize that I'm not in my bedroom at the Ansonia or in one of the cheap motel rooms that Jackie reserved for us. I sit up and reacquaint myself with my room. The Liz Claiborne linens on the bed and windows. The Bose home theater system. The walk-in closet filled with clothes bought at LoDo boutiques such as Serina Gray and Triage yet smuggled home in shopping bags from Foley's and Dillard's. (Did I leave the door ajar? *¡Voy a matar a Oscar!* He's been going through my things again.)

My eyes fall on the Louis XVI vanity table Papá bought me for my fifteenth birthday. Mamá was so angry with him for giving it to me two months early. She wanted to present it to me during my *quinceañera,* a major production that would have outdone the Big Dinner. But Papá couldn't keep it from me. He knew I would love it as much as he did and for the same reasons. Most girls would fall only in love with the air of it all, but my father understood how much I would appreciate the brown and gray marble tabletop, the fluted legs, and the floral basket crowning the center mirror.

My parents had hidden the vanity table in my father's office thinking I would never discover it because they had no idea how often I was in there. But after going into Papá's office looking to "borrow" a photography book from his library and finding the table, I ran into the family room to ask my father, "*¿A dónde conseguiste esa mesa tan bellisima?* I wish I had something like that!" Eager to confess, Papá told me the table was actually my birthday present. At my insistence, we set out to carry the vanity table from his office to my room. We fawned over the table and my father told me that Mamá thought it was gaudy. As we lugged the table down the corridor, Papá and I teased Mamá in her absence about having no taste, and we guessed that she would chide us for confusing high prices and old age with good taste.

My mother came home with Oscar from his playdate in time to catch us in the midst of all this *cargando importuno* and threw a fit that impressed even my little brother, who at seven was the master of tantrums. The argument did not end when my father and I finally got the vanity table into my bedroom but continued for almost a half hour in Papá's office. I pressed my ear to the door, listening to my mother complain about how he ruined my big *quinceañera* surprise and my father apologize over and over again for it and knowing that he was not the least bit sorry.

About a month later, my father had a heart attack in his office at the company. Papá had been dead slumped at his desk for several hours before Marie found him. We cancelled the *quinceañera,* which is the only blessing that came from the untimely loss. *Nunca quería esa fiesta estúpida,* but I could never tell my mother that. She thought I genuinely liked the girls I had selected to be my *damas* when I doubted they would even bother to pretend to like me if I didn't attend the same school and had the same charge cards. *Dios perdóname,* I'm not saying they were bad girls, but I cannot pretend that I received much from their friendship. I gave them multicultural cool. They gave me a great deal of anxiety over when I might say or do something that would remind them that, despite my parents' income bracket, I was far from one of them.

That's why regardless of all our differences, Jackie, Hazel, and Irena mean so much to me, and I realize that it goes beyond the fact that we are all Latina. Irena always says that our essence is made of those aspects of our humanity that would be the same regardless of things like our race or class. Even if Jackie had been born a white man, she would still be the clown-bully who is unafraid to speak the unsaid. She probably would be like Michael Moore or Tim Wise. If Hazel were born a straight *blanquito* into a Norman Rockwell family, she would probably be a lot like that guy Jimmy we met in Des Moines: still a romantic yet not hopeless soul ready to love and eager to forgive. And Irena, she would be . . . well, I don't know who she would be like since I refuse to have anything to do with her occult hobbies. But if Irena had been a black man who was raised by a single mother, she would be compassionate and generous and . . . She would be *Kharim*!

Jackie, Hazel, and Irena certainly are not my friends because I have money. I realize these three are my friends *despite* the fact that I do.

In fact, until I met Jackie, Hazel, and Irena, I had no friends—true or false—who cared as much as I did for the welfare of people who were not part of my everyday life. Any doubts I had about why were laid to rest when I got that e-mail from Jackie with the subject *Road Trip!,* inviting me to drive with them to the Gamba Adisa Conference. She never asked if we could go in my SUV; I volunteered it. When I offered to spring for the occasional hotel room as a break from all the economy motels, Jackie politely declined, saying that if it were all the same to me—and never assuming that it was not—they all preferred to split the cost of a room at a rate everyone could afford. And when, at a planning meeting at the Olympic Flame, I asked if there was anything I could bring that we might need with the secret intention of buying whatever she suggested if I didn't already own it, Jackie said, "If you don't mind the rest of us using your blow dryer, iron, and stuff like that, pack them so we can share them, save space, and travel lighter." I became more excited about being with them even if it meant staying in motels and keeping restaurant meals to a minimum. I wanted to bond with the three of them and make more friends like them from around the country at the conference. Now not a single one of us may make it to San Francisco.

But I am going back to Omaha.

I finally jump out of bed and walk over to my bureau. Ripping open the drawers, I find clean clothes. I think that I should bring some fresh clothes for the others, too, so I walk into my closet and find a small overnight bag. For the life of me, I don't know what I have that might fit Jackie in size or personality! Perhaps my mother still has some of my father's T-shirts that she can wear if she did not give them away to Goodwill.

Then the idea hits me!

I rush back into my closet and tear it apart until I come across the box in which I keep my hood hair dryer. I carry the box to my bed and drop into it any and every portable appliance that I might be able to pawn for money on Larimer Street. And if that doesn't work, I'll go to Colfax and sell it on the street myself! I toss into the box the radio, the alarm clock, the DVD player . . . the same rush that I experienced when I bought them comes back to me. I start to wonder how I might be able to take the television because this baby's a thirty-two-inch flat screen. I can get good money for it, but there's no way I can take all these things on the bus. First, I have to get enough cash for a cab ride downtown, and I am running out of time.

JACKIE

University of Nebraska
Medical Center
Omaha, NE
Tuesday, June 20, 3:06 P.M.

Let's see if I can remember how to do this. If I hadn't promised Lourdes, I wouldn't bother, but I keep my promises. It doesn't matter that she would never know. I would know, and that's enough. The thing is I haven't recited the rosary since I got kicked out of Catholic high school for checking the principal, Sister Maguire. She was only going to suspend me for the rest of the week for popping Mercedes in the mouth for dissing Hazel, because everyone knew she was a premium snot. I could tell by the smirk on her face that Sister Maguire was secretly thanking me for taking Mercedes down a few notches and was only suspending me for appearance' sake. I guess she knew I knew that because as I was walking out the door she said to me, "You're not as smart as you think you are, Jacqueline."

To which I said a little too loudly, "Apparently not or I'd be at the Bronx High School of Science instead of this place." I didn't even know until I got home that she had called my father at his job to tell him I was no longer welcome at Scanlan. She said it was because of the fight, but Dad knew better. Catholic schools don't kick out kids whose parents pay their tuition in full and on time over one fight. Bad enough the black girl with the immigrant parents was at the top of her class, but she had the audacity to let everyone know it.

Okay, so on the crucifix, I'm supposed to make the Sign of the

Cross obviously and then recite the Apostles' Creed. Funny, I remember the name of the prayer and its point—it's pretty much a laundry list of basic Catholic beliefs, so reciting it is basically a profession of faith—but I can hardly remember all the words. The beginning's a snap. *I believe in God the Father Almighty, Creator of Heaven and Earth, and in Jesus Christ, His Only Son, Our Lord who was conceived by the Holy Spirit, born of the Virgin Mary, suffered under Pontius Pilate, was crucified, and was buried.* I can't remember the rest, and that kind of bothers me for some reason. Can't be because I still believe in all this stuff, 'cause I don't. I mean, I believe Jesus existed, that he was a cool guy who always rooted for the underdogs. I believe he said things—simple yet profound things—that if people actually heeded, the world wouldn't be such a fucked-up place.

And I'll never tell Lourdes this, and maybe it's kinda wrong to think this while I'm sitting in this chapel holding her rosary in my hands, but I also believe that either Jesus started to believe his own hype or lost his mind. I haven't determined which. How else can you explain why he started saying he was the son of God and recruiting people like Jim Jones and whatnot? But I also believe that regardless of whether he started to feel himself or lose his mind, Jesus still was a harmless guy with a good heart. He wasn't like self-proclaimed prophets nowadays, asking his flock to fill his cup with gold and silver so he could roll through Galilee on a two-humped Bactrian camel wearing a purple silk robe and flossing gold and ivory. Maybe if he had, the government wouldn't have been like, "Yo, we need to check this cat." They wouldn't have knocked the hustle and let him be so long as he was rendering to Caesar what was Caesar's and all that. Anyway, whether the man was sane or not, I never doubted that Jesus existed, and that he was one of the most extraordinary beings to walk the earth. If you have to emulate someone, he's not a bad choice. Not the only choice, of course, but right now I could stand to be a little more like him.

I guess that's my post-Catholic take on the Apostles' Creed, God, and it's going to have to do. I don't believe in that kind of mythology anymore. I don't remember when I stopped. Maybe I never truly did.

But I do believe in you sometimes even if not in the way Lourdes does. She's got this *abuelito* in the sky image of you. In Lourdes's idea of heaven, folks bounce from cloud to cloud, living out their fantasies, reuniting with their loved ones and the like, and then at dinner time they all convene for story time. I mean, she doesn't call it that, but Lourdes believes you gather everyone and regale them with explanations of life's mysteries. Like you break down the science behind how you created the world, flooded the earth, parted the Red Sea, built the Grand Canyon, and things like that. Me, I'd want to know how you could let the Yanks choke in the 2004 World Series—getting swept by the freakin' Boston Red Sox after eighty-six years, no less. My guess is that JC lobbied you pretty hard on that one, and I can't say I blame him since despite being a die-hard Yankee fan, I'm a relentless champion of the underdog myself, although admitting that a tiny part of me was happy that the BoSox won would be a surefire way to get my ass disowned. Well, it's not like at this rate I'm going to heaven to find out what the deal with that was anyhow so, yeah, like I was saying, I don't buy Lourdes's idea of you.

Now Irena thinks of you as a force, but I kind of like the idea that you have some human qualities to you. When I was a kid, I saw *Romero* once, and ever since I always imagined you as Raul Julia except with long white hair and no glasses. I like the idea that you have a face. A temperament. A sense of humor. Everything humans have but much better. Definitely much more intelligent than we are. Like I believe that you created the world and set it in motion, allowing evolution to do its thing. I know you invented tsunamis, but I'm pretty convinced that cancer's our doing. Not too sure about AIDS though. At least, I don't buy that you created it to punish anyone, let alone any particular group of us. Sure, every once in a while you shake things up in our individual lives just to remind us that free will has its consequences, so that we better not take it for granted and should use it wisely, but I don't believe—at least I don't want to—that out of some righteous impulse, you fuck us up just for kicks. After all, we do that just fine with no help from you. As you know, I've outdone myself on this trip, and my poor friends . . .

"Jackie." I turn toward the doorway of the chapel, and there stands Hazel. I almost don't recognize her, because she's gone off and changed her hair color again! I like Hazel's new hair color because it's not really new at all. If she lets it grow, it'll look just like when we were in high school.

I hastily make the Sign of the Cross, genuflect, and meet Hazel in the back of the chapel. "Let's go outside. I'm tired of being cooped up inside." She hooks her arm through mine. "Besides I have to talk to you about something."

She leads me to the atrium. Now that things have settled, Hazel probably wants to lecture me for what I did to Irena and the impact it had on Lourdes. I'll eat it. I'm not looking forward to it, but I have it coming, and I'd rather she light me up now than wait until Lourdes gets back from Colorado.

As we sit down in the atrium, the sun catches the hair on Hazel's crown. It shines so brightly, I can't resist sliding my fingers through it. "Haven't seen your natural hair color since we were sixteen." Homegirl colors it twice in less than a week, and it still glides through my fingers like silk. If Hazel weren't my favorite person on the planet, I'd resent the shit out of her.

"This is about as natural as it's gonna be till I grow it back."

"It's such a perfect match, no one's going to notice." I glide my fingers through her hair again. "It's so shiny and soft. How do you pull that off?"

"By not doing it myself," she laughs. "I found this place on the south side called Salón de Chelena."

"Found some sisters to do your hair, huh?"

"There are so many here, Jackie. From all over. Mexicans, Cubans, Salvadoreans, Venezuelans, you name it. In Omaha! I wish we could spend more time here really getting to know the city instead of—"

"Yeah, I know." Then it hits me. "How much did that cost? No way you got your hair done at a time like this!"

Hazel pulls out a piece of paper and hands it to me. "I stopped by Kinko's to check my e-mail, and I got this." As I read the printout, her voice quickens. "Jackie, please believe me. I only reached out to Wil because I wanted to support you. If I had known that he would take it . . ."

I shrug and stand. Like Wil wrote, I should've called him my damned self. I want to rip up the e-mail, but instead I fold it up and shove it in my back pocket. I've got enough things on my mind without having to grapple with the fact that not only did my boyfriend effectively dump me via e-mail, the e-mail was addressed to my best friend. "Let's check on Irena."

Hazel grabs and pulls my hand. "C'mon, Jackie, let's talk about this."

"There's nothing to talk about, Haze. This was inevitable. And I'm not upset with you at all. I know why you e-mailed him."

"You do?"

"You're my best friend, and you know Wil loves me . . ." I had never said those words before. The worst thing about saying them is that I finally can only now when it's too late.

"I didn't call Wil because he loves you." Hazel stood up to face me. "I called him because *I* love you."

"That's what I said—"

"No, you said that I called Wil because he loves you, but that's not why I did it. I called Wil because I love you."

"I know that." Of course, Hazel loves me. She's my best friend. No, she's more than that. Hazel's my sister. Even though she agrees with me that Wil should not be playing Daddy Dearest to Eric knowing that Sheila wants him back, she put her feelings aside and called him because she knew he would help me. I never told Hazel that I called him. I was too embarrassed. And if Wil didn't come through for me, that would be much worse. He did come through for me, but made it clear that this would be the last time he would be there for me. I never should have doubted him in the same way I never doubt Hazel.

Hazel reaches out and turns my face toward her. "No, Jackie, listen to what I'm saying to you. I love you." She caresses my cheek, touching me in a way she never has before.

And suddenly, I understand.

I absolutely cannot deal with this right now!

But when I get up, Hazel yanks at my arm. She stands up and gets in my face. Not in a romantic way either. She just told me she loves me, so why does she look like she wants to sock me into next week? "Don't you dare fuckin' run from me."

I try to break free from her, but Hazel tightens her grip on me. She's turned into the Terminatrix, and I'm not feeling it. Hazel knows how I feel about being manhandled. Or womanhandled. Whatever. I don't like being handled period, and she knows it. "You of all people should know better." I finally break free and back a few steps away from her. "Irena's sedated in a hospital thousands of miles away from home. Lourdes took a train across the country by herself with nothing but a calling card in her pocket. Wil quits me for *not* doing something . . . Chances are that when we get back to New York, none of them will have a thing to do with me. Hazel, you're the only person in this world who is strong enough to stand me. What kind of *pendeja* would I have to be to get that involved with you so I can drive you off, too?" I feel eyes all over me, and sure enough when I look around, I see these strangers staring at Hazel and me while pretending to ignore us. Why do people freakin' bother? I turn around and yell, "Can we have our business back, please? Thank you!"

I turn back to Hazel, and the sad eyes I usually see are beaming with anger. Not annoyance or frustration. Pure anger. The last time Hazel was this angry at me, we didn't speak for two weeks. We were fourteen, and she came out to me. At first I iced her. It took me a few days to realize that my discomfort with her sexuality was not about Hazel but about myself. I went to Hazel to own up to my shit and apologize to her, but she would have nothing to do with me. It almost killed me. I missed her so much because I never had—and still do not have—a truer friend. I just can't have Hazel mad at me. Least of all now.

Hazel peers into my face and says, "No wonder Wil left you. If you would lay that bullshit on me after nine years of putting up with your ass, I can only imagine the drama you try to run on that poor man. Why can't you be honest?"

I have no idea what the hell she's talking about. "I am being honest. If anything, my freakin' problem is that I'm too honest. You're the only person I know who can deal with me honestly."

"Then stop making me feel like an idiot for being in love with you."

"What do you want me to say, Hazel?" I throw my hands up in the air and recite all the lines men have given to me. "I'm sorry, but I'm already with somebody. I really like you a lot, but I just don't see us that way. You're awesome, but I'm just not ready for this right now." Now the sadness seeps back into Hazel's eyes, and my heart pounds against my chest because for once I have no answers. As hard as I tried to act as if I didn't care, is that how I looked at the guys who gave me these excuses when they realized that despite what they're supposedly looking for, they find themselves attracted to me? But I'm not like those gutless men. I knew what they meant when they were saying those things to me. "You've got all the right ingredients, but you're in the wrong package." But that's not what I'm trying to say to Hazel.

I walk back to her and put my hands on her shoulders. "Hazel, I couldn't love you more if you were my sister. Most days I love you more than my own flesh and blood. To tell you the truth, I really don't think a man exists who I could love more than you. But the love I have for you is just not the same kind of love I have for Wil."

Until I say that, I realize that I have never expressed my love for Wil either. I've been so afraid to admit it to myself. I think *I love that man* in the same way I think *I love fettucine Alfredo* or *I love the movie Krush Groove.* I never take my own thoughts seriously, let alone say them aloud to anyone. Now the best friend a woman could ask for tells me that she is in love with me, and all I can think about is how in love I am with this man I just drove out of my life.

I suck.

"That doesn't make you feel any better, does it? I'm sorry, but it's the truth. Know what else is true? You deserve better, Hazel. You haven't been with a single person yet—male or female—who's worthy of you, and wanting me? That's just stooping to a new low. Not because I'm your best friend or because I'm straight or because I love Wil or anything like that. Even if all that weren't true, I still wouldn't deserve you."

Hazel stares into my eyes with such intensity, I expect their greenish gold to darken into a murky brown. "You're right, Jackie. I do deserve better. We all do." I don't know what I expected Hazel to say to me, except not that. Nor can I read her. My best friend for the past nine years, and I don't know whether she's teasing or checking me or something different and worse. The shit's not cool.

I try to laugh. "Gee, Haze. Love me a little less, why don't you."

Hazel doesn't laugh. She says, "Yeah, why don't I? You walk around like Little Miss Confidence. *Straighten my hair, paint my nails, or wear a dress just 'cause you say so? Fuck you!*" I might have enjoyed her imitation of me had she not been so damned accurate. "*I'm not gonna watch my language or lower my voice. This is who I am, so deal. And if you actually love that about me, well, fuck you twice.* How's that for honesty?"

Then like everyone else in my life who matters, Hazel walks out on me.

LOURDES

6403 S. Blackhawk Way
Aurora, CO
Tuesday, June 20, 4:23 P.M.

With my duffel bag hanging from my shoulder and my hair still wet from my quick shower, I haul the box filled with my sellable gadgets to the front door. Then making the Sign of the Cross, I walk into the kitchen and reach above the sink where Valería keeps her cookbooks. I pull open the back cover of one book, and there is the wrinkled envelope with *ABARROTES* written across the front in her blocky print. In the envelope is about a little under a hundred dollars in bills, a bunch of coins, and a stack of receipts.

Ay, no puedo. Even though I don't think of it as stealing from Valería—it's my mother's money. Money that she gives Valería to buy our groceries. Groceries to feed herself as well as Oscar and me, and none of us are here now. *Pues, yo estoy aquí, pero* I'm not staying.

The only way I can do this is if I let Valería know. I can't let her find out about it when she returns from vacation, goes to the cookbook for cash to go shopping, and finds it missing. And leaving a note doesn't feel like enough. So I walk over to the telephone and dial her cell phone number.

The call goes directly to her voice mail. As I wait for her briefly bilingual greeting to end, I picture Valería sitting on the beach with a margarita in one hand and her open cell phone in the other. As the caller ID displays our home number across the screen, she scoffs at it and snaps her phone closed. Good for her! And not just because it benefits me.

The greeting beeps, and in Spanish I ramble everything I believe I need to say. That I hope she is having a fabulous vacation because no one deserves that more than she does, and that I'm only calling because I have an emergency situation and need to borrow the grocery money, and not to worry that it's only a temporary loan until I get the money I'm expecting from someplace else, and that once I had it, I would send her a money order for the full amount immediately. I take a breath then say, *"Y te extraño y quiero muchisimo."* I pray that Valería doesn't think I said that because I borrowed the grocery money without first getting her permission. She has to know that I truly do miss and love her. *Claro que sí que ella lo sabe.* And I know she loves and misses me, too, although I also have no doubts that when Valería gets my sincerely loving but undeniably suspicious message she will be thanking God that she is on vacation.

I fold the cash and stash it in my pocketbook. Then I scan the photographs and magnets that dot our refrigerator for the business card to one of the local taxi companies. Just as I find one and dial the number, the front door slams. "What is this box doing here?" my mother yells. "Lourdes! *¿Lourdes Rosalia Becerra Chacón, dónde estas?*" Her Stuart Weitzman pumps clack across the hardwood floors toward the kitchen.

¡Ay, no puedo! I cancel the call but take the telephone with me when I rush into the living room. "I'm here, Mamá." When she sees me, she stops walking. My mother takes the stack of accordion files tucked under her arm and places it on the coffee table. "You're home early."

"Thanks to your escapades, I haven't been able to concentrate at the office, so I decided to come home, deal with you, and then finish the rest of my day's work from here." She notices the telephone in my hand. "Who are you calling?" But before I can even answer, my mother gestures for me to take a seat on the sofa. "*Siéntate.*"

But I cannot move. "No."

"Excuse me."

I rush to the front door. "It's not that I don't want to sit down and talk everything out with you, but . . ." I stop to turn around and face my mother, and it scares me how angry I suddenly am. Is this how Irena felt when Jackie pushed her to the breaking point? No wonder she became so sick. It had to come out somehow. For once I see some merit in the things that Irena says about the mind-body-spirit connection and how emotional unrest leads to physical disease. And thinking about Irena just makes me even more furious. "You should've talked to me before you went to the office. Now I don't have time to talk because the next train to Omaha leaves at—"

"I told you that you're not going—"

"Yes, I am, Mamá!" I've never interrupted my mother, let alone raise my voice to her, *y no me gusta.* I don't like it one bit so I hope my mother does not force me to do it again. "My friends need me."

"They're using you for your money."

"No, they're not. *Sí, necesitan dinero,* but whether or not I can give them any, they want me to go back. How can you say such things about people you've never met?"

"I'll give you that one, Lourdes. I didn't know a thing about these so-called friends except that one is sick, the other has a filthy mouth, and the last . . . she's a complete mystery to me!"

"Her name's Hazel. I mean, Carmen. But we call her Hazel."

"Carmen, Hazel, Jezebel . . . *¡a mí no me importa el nombre de ella!*"

"But you should care, Mamá. You should know all their names, what they look like, where they're from. And maybe you should assume that because they're my friends they just might be good people." I am more furious than ever but with no one but myself. "They're not the ones who lied to you. I did, and I'm sorry. It's nobody's fault but my own that you had to find out about us this way."

"What do you mean find out about us this way?" Suddenly, my mother gasps. "*Ay, Dios mío.* You're a lesbian!"

"*¡Ay, Mamá, no soy lesbiana!* But would it be so horrible if I were?" I look into my pocketbook, *y gracias a Dios,* I find several envelopes of photographs. Some are the photographs I printed out at a Cleveland drugstore, and others I took long before our trip. I sift through for a picture of Hazel. Of course, she looks amazing in all of them, but the one I took of her wearing her bathrobe and leaning on my balcony at the Ansonia during a slumber party is worthy of *Life.* The way Hazel holds her cigarette as the breeze blows through her hair, she looks like a golden age Hollywood starlet like Hedy Lamarr or Lauren Bacall. "This is my friend Hazel, and she is a lesbian. She cuts and styles my hair and never lets me pay for it. She's the one I call when I want to go shopping or dancing." I try to hand it to my mother, but she refuses to take it so I just balance it on the back of the sofa. "The more I get to know her, the more I question the Church's position on homosexuality. If Heaven is supposed to be such a joyous place, then I don't understand why God would create someone like Hazel just to keep her out of it. She's filled with so much love, and it makes no sense to me."

I flip to the photographs until I find one of Irena on a merry-go-round horse at the carnival. "*La flaquita*'s name is Irena. I've mentioned her to you before. We're always debating about religion because . . . well, she hates it. But Irena has this beautiful spirit. She may not belong to any organized religion, but she's the most spiritual person I've ever met." *Me pongo a llorar,* and I just let the tears flow as I continue. "I used to pride myself on being of service to and having compassion toward others, but I have nothing on Irena." I almost tell my mother that Irena's the friend who is sick, but I feel that would misrepresent her. Despite the girlish setup of the photo, Irena appears wise and strong, and that's the impression of her that I want to leave with my mother.

Then I find a picture of Jackie. She may not be as beautiful as Hazel or as cute as Irena, but it amazes me how photogenic she is. In every single picture I have of her, she is absolutely striking. The camera never fails to capture her essence because it's so filled with both power and vulnerability. I laugh because Jackie threatened my life every time I tried to take a picture of her alone, and I had to steal every shot I have of her by herself. In each and every one, she looks like a warrior princess. Her back is always straight and her neck long. Jackie's skin is flawless. In my favorite photograph of her, she's reclining on the hood of the car with her back against the front window, her hands folded behind that mass of dark curls and her long, toned legs straight yet crossed in front of her. She leaned back and looked directly up at the sun like an urban goddess.

I hand this photo to my mother. "*La negrita* is Jackie. She's the one you spoke to on the phone, and she almost came home with me. Even though she didn't, she's the reason I'm here. And not just to get them money, but for my own good. I could call her right now, and she would make the nine-hour drive to come get me. Jackie sometimes gives me a hard time, but God help anyone else who tries to mess with me." Then I add, laughing, "Even you, Mamá." Her head snaps back with indignation, but before she can interject I say, "I've never had a friend with as much courage or loyalty or integrity, so if I have to put up with her teasing every once in a while, *pues lo hago* because her friendship is worth it.

"So these are the women I'm traveling with. My friends. And I have to get back to them because—money or no money—they need me. I don't know what I'm going to do for them, but I know I'll be of better use to them in Omaha without almost no money than here in Aurora with plenty of it."

I place the rest of the photographs on the sofa and walk around my mother and back into the kitchen. I redial the cab company, tell the dispatcher that I want to go to the Ballpark, since the Larimer Street pawnshop I saw is near there. He takes my address and tells me that the taxi will be in front of my house in five minutes.

When I walk back into the living room, my mother is gone. *¿Pues que voy hacer?* Continue with my plan. I collect my photographs, throw open the front door, and drag the cardboard box into the driveway. The cab arrives on time, and the driver gets out to pick up my box and place it in the trunk. I climb into the backseat and say, "The Ballpark, please." A sharp rap at the window makes me jump. My mother continues to bang on it even though she knows she caught my attention.

I roll down the window. "*¿Señora?*" After what I have said and done, the least I can do is show her respect. My heart races with anticipation for both the best and the worst at once.

My mother sticks her upturned palm through the window. "Give me your credit cards."

"Mamá, you already cut them off, remember. They even confiscated one from me. The other one is of no use to me."

"Then you don't need it, do you?"

Dios perdóname, pero odio a mi madre en este momento. I really do. No commandment demanding that I honor my mother can change the fact that right now I genuinely feel that she hates me, and I hate her right back. If that's such a big sin, it's hers and not mine.

I reach into my pocketbook and pull out my wallet. I open it and take out the essentials—my driver's license, school ID card, and the grocery money. Everything else, from the department store charge cards to the receipts for purchases I made on the trip, I leave behind and hand the entire wallet to my mother.

"Lourdes . . ."

"Drive." The cabbie throws the car into first gear and lurches away from the curb. I hear my mother calling my name, but I refuse to turn. Maybe in the near future I will think of this moment with guilt or shame or embarrassment, but right now it feels damned good to show my mother what it feels like to be treated like this. *Quizas voy al infierno por esto,* but after I imagine Lucifer folding a linen napkin into a bishop's mitre and setting it on my dinner plate, I realize that I'm starving, and I make a note to buy myself something to eat before I get on the train back to Omaha.

JACKIE

University of Nebraska
Medical Center
Omaha, NE
Tuesday, June 20, 7:43 P.M.

I knew Irena had a little diva inside her, but she surprises even me when she insists on checking out of the hospital tomorrow morning. The whole steroid thing really pisses her off. Although I've been checking my attitude around her, I have to remind Irena to show Dr. Taylor a bit more appreciation for blocking her path to the other side. She apologizes and thanks Dr. Taylor for her conscientious treatment, but still demands to be discharged against medical advice. Irena obviously gets off on rebelling against the medical establishment, and I have to admit, for a while there she gives a good show.

At least she's started speaking to me. She had Shonda come get me from the chapel. Although I gave up on praying the rosary, I kept them on and just chilled in the front pew. The place grew on me, I guess.

When I came to Irena's room, she opened her journal to the apology I had scrawled in it. Irena refused to talk to me, but I knew if I wrote that I was sorry in her journal, she would see it. Only after I finished it did it occur to me that I shouldn't have done that. So I braced myself for the blast I had coming. Instead Irena said, "Could you redraw this in our collective journal?" And that broke the ice. I catch her up on everything—Hazel's revelation was no news to her at all, and how she picks up on these things I'll never freakin' know—and she tells me about the letter she wrote to her father. One down, two to go.

"When does Lourdes get back?" Irena now asks as I help her pack her things.

"Five thirty tomorrow morning. Hazel's going to pick her up then come get me. The three of us will go to the motel to get our stuff and settle our bill. Then we'll come get you."

"You think we can make up the time?"

"Make up time for what?"

"To get to the conference in time, silly."

"You're kidding, right?"

"No."

"Rena, the only place we're headed is back to Jersey City."

She stopped packing to start pouting. "You mean there's absolutely no way we can make it to the conference?"

"Only if we fly." No chance of that happening. We don't have *that* much money. Irena goes back to packing, and I think that squashed it.

But then Irena says, "You mean, even if we pushed through it . . ." She reaches into her suitcase for a forest green folder with the recycling symbol on it and pulls out some stapled pages. Irena flips through printouts from Juno, MapQuest, Hotels.com, and other Internet sites until she finds the page she wants. "Look, Frisco's only a day from here. If we drive nonstop, we can make it, Jackie."

This chick's crazy. "First of all, there's no way any of us is letting you drive, so we're down to three drivers," I say. "I know no one's been through more in the past couple of days than you, but c'mon, Irena. That's a lot to ask of us."

"I know," says Irena. She takes a deep breath. "But I'm asking."

"Why don't you just want to go home?"

" 'Cause I'm not ready to, that's why. None of us really is. We're almost there, Jackie, and I don't know about the rest of you guys, but I'm not ready to give up."

I don't want to give up either. I'm certainly not ready to go home. I can't imagine that Hazel or Lourdes are either. And I can see us pushing through, trading the wheel every few hours until we see the silver beams of the San Francisco Bay Bridge. In fact, I want to be the one behind the wheel when we reach the bridge just as the sun comes up. To be the driver who wakes up the others to let them know we finally made it. But I don't see us making it anymore, and I don't mean to San Francisco.

"Even if we drove nonstop, Irena, we'll have missed so much. We'll be lucky if we make it to Frisco in time for the closing ceremony. I don't know if it's worth all the trouble."

"I think it is." The way Irena's smiling at me I can tell she knows that I believe so, too. "I know it's not only up to me, but Hazel and Lou will sign on if you back me up."

When she says that, I understand why she wants it so badly. It isn't really just about her. Irena wouldn't push for this for her own sake. She wants it for all of us. Irena probably had one of her intuitive moments where she saw the four of us getting to Frisco and experiencing this miraculous sense of reward. A few days ago, I would have nixed the idea—no matter how psyched I was about it—if I had sniffed the slightest hint of a holistic rationale. Throwing down shots of espresso, blasting hip-hop, and eyeballing the bushes for 5-0 just for the adrenaline? I'm all about that. But going through all of that on the promise of some kind of spiritual rush at the end of the rainbow? Uh, yeah.

"So what do you think, Jackie?"

"Rena, I'm not sure."

"Please. Let's just go."

Irena's expression sounds familiar, but I can't remember where or when I had heard it before. Not being able to place it, however, doesn't stop it from getting to me. It lifts my spirits and breaks my heart all at once.

"Cali, here we come." Irena squeals, jumps, and hugs me like she just won the lottery. "But we need to rest tonight and leave on time tomorrow. I mean it, Rena. Nine A.M. sharp!"

I beat her off me and head into the corridor to get us something to drink from the vending machine. As I smooth out a dollar and slip it into the machine, I replay Irena's plea. What does it remind me of? *Let's just go.* With that saddest of smiles. Like something out of a movie. As Irena's apple juice clunks into the tray at the bottom of the machine, it hits me.

It's the last thing Thelma tells Louise right before they drive off the cliff and into the fuckin' Grand Canyon.

IRENA

San Francisco State University
San Francisco, CA
Thursday, June 22, 10:34 A.M.

Eager to experience as much of the conference as possible, I say to Lourdes, "Let's forget about the schedule and just walk around. If we find something we like, we'll stay."

"*¡Pues vámonos!*" Lourdes grabs my hand and yanks me down the hallway toward a random door.

"Okay, but don't just go busting in." She pulls open the door, and we slip into a room full of about two dozen other people. They had pushed all the folding chairs against one wall and had assembled along the opposite side of the room. In the front stand two women as different as can be. One is African American and about my age. She wears a very short Afro, thick glasses, and a beautiful sarong with the colors of a ripening mango. The other one is white with long dark hair peppered with gray and braided down her back. She has on a Gamba Adisa T-shirt and jeans, and I guess she's in her forties.

"Come, come," she says as she waves Lourdes and me into the room. "We're about to start the power shuffle."

The African American woman strides over to an easel with newsprint scrawled in purple marker. "Take a moment to read the guidelines, and then we'll begin."

As Lourdes and I take our place among the other participants crowded along the wall, I quickly scan the guidelines.

POWER SHUFFLE—AGREEMENTS FOR PARTICIPATION

- *Honor confidentiality. What is said here, stays here.*
- *Respect yourself and others.*
- *Speak only from the "I."*
- *Dialogue not debate. Agree to disagree.*
- *You have a right to pass.*
- *Take responsibility for your own learning. Ask for what you need.*
- *Feel free to express your emotions.*
- *Avoid interpreting other people's experiences.*
- *No "rescuing"!*

I grow excited about the exercise. I have heard about the power shuffle but have never done it before, neither as a participant nor facilitator. I look forward to experiencing it, knowing that I will want to take it back to the center and share it with the women there.

"Remember," says the older facilitator. "Participate as much or as little as you feel comfortable, but Rashida and I strongly encourage you take risks with this exercise."

"You don't have to identify with any group that is called, but do take notice of any feelings that come up when you choose not to identify yourself," says Rashida.

A middle-aged woman—honestly, I can't tell if she's Latina, southeast Asian, Arabic, or what—raises her hand. "What if you're not sure about which group you belong to?"

"Excellent question," says Rashida. "Each of you has to decide for yourself where you should go." She pauses for more questions, and when none are forthcoming, she says, "Doreen, I think we can start now."

Doreen looks down at the sheet in her hand and reads, "Please step to the other side of the room if you are a woman." With the exception of the six men in the workshop, the group ambles to the other side of the room like cattle. Some of us start giggling, feeling both silly and nervous. Silly because it seems like such an obvious question yet nervous because we know that at a conference like this, nothing is ever as obvious as it seems. Rashida raises her finger to her lips, and I realize that silence is an important part of the exercise. I settle down and motion Lourdes to do the same.

When we make it to the other side of the room, Doreen says, "Notice who's standing with you." Lourdes and I look at each other and smile. "Notice who's not." Then I look across the room and take in the guys we left behind. But one of them is not a guy at all. I mean, her hair is marine short, but her bosom and hips are unmistakably full under her large T-shirt and baggy jeans. Then Doreen says, "Notice how you feel," and the point of the exercise begins to sink in. I like it. And I don't.

"Come back together again." As we women drift across the floor to rejoin the men on the other side of the room, we leave the silliness behind but take the nervousness with us. Everyone is tense with anticipation, waiting for Doreen to read the next statement.

"Please step to the other side of the room if you are a person of color." I hustle to the other side and fold my arms across my chest. "Notice who's standing with you." Lourdes is standing on my left side. On my right is a young woman about my age who looks like she might be Latina, too. Or maybe she's biracial. If not for the texture of her brownish blond coils, she probably could pass for a white woman. But here she stands next to me, her arms folded across her chest, too. I quickly glance at the others on my side of the room and catch a black woman staring at me. She shuttles her eyes away from mine, but I keep my gaze on her. "Notice who's not." Get to the next question because I've got a lot going on here. "Notice how you feel." Defensive, Doreen. That's how I feel. I may have pale skin, blond hair, and blue eyes, but that doesn't make me white. I mean, I'm white, but I'm not *white.* Maybe I don't get followed around stores like Jackie or get confused as the help like Lourdes, but I'm no Anglo. Before I can untangle all the other thoughts and feelings rushing into my head, never mind process them, Doreen says, "Come back together again."

I barely reach the other side when Doreen says, "Please step to the other side of the room if you are Latina, Chicana, or *mestiza.*" So I spin on my heel and head back to the other side of the room.

As I do, I look for Lourdes and I see her lingering. Did she hesitate? But she's Latina. Chicana even! But come to think of it, I don't think I've ever heard Lourdes refer to herself as Chicana. Perhaps that's why she hesitated. I don't know. "Notice who's standing with you." We all look at each other, and who's in front of me but the black woman who had just been staring at me. That's right . . . for all I know, she could be *cubana,* too. Or Dominican. Or Puerto Rican, Colombian, Panamanian, Brazilian . . . Just about anything, couldn't she?

And I barely hear Doreen's instruction to notice who's not standing with us because now I'm stuck on the fact that Chicanas were named while the rest of us are lumped under Latina. I mean, I get how their unique history with the United States makes such a distinction so important, I really do. But as a *cubana,* can't I say the same? Can't Jackie? Or Hazel? What's that about? "Notice how you feel." Is, like, nationalistic an emotion? Because that's how I feel. Not to mention somewhat indignant and righteous. And now even a bit petty. "Come back together."

Doreen reads down her list of statements, mentioning all the other racial categories. And even though we're supposed to be as aware of one another as much as ourselves, I surprise myself so much with my own identifications that it becomes too much to also keep track of who's standing with me and who's not. Like when she calls for Native Americans or people who have at least one parent who is full-blooded Native American, I stay put even though I know that being Cuban means that I have some Native ancestry. When Doreen starts, "You're African American, or black . . ." I dig my heels in only to sail across the room when she finishes, ". . . or of African descent." I mean, I'm Cuban. Despite how I look, that makes me of African descent. I know there are some people who are "noticing" me, some affirming my identification while others are criticizing it. And I don't give a shit. It seems like the right thing to do. Had Doreen left it at "black" or "African American," I would have kept my white ass on the other side of the room. But she said African descent, and so this is where I belong. It feels right standing here regardless of whether others believe I belong here or not. And yet for the second I considered claiming my Native American heritage, I felt like such a poseur that I decided not to walk across the room. Funny, Lourdes didn't either.

Doreen continues through a series of statements about age, national origin, sexual orientation, religion, class, education, and language. We shuffle back and forth across the room, and I sail through these and focus more on who's standing with me and who's not. She even offers a few statements about disabilities and I find myself starting to enjoy unveiling myself and having my assumptions challenged as others in the room do the same.

Then Doreen hands Rashida the paper and steps to the side. Rashida proceeds to read from the sheet, but now the questions focus less on the textbook constructs and other things. Things that are relatively easier to identify in oneself yet so much more difficult to admit in a roomful of strangers.

"You come from a family where alcohol or drugs are a problem."

"You or a member of your family has ever been labeled mentally ill or crazy."

"You or a member of your family has ever been incarcerated."

"You come from a family where physical, verbal, or emotional abuse is a problem."

Fewer and fewer people trek across the room. I can see people deliberate, hesitating before deciding to move to the other side or stay in place. With some I can even sense their internal struggle after making the decision to stay or go when Rashida says, "Notice how you feel." Faces tighten and tears stream. People second-guess their identifications and then grow self-conscious, wondering if their doubts are transparent to everyone else in the room as they notice who is standing with them and who's not.

I know Rashida is going to ask *that* question, and I have no idea how I am going to answer. Not because there is any doubt in my mind as to what the answer is. There is no doubt what the answer is, and that's why I'm dreading the question. And I guess that's why they call it the power shuffle. Each of us has power in some circumstances and is rendered powerless in others, and often the distribution of power is based on nothing but perception. And perception is fueled by things like assumptions, judgments, and even silence.

"You have been raped or forced to have sex against your will."

Everyone is still until an elderly white woman with a cane begins to cross the room. For the past few statements, she had been a fixture in the back of the room. As she ambled across the floor by herself, I have so many questions about her story. How old was she when it happened? Did it happen more than once? Was she assaulted by someone she knew? I imagine her telling this story at a Take Back the Night speakout when my inner voice interrupts my visualization. *Why are you still standing here?*

So I begin to walk across the room. Without thinking about it, I quicken my pace until I am next to her. I don't want her to be alone in revealing this truth, any more than I want to be alone doing the same. I find myself wanting to offer her my arm, but I fight the urge, reminding myself *No rescuing!* The woman turns to look at me. Through the deep wrinkles around her eyes, I see that they are the same shade of blue as mine. She switches her cane to her other hand and takes hold of my elbow, silently asking me for what she needs. I offer her my arm, and she squeezes her speckled hand around my forearm.

Only when we reach the other side of the room, and Rashida says, "Notice who is with you," do I realize how many people have followed us. Of the two dozen or so people in the workshop, ten of us have crossed the room. That's more than the 18 percent the statistics say because after all, the statistics are based only on self-reports and almost 40 percent of rapes go unreported to the police. And among the ten of us are two of the six men in the workshop. I mean three because the man with the bosom and hips is with us as well. With me.

"Notice who is not." I look across the room and catch eyes with Lourdes. Although she's crying, she tries to smile. "Notice how you feel."

Lourdes isn't crying because she feels sorry for me. She's crying because she's proud of me, and I know this not because my intuition is strong. I know this because I feel proud of myself, and that's the reason I'm crying, too.

HAZEL
San Francisco State
University
San Francisco, CA
Thursday, June 22, 2:17 P.M.

While scanning the bulletin board, searching for interesting workshops that might still have openings, I run across a sign-up sheet for the open mic following the closing march. I scan the instructions:

CLOSING RALLY OPEN MIC—SIGN-IN SHEET

Each performer will have FIVE MINUTES. Including your personal info is optional, but it helps Gamba keep diversity alive! The show will go on for as long as there's an audience. Caution: we WILL discriminate against the self-absorbed, so keep to the time limit. (In the spirit of solidarity, don't make us remind you!)

Name	Race, Age, Etc.	Talent
Ashleigh Park	Straight (but not narrow), African American–Korean, 19	Spoken Word
Crystal	Heterosexual MTF transgender Pinay	I want to recite a poem I wrote in

	immigrant goddess, 24	memory of Gwen Arujo. It's only three minutes. Thank you!!!
Sonia Guzmán	Bi, Xicana, 43, low-income single mother of twin boys, legally blind	Drumming
Melody and Malika	Interracial (Irish/Italian and African American/Haitian) lesbian couple, childless (for now) both of us are 31.	Melody dances while Malika sings and plays guitar.

On the next free line, I write:

Hazel Flores	Queer, abled Nuyorican, 22	Kick-Ass Singer!

Somehow this gives me the courage to browse the list for Geneva's panel, which is happening right now. The fact that we missed so much of the conference yet still arrived in time for me to hear Geneva speak makes me feel compelled to find her. What would Irena call it? Synchronicity.

Geneva's panel takes place in the very last room down the hall. The handwritten sign outside the door reads *Sister Outsider—Multiracial Organizing in Queer Communities.* Just as I reach for the door handle, the door sails open and two sisters rush out.

"I can't believe she said that shit!" said the light-skinned one with the buzz cut and almond-shaped eyes.

Her friend with the chocolate tone and shoulder-length locks with blond highlights says, "Some of them think they're so far along that they're beyond criticism."

My hope that they're not talking about Geneva surprises me. I scour my pocketbook for my handheld mirror. I find my lip gloss only to decide that I don't need to reapply it, so I drop it back into my bag without even opening it. I comb my bangs with my fingers, and suddenly going back to my natural hair color feels like an accomplishment. I close the compact, put it back in my bag, and slip into the classroom.

The tension in the packed lecture hall immediately envelopes me. I find an abandoned seat in the back row. A white woman—one of two on the panel of five, including the moderator—is speaking. "I know this is difficult to hear, but we have to get past these divisive identity politics. They've outlived their usefulness, and the sooner we accept this, the more successful we will be in moving our agenda."

The speaker seems familiar to me. I lean toward the woman next to me and ask, "I'm sorry, but who's that speaking?"

"Pamela Cheevers."

Now I remember the speaker's face from the photo on the back cover of her widely acclaimed collection of essays. Geneva had so many issues with the book, I didn't dare ask to borrow her copy. Instead I borrowed it from the university library and kept to myself how much I loved Pamela's poignant stories of coming-of-age—and eventually coming out—during the eighties as the only white kid in the West Indian section of Crown Heights. It surprised me how much I related to Pamela's experiences, much more so than I did with any of Geneva's tales about growing up middle class in a suburb of Atlanta. Geneva dismissed the book as the lesbian *8 Mile,* and at the time I told Geneva that had she written something similar, her book never would have been as widely reviewed let alone made the *Times* bestseller list, even though Geneva's a more compelling writer. I genuinely believed that and still do. But I also believe Geneva was a bit jealous of Pamela's success, although I kept that to myself, too. She never asked me how I knew that she was a better writer than Pamela Cheevers.

Geneva reaches for her microphone just as the other white woman on the panel begins to speak. "What you have to understand, Pam, is that the ability to demand an end to identity politics is itself rooted in a position of privilege," she says. Applause scatters across the room, and the woman sips from her bottled water until it ends. "It's easy for a white person to tell a person of color that race is now an obsolete social construct. That's no different than a man arguing that sexism is dead because women have made some gains. Don't forget how it feels to have a heterosexual tell you, 'If you just stopped being so *out,* your lifestyle would be more acceptable.' "

"It's not the same thing, Kathy."

"Isn't it?"

"Professor Boyd has been patiently waiting to speak for some time now," says the moderator. She seems white, too, but wears a traditional Native American blouse adorned with beads and ribbons. "Geneva, your thoughts?"

Geneva adjusts her glasses on the tip of her nose and clasps her hands in front of her. According to the schedule, this workshop is slated to end in about eight minutes, but I have seen her a dozen times in a setting like this and know that the dialogue is only beginning. When Professor Boyd straightens her glasses and folds her hands, it means only one thing. We are about to enter the Geneva Zone.

"It both disheartens and yet fails to surprise me that in a workshop about multiracial organizing in queer communities, two white women are dominating the discussion." This time the applause comes on the backs of whistles. The white girl next to me leans toward her friend sitting on her left and whispers, "I was just thinking the same thing." Then she looks over to me and shrugs. I smile and shrug back, wondering if she thinks I'm white, too. If you ask me, I couldn't read more Puerto Rican if you tattooed a *coquí* on my forehead, but this wouldn't have been the first time I would be taken for white. In fact, I'm usually mistaken for white by white folks who want to sleep with me, men and women alike.

Geneva waits until the cheers subside and then continues. "I agree with Pam that we have to recognize the limits of identity politics in moving a queer liberation agenda. However, Kathy's right that we have to acknowledge the role it plays in giving marginalized groups a base of strength. So the key's to put identity politics in perspective. We can't act as if differences don't exist in the hopes that if we pretend to be color-blind or dismiss sexual orientation as a private matter or what have you, all the isms and their effects will fade away." I look around the room, and Geneva has the majority of the attendees regardless of race hanging on her every word. "By the same token, we can't be so invested in our personal identities that it becomes impossible to collaborate with others who don't share them. That solves nothing nor does adopting a naïve we-are-the-world attitude when someone expresses pride in belonging to a group that has been the object of intolerance and terror. So my challenge to everyone here is this: How do we use our identities as foundations that ground us, yet push ourselves to reach past them in order to build alliances across our differences? Let's stop wasting our time debating the relevance of identity politics because *this* is the question that we have to answer."

She barely finishes when virtually every woman in the room stands on her feet to clap, cheer, and stomp, myself included.

The moderator apologizes that we have no time for the Q&A, so participants should proceed to their next sessions. Instead attendees flock to the front of the room to speak to Geneva. By the time I reach her, about a half-dozen women have already encircled her; some are holding copies of her book, which her publisher must have sent out just for the conference, as the official publication date is still weeks away.

A young woman asks Geneva to autograph her book, then says, "I'm the head of the lesbian and gay organization on my campus, and I could really use your advice, Professor Boyd . . ." Here we go again. How many times did I have to wait for Geneva at the end of her classes while she dispensed wisdom to burgeoning lesbian activists? I laugh to myself because even as I feel such affection toward Geneva right now, I don't miss being in this position one bit. That's when I notice who might have taken my place.

Pressed to Geneva's elbow is a young Indian woman about my age. People call me beautiful, but I have nothing on this girl. She radiates gloriousness in nothing but a fringed denim skirt and T-shirt that reads SASSE—South Asian Sisters for Sexual Equality. She brushes her spiky dark bangs out of her huge black eyes, and I feel a slight twinge of jealousy. With five more students waiting to speak with Geneva in front of me, I decide to wait for her outside. I leave the room and find a cluster of lounge chairs not too far from the door. I look around and sneak a cigarette out of my bag, dropping it out of sight every time the door opens and a new group of conference attendees drifts out on their way to the last session before the closing rally.

So for one last time I sit in the hallway of another university waiting for Geneva. I stub out one cigarette and reach for another. Twenty minutes pass and she finally emerges from the lecture hall carrying a stack of folders and books with Pamela Cheevers on one side and Ms. SASSE on the other. Geneva puts her hand on Pamela's shoulder and whispers something in her ear that makes Pamela laugh. They sign each other's books and trade business cards. Then Geneva gives Pamela a warm hug, and she and her friend make their way toward me. I stand up, and despite my drastic change in hair color, Geneva recognizes me.

"Carmen! I was wondering if you were here. Did you make it to my panel?"

"Yeah, we just got here," I say. "Long story. Don't want to get into it right now."

"Oh." Geneva turns to her companion and says, "Trishna, this is Carmen. I believe I've mentioned her to you." *You know you damned well have!* "Carmen, this is Trishna."

I offer Trishna my hand. "Such a pretty name. Is that, like, Hindu for 'gorgeous'?"

Trishna laughs and shakes my hand. "Oh, thank you. Actually, it means 'desired one'."

"I bet."

Trishna blushes a shade of red that makes her even more beautiful. When she giggles, Geneva puts her arm around her shoulder. "Honey, why don't you head back to the hotel, and I'll catch up to you."

"Okay, do you want me to take that for you?" Trishna asks, motioning for Geneva's portfolio.

"Please, thank you." Geneva hands her the portfolio but then motions for Trishna to return it. "Let me get something from there first." She reaches into the bag and pulls out a copy of her book.

"You know she can't go anywhere without one of those should she run into an adoring fan," I say.

Trishna giggles again. She obviously understands exactly what I'm driving at. Geneva might have wasted no time trying to replace me with another starry-eyed bombshell, but like me this one's smarter than she thinks. I give it six months. Then Trishna says, "Nice to meet you, Carmen." The way she's smiling at me, I now give it three months.

"Likewise, Desired One."

Geneva and I watch Trishna as she walks down the corridor until she disappears around the corner. Then Geneva turns back to me and smirks. "Were you just flirting with my hostess?"

Hostess, my ass. And, I never meant to flirt. I mean, I never mean to flirt. I just do. "That's what you get for messin' with students," I say.

"I was doing no such thing—"

"When are you going to find someone your own age?"

"Carmen, I'm really not comfortable with—"

"You'd think you'd learn your lesson."

Geneva finally realizes that I'm having a little fun at her expense. Mine, too. "I'm glad you're here. It's really good to see you."

"It's good to see you, too." This I mean. "You were great in there as you always are."

"Does that mean you've read my book?"

"I was waiting for you to send me my own autographed copy."

"Here it is." Geneva hands me the book. I pull back the cover to find the inside blank. Perhaps this was presumptuous, but I had expected that she would not only have signed it but included a warm, personal note. "Keep going." I flip until I reach the dedication page. *For Hazel.* Then Geneva had written down the page. *You have inspired me with an intelligence that cannot be found in between the pages of any book. You have moved me with a compassion that cannot be captured in words. You have loved me with an acceptance that cannot be forgotten. These things will stay with me always even though you have decided that you cannot. For that I am forever grateful. Always, Geneva.*

I might have kept my cool had Geneva not taken that moment to reach out and brush a few strands of hair off my face. The tears roll forward as if she pulled a lever inside of me. "You were right." I take a deep breath. "I made a big mistake."

It takes Geneva a few seconds to understand what I mean. "No, honey, you didn't." Then Geneva pulls me toward her, and for the first time since I've known her, she lets me cry on her shoulder.

LOURDES

Market Street
San Francisco, CA
Saturday, June 24, 4:11 P.M.

Before the rally begins, I find the Catholics for Choice contingent to lend them the banner. Then I just weave throughout the crowd, snapping random shots at whatever inspires me. So much so that I have to resist the temptation to use all the film I have left. I need to save some for Hazel's performance at the open mic and our ride back to New York City.

The march down Dolores Street begins *y esa negra siempre tiene alguna sorpresa.* Leave it to Jackie to be the only woman to march with Men Against Machismo! They're mostly a group of black and Latino men, and they come stepping down the street like the fraternities in that Spike Lee movie. Jackie's marching behind the members, holding the banner and leading the chant with a bull horn.

Racism, sexism, two walls, same prison.

"Jackie!"

Without breaking the rhythm of the chant, she looks for me. I run out of the crowd to kneel before her and take a close-up shot. She calls for one of the men to take over the bullhorn, then says to me, "Wait until you see this!"

Jackie along with five members of Men Against Machismo break out in the step routine. *¡Qué tremenda!* She must have spent what few hours we had learning and practicing the choreography.

I use half a roll on that alone, taking a few shots of the crowd cheering for good measure.

About a half hour later comes the Cubanas for Cuba float. *Esa loca* Irena is on it. She holds a sign that reads *End the Embargo* and chants along with them *in Spanish!*

P'arriba, p'abajo, bloqueo pa'l carajo.

I laugh and take a few shots. A girl next to me with burgundy hair and a nose ring nudges my arm. "What did they say?"

"They're pretty much saying . . ." As much as I don't like to curse or swear, it feels like a more serious sin to offer an inaccurate translation. ". . . to hell with the blockade against Cuba."

"I hear that!" The girl hoots and pumps her fist in the air. "Can you teach me how to say it?"

Ay, Dios, perdóname, but not only did I teach her how to say *P'arriba, p'abajo, bloqueo pa'l carajo,* I enjoy it.

I go through almost four more rolls during the march, which was open to all who wanted to participate. Most of them I use on the Parade of Stereotypes and the crowd itself. For the Parade, people dress up in exaggerated costumes as their "favorite" stereotype to show just how ridiculous they are. One Latina wore an amazing costume where on her left she resembled *la Virgen de Guadalupe* but on her right she is dressed in a bright red tube dress and black fishnet stockings. How she was able to put so much padding on only half of her butt, I'll never know. Not to be outdone, a pair of Japanese twins—one dressed as a Geisha holding a toy ball and chain and the other dressed as a dominatrix cracking a whip—have tied themselves to one another back to back! A black guy comes by in pants so huge, he can barely walk, and the crowd laughs as he tries to bop in them. He also carries a giant fake marijuana cigarette under one arm and a toy rifle in the other. When he notices that I'm taking pictures, he flashes me a big grin and gives me a hilarious gangster pose. A black woman dressed as a body builder and holding a barbell made of Styrofoam rushes into one of his shots. The round weights at the end of her homemade barbell are actually globes. *¡Qué creador!* I love it!

The black man pretends to throw a tantrum. "Just like a Strong Black Woman to try to upstage a brother."

"Just like a Dangerous Black Man to whine about it."

I take a few great shots of them pretending to box around each other while trading quips about who is more oppressed. "Okay, show me the love now," I say, and they put down their props to give each genuine hugs and kisses.

Suddenly, two women sail by in a golf cart stacked with suitcases with a *Just Married* sign on the back, dragging streamers of tin cans behind them. The crowd roars with laughter. Now it's my turn to tap the girl next to me. "I don't understand."

"There's a joke that lesbians like to move in together by the third date."

I giggle and take a few pictures of the couple in the golf cart only to be distracted by another female couple. The fair-skinned one is dressed from head to toe like an Orthodox Jewish man and is counting a thick stack of play money. She is arm-in-arm with a girl of Arab descent who has used cardboard rolls of paper towels to make a belt of fake bombs wrapped around her waist. Some people in the crowd point at them and whisper, and I can sense that some are offended. I'm not. I think they're the bravest couple I've seen so far, and I take about six pictures of them.

An Irish man carries a blowup toy of a gigantic whiskey bottle and wears a red clown nose. Behind comes a group of Italian men dressed like Tony Montero, wielding pipes and crowbars. One of them even pretends to chase the black guy around the crowd. They start to laugh so hard at themselves, they have to sit on the curb to rest. The Strong Black Woman hands them each a water bottle. I catch a picture of the Dancing Mobster and the Dangerous Black Man toasting one another before throwing back long gulps of water. A white woman wearing a business suit, a tight bun, and faux combat boots like Jackie wears marches by with a white man in a headlock. It takes me a moment, but then I get it. She's the Ball-Busting Femi-Nazi!

I can't bring myself to laugh when I see the white man dressed as priest holding hands with another man dressed in overalls and sucking on a pacifier. I have to accept that I'm the minority on this one because everyone else adores them. I swallow my reservations and push myself to take a few photos of them. And as I do, I find myself smiling at how absurd it all is. After all, this is the point of the parade. If we are neither laughing at one stereotype nor squirming at another, we're missing the point that we are all fair game.

Even though I have two more years before I graduate, I already have a fantastic idea for my senior portfolio in my new major.

JOURNAL—DIVAS DON'T YIELD

Just reflecting on the intentions we made at the ritual—to learn something new, find love, and release fear—and wanted to check in to see how you guys thought you were faring. —IR

I feel that I've traded one set of fears for another, but I've also learned that not only should I tackle my fears head on, I'm quite capable of doing so. I'm praying on how, and I have no doubts that I will find the answer. —LB

I wanted to find love, and I did. It just wasn't the kind of love that I was looking for. In fact, it's more accurate to say that I discovered a love that's always been there. So I guess the lesson I still have to learn is how to appreciate that love. –CHF

I learned a whole bunch of stuff. What I'm going to do with it, who knows? Still trying to get a handle on it all, so bear with me —JA

Here I was anticipating elaborate reflections when I should have been open to the possibility that you are all processing everything that has happened and perhaps need space to do that. My bad. Just know that you're not alone in your transitions, and that if and when you are ready to share more, the rest of us will be here with open ears, minds, and hearts. Aché. —IR

Aché –CHF

Amen. —LN

Word. —JA

HAZEL

Dolores Park
San Francisco, CA
Saturday, June 24, 7:51 P.M.

My stomach jumps with both relief and nervousness when the emcee of the open mic tells me that the band knows the song I want to sing. "They love Cree Summer. Sing any song you want from that album," she says. "Just let us know."

" 'Miss Moon' is perfect."

"Okay, you go on right after the Pinay dancers."

The Pinay dancers are on stage now! I look into the crowd to where I found Jackie, Lourdes, and Irena standing, but they're gone. Then I find them again as Jackie leads them to the front of the stage while Irena appears to explain to folks that a friend of theirs is performing next. Lourdes adjusts the zoom lens on her camera.

The Filipino music stops, and the crowd bursts into applause for the Pinay dancers. They take their bows and jog off to the left of the stage. The emcee thanks them for their performance then says, "Next up we have a gorgeous—and I do mean gorgeous—singer from the Big Apple who is going to sing one of my favorite songs. Give it up for Hazel Flores."

The audience claps as I make my way to center stage. Jackie yells, "Bring it, Hazel!" I laugh and adjust the microphone. After getting permission from the emcee, Lourdes climbs onto the stage to take photographs. I consider introducing the song but then decide it can stand on its own. Instead I signal the band, and it plays the opening chords. Many in the crowd recognize the song and cheer, including Irena, who claps and sings along. By the time I reach the bridge, the crowd is singing with me.

I'm not sorry for the fire . . . inside my heart
I'll be howling . . . for Miss Moon.

Everyone in the audience who knows the song is serenading someone they love, from honeys and homegirls to mothers and mentors. Jackie stands at my feet, and I look into her eyes and sing. *Miss Moon, Miss Moon, Miss Moon.* She knows this song is for her although she is unsure what it means. That's okay. I know.

I finish and the crowd bursts. Some even howl like wolves just like in the song. Jackie leads them in chanting my name. "Hazel, Hazel, Hazel . . ." I take a quick bow and rush off to the left side of the stage. As I walk through the crowd, people shower me with smiles and thanks for my song. I have never sung before an audience before, and the response is intoxicating.

The compliments flutter around me as I make my way toward Jackie and the others. An a capella group that performed earlier yell, "Brava!" as I pass by, and I can tell they're genuinely impressed and not just caught up in the spirit of sisterhood, although I would have liked that just fine.

A mass of corkscrews zips by me in the distance, and my eyes follow it. Before I can confirm if it belongs to Jackie or not, strange arms fling themselves around me. Someone ambushes me with a hug, and it takes me a moment to pull back far enough to see the face of a striking brunette with butterscotch skin and crescent eyes that turn upward with her glistening smile. I expect her to step back in embarrassment and apologize that she had confused me for someone else.

Instead she says, "I just had to hug you 'cause 'Miss Moon' is one of my favorite songs, and you have such a beautiful voice." Her New York accent's unmistakable. "Hearing you sing that song was like . . ." And like a true New Yorker, she flails her arms around as if searching the air for the right word. "You really touched me. I mean, I sing in the shower and the water runs cold."

I laugh. "Thank you, that's so sweet of you to say. Is it me, or are you from New York City?"

"Born and raised in Quisqueya Heights. Still live there. You, too?"

"Can't you tell?"

"Well, yeah now that you mentioned it." We both laugh. "But you're Puerto Rican, right."

"Right. You're Dominican?"

"Yes, yes, yes! Thank you! All week when folks have found out that I'm from New York, the first thing they say is, 'Oh, so you're Puerto Rican.' And I'm, like, nooooo. I mean, there are other kinds of Latinas in New York. Not that I don't love my Boricua sisters. The love of my life was Puerto Rican."

"Oh." My heart sinks so fast, I swear she can hear it. The purpose of this entire week was to connect with amazing women, and I've been crossing signals the second I climbed into that raggedy Tempo. Then I realize she said *was.* "What happened to her?"

"Bitch left me for another *dominicana.*" And she laughs without a hint of bitterness and looks over her shoulder. "They're back there somewhere. We all came out here together."

When she faces me again, I beam a smile right into her eyes. "Doesn't mean that the love of your life is not Puerto Rican?"

She offers me her hand, which is as smooth as a pearl. "My name's Maria. But they call me La China 'cause you know . . ." and she points to her eyes.

"My real name's Carmen, but they call me Hazel because of you know . . ." and then I point to my eyes. Long after we laugh, we're still holding hands.

JACKIE

Mary Hall Ward
San Francisco State
University, CA
Sunday, June 25, 4:03 A.M.

I decide to stay up for Hazel, who wanted to hang out longer with China and her friends and catch up to Trishna and her peeps. They went to some place called El Rio and invited all of us along. I thought about it. On the one hand, I've never been to a lesbian club, and I'd be lying if I didn't say I'm curious. On the other hand, I couldn't shake the feeling that I was eavesdropping on a private conversation. Curiosity felt better so I headed back to the dorms with Lourdes and Irena. If she had not been so tired, Irena would have been all for it. Nothing fazes that girl. She's something else. I think Lourdes would have preferred to skip the club, but if Irena and I had wanted to go, she would have kept her reservations to herself and tagged along. But I'm the one who chickened out.

So I just lie awake in bed, staring at the beam of light being cast across my bed by the streetlight outside my window. I know Hazel's safe—probably the safest she's felt in a very long time—but I wish she would hurry up and come back. The idea of her staying out all night traipsing the streets of Frisco without me isn't sitting well with me. China and her friends seem okay, but Hazel just met them.

She finally strolls in a bit after four in the morning. "Hey," I say.

"You still up?"

I feel Hazel's fingers caressing my hair. I grew this mop to remind boys of the difference between them and me, and yet I really hate to take care of it. Not when taking care of it means drowning it in relaxing cream and smothering it with a hot flat iron. That's not me, but I can't bring myself to hack it off. That wouldn't be me either. Years later and I'm still stuck in this fucked-up place with this nest on my head. "Have you talked to Wil?"

"Nope."

"Why not?"

"It's over."

"Not necessarily."

"What am I supposed to say? I know I'm an insecure bitch, but you should've come?"

"If that's how you really feel, yeah."

"That'll help."

"Not if you start with something else. Because that's not all you feel, is it? Remember what we all wrote in the journal? You can start with *Thank you.* Then follow up with *I'm sorry.* Bring it home with *I love you.*"

"He's through loving me."

"I doubt that."

"Doesn't mean he wants to be with me."

"Well, guess what?"

"What?"

"Love him anyway."

Where would you like to be by the time you're thirty?—LB

By the time I'm thirty, I'll be a civil rights attorney with my own practice with an office, staff, and infomercial. (Just kidding on that last one.)—JA

When I'm thirty, I'd like to own my own salon, maybe even two, and I'd really like to be in a long-term relationship.—CHF

Jackie and I were just talking about this! I want to have my own social work practice and start a nonprofit organization. I don't necessarily want a long-term relationship, but if it happens, so be it. It'll be hard to run a practice and create a nonprofit as it is without having to account for another person's needs.—IR

Am I the only person who wants to get married and have children? Of course, I want to have a career, too. Pero Hazel se me olvidó! I thought we were going into business together. ☹ What happened to our full-service photography studio?—LB

I'm not the marrying type, but yeah, I'd like to still be with Wil, and I'd like us to open up a family practice. He can do the corporate stuff and bring in the loot while I do the crusader thing. But let's be realistic. What's the likelihood that we'll still be together 8,9 years from now. OK, we all said where we wanted to be . . . now where do you think you will actually be?—JA

Lou, we can TOTALLY go into business together. I'll probably need you if I really do hope to have my own salon nine years from now. In the worst-case scenario, I'll still be working on it, probably renting a chair at an upscale salon while I save my money, do the research, build my credit, etc.–CHF

Well, if I don't have a studio by the time I'm thirty, I don't think it's unrealistic to say that I'll at least be a working photographer or maybe a photojournalist. And I really do believe I will be married and have children by then.–LB

I definitely will at least have my nonprofit. That's more important than the practice, so if I can't make both happen, that would be my priority. And even if I don't have a full-fledged practice with an office and assistant and all that, I still can see myself with a few clients . . . like maybe the three of you.—IR

C'mon, I'm not going to be with Wil, that's obvious. But I definitely am going to have my practice. Believe that!—JA

"You sure you want to do this?" Even though I want Jackie to go through with this, it has to be for the right reasons. She asked me if I would cut her hair before we went to Sangria's tonight, but I have to be sure that it will make her feel better.

"No, but I trust you." Jackie closes the lid of the toilet and sits down on it.

I unzip my bag and pull out the Mehaz styling shears. I've told Jackie time and again that she can take care of herself—that she *has* to take care of herself as a way of loving herself—without throwing away time and money and capitulating to society's narrow standards of beauty. Now she finally listens to me, and I guess that's because I started walking my talk on this trip. I had kept telling myself that changing my hair color or style was a way to love myself when it was really a desperate attempt to change myself, to make others love me. Jackie ignored what I said because she noticed how it contradicted what I did, just like a perceptive but rebellious child. "I promise that I'm only going to take off enough to get rid of the split ends. That's all you need."

"Bound to be a lot though, 'cause it's been eons since I let you trim it, and you know I don't let anyone else but you touch my hair."

She's right, but I don't want her to panic. Jackie's hair'll be much shorter, but it'll be beautiful. "It'll still be relatively long," I say. "About shoulder-length."

Jackie blows air out of her cheeks, and I start to cut her hair. Black coils sail toward the floor, a few catching onto the motel towel draped around her shoulders. "Remember that time I washed my hair, like, a gazillion times thinking it'd get just like the girl's in that commercial?"

I smile as I clip away a few more strands. Jackie has so much hair. The follicles are thick, too. Hollywood actresses pay thousands for extensions to get the body and volume she naturally has. "You were yelling, 'The fuckin' box says rinse and repeat, but look at me. My hair's so dry, I look like a porcupine on speed. I'm fuckin' suing Pantene.' "

Jackie and I laugh now, but we didn't then. That day I pulled her hair into a ponytail and braided it; then Jackie put on a baseball cap and went home. Later that night it came to me to add more conditioner in her hair but not to rinse it out despite what the directions on the bottle said. So I climbed out of my window and up the fire escape to Jackie's room. I peeked through her window and saw Jackie lying in bed wearing her street clothes, including the baseball cap. She had streaks on her face from having cried herself to asleep. I went back to my room and waited for her to knock on my window the next day. When Jackie did—wearing a different baseball cap to match her T-shirt—she jumped into my room asking me, "You want to go see *There's Something About Mary* or *Armageddon*?" As if nothing had happened the day before. At that time I decided not to mention that we try adding more conditioner to her hair nor did I tell her that I had seen her the previous night.

"You've been hounding me to moisturize ever since," says Jackie.

"But do you listen to me?"

"Sometimes." Someone knocks, then swings open the bathroom door. Lourdes slips in with Irena behind her. By the look on their faces, we can tell they've been arguing again. "What's with you two now?"

Irena says, "She went overboard again."

"I just wanted to give Jackie a few options."

"She doesn't want that stuff!" says Irena.

"*Dejes que ella decida.*"

"*¡Ya!*" I scold them. "Let's see what you got." Lourdes hands me the white plastic shopping bag. I reach into it and stack the products along the counter. A large toothcomb and leave-in conditioner like I asked. Curl activator. Two Clairol hair colors—amber shimmer and cocoa infusion. Aerosol hairspray with alcohol in it, so that's a no-go since it'll dry Jackie's hair. And finally a no-lye relaxer kit. "So what you think, Jackie?" I hope she doesn't ask me to straighten her hair. When given the love they crave, her natural curls are so beautiful. But I intend to support Jackie's choice no matter what it is.

Jackie stares at the products for a moment then says, "Let me see that." She motions for the hair color, and Lourdes hands both choices to her. She surveys the colors, then places the packages on her lap. "And that," she says, pointing at the relaxer. Lourdes hands it to her, and she reads the back of the box. Jackie lines all the products along the edge of the tub. "I'm just going to let Hazel trim and condition it. Maybe use some of the activator." Irena applauds. Then Jackie adds, "But I appreciate your looking out, Lou. I think you should try this." She hands her the amber hair dye. "I bet you can work that."

Lourdes takes the box and turns toward me smiling. "Can I go next?"

"Of course, sweetie." I pick up the toothcomb. "I'll be done with Jackie in about fifteen, twenty minutes."

"You gotta love the wash-n-go," says Jackie.

"I'm going to see if we need a reservation for Sangria's," says Lourdes, skipping past me out of the bathroom.

With a big grin on her face, Irena closes the door behind them. Then she swings it open again. "Save me a lock for the journal."

"Okay," I say, and she leaves.

Jackie rolls her eyes, "*Loca.*"

"Ready?"

"Like I said, I trust you. Make me beautiful."

"And like I said, you already are."

"Whatever." I slap the comb against the back of her neck. "Ow!"

Jackie smiles. "I'm going to get my girl Li'l Bit after you."

JOURNAL—DIVAS DON'T YIELD

If there's one thing that you could change about your childhood or upbringing, what would it be and how do you think that might have made your life different? Remember the risks and assumptions involved before you answer. I think I would have liked to have my mother in my life. That means either I never would have come to the U.S. or she would have left Cuba. And that might mean that one of us might have been unhappy, but I'd like to think that our being together would have been enough to overshadow any kind of material or emotional hardship.—IR

I definitely would not have wanted to lose my father. That means that Valería might have never come into our lives because I'm pretty positive that my mother would have been a housewife. She only took over the company because she had to. Although I think of Valería as my favorite aunt, an aunt can never replace a father.—LB

This is a tough question for me because there are so many things I would like to change about my childhood. But even if I could change the fact that my father got addicted to heroin, caught HIV, and went to prison, would I want to? Because the truth is, I think he became a better father to me because of all those things. So the only change I can think of that probably would have had a major, positive impact on my life is going to live with my grandmother as soon as I was born. I never would've had to experience all that drama firsthand, I seriously doubt that I would have missed my mother, and I still would've met Jackie.—CHF

I wouldn't change anything. You know the saying . . . stick to the misery you know. Just kidding. Not about not changing anything because I mean that. I have no clue whatsoever why my mother left, but if she could do something like that, imagine how much worse I'd be if she stayed? It's like what Hazel said (no offense, hon). My father, brother, and I turned out just fine without her, so why risk changing that?—JA

No offense taken, sweetie. I know exactly where you're coming from. Lourdes, I have no doubt that your mother misses your father terribly, but do you ever wonder if your mother felt fulfilled as a housewife? Just curious, not trying to start any trouble. It's just that things are rarely so black-and-white. Least of all family.—CHF

That's right, Hazel! Now you know why I asked the question. Jackie, funny how your answer made me appreciate what did happen to me as a child. Thanks for that. Lourdes?—IR

Tengo que pensar mas sobre esto.—LB

IRENA

Interstate 80
Philadepia, PA
Friday, June 30, 4:27 P.M.

When Lourdes take the wheel in Philadelphia, Jackie joins me in the backseat. Lourdes ejects my Cree Summer CD and replaces it with one of Shakira's earlier albums. She and Hazel immediately start to sing along. I want to, but the song's in Spanish.

"Hazel, pass me the album," says Jackie. "Don't know why I didn't think of this ages ago." Hazel passes her the CD, and Jackie flips through the liner notes. She hands them to me, pointing to the lyrics of the song Shakira is singing. Such a cool idea!

I sing along as best I can, and I even start to understand the words, too. A few songs later I notice that Jackie's not singing. She just bobs her head but stares out the window. At one point, she catches me looking at her. She gives me a weak smile and turns back to the window. I put my hand on her knee, and Jackie faces me again. "You know what?" I say. "I think for one semester, I'm not going to take Spanish."

"Not working for you?"

"No, it feels like using a map to go someplace I've been to before a long time ago. I'm just driving in circles staring at the thing when I should just keep my eyes on the road and look out for something familiar."

"I feel you."

Hazel looks over her shoulder at us. "So how're you going to learn it well enough for your trip to Cuba next summer?"

"I'll just listen to records like this. Watch some *novelas.*"

Lourdes laughs. "You'll learn some phrases you can really use that way." She turns down the stereo.

"Exactly! I mean, I've got to have something else to say besides '*¿Dónde está el baño?*' " I say, tapping into my Inner Gringa and making no effort to pronounce the words with the appropriate accent. Lourdes and Hazel laugh while Jackie just smiles and returns to staring outside the window. I follow her gaze to a large green sign that reads NEW YORK—95 MI. "Speaking of which, I really gotta pee." Everyone groans, and I understand because we're so close to home, but that's precisely why we should stop. "It's the asthma medication! Just pull over as soon as it's safe, and I'll run into the bushes."

Lourdes makes a face, but she flicks on the right-turn signal. Eventually, she pulls the Tempo over to the side and parks. When I'm finished taking care of myself behind some bushes, I find Jackie sitting under a tree, yanking grass from out of the ground. Next to the car and out of earshot, Hazel smokes a cigarette while she chats with Lourdes. I walk over to Jackie and sit down next to her.

"Between you and me," I say, "the real reason I needed to stop was because I needed time."

"Time for what?"

"That's what we call a co-counseling session. You say, 'I need time' or 'I can give you time.' Throughout this entire trip, I've been missing my father, but I'm still angry with him, too. I need some time to sort through my feelings and prepare myself to see him."

"Gotcha." Jackie's eyes dart after the cars racing past us on the interstate. If she thinks she's going to get out of this, she's got another thing coming. "You promised me, Jackie," I remind her. "Remember? In the hospital? Did you think I'd forget?"

"No." She finally looks me in the eye and gives me a crooked smile. Like she respects me for holding her to her promise.

"Besides I think you could use some time, too." I crawl in front of her so we can sit facing one another. I hold out my hands, and I sense Jackie growing nervous. She rubs her grassy hands on her knees.

"So how does this thing work?"

"It's super easy. We each take turns asking each other three questions. The first is, 'What's good?' "

Jackie laughs and bobs her head as if she's listening to a hip-hop track. "What's good, ma?"

I laugh, too. "We ask each other what's good, what's coming up, and what are you looking forward to. One person answers the questions, and the other just listens. Sometimes the listener might echo the answer or ask a follow-up question. One of the tenets behind co-counseling is that we naturally have the ability to heal ourselves and one another. So just follow your instincts, and you'll do just fine."

"That's all?" Jackie slips her hands into my open palms. "Okay, so who goes first?"

Ordinarily, I like to go first to be a model and make the person who's new to co-counseling feel safe. But my gut tells me this won't work with Jackie. She'll give me what I need, I have no doubt, but after I have my emotional release, she'll either make an excuse not to go or put up her guard. She has to go first. "You go first."

"Does that mean I ask or answer?"

"I ask, and you answer."

"Okay. Do I have to, like, close my eyes?" Before I can answer, Jackie closes them.

Now I know I made the right choice. "Only if you want to, hon. Whatever's comfortable for you." Jackie's eyes pop open. I take a deep breath, and she does, too. "So, Jackie, what's good?"

"My ass is going home."

We both laugh. "And what's good about going home?"

"My dad," she says, smiling. "My brother, too, believe it or not." She chuckles at that. "My bed." Then her hands tighten around mine. Jackie's going there fast, and she doesn't even know it.

But I want to be sure so I ask, "What else is good about going home?" Jackie swallows and avoids my eyes, and I know it's okay to move on to the next question. "What's coming up, Jackie?" She shakes her head. I bet by *coming up* she thought I meant her to-do list. If Jackie knew I was referring to the problems that sit nagging in the back of your head while you insist that everything's perfect, she might have never agreed to do this. But I've got her now, and I'm here for her. "What are you afraid of?"

"C'mon, Rena, I'm really trying not to go there, okay?"

"Home?"

"No. You know. There."

"What's so bad about going there?"

Jackie scoffs. "I might not fuckin' come back!"

"Of course you will. You really think you're going to go insane?"

Now Jackie's laughter is laden with discomfort. "No."

"That's right. You're not going to go insane. If anything, you're going *into* sanity."

"I like that," she says like an impressed little girl. "That's cool."

"The point of going *there* is to find your way back, right?"

"Right."

"So what's coming up for you about going home?" She can barely speak so I have to push. "Wil."

"He's not going to be there when I get home. I mean, not for me."

"How can you be so sure?"

"Because he told me so."

"He told you that? Wil actually said, 'Jackie, I'm not going to be here for you.' "

"Maybe not like that, but I know what he means. And Wil always means what he says."

"He's real."

"So real, Irena. It's one of the things I love about him."

"You're real, too. That's probably one of the things he loves about you."

Jackie stays quiet. Then she drops her head. "But Wil's honest."

"So are you."

"I mean, he's honest with himself as well as me. Me, I'm just a fuckin' mess."

As much as she fights to maintain her composure, the tears force their way to her eyes. "Yeah, Jackie, you're such a fuckin' mess." I hear her catch her breath in her throat. "You're the only childhood friend that Hazel still has, the only one who didn't turn her back on her when she came out. You're the fuckin' mess who kept telling Lourdes, 'You're nobody's fuckin' doctor, you're a photographer.' And you gave her the courage to face her mother."

Jackie shakes her head violently. "She wouldn't have had to go to Colorado if I hadn't . . . Irena, I'm so sorry. I'm so, so sorry." Her voice cracks with regret, and her tears intensify.

"But if not for you, I wouldn't be on this trip at all. I wouldn't be planning to see my mother next summer. I never would've been at Take Back the Night. I never would've broken my silence at this conference and with my father." Jackie finally looks at me because I had yet to tell her this. "I love you, Jackie. And Hazel and Lourdes do, too. And so does Wil. That's how much of a fuckin' mess you are."

"You shouldn't." Jackie buries her face into her hand and collapses into sobs. I pull her head into my lap and stroke her hair. "My own fuckin' mother . . ."

"Of course we should. And we do. So should you."

Hazel and Lourdes kneel down on either side of me, and we create a safe space for Jackie to finally release all that pain.

IRENA

La Habanita de Rodriguez

Jersey City, NJ

Friday, June 30, 7:15 P.M.

"Make that left, and you should see it right on the corner."

Lourdes follows my directions, and we immediately see the lights above the bodega's awning—LA HABANITA DE RODRIGUEZ. My heart pounds as I see my father unlocking the icebox beside the entrance as a kid about eleven years old waits. Dad reaches in, pulls out a bag of ice, and hands it to the kid, who gives him a bill. Before he can go inside, one of his cronies calls his name and approaches him. They stop to chat.

"Your pops is tall," says Jackie.

"Yeah, I take after my mom." Lourdes double-parks across the street. "Guess this is it." I lean into the front seat to give Lourdes and Hazel their hugs and kisses. Then I pull back and look at Jackie.

"See ya Monday," she says.

"What's Monday?"

"Kickboxing."

"That's right." I reach over her to give her the biggest hug of all. "Bring me some good news."

Jackie presses her lips against my cheek. "You, too."

She means about my father, but that's because she doesn't know what I'm thinking of doing. Every other Saturday, Kharim comes to the center and holds a free legal clinic for the clients. If I can find the courage, I'm going to ask him if he wants to have lunch with me. Just a friendly lunch. Not a date. Maybe I should just bring him lunch. Or offer to get his lunch. No, that's a horrible idea. I mean, if I'm getting my own lunch . . . Anyway, I'll do something. Something small. But definitely something.

I climb out of the Tempo. My father's still talking to his friend, so he still hasn't noticed me. I walk to the back of the car to take my bag out of the trunk. Lourdes waits as I cross the street. "Dad."

My father finally looks my way. "Irena!" He opens his arms. I drop my bag and run into them. As I cling to him, I glance over his shoulder in time to see the Tempo turn the corner with Jackie giving me a thumbs-up from the backseat.

LOURDES

Ansonia Hotel at
73rd & Broadway
Upper West Side, NY
Saturday, June 30, 8:43 P.M.

I thought it would feel great to be home, *pero me siento muy inquieta.* The second I open the door, I see the bag I had packed but had to leave behind. I bring it into my bedroom, toss it onto the ottoman, and unzip it. The facial sauna, the paraffin wax spa . . . I guess we really didn't need these things on our trip, but I can sure use them now. So I take everything into my bathroom and run a hot bath.

But an hour later I lie on my bed in my robe feeling not too much better. I have this tension that cannot be soaked, exfoliated, or massaged away. I climb out of bed, walk over to my desk, and click on my Mac. As I wait for it to boot, I straighten the papers on my desk. On the top of one stack, I find my incomplete change-of-major form. I reach for a pen and fill it out, writing *Visual Arts* in the space marked *New Academic Information.* Because I cannot wait until Monday, I find an envelope and stamp. I copy the address of the registrar across at the bottom of the form onto the envelope. Then I throw on a Fordham sweatsuit, grab the envelope and my cell phone, and walk out of the apartment.

As I make my way to the closest mailbox, my telephone rings. I glance at the caller ID display and then answer it. I'm home, and it's time. "*La bendición, Mamá.*"

"*Qué Dios te bendiga. ¿Dónde estas ahora?*"

"I'm just walking down Broadway."

"So you're back in New York."

"*Sí, sí, sí.* Jackie and Hazel just dropped me off about an hour ago."

My mother sighs. *Se lo que ella esta pensando. Can't you sit for a minute before taking to the street?* "Where are you going now?"

"Just to drop something in the mailbox." *Respiro.* "A form to change my major."

"To what?"

"I've decided to major in visual arts. With a concentration in photography." Mamá takes so long to respond that I wonder if my signal faded. "Hello? Mamá?"

"I'm here. Lourdes, have you thought this through? Are you going to be able to find a good-paying job when you graduate with that major?"

"Mamá, Fordham's a great liberal arts college. I could afford to major in finger painting and . . ." *Mentira.* If I'm going to come clean to my mother, I should start by being honest with myself. "Well, the way the economy is nowadays, I'm probably going to have to go to graduate school, too." Either my mother is huffing or she's laughing, *no puedo decir.* "Mamá, are you happy?"

"Of course, I'm not happy—"

"No, I mean with what you are doing. I know that you are great at what you do. Maybe even better than Papá was. But does it make you happy?" Once again, I wonder if the signal has faded because my mother does not answer for a long time.

Before I can ask if she's still there, I hear someone come into her office. I overhear Mamá sternly tell whoever it is, "Not now. I'm on the telephone with my daughter. I'll call you when I'm finished with her." Then she gets back to me. "*M'ija,* are you still there?"

My heart feels as if it is bursting at the seams to hear her call me *m'ija.* "Look, Mamá, I know you're really busy. So can we talk some more about it when I come home in August? Maybe we can compromise."

"You're still coming home in August?"

"*Claro que sí.* I thought I'd come home and help you at the company." I reach the mailbox. "And I was thinking that when school starts, I'll just find another job here and help you pay for school. I can move into a cheaper apartment or into university housing. Maybe Irena and I can find a place together. And Mamá?"

"What?"

"I'm really good. Let me develop and send some of the pictures I took at the conference with the 35mm. You'll see. Or I can even e-mail you some of the ones I took with my digital camera." Never mind that pride is a deadly sin. It can't be worse than suppressing a gift that God has given me. "They're great."

Mamá sighs. "You got this from your father, you know. This artistic streak. Not only did he teach me everything I know about art, but I think he also wished . . ." She sighs again. "Well, let's discuss it when you're home. First thing when you get back to the apartment, I want you to go online and buy your ticket."

"I can't, Mamá. I have no credit cards, remember."

"Oh. So I'll buy your ticket and send it to you." She pauses and says, "And in the meantime, you can e-mail me some of your photos."

¡Gracias a Dios! "Sí, señora," I say as I open the mailbox and drop the envelope. "First thing when I get back home." And this time I mean it.

Jackie drives me home without saying a word. Usually when she's quiet, I still know what's on her mind, but now I have no clue. Maybe she's wondering what I'm thinking and has no clue either. Oddly, I take some comfort in that.

She pulls up to the front of my building, pops the trunk, and gets out of the car. When I reach the back of the car, Jackie has pulled my bags out the trunk and set them on the ground. "You need help getting these upstairs?"

"No, I can handle them."

"Bet you've got a dozen messages and e-mails from La China waiting for you." The thought must have made me smile because now Jackie's pointing and grinning at me.

"I'm not going to jump into anything right away," I say, and it surprises me that I actually mean it. "I mean, I like her. And her friends. But I need to spend some time by myself."

Jackie folds her arms as if she's cold even though it's a warm June night. "Hazel, are we cool?"

"Sure."

"I mean it. I need to know that nothing's changed between us."

"But things have changed. Even though I'm not going to jump into another relationship anytime soon, I've got to make some new friends. Hang out with some women who are more like me."

Jackie looks crushed. Still she says, "Just so you know that no matter what, I'm always going to have your back."

"And no matter what, you and I will always be girls."

"So can your girl get a hug?"

"Any time." Jackie and I embrace. At this moment, I know that even though we have some rough patches ahead of us, we're going to be friends for life. "You know what? Why don't you come upstairs for a minute? I have the perfect thing for you to wear when you go see Wil."

Jackie shakes her head. "Nothing of yours is going to look good on me," she says.

I reach across and tug at a healthy spiral of hair sitting on her shoulder. "Trust me."

JACKIE

1783 Willis Avenue
South Bronx, NY
Sunday, July 2, 2:56 P.M.

I convince Raul to let me have the Tempo for a few more days so I can pick up my things from Wil's place on the weekend. I was just going to go the apartment, toss my things in a cardboard box, and leave behind the key he gave me. Hazel had a fit when I told her this. "You have to let Wil know you're coming," she said. "You have to give him the choice to be there. And if he is, that says a lot. You're almost there." Truth is, I only give him a heads-up because the last thing I need is to walk in on him with Sheila and Eric playing house.

When I turn the corner, another stickball game is in progress. Wil's giving Li'l Bit pointers as she scrapes a broomstick against the curb. Next to the pile of straw they removed sits a roll of electrical tape and a pair of large scissors. I park the car across the street and make my way toward them.

Li'l Bit spots me first. "Jackie's back!" She drops the stick, rushes toward me, and throws her arms around my waist.

"Wow, kid, you grew a whole foot in two weeks."

"Hey, Bit, you're up!" I look toward the voice. Sheila's son, Eric, waves her over.

"My bat ain't finished," she yells.

"Use mine then."

Without another word to me, Li'l Bit runs off. I walk over to where Wil sits on the curb and pick up Li'l Bit's stick.

"Welcome back." He offers me the electrical tape.

I take the tape from him. "Thanks." I pull out a few inches of tape off the roll and Wil cuts it for me. Then I wrap it around the handle of Li'l Bit's bat.

"Nice dress."

I smooth the sundress Hazel lent me and bite the urge to say *This old rag.* Hazel always gets on my case about taking a compliment graciously. "Thanks." I busy myself pulling off another piece of tape on the roll to avoid looking him in the eye.

But I can hear the surprise in Wil's voice. "Very nice dress. With your legs, you should wear skirts and dresses more often." Then I feel him tap my calf with the handle of the scissors. "Glad to see you haven't given up on your boots though." Hazel gave me hell for insisting on wearing them, but they make me comfortable. This conversation's going to be tough as it is without stuffing my big feet into a pair of stilettos and literally falling all over the man in an attempt to be something I'm not. "I always thought they were sexy."

This better not be his idea of letting me down easy. I feel like a fool thanking him yet again, so instead I hold out the roll of tape so he can cut it for me. We do this for a few minutes while watching the game in silence. Li'l Bit gives the ball a good whack and races toward first. The other team has no chance of catching her. Eric runs to her and gives her a high-five.

Wil says, "You taught her well."

"But you were giving her tips while I was away, right?"

"She didn't need them." He pauses, then says, "A few hours after you left for Frisco, Li'l Bit shows up at my door, telling me that you promised her that I would show her how to wrestle."

I realize that I never gave Wil a heads-up about that. Hell, I never thought the child would come knocking on his door to make good on the offer. "Sorry 'bout that."

"No, it's okay," Wil says, smiling. "Anyway, Eric's there, so I tell her to come on in. Next thing I know, Li'l Bit accomplishes the impossible. She convinces Eric to shut off that damned Xbox and go outside to play. I couldn't believe it."

"Me neither." Wil bought Eric that Xbox for his last birthday.

I wasn't crazy about that, but I held my tongue. At least, I did until Wil insisted that Eric leave it at his apartment. Jackie, stop thinking about the past and listen to the man.

"So I take my laptop to the fire escape so I can keep an eye out on them while I work, and the kids are playing some crazy, freestyle tag where, like, everybody's It. And I watch Li'l Bit, thinking, 'That little girl's so fast. She can catch anyone she wants, but nobody can catch her. Bet Jackie was just like that when she was that age.'

"Next thing I know, Eric is chasing Li'l Bit, and I'm thinking, Forget it, Li'l Man. You're wasting your time. And I realize he's chasing her 'cause he likes her. Just when I start to feel sorry for him, *tag.* Eric catches her. He just opens his arms and throws them around her. And by the way Li'l Bit's laughing, it hits me. She let him. She likes Eric, too, so she let Eric catch her. He never would have caught Li'l Bit if she had not let him. So I found myself wondering, 'Did Jackie ever let anyone catch her?' "

"No, I didn't." I unzip my fanny pack. "Speaking of Eric, I brought him back a souvenir from our trip."

"You did?" I pull out the Roberto Clemente card and hand it to Wil. Only then do I notice there are other cards in there. I don't remember saving any more cards. "Wow, Roberto Clemente," says Wil. "He was the man! Who else you got in there?"

I pull out the other cards and start to laugh. They're tarot cards. "Irena must have snuck these into my bag when I wasn't looking." Each is an ace of a different animal. Wil looks over them as I look through them. A flying dove. A smiling dolphin. A charging bull. A growling lioness.

"What do they mean?"

"Let's just say they're pictures of us on our trip."

Wil takes the lioness. "This must be you."

I sigh and say, "Look, Wil, I know I'm always fighting you, and we both know why. I fight you because I love you and it scares the shit out of me. But I'm working on it. Whether you want to give us another chance or not, I just wanted you to know that I do love you, and that I'm sorry, and that I really am working on it."

I say my peace and shut my mouth. Wil just stares at me. Irena warned me not to rush to fill the silence and demand a response. But if he doesn't say something soon—anything—he'll have said more than I can take.

"I don't think I've ever been with a woman who's apologized to me for anything," he says. "You're the first."

"Just trying to be a woman about mine."

"I'm sorry, too, baby." Wil puts his arms around me. "And I love you, too. We'll figure it out."

Then I give Wil two weeks' worth of kisses even when the kids stop playing stickball to tease us.

DIVAS DON'T YIELD
divasdontyield@yahoogroups.com
6 New Messages

Jackie's B'Day Party Since Jackie and Wil are not going to the Bahamas, I decided to throw one last party for her at the Ansonia before Irena and I move to our new apartment in Washington Heights. Jackie's birthday is on a Friday so does the 18th work for everyone? Jackie, no te pongas a discutir. This is going to be our last time to get together before classes start, so we party with you or without you. You might as well e-mail me a guest list and plan on being there.	Lourdes Becerra LuLuLinda@aol.com July 17, 2006 5:07 PM E.S.T.
Re: Jackie's B'Day Party Y'all are too much! Seriously, the 18th sucks because my first-year orientation is that day, and Wil's got some surprise cooked up for me that night, too. So can we do Saturday? Lou, you already know who to invite. K, Julio, Levell, todas las colegas, the usual suspects. We also have to celebrate Hazel's new gig, so she should invite her other homegirls, too. The place is sure damn big enough!	Jackie Alvarado jacqueline.alvarado@nyu.edu July 17, 2006 5:29 PM E.S.T.
Re: Jackie's B'Day Party The 19th is perfect for me. So far my new job at the salon in SoHo is awesome! The owner really likes me so	C. Flores Hazel1985@hotmail.com July 17, 2006 7:12 PM E.S.T.

not only did she rent me the chair, she's showing me aspects of the biz. China swears she wants to get in my pants, but never mind. And these people can tip! I'm telling you, the New Year's Eve party is going down at my new place this year. Mark my words.	
New Year's Eve at Hazel's (and China's?) I'm down with that!	Jackie Alvarado jacqueline.alvarado@nyu.edu July 18, 2006 8:34 AM E.S.T.
Re: New Year's Eve at HAZEL'S Don't you start nothing. I said I wasn't jumping into anything, and I mean it. Of course, I hope China will be there. ☺ But let's not get it twisted . . . there's only going to be one name on that lease!	C. Flores Hazel1985@hotmail.com July 18, 2006 2:12 PM E.S.T.
Planning for Next Summer Wow, I know I just saw you guys last week at the Cree Summer concert at Central Park, but I miss you sooo much. It's going to be tough not to see you two almost every day. So I've been thinking . . . anyone want to come with me to Cuba next summer?	Irena Rodriguez Arroyo DreaminginCuban@juno.com July 18, 2006 6:48 PM E.S.T.

GLOSSARY OF SOME SPANISH TERMS AND SOME CULTURAL REFERENCES IN *DIVAS DON'T YIELD*

(In order of appearance)

Reiki *(p. x)*—(pronounced RAY-KEY) a Japanese healing art in which one channels energy by laying hands on specific parts of the body.

Starting Over *(p. 6)*—In this daytime reality TV show, several women from all walks of life live under one roof as each confronts a particular issue in her life with the help of life coaches. It's *Oprah* meets *The Real World.* No TV show is more Irena than this one.

narcocorrido *(p. 6)*—a song—usually a ballad—about the U.S.–Mexican drug trade.

Que piensan *(p. 7)*—What do you think?

No se preocupen *(p. 7)*—Don't worry.

No me dejen ser la unica en el viaje que no fuma *(p. 8)*—Don't let me be the only non-smoker on the trip.

Un abrazo fuerte a todos *(p. 8)*—Tight hugs to everyone.

capoeira ***(p. 11)***—a martial art developed by enslaved Africans in Brazil. Some believe that break dancing hails from capoiera.

botánica (p. 11)—a store in which one can purchase materials needed to practice religions such as Santería and voodoo that originated in Africa.

bruja (p. 13)—witch

Dios, perdóname (p. 22)—God, forgive me.

porque no quiero faltarle el respeto (p. 24)—Because I don't want to be disrespectful.

¡Qué escándalo! (p. 24)—What a scandal!

La bendición **and** ***Qué Dios te bendiga (p. 27)***—It is customary in many Latino cultures to greet an elder by requesting a blessing (*la bendición*) and, of course, for them to ask God to grant it.

Me voy al infierno, lo sé (p. 29)—I'm going to hell, I know it.

negra (p. 32)—Black. Among many Latinos, the term is not only used to describe something but often as a term of endearment. In fact, those of Caribbean descent are particularly known to call anyone we like with the slightest hint of melanin *negro* or *negra.*

¿Qué tú quieres que yo diga? (p. 35)—What do you want me to say?

¿Qué te pasa? (p. 35)—Literally, this means, "What's going on with you?" It is often said, however, in the same tone of voice as you might say, "What the hell's your problem?"

me muero (p. 37)—I'll die.

bogart *(p. 42)*—In hip-hop slang, it once meant to monopolize a cigarette the way Humphrey Bogart did. Now it's pretty much used when someone attempts to hog, hoard or hone in on anything.

orishas *(p. 43)*—the deities of the Yoruba religious system which are believed to be the manifestations or emissaries of God.

Aztlan *(p. 45)*—The term used to refer to the seven states of the southwestern U.S. by those who believe they should be returned to Mexico.

¡Déjame quieta ya! *(p. 45)*—Leave me alone already.

No quiero que empezamos a discutir *(p. 56)*—I don't want us to start arguing.

¿Porqué ella se puso tan enojada? *(p. 56)*—Why is she so angry?

¡Te cogí! *(p. 89)*—Busted!

Vírgen, dame paciencia *(p. 93)*—Virgin Mother of God, please give me patience.

Dicen que soy . . . *(p. 100)*—They say I'm your poisoned apple, they say I'm the shipwreck of your soul . . . (something like that) . . .

La basura de una mujer . . . *(p. 104)*—One woman's garbage . . .

La Malinche *(p. 122)*—An Aztec woman who served as an interpreter, advisor, and eventually mistress to Hernán Cortés as he colonized Mexico for Spain. Because of this, some consider her a traitor and harlot. But since she was offered to Cortés as a slave and allegedly used her influence in negotiations to spare Mexican lives, some consider her a complex heroine.

Padro nuestro . . . *(p. 174)*—Our Father, Who art in Heaven . . .

Padre Albert *(p. 188)*—Father Albert Cutié is an immensely popular priest based in Miami who has a television show, radio program, and syndicated column. Think of him as the Catholic Dr. Phil.

MALDEF *(p. 189)*—The Mexican Legal Defense and Education Fund.

National Council of Las Raices *(p. 189)*—What Irena meant to say was the National Council of La Raza.

malcriada *(p. 192)*—Literally translates into "poorly raised." It's the term we use to refer to someone who is spoiled, undisciplined, or otherwise behaves as if her mother didn't teach her how to act right.

Pinay *(p. 295)*—Filipina (drop the *Fili* and add a *y* at the end.)

Cree Summer *(p. 309)*—You will remember her as Freddie on the popular 1990s sitcom *A Different World.* As a musical artist, her work is very eclectic and can be described as a cross between Lenny Kravitz and Frank Zappa. The song "Miss Moon" is an ode she wrote for her friend Lisa Bonet, who was once married to Lenny Kravitz (who produced her album and co-wrote some of the songs).

respiro *(p. 330)*—I take a breath.

Divas DON'T YIELD

Sofía Quintero

A READER'S GUIDE

A Conversation with Sofía Quintero

Q: Were the women in *Divas Don't Yield* based on people you know?

A: Absolutely not! Don't get me in trouble. Seriously, none of the characters were based on people that I know, nor were any of them composites of people I know. At best, there are aspects of myself in each of them—things that I like, don't like, and want to be like. Other than that, I really strived to create four unique beings in these characters. This novel first came to me as a screenplay, and it was such a compliment to have women of all backgrounds approach me at readings to say that these characters reminded them of themselves or women they knew.

Q: You tackle a lot of controversial issues in this novel. Did you have an agenda while writing it?

A: I think every artist has an agenda whether or not she owns it or is even aware of it. So the answer is yes, without regret or apology. I had multiple objectives, but my overarching goal is to create stories with Latina characters that raise issues such as race, class, sexual orientation, and spirituality, which all humans must grapple with regardless of how we identify ourselves. After all, I may not be a working-class Portuguese girl in Connecticut or a twelve-year-old boy in Oregon coming of age during the fifties, but I still relate to the characters in *Mystic Pizza* and *Stand by Me.* I also wanted to contribute some depth to the chick-lit genre while retaining its accessibility, particularly the elements of humor and hope. Real women have meaningful issues. We have viewpoints that influence the way we move in the world and impact the way others interact with us. It's those underlying things that make the desire for a romantic relationship or the quest for the corner office interesting to me, rather than those pursuits in and of themselves. For me it's those "inner" stories that can make the most mundane plotlines resonate.

Q: What inspired you to write *Divas Don't Yield*?

A: I wrote the screenplay on which *Divas Don't Yield* is based during the Latin pop explosion of 1999. While most folks were "*Living La Vida Loca,*" the whole thing irked me on many levels—the lack of diversity and the fleeting nature of it all, to name only two. Wanting to be part of the solution and recognizing the power of telling our own stories, I wrote the screenplay in the hope of creating a film that would break out not one but *four* new Latina talents, including an Afro-Latina and an out lesbian. But as much as people liked the script, no one wanted to take a gamble because there were no roles for the smattering of Latinas the film industry deems bankable. I wish I had known that the publishing industry would have been more courageous in this regard and written the story as a novel from the start.

Q: Is there one character you relate to more than the others?

A: As I said, there's a bit of me in all of them, or at least there's an aspect of each character that I wish I had. For example, I envy Hazel's openness to love and Jackie's physical fearlessness, and I certainly have Lourdes's penchant for gadgets and Irena's fascination with the occult. If I had to choose one character with whom I had the most in common—the good, the bad, and the ugly—it'd have to be Jackie.

Q: If you were to meet Jackie, Irena, Hazel, and Lourdes at a party, do you think you'd want to be friends with them?

A: Now here's the funny thing. I don't know, if I met Jackie, how I would feel about her. Depending on what she said, Jackie could just as easily win me over or totally rub me the wrong way. Same with Lourdes. If she wanted to talk clothes and shoes, I'd flee the room. But if she wanted to discuss philosophy or gadgets, I could talk to her for hours. I think I would take to Hazel, and I definitely would like Irena.

Q: Have you ever gone on a road trip from New York to San Francisco?

A: No. Although I tried, I was unable to make it happen for various reasons, and that made writing the novel a challenge. You can fake the funk with a screenplay in ways you can't in a novel. Now that the novel is written, I'm almost afraid to make the trip. Would all the missed opportunities and gaps or discrepancies in my research dampen my enjoyment of the trip? Never say never. Maybe I'll just take another route than the I-80. I have been to most of the cities on the women's itinerary; you can probably guess which ones. I bet if I were to take the trip, I'd start to yearn, not for a sequel, but a revised edition!

Q: Do you see yourself as a Latina writer, as a writer, as a black and Latina writer? Why or why not?

A: I see myself as all of the above. I'm not Latina today, black tomorrow, and a writer on Friday. I am Latina, black, a writer, and many other things every single day. The way I see it, how I identify is not the issue, but rather the problematic assumptions that some people may make because of the way I identify. If when I say, "I'm a Latina writer," someone thinks, "Then her books won't interest me because I'm not Latina," the issue is not my identification but that person's racism. No artist wants to be pigeonholed, but I think there's a fundamental difference between wanting to appeal to as many different audiences as possible and downplaying aspects of one's identity to cater to narrow-minded thinking. It makes it seem as though certain aspects of one's identity are somehow alien to universal humanity.

Q: What was the best thing about writing *Divas Don't Yield*? What was the most challenging?

A: In the best moments, writing this novel was immensely cathartic. I found great joy in making the differences among the four women meaningful rather than incidental and in giving voice and representation to certain groups in our society who tend to be marginalized and silenced. And I had my own emotional releases through the process of writing *Divas Don't Yield,* whether laughing at Hazel's sudden yet astute observations at the end of a melancholy passage or crying during Irena's breakthrough during the Power Shuffle. The most difficult thing was writing this novel when I had not actually made the physical trip myself. If I had my way, there would've been at least four scenes—one for each character—on every night and in every city. Sometimes actually having been to the city in question was just as challenging because there was so much I wanted to incorporate that I had to let go for one reason or another.

Q: Will there be a sequel?

A: I have mixed feelings about that question. On the one hand, I'm not a fan of sequels either as a producer or consumer of popular media. Sequels should strive to be as good as if not better than the original, and that's hard to achieve if the story was not conceived with multiple installments from the start. On the other hand, I love these characters and would like to explore how they evolve (or not) at life's different stages. What if Jackie got pregnant? How does Lourdes lose her virginity? What if Irena fell for Kharim? What if Hazel's father was paroled? I'm going to leave this up to the fans though. If the demand is high enough, I can be convinced to write a sequel. But without encouragement that borders on insistence, I don't see it happening, because once I finish a story, I'm usually more than ready to move on to the next one. There's plenty more where this came from!

Q: If not a sequel, what else?

A: On the writing front, I'm finishing my second novel for One World. The working title is "Oshun's Arrangement," and it's about a young woman who becomes the paid companion to three college seniors. Sounds racy, doesn't it? I'm not going to say another word. I'm also teaming up with Berta Plata, Mary Castillo, and Lynda Sandoval for a Chica-Lit anthology of novellas about sisters and their secrets as well as contributing a short story to an erotica anthology by Latina authors. My story will be informed by my experiences as an, ahem, romance consultant (translation: neighborhood sex toy vendor). Author and filmmaker Elisha Miranda and I are forming our own multimedia production company called Sister Outsider Entertainment, and we're already in talks to write and produce several television, film, and theater projects. And of course, there's always exciting things going on at Chica Luna, the nonprofit organization I co-founded. Just visit sofiaquintero.com to get updates on these and other projects.

Reading Group Questions and Topics for Discussion

1. Hazel, Irena, Lourdes, and Jackie are four diverse Latina women. How are they similar to the Latinas you might have encountered? How are they different?

2. Each of the women has a challenging thing to learn and accept about herself. What is the challenge facing each of them? What forces each woman to grapple with that challenge? Did any particular journey remind you of one of your own?

3. Jackie doubts the holistic treatments and New Age philosophies that Irena believes can improve her life. Lourdes actually fears these alternative approaches to health and spirituality. Whose perspective, if any, is most like yours? How do you deal with people who think differently than you do about these subjects?

4. Do you consider Wil's commitment to his ex-girlfriend's son, Eric, a betrayal of his love for Jackie? Why or why not? If you were in Jackie's boots, how would you deal with this situation?

5. Although Lourdes sees herself as generous, the way she handles her money sometimes creates tension between her and her friends. Does Lourdes put her money where her mouth is?

6. Have you ever had close friends of different socioeconomic backgrounds? What kinds of issues, if any, did it create, and how did you deal with them?

7. Why does Irena's father try to discourage her from keeping in touch with her mother in Cuba? Do you think Irena should go to Cuba next summer? Why or why not?

8. Do you believe Hazel genuinely fell in love with Jackie? Why or why not?

9. Have you ever believed you were in love and later found the opposite to be true (or vice versa)? What made you realize that, and how did it affect your relationship to the other person?

10. How did each of the women's relationships with their mothers—especially Jackie and Hazel's—impact their lives? In what ways is each of the four women her father's daughter?

11. Lourdes struggles to find the courage to pursue her true passion, which she knows is art and not medicine. What stands between Lourdes and her passion? Have you ever pursued a passion despite multiple barriers?

12. At the conference, Irena participates in an exercise called the Power Shuffle, which challenges participants to examine different aspects of identity. In the space of a few minutes, she experiences a range of thoughts and feelings about her different identities. How did you react to Irena's experience? Have you ever experienced a Power Shuffle? Would you want to? Why or why not?

13. Jackie is a big proponent of tough love and truth-telling. Sometimes it works, and at other times it backfires. Are you an advocate of tough love or truth telling? Why?

14. Lourdes is a very devoted Catholic, but she's a pro-choice activist. What enables her to reconcile her beliefs? Do you hold a political viewpoint that contradicts your religious upbringing? How do you reconcile your beliefs?

15. If you were to meet these women at a party, would you want to be friends with any of them? Who? Why? With whom do you have the most in common? The least?

16. The women have a range of opinions on everything from pop-culture icons like Jennifer Lopez to social issues such as race and religion. Which opinions mirrored your own? With whom and on what did you vehemently disagree?

17. What do you see in the next five years for Jackie, Hazel, Lourdes, and Irena? Ten years? Have they resolved the issues that arose during their road trip? Do they accomplish their goals? Are they still friends?

ABOUT THE AUTHOR

Self-proclaimed "Ivy League homegirl" Sofía Quintero is an activist, educator, writer, speaker, and comedienne. Born into a working-class Puerto Rican–Dominican family in the Bronx, where she still resides, she earned a BA in history-sociology from Columbia University in 1990 and her MPA from the university's School of International and Public Affairs in 1992. After years of working on a range of policy issues from multicultural education to HIV/AIDS, she decided to heed the muse and pursue a career in entertainment.

The novel *Divas Don't Yield* began as the screenplay *Interstates. Interstates* was twice a finalist for the Sundance Institute's screenwriters' lab and won the 2001 San Francisco Black Film Festival Screenplay Competition. Her second screenplay, the baseball comedy *M.L.B.,* was a finalist for the ABC New Talent Development Award in 2003. She is at work on her third screenplay, *The Macktress,* which is a cross between *Boomerang* and *Brown Sugar* with a feminine twist.

As a stand-up comedian, Sofía placed in the 2002 Bud Light New York's Funniest Female contest. She taught youth *Screenwriting for Personal Growth and Social Change* and *Comedy with a Conscience* at the Y's Writer's Voice in New York City. She wrote and performed in "Soul Latina"—a night of comedic monologues and skits produced by Latino Flavored Productions—at the New

York Comedy Club in 2003 and again at the Nuyorican Poet's Café in 2004. In addition to writing "The J.Lo Drop Squad," she played Rosie Pérez who leads Michelle Rodriguez, Rosario Dawson, and Salma Hayek in a plot to kidnap and reprogram Jennifer Lopez.

Under the pen name Black Artemis, Sofía also writes hip-hop fiction. As Black Artemis, she wrote *Explicit Content,* the first novel about young women in the hip-hop industry, which was published by the New American Library/Penguin in August 2004. Her second Black Artemis novel, *Picture Me Rollin',* hit bookstores in June 2005 while the third one *BURN* is scheduled for August 2006. Sofía's novella "The More Things Change" appears in *Friday Night Chicas,* the first chick-lit anthology by and about Latinas. She is also at work on two other novellas as well as her next novel for One World.

In 2001, Sofía co-founded Chica Luna Productions to identify, develop, and support other women of color seeking to make socially conscious entertainment. She wrote two short films that Chica Luna produced and that have won acclaim on the festival circuit—*Corporate Dawgz* (a comedic ode to white folks who "get" it) and *Blind Date* (a dark romantic comedy with a dirty mouth). To learn more about Chica Luna and other women behind it, visit www.chicaluna.com.

Sofía is represented by literary agent Jennifer Cayea at Nicholas Ellison, Inc., and is regularly invited to speak and perform at colleges and universities throughout the United States via her speakers' bureau SpeakOut. Visit the *Divas Don't Yield* website at www.sofiaquintero.com, where you can read blogs for Jackie, Hazel, Lourdes, and Irena, as well as contact Sofía and get updates on her other projects.